Praise for Beth Wiseman

"The importance of finding peace and acceptance, especially within oneself, is a central theme in this book, the second in Wiseman's Daughters of the Promise series. Well-defined characters and story make for an enjoyable read."

—*Romantic Times*, regarding *Plain Pursuit*

"Beth had me sucked into the story from page one. Her Amish descriptions are dead-on accurate, and her characters are real and engaging. You will love *Plain Pursuit* whether you are a new Amish reader or a seasoned fan of the genre. I look forward to the next book in the series, *Plain Promise*."

—Amy Clipston, best-selling author of *A Gift of Grace*

"Wiseman's voice is consistently compassionate and her words flow smoothly."

—*Publishers Weekly* review of *Seek Me With All Your Heart*

"In *Seek Me With All Your Heart*, Beth Wiseman offers readers a heart-warming story filled with complex characters and deep emotion. I instantly loved Emily and eagerly turned each page, anxious to learn more about her past—and what future the Lord had in store for her."

—Shelley Shepard Gray, best-selling author of the Seasons of Sugarcreek series

"*Seek Me With All Your Heart* by Beth Wiseman is a heart-stirring story of second chances and learning to trust God in difficult circumstances. You won't want to miss the start to this new Amish series!"

—Colleen Coble, best-selling author of The Mercy Falls series

Healing Hearts

Other Novels by Beth Wiseman

The Daughters of the Promise series

Plain Perfect

Plain Pursuit

Plain Promise

Plain Paradise

Plain Proposal

The Land of Canaan series

Seek Me with All Your Heart

The Wonder of Your Love

Novella found in:

An Amish Wedding (Available December 2011)

Healing Hearts

THREE AMISH NOVELLAS

BETH WISEMAN

THOMAS NELSON
Since 1798

NASHVILLE   DALLAS   MEXICO CITY   RIO DE JANEIRO

Glossary

aenti – aunt

baremlich – terrible

bruder – brother

daadi – grandfather

danki – thanks

Deitsch – Pennsylvania Dutch language

Die Botschaft – a weekly newspaper serving Old Order Amish
    communities

dippy eggs – eggs cooked over easy

dochder – daughter

dumm – dumb

dummkopf – dummy

Englisch or *Englischer* – a non-Amish person

fraa, frau – wife, Mrs.

guder mariye – good morning

gut – good

hatt – hard

haus – house

in lieb – in love

kaffi – coffee

kapp – prayer covering or cap

kinn, kinner – child, children

lieb – love

maed, maedel – girls, girl

mamm – mom

mammi – grandmother

mei – my

nee – no

onkel – uncle

Ordnung – the written and unwritten rules of the Amish; the understood behavior by which the Amish are expected to live, passed down from generation to generation. Most Amish know the rules by heart.

Pennsylvania Deitsch – Pennsylvania German, the language most commonly used by the Amish

rumschpringe – running-around period when a teenager turns sixteen years old

snitz pie – dried apple pie

sohn – son

ya – yes

wunderbaar – wonderful

Contents

A Choice to Forgive

To my husband, Patrick . . . my forever love.

Chapter One

Lydia opened the front door, expecting her friend Sarah or one of the children's friends. Instead, a ghost stood in her doorway, a vision from her past—*Englisch* in appearance, Amish in her recollection of him. A man long buried in her heart and in her mind, he couldn't possibly be real. But his chest heaved in and out, and his breath clouded the air in front of him, proof that he was no apparition. He was real. *He* was Daniel Smucker.

Up till this moment, Lydia was having a routine day, busying herself with baking and household chores. On this Thursday afternoon she was enjoying some solitude while her children visited her sister Miriam for a couple of hours. Chilly November winds whipped around the farmhouse, hinting of a hard winter to come, but a cozy fire warmed the inside of the hundred-year-old structure. Aromas of freshly baked pies and cookies wafted through the house—shoofly pie and oatmeal raisin cookies— just like her mother used to bake when Lydia was a child.

Lydia smoothed the wrinkles in her black apron, tucked strands of dark-brown hair beneath her white prayer covering, and headed to the front door, thankful to God for all that she'd been blessed with. Three beautiful children, a lovely home, and a church community that encouraged her to be the best Amish woman she could be, especially since the death of her husband two years ago.

Elam's fatal heart attack shocked everyone, especially since there was no family history of heart problems. After he died, Lydia had struggled to get out of bed each morning, but with the help of the Old Order district, she and the children were doing much better.

Today she was trying to keep her thoughts in a happy place, one filled with hope for the future, the promise of good times with friends and family during the upcoming holiday season, and a blessed Christmas to celebrate the birth of their Savior.

Then she opened the door, and this man's presence threatened to steal all that she'd been working toward.

"Hello, Lydia."

He stood tall before her in black breeches and a black coat buttoned to his neck. His half smile was enough to produce the boyish dimples she remembered from their youth. His sandy-brown hair, now tinged with gray at the temples, reminded her how much time had passed since she had seen him—eighteen years.

His voice was deeper than she remembered. But his slate blue eyes were unmistakably the eyes of her first true love, tender and kind, gentle and protective, reflective of a man she'd known as a nineteen-year-old girl. And now he stood shivering on her doorstep, clearly waiting for an invitation to come in out of the cold.

But Lydia couldn't speak. She couldn't move. And she didn't want to ask this man into her home—this man who had once promised to marry her, then disappeared from her community and her life in the middle of the night. And on Christmas Eve, no less.

But that was a long time ago, and she'd gone on to marry

his brother. Thank goodness Elam had been there to comfort her after Daniel's desertion. Elam, the man she was meant to be with, whom she'd married and shared fifteen wonderful years with.

"Do you think I could come in for a minute?" Daniel finally asked, teeth chattering. "My ears are frozen." His smile broadened.

Lydia swallowed hard and took a deep breath. She was trembling, but not from the frigid air blowing in from behind him. Had he come to ask for forgiveness after all these years? Curiosity compelled her to motion him through the threshold.

As he brushed past her, he began to unbutton his coat and then hung it from a peg on the coatrack near the door—the coatrack *Elam* built. She scowled as she reached for the garment to move it, but stopped herself when she realized there was nowhere else to hang it up. Her arm fell slowly back to her side, and she watched Daniel walk toward the fireplace as he scanned the room—a room filled with memories of the life she'd lived with Elam.

Daniel warmed his palms above the flames for a moment and then focused on her husband's collection of books on the mantel. He gingerly ran his finger along each one, studying the titles. Lydia cringed. *Those are Elam's things.*

"You've made a fine home, Lydia." He pulled his attention from the books and turned to face her.

His striped *Englisch* shirt reminded her that his Amish roots were long gone.

"You are more beautiful than I remember."

Lydia couldn't recall the last time she'd thought about

Daniel, but suddenly old wounds were gaping open. "What are you doing here, Daniel?"

He walked toward her as if he might extend his arms for a hug. She backed away and walked to the other side of the room.

He raked his hand through his shaggy hair, hair not fit for an Amish man. He wasn't Amish, she reminded herself, and hadn't been for many years. What length he chose to wear his hair was of no concern to her.

"I just thought you should know that I have talked to my family, and also to Bishop Ebersol. I'll be baptized back into the community two Sundays from now."

Lydia's heart was thudding against her chest. Had she heard him correctly?

"I'm back for good," he went on. "I'll be making my home at the old Kauffman farm up the road, eventually. Right now, I'm staying with my parents." He smiled again.

"*Ach*, I see." She nodded, then turned away from him and took a few steps. She folded her arms across her chest and tried to steady the quiver that ran from her toes to the tip of her head. "What made you decide to come back?"

She heard his footsteps close the space between them, and as he hovered behind her, she recognized his scent. Oddly, it was as though he still used the same body soap, toothpaste, and whatever else made him smell the way he did. She breathed him in, closed her eyes, and imagined his arms wrapped snuggly around her waist, his lips nuzzling her neck, the way he'd done so many times back behind the barn following the Sunday singings.

Lydia silently chastised herself for having such thoughts. She blinked away any signs of distress and turned to face him.

Daniel shrugged. "It's time. My family is here. My roots. I want to live out the rest of my life here."

He sounded like an old man on a course with death, not a man of a mere thirty-eight years.

"But you can't just go be *Englisch* for eighteen years, come back, and expect to just—to just be welcomed back into the community. You've been shunned, for goodness' sake." She shook her head. "I don't understand."

"You know as well as I do that if I seek forgiveness from the bishop—which I have—and commit myself to the *Ordnung*, then I can be rebaptized into the community. And that is what I choose to do."

This can't be happening, Lydia thought, as she soaked in what he was telling her.

"I'm hoping you'll forgive me too," he said softly, with pleading eyes.

Lydia knew that forgiveness freed the soul of an unwelcome burden, and she'd forgiven Daniel many years ago. So what were these resentful feelings spewing to the surface now?

"If God can forgive me, if the bishop can forgive me . . . maybe you can too."

"I forgave you a long time ago, Daniel." *Even though you left me one night without a word.*

Daniel breathed a sigh of relief. "I'm so glad to hear that. I know that leaving a note wasn't the best way to handle things."

It was a terrible way to handle things. Lydia recalled Daniel's hand-scribbled missive. He'd left a similar letter for his parents, telling them all that he could no longer adhere to the strict guidelines of the Old Order district and that he would be heading out into the *Englisch* world.

She quickly reminded herself what a wonderful life she'd had with Elam for fifteen years, a life she wouldn't have known if she had married Daniel. Nor would she have Anna Marie, now sixteen; Jacob, who'd just turned twelve; or nine-year-old John. "I suppose everything turned out as it should."

Daniel's brows drew together in an agonized expression, but he didn't say anything.

Lydia studied him for a moment, wondering exactly how much his being here would affect her and her family. Quite a bit, she decided. And she knew that to harbor any bad will toward Daniel was not only wrong in the eyes of God, but it would also hurt her more than anyone else. She would need to pray hard to keep any bitterness away.

"I just thought you would want to hear the news from me," Daniel finally said.

Lydia nodded, then walked toward the door, hoping he would follow.

Daniel reached for his coat on the rack. He looked like he had more to say, but Lydia didn't want to hear any more. His presence was enough of an upset for now. As she reached toward the doorknob, the door bolted open, almost hitting her in the head. She jumped back and bumped right into Daniel, whose hands landed on her hips. She slid sideways and out of his grasp instantly.

"*Aenti* Miriam sent this lemon pie," Anna Marie said. She handed Lydia a pie as Jacob and John bounced in behind her.

John closed the door behind him, and all three of her children stood barely inside the doorway, waiting for an introduction. And Lydia realized that Daniel's return was going to complicate her life in more ways than one. Her children had a right to know their uncle, but did Daniel really deserve to know her children? He hadn't even shown up for Elam's funeral. His only brother. But her children were waiting, and so was Daniel.

"Children, this is Daniel, your *daed*'s *bruder*."

Lydia watched as Anna Marie, Jacob, and John in turn extended a hand to Daniel, who smiled with each introduction. Lydia wondered if maybe she was dreaming all of this. A disturbing dream, one she hoped to wake up from any minute.

"Very nice to meet you all," Daniel said.

"Your *Onkel* Daniel will be making his home here in Paradise, at the old Kauffman place," Lydia said. Not even a half mile down the road. "Right now, he is staying with your *mammi* and *daadi*." Lydia steadied her voice and tried to appear casual in the presence of her children. "He is being rebaptized into the faith."

Lydia's sons nodded, then excused themselves. But Anna Marie eyed Daniel with suspicion. "You are dressed *Englisch*," she said.

Daniel shifted his weight. "Uh, yes, I am. I haven't been in town long, but I'll be stocking up on the traditional clothes."

Anna Marie narrowed her eyes into a scrutinizing gaze. "Where've you been?" She paused, but before Daniel could answer, she added, "Why weren't you at *mei daed*'s funeral?"

Good question, Lydia thought, as she waited to hear Daniel's answer. Elam had told the children that their uncle chose a life with the *Englisch,* and that he was shunned for doing so after baptism. But he never told them that their mother almost married his older brother before she married him.

Daniel rubbed his forehead, and Lydia could see the regret in his expression. "It's a long story," he said.

Anna Marie, a spirited girl in the midst of her *rumschpringe,* questioned everything around her. Daniel's return was no exception. "I have time," she said. She edged one brow upward and lifted her chin a tad.

Lydia cupped her hand over her own mouth to hide the grin on her face. Anna Marie reminded her so much of herself at that age. She glanced at Daniel, who seemed rattled by the inquisition.

"I'm sure I'll be seeing lots of you. We can talk later," he said to Anna Marie. His eyes shifted to Lydia.

Lydia pulled from his gaze, and his words echoed in her mind. *I'll be seeing lots of you.*

She and the children had remained close to Elam's parents and his two sisters and their families. Of course, his family would be including Daniel in all of their activities from now on, which would indeed mean that Lydia and her children would see him often. It wouldn't be fair to the rest of the family to keep away just because Daniel was in the picture now. Lena and Gideon had been wonderful to their grandchildren, and to Lydia, since Elam's death. So had the rest of the family. But they all had to realize how strange this was going to be for her.

"Fine." Anna Marie responded flatly to Daniel's offer to talk later. "*Mamm,* I'm going to go finish sewing Jacob's shirt upstairs." She studied Daniel hard for a moment. "Nice to meet you." And she headed up the stairs.

"They're beautiful children," Daniel said when Anna Marie was out of earshot. His tone was laced with regret.

"*Ya*, they are." Lydia pulled on the doorknob and swung the door wide, allowing the chilling wind to coast inward. She had no parting words.

Daniel pulled his coat from the rack and slipped it on. When the last button was secure, he looked down at her, towering over her five-foot-five frame. "I know this is a shock for you," he said.

"It's fine." She tried to sound convincing, unaffected. There was a time when Daniel knew her better than anyone. She wondered if he could see past her words now and into her heart, where everything was anything but fine.

He walked out the door, then turned to face her.

Lydia started to close the door, but Daniel put his hand out, blocking her effort. "Lydia . . ."

Her cheeks stung from the wind, but she waited for him to speak.

"I've come home to start a new life." He paused, fused his eyes with hers. "Thank you for forgiving me."

Lydia forced a smile, then pushed the door closed. She stood still and faced the door, not moving, as an angry tear rolled down her cheek.

Had she really forgiven him?

Chapter Two

Nothing about Daniel's life had felt right since the day he left Lydia. But leaving Lancaster County was the right thing to do all those years ago, no matter how much the separation had pained him and hurt those he loved. If Elam were still alive, Daniel would have never returned home, despite his longing for family. His love for both his brother and Lydia had overshadowed his own desires.

He regretted not receiving his mother's letter in time to make it to Elam's funeral, but he'd moved too many times for his forwarded mail to catch up with him. By the time he'd gotten word, the funeral had long since passed. He recalled his sobs of regret, his feelings of despair at the news, and his confusion as to what Elam would want him to do. But it took another two years before he was ready to come home. Hopefully, he could be a friend to Lydia and a good uncle to the children. To speculate about more after so many years seemed far-fetched and out of reach at the moment.

Daniel parked the rental car in the designated parking area at Avis. It was strange to think this was the last time he would drive an automobile for the rest of his life. Change was on the horizon, and he continued to hope and pray that he was making decisions that were right in the eyes of God.

His parents openly wept when Daniel told them the truth about the night he left the community—that Christmas Eve so long ago. Their forgiveness partially plugged the hole that had been in Daniel's heart since then. But if things were going to be right for all of them, Lydia would need to know the whole story too—a secret that Daniel had carried for eighteen years, and one that Elam took to his grave. Daniel worried whether his confession was a betrayal of his brother. He could only pray that now Elam would want him to step forward with the truth.

Lydia's olive skin still glowed, just as he remembered. The dusty rose of her cheeks and full pink lips lent a natural beauty to her delicate face, a face that reflected the perfect combination of strength and femininity. Her dark-brown hair, barely visible from beneath her *kapp*, hadn't speckled with gray over the years like his own, and her deep brown eyes still reflected her every emotion. She still moved with grace and poise. And she still rubbed her first finger and thumb together when she was nervous, something she'd done more than once today.

But did Lydia have enough forgiveness in her heart, not only to forgive him, but also to forgive her own husband—a man no longer in a position to explain his choices? Could she forgive two brothers who had betrayed her one Christmas Eve so long ago?

Daniel climbed out of the car and closed the door.

I hope so.

Lydia heard a knock at the door shortly after Daniel left.

Please don't be Daniel again.

She was relieved to see Sarah Fisher, but one glance at her friend's face told her that Sarah had heard the news of Daniel's return. Sarah scooted past Lydia into the den. Lydia followed her in and closed the door behind them.

"Have you heard?" Sarah asked, breathless.

Lydia gulped and fought the tears welling on her eyelids. "*Ya*. He was here."

Sarah put both hands to her mouth. "Oh no. Are you all right?"

"*Ya*. It was a shock though." Lydia shook her head, then stared hard into her friend's eyes. "It was so long ago, Sarah. But after seeing him, it feels like just yesterday that he left. How can the pain bubble up after all these years?" She swiped at her eyes and hung her head.

Sarah walked to one of the wooden rockers near the fireplace and sat down. Although fifteen years Lydia's junior, she and Lydia were close friends, and Lydia knew Sarah would sympathize with her distress. Lydia took a seat in the other chair.

"You were *in lieb* with him once," Sarah said soothingly. "It's only natural to have these feelings."

Lydia yielded to the tears as heaviness settled in her chest. "I will have to see him all the time. His parents are the children's grandparents. He'll be at church services, family gatherings, social get-togethers—" She searched Sarah's eyes for answers. "It will be awkward."

Sarah seemed to be choosing her words carefully. She reached over and touched Lydia's arm. "*Mei* friend, is there any chance that you and Daniel—"

"No! I could never have a life with Daniel. I don't even know him anymore. He lived his life in the *Englisch* world, the world he chose." Tears ran down her face, and her voice choked in her throat. "Besides, I loved Elam with all my heart. We had three beautiful children together. We had a *gut* life. I would never, never . . ." She shook her head, determined to stay true to her words.

Sarah patted her arm. "But you did love Daniel very much once."

"*Ya*, I did. But he left me, Sarah. We had so many plans, and to this day I can't understand his choice." She paused. "I don't want to have any bad feelings toward him. I forgave him a long time ago." *I did. I know I did.* Lydia looked up and stared into her friend's hazel eyes, sympathetic and kind. "I loved *Elam*, Sarah."

"Of course you did."

Sarah understood about love and loss, and Lydia suddenly regretted dumping all this on her young friend. She attempted to pull herself together. "What about you, Sarah? How are you doing?"

Lydia knew that the approaching holidays would be a hard time for Sarah. Her friend had lost a baby last Christmas Eve, and Lydia knew the miscarriage still lingered painfully in Sarah's heart.

"I'm all right," Sarah said. She tried to smile.

Lydia knew Sarah better than that, but before she could say more, she heard footsteps coming down the stairs. She quickly gathered the edge of her apron and blotted her tear-streaked face. "I don't want the children to know of this."

Sarah nodded.

"What's wrong?" Anna Marie asked when she entered the den.

"Nothing." Lydia tried to sound casual. "Just chatting with Sarah."

Anna Marie narrowed her eyes in her mother's direction. "You've been crying. What is it, *Mamm*?"

"I'm fine, Anna Marie. Did you finish your sewing?" She held her head high, looked at her daughter.

"*Ya*, I finished." Anna Marie cupped her hands on her hips and blew out a sigh of exasperation. "Why? Do you need me to do something else?"

Lydia cringed at the sound of Anna Marie's tone—and she needn't show such disrespect in front of Sarah. She sent her daughter a warning with her eyes and said, "We need to put labels on the jams and jellies later, and bind more cookbooks. I also have some soaps packaged to sell. Pauline Sampler said she has sold everything we've brought to her store."

"That's *wunderbaar*," Sarah chimed in.

"A true blessing." Lydia walked across the room to a small table, where her loosely bound cookbooks were piled. She picked one up. "We've sold enough of these to pay for all of our winter supplies this year. The *Englischers* seem to love them."

Anna Marie stomped across the den toward the kitchen. "I'll go put the labels on, but I don't know why Jacob and John can't help more. Plus I'm tired of putting cookbooks together." She twisted her head around. "And I know you are not telling me something. You treat me like a child."

"We do not talk that way in this *haus*, Anna Marie," Lydia said as her daughter rounded the corner.

Sarah stood up. "I should probably go," she said. "I still need to stop by the market. I just wanted to check on you."

Lydia walked alongside her. "Ever since Anna Marie began her *rumschpringe*, she is testy with me."

Her friend smiled. "It's her age."

"I reckon," Lydia conceded.

She hoped and prayed that Anna Marie wouldn't do half of the things she'd done during her own running-around period. The thought instantly brought her back to Daniel, and recollections of the time they spent together in their teenage years. Then the reality of his return punched at her gut, and she grabbed her side.

Sarah leaned in for a hug. "Everything will be fine, Lydia. You will see."

Lydia returned the embrace, unsure how her friend could possibly think things would ever be fine again.

Later that same afternoon, Daniel's father was in the front yard when Daniel pulled up in his new buggy, led by Sugar, a fine horse he'd purchased from Levi Lapp. It was surprising how quickly it all came back to him—gentle flicks of the reins and the subtle gestures necessary to guide the animal.

"He's a fine horse," Gideon Smucker said. He looped his thumbs through his suspenders and pushed his straw hat back to have a better look. "How does he handle?"

"*Gut*. I had no troubles." Another surprise—how easily his Pennsylvania *Deitsch* was coming back to him as well. Daniel could tell that it pleased his father to hear him speak the dialect.

"And I see you are back in plain clothing and got yourself a proper haircut," his father added. He eyed Daniel's black pants, dark blue shirt, and straw hat, then nodded his approval. But his face quickly grew serious, and he stroked his gray beard. "Did you talk to Lydia?"

"Just briefly." Daniel paused, secured his new horse, and then walked alongside his father toward the house. "She was surprised to see me, to say the least."

"*Ya.* I reckon she was."

He pulled the door open for his father. As Gideon Smucker shuffled across the wooden floor in the den and headed toward the kitchen, Daniel breathed in the smells of his childhood home, flooding his mind with precious memories—and awful pangs of regret.

He continued through the den behind his father. The years that had passed were evident in the older man's stance. His shoulders curled forward, forcing him to bend over slightly at the waist as he walked.

The house was almost exactly as it had been when Daniel left—two rocking chairs to the right side of the fireplace, a dark green couch against the far wall, and the rug in the middle of the floor, now much more weathered and lacking the vibrant colors Daniel remembered. He'd played a lot of card games on that rug with his sisters. When he first saw Bethany and Eve upon his return three days ago, he'd been so proud of the fine women they'd become. They were just kids when he left—Bethany ten and Eve twelve. Now each woman had two children of her own. More regret plagued Daniel's heart for all that he had missed.

He pressed his lips closed and breathed in the familiar smell of fresh bread baking, then headed to the kitchen.

"Smells mighty *gut*," his father said to his mother as he took a seat in one of the wooden chairs surrounding the table—a long, wooden structure that could seat ten comfortably.

Daniel stood in the kitchen. A stranger in what used to be his home. But when his mother turned around and smiled in his direction, it calmed Daniel, just the way her smile had when he was a child.

"Sit down, Daniel," she said warmly. "I'll serve you up some butter bread. Got plenty of jams there on the table too. Supper won't be ready for a bit. Havin' meat loaf." She paused, fused her green eyes with Daniel's. "Is it still your favorite, no?"

Daniel recognized the same regret in her voice that he himself felt. "It is still my favorite," he assured her. He sat down in a chair across from his father, but he couldn't seem to pull his eyes from his mother. Her warm smile was exactly the same, but most everything else about her face was different. Deep lines webbed from the corners of her eyes, and similar creases stretched across her forehead. Daniel wondered how many of those wrinkles had his name on them. Like his father, Lena Smucker was much thinner than he remembered, and frail.

Daniel was lost in regret for what he'd done to his parents. The event itself. And then the lie. But he reassured himself that his choice at the time had been best for all of them.

As if reading his mind, his father said, "You said you spoke with Lydia. Did you tell her the truth about why you left?"

"No. Not yet." It had been hard enough to tell his parents and the bishop.

"The sooner you do that, the better. You owe her an explanation." His father shook his head. "It was so wrong what you boys did—the both of ya. I'll never understand—"

"Gideon, please . . ." *Mamm* spun around and faced the two men, a wooden spoon dangling from her hand, dripping brown sauce onto the floor. "Let's please don't do this now. Please." Her voice begged Pop to let the conversation drop.

Gideon's mouth thinned with displeasure, but he stayed silent.

Daniel knew that his father's response to his confession could have been much worse. His anger seemed padded with gratitude that Daniel was home now.

Bishop Ebersol, too, had accepted the news much better than Daniel expected. But Daniel knew who his harshest critic would be. Lydia. Daniel and Elam made decisions one Christmas Eve that changed the way all three of them would live their lives, with no consideration of Lydia's thoughts on the matter. And for that, she might never be able to forgive either of them.

∽

Three days later, Lydia went to bed early after spending a quiet Sunday with her children. Thankfully, she hadn't seen Daniel since Thursday, but she couldn't shake the memories that continued to flood her mind, which kept her tossing and turning until much too late. She'd barely been asleep an hour when she bolted from her bed at eleven o'clock. Mother's instinct. Something was wrong. She scurried into her robe, pushed back tangled tresses, and blinked her eyes into focus as best she could in the dark.

She grabbed the flashlight she kept on her nightstand and made her way down the hall. She quietly pushed open the door to John and Jacob's room and pointed the light toward them, enough to see that they were both sleeping soundly. After breathing a sigh of relief, she closed the door and took a few steps to Anna Marie's door on the opposite side of the hallway. She stood still for a moment and recalled all the times she'd sneaked out of the house during her *rumschpringe*—most of those times to meet Daniel.

She rubbed her left temple and tried to push away the visions of him, but Daniel's presence in her home—in her and Elam's home—kept replaying like a bad dream, the kind you can't wake up from. She squeezed her eyes closed and took a deep breath, blowing it out slowly.

Please, God, let her be in there. Times were much different now than during her running-around period. The *Englisch* world was a far more dangerous place.

Lydia's heart pounded. She hesitated for a moment, then pushed the wooden door wide and shined the flashlight.

Anna Marie wasn't there.

After searching the entire house, and even outside, she finally went back into John and Jacob's room. She knelt down beside her older son.

"Jacob. Jacob, wake up." She shined the light on his quilt, away from his eyes, but illuminating his blond locks.

"*Mamm?* What is it?" He rubbed his eyes with one hand and pushed the flashlight away with the other. "It's too bright."

"Jacob, I can't find your sister. She's not in her room."

Jacob sighed. "*Ya*, she does that sometimes." He attempted to roll onto his side.

Lydia poked him on the shoulder. "She does what? Tell me, Jacob."

"She sneaks down the stairs and leaves," John said from across the room.

Lydia bolted up and turned the light toward John, who immediately shielded his eyes. His own blond hair spiked upward. Only Anna Marie had inherited her mother's dark hair.

"What?" Lydia looked back and forth between the boys. "What do you mean?"

Was it possible that both her sons were aware of this treason going on right under her own roof? Why didn't they tell on their sister? Lydia could recall a time not too long ago when both younger boys wouldn't miss an opportunity to snitch on their older sister—most recently, when Anna Marie had purchased a portable phone at the store in town. Her daughter had prepaid minutes and spent hours on the device before Lydia found out. The boys told on their sister when she wouldn't let them use the phone.

"Why haven't you told me about this?" she demanded. She flashed the light from one boy to the other.

Young John shrugged, but Jacob spoke up. "She said we'd be havin' our *rumschpringe* some day, and if we told on her, she'd tell on us."

Lydia stomped her foot. "Neither of you made a *gut* bargain, since Anna Marie will likely be gone and married before either of you have your *rumschpringe*! Shame on you both for keeping this from me. Anna Marie could be in danger, or—"

"I reckon she's with Amos Zook." Jacob sat up and rubbed his eyes again. "She done took a fancy to him months ago."

Amos had driven Anna Marie home from Sunday singings on several occasions, but Lydia didn't think they were officially

22   BETH WISEMAN

courting. They seemed like an unlikely couple to Lydia. Her daughter was very outspoken and social, always right in the middle of any youth activities, especially volleyball after the Sunday singings. Amos stayed more to himself and could often be found on the sidelines. He seemed a very nice boy, but a bit timid.

Again her mind raced back eighteen years—to how unmatched everyone thought she and Daniel were. Lydia had been spirited, like Anna Marie, but mostly followed the rules. Daniel was softspoken until he felt an injustice had occurred, and then he reacted in a way that often got him into trouble.

She recalled a time in the eighth grade, when Daniel thought the teacher had treated a student unfairly in class, reprimanding the boy unnecessarily in front of the other students. Daniel voiced his feelings to the teacher—in front of the entire class. He told Lydia later that his behavior earned him a paddling from his father when he got home, but he said he had no regrets.

When they were a little older, Daniel even approached the bishop when a member of the community was shunned for installing a small amount of electricity in his barn, claiming it was necessary for his business. The man was a carpenter, but because of arthritis in one hand, he could no longer operate some of his nonpowered tools—devices not available in gas-powered or battery-operated versions. He refused to disconnect the power, and the bishop had been unsympathetic and upheld the shunning. Daniel voiced his opinion about that too.

Lydia shook her head, trying to clear the images from her mind.

She sat down on the side of Jacob's bed and looked hard at her son. "You best tell me where your sister is, if you know."

Jacob avoided her threatening stare and scratched his chin.

"Jacob!" Lydia snapped.

Her son rolled his eyes. "She's going to be real mad at me."

When did her children start being so disrespectful? Jacob would have never rolled his eyes if Elam were in the room.

"You best stop rolling those eyes at me," she demanded. "*I will be mad at you if you don't tell me where Anna Marie is.*"

Jacob twisted his mouth from side to side, then said, "The old oak tree."

"How do you know this?"

Jacob shrugged.

"I will deal with you later, more than likely out by the woodshed!"

Elam had spanked all the children from time to time, out by the woodshed, but Lydia could never bring herself to discipline them in that way. Maybe she should. Maybe if she had, Anna Marie wouldn't be at the old oak tree—with Amos Zook.

A muscle quivered in Jacob's jaw, and his hurt shone in his sleepy eyes. Lydia knew her comment was fueled by fear. She reminded herself that Jacob was barely twelve, a long way from being a man, but too old for her to make idle threats. She pushed back his hair, then leaned down and kissed him on the cheek.

"I'm sorry I snapped at you, Jacob. I'm just worried about Anna Marie."

Jacob responded with a lazy half smile. "I know, *Mamm*."

Lydia patted his knee and then stood up. She pointed her finger back and forth between her boys. "Don't you boys ever do this." She blew them both a kiss. "Watch your brother," she said, and walked out the bedroom door.

Lydia went to change out of her nightclothes. She couldn't believe that the teenagers were still going to the old oak tree off Leaman Road. So many times she'd met Daniel there. . . .

She hoped that the innocent encounters at the old oak tree hadn't escalated into something else over the years.

But times were different. And Lydia's heart was heavy with worry.

Chapter Three

Daniel couldn't sleep, and it was no wonder. Ever since he'd seen Lydia again, his mind twisted with longing, regret, and feelings that he'd suppressed for almost two decades. And yet, when he'd laid eyes on his first love a few days ago, it was as if no time had passed at all.

But the years *had* passed, and they weren't the same people anymore. Lydia wouldn't approve of the life he'd led in the outside world. Daniel himself didn't approve of the choices he'd made.

He turned onto his side and buried his face in the white pillowcase, appreciating the fresh smell of line-dried linens. A small gas heater warmed his childhood bedroom, and the aroma of meat loaf and baked bread hung in the room like a reminder of all he'd missed. How different his life would have been had he not left this idyllic place.

Instead, he'd moved in with Lonnie, an *Englisch* buddy he'd met during his *rumschpringe.* Lonnie gave Daniel a place to stay until he could get his own apartment, but Lonnie also introduced him to a world he hadn't known anything about prior to him leaving the Old Order district—a world filled with alcohol, drugs, parties, and women. Even though he'd never felt comfortable there, Daniel had allowed himself to live that life for much too long. Almost six years. He took odd jobs to get by, mostly carpentry work since that was all he really knew. But with each step he took further into the *Englisch* world, he felt more and more detached from all he'd never known. Most important, from God.

Then he'd met Jenny, a beautiful woman who'd been raised Catholic. Jenny had a strong faith, and his friendship with her was a turning point for Daniel. He said good-bye to a way of life in which he'd merely been existing. He dated Jenny and ultimately reestablished a relationship with God. He thought about Lydia often during that time, comparing the two women. Perhaps that's why he'd never asked Jenny to marry him. For almost two years he found a sampling of what he remembered from his youth, a certain calm that settles over a man when he is living the way the Lord wants him to live. He went to work every day, spent time with Jenny in the evenings and on weekends, and even attended church with her.

But when Jenny was killed by a drunk driver, Daniel in his grief wasted no time returning to his old ways. His relationship with God suffered, and accepting anything as his will became a challenge. How could his Father have put him on this path of self-destruction, when all Daniel had ever wanted was to do the right thing by God and by others? For the next seven years he moved from place to place, working at jobs that barely afforded him enough to live on. With each year that had passed, it was harder and harder to remember the peace he'd known when he was young.

But then Daniel met Margaret. When he was as down on his luck as a man could be, seventy-year-old Margaret took him in and showed him another way to live. Daniel felt a connection to this wise woman that he could only explain as divine intervention.

He started out doing handyman work in exchange for room and board, but eventually he became to Margaret like the son she'd never had. They'd often drink hot tea late in the evening, and Daniel would tell her all about his childhood. Margaret listened intently, never pushing Daniel to confide more than he was ready to share. But eventually he told her everything, even what had happened that fateful Christmas Eve. When Margaret passed peacefully in her sleep four years later, Daniel was in a new spiritual place, and it was time. Time to go home.

He tossed and turned again. He closed his eyes to pray, but his communication was interrupted when he heard horse hooves, faint at first, then louder.

He glanced at the clock on his bedside table. A quarter to midnight. He threw the covers back, stepped onto the cool wooden planks, and then crept across the floor, purposely stretching his legs wide to avoid two slats in the floor that creaked loudly enough to wake his parents—something he'd found out in his youth.

His pants were thrown across the bed instead of hung on the rack or stowed in the dirty clothes bin. His mother would be appalled by his sloppy housekeeping. He pulled on the dark trousers, then grabbed a crisp white shirt from the rack and buttoned it on his way down the stairs.

By the time he reached the door, the visitor was already on the porch. Lydia. And she was frantic.

"What's wrong?" he asked, opening the screen for her.

She just stood there.

"I need your *daed*. He's the only person Anna Marie listens to these days." Lydia cupped her cheeks with both hands. "I hate to wake him and Lena. I should just go myself." She turned to leave, then swung back around. "But I'm so afraid . . . and if anyone can get through to her, it's Gideon."

Daniel wasn't sure what to do. Lydia couldn't even stand still, twisting about, shaking her head. He felt guilty for thinking how beautiful she was even in her desperate state and with her daughter in some sort of trouble.

"What are you afraid of? Do you know where she went?" Daniel glanced down and realized his appearance. Shirttail hanging, barefoot, slept-on hair.

Lydia finally brushed past him and into the den, shivering. Her black cape and bonnet were not enough protection from the night air. "I'm going to go wake him," she said, stepping around Daniel.

"Wait." He gently grabbed her arm. "Don't wake Pop. I'll go with you to look for Anna Marie."

Lydia pulled out of his hold. Anger swept across her face, and her hands landed on her hips. "I don't need to *look* for her. I know where she is." Then her face softened a tad. "I—I just don't know what to do when I get there. It will be awkward, and I—"

"Where is she?"

Lydia looked down for moment. When her eyes finally lifted to meet his, a blush engulfed her cheeks, and she gazed into Daniel's eyes. "She's at the old oak tree—with a boy."

Daniel stifled a grin. "Kids still go there?"

"*Ya.*" She pried her eyes from his. "And you know what they do there."

Daniel didn't know Lydia as a mother, only as a young

woman with dreams—dreams she had fulfilled with someone else. He didn't recognize this maternal Lydia, whose eyes shone with worry. "They kiss," he said softly as his eyes homed in on Lydia's lips.

Then her eyes met with his in such a way that Daniel knew Lydia, too, was recalling the tenderness they'd shared, innocent kisses beneath moonlit nights, stars twinkling overhead. It was no surprise that young love still flourished underneath the protective limbs of the old oak tree.

"Times are different now," she whispered. "Elam and I . . ."

She paused, and now it was Daniel who couldn't look her in the eye. They'd had a life together, Elam and Lydia. Three children. To hear her refer to them as a couple was difficult.

"Elam and I," she went on, "tried our best to protect the children from outside influences, but with Anna Marie in her *rumschpringe* and all—I'm just worried. Times aren't the same as when we were . . ."

"Under the old oak tree?"

"*Ya*," she said softly.

Daniel stepped forward and reached for the words. "Lydia, I'm sure that you and Elam raised Anna Marie properly, and given that, I'm sure you have nothing to worry about. Why don't you let me go with you to get her?"

"No," she said, straightening to attention.

"Pop sure looked tired when he went to bed. Sure you want to wake him?" It was a stretch. His father hadn't looked all that tired, but suddenly Daniel was desperate to go with her, to be a part of her life.

Lydia took a deep breath. "No, I really don't want to wake

30   BETH WISEMAN

him, but he has been so *gut* with Anna Marie since Elam died. She listens to her grandfather, and mostly she just gets angry with me. Besides, what would I say to her and Amos?" She scrunched her face into a scowl, then rapidly shook her head back and forth. "Anna Marie shouldn't be in such a place."

"The old oak is a beautiful place." But Daniel could see in Lydia's face that somehow what seemed fine for her so many years ago did not seem okay for her daughter. "I'm sure Anna Marie is using good judgment, Lydia. Let me put my shoes on and grab a jacket. I'll go with you."

Her forehead creased, and she pressed her lips firmly together. "All right," she finally said.

Daniel hurried up the stairs, quietly as he could. In his room, he fished around in the dark for his shoes and then remembered the flashlight on his nightstand. He shined the light around the room until he located his black tennis shoes in the far corner, then pulled a pair of black socks from the chest of drawers. He sat down on the bed, stretched the socks over his cold feet, and slipped his shoes on, his stomach rolling with anticipation.

He tiptoed to the bathroom, swooshed mouthwash, and spit, wishing he had more time to groom himself properly. But she was waiting.

Daniel walked briskly down the stairs, shining the light as he walked. When he hit the floor in the den, he stopped abruptly, his heart thudding against his chest. *Where is she?*

Her scent tarried in the room, but he knew before he even reached the window that she was gone. He gazed out into the night just in time to hear a faint whistle, the pounding of hooves against the dirt, and to see her buggy begin its descent down the dirt driveway.

Daniel flung open the door and hurried onto the porch. He opened his mouth to yell out to her, but remembered his parents asleep upstairs.

"Lydia," he whispered instead, as he watched her disappear into the darkness.

Chapter Four

Lydia maneuvered her buggy across Lincoln Highway, propelled by the kind of determination that only a fearful mother could understand. Her glove-clad hands trembled as she neared Leaman Road, and she fought to keep a steady hold on the reins. As the lights from the highway grew dim behind her, Lydia pushed forward into the darkness of the cold night, wondering why her daughter and Amos would be so silly as to choose the old oak tree in this frigid weather.

But, of course, she knew why.

Lydia recalled the massive trunk and the sprawling branches that stretched upward, then draped to the ground. She remembered the way the moonlight charmed its way between the forked offshoots, gently illuminating those seeking to bask in the magic of the moment. Lydia could almost feel the misty dew dusting her cheeks, clouding the air around her—around her and Daniel—and the tenderness of his lips against hers. She should never have gone to get Gideon, knowing there was a chance she'd run into Daniel.

She pulled back on the reins, slowed the buggy, and pulled to the side of the road, trying to remember what it was like to be sixteen and in love, and how she would have felt if one of her parents had ever approached her when she was under the old oak tree with Daniel. Lydia leaned out the window, making sure she was completely off the road, and clicked off the lights on the buggy.

She had shared tender moments of first love with Daniel underneath that tree. Did she really want to ruin that for Anna Marie by charging in there like a hysterical shrew, demanding Anna Marie hightail it home, and destroy what Lydia knew deep in her heart was an innocent encounter between a boy and a girl enjoying the thrill of sneaking out during their *rumschpringe?*

She'd raised Anna Marie well, and despite the recent distance between them, she knew her daughter would make wise choices. Perhaps she should trust her, let her enjoy this special moment, and then make it clear to her tomorrow that sneaking out was unacceptable. Even more improper on a Sunday.

Lydia smiled, thinking how her parents would have never taken that approach. Her mother would have sent her father to drag her home, and she would have been humiliated beyond recovery. *Thank goodness we never got caught.*

She wrapped the thick, brown blanket tightly around her, hoping Amos had been smart enough to at least bring a blanket, the way Daniel always had. Lydia sat in the buggy and recalled the events of the day, still not confident enough to ride away and leave the two teenagers. In the distance she could see the spanning might of the old oak against blue-gray skies.

Part of her still wanted to storm forward and drag Anna Marie home—the motherly part of her. But the woman inside of Lydia beckoned her to let the girl be, just for tonight. Recollections invaded Lydia's mind, sending her back to a place and time with Daniel. For a few moments she lost herself in the past, a place she seldom chose to visit.

Then pangs of guilt stabbed at her insides, and she reminded herself that she'd married another, and that such memories should be squelched in honor of Elam. Daniel had betrayed her, and she had married his brother—a wonderful man who had picked up the pieces of her broken life and patched her back together. Over time, Elam's patchwork grew stronger and became a thick barrier of resistance against the memories she harbored of Daniel. And she'd fallen in love with Elam.

Why did Daniel have to come back? After all these years, she'd never considered the possibility that he might return. The way he looked at her today, the sound of his voice, his touch—it rattled her. She could feel her heart starting to spider with tiny cracks, threatening to tear down the protective armor where memories of Daniel had lain dormant for all these years.

Her thoughts were interrupted by a faraway rustling, and Lydia watched as Amos's buggy began the trek from the tree to Leaman Road. She considered trying to turn around and get back on the road ahead of them, get home, crawl into bed, and talk with Anna Marie in the morning, but instead she stayed where she was.

It was several minutes later when the headlights from Amos's buggy drew closer, and she shielded her eyes from the light in front of her. As they passed by her, Amos did not look her way, nor did Anna Marie. But they knew she was there, and that's all that mattered.

Lydia doubted Anna Marie would be sneaking out again, at least for a while. And no one had been embarrassed or humiliated, and her daughter would be home soon enough. She knew the Zooks well. Amos was a good boy, and he would be a fine choice for courting Anna Marie. Although tomorrow Lydia would need to sit down and establish some boundaries for her daughter.

Lydia twisted her neck around and waited until Anna Marie and Amos had safely crossed Lincoln Highway, then she motioned her horse into action. But she didn't turn the buggy around. Instead, she headed toward the old oak tree.

~

Daniel made his way down Leaman Road, unsure what he'd walk into but determined to be there for Lydia if she needed him. Maybe in some tiny way he could start to make up for his own past by helping her with her children in the absence of Elam.

But as he neared the old oak tree, wondrous recollections of his time there with Lydia paraded through his mind, mixing with a sense of anguish over the life he'd missed out on. He reminded himself, the choices were his to make.

He turned onto the worn path created by generations who had sought privacy beneath the tree, where he had first told Lydia that he loved her. As he traveled down the winding trail, it felt like he was entering a time warp, a magical place where the past stayed the past and you never had to leave.

Daniel pulled up beside the only buggy parked near the tree. Since all the buggies looked almost exactly the same, he wasn't sure who he would find. Maybe Lydia had changed her mind about coming out here, and Daniel was about to intrude on Anna Marie and her beau, which certainly was not his place. He stepped out of the buggy, closed the door, and knew that whoever was beneath the branches was certainly aware of his presence.

With slow, intentional steps he moved forward, tucked his head to pass under a low branch, then straightened within the magical dome. He filled his nostrils with the familiarity of the air around him, a sweet, dewy fragrance that he'd never smelled anywhere else. Lydia used to say that no one left the old oak without falling in love.

He blinked his eyes several times, adjusted to the darkness, and briefly wondered if he was dreaming. But there she was—his Lydia—standing alone, delicate rays of moonlight brushing her cheeks, her eyes twinkling mysteriously, and Daniel wondered if there was enough magic in the night to re-create what they'd shared so long ago.

"Is everything all right?" he asked. She had the strangest look on her face, and he couldn't help but wonder if her thoughts mirrored his. "When I came downstairs, you'd left, and I just wanted to make sure you were okay."

She didn't respond, but took two steps toward him.

"Lydia?" he said after a few moments. She took another step toward him, her eyes hazy with emotion.

"Do you remember the first time we came here?" she asked.

Of course he did. He remembered every single time he'd been with her anywhere. "As if it happened yesterday," he said, hoping his eyes would convey the importance of his statement.

"You promised to love me forever," she said as her lips curved slightly upward.

But her brown eyes narrowed, confusing him. She leaned close to him and looked up, putting her lips within a few inches of his chin. He could feel her breath, and she smiled again. But something about the smile caused Daniel to feel uneasy.

"You lied," she added simply. Then she backed away from him, but she never took her eyes from his.

You lied. You lied. You lied. The words echoed in Daniel's head, reverberating against the part of his brain that was trying to decipher whether or not he really had lied. He'd always planned to love her forever.

"I didn't lie," he said with boyish defensiveness. "I wanted to love you forever, but . . ."

She shook her head feverishly. "It really doesn't matter," she said, and then shot him the same confusing smile. "I found my true love. If you hadn't left, Elam and I would never have married and had three wonderful children." She arched her brows proudly.

Daniel hung his head for a moment, then raised his eyes to hers. "I guess you're right." He couldn't deny the truth in what she said. Maybe his leaving was meant to be.

He filled his lungs with the atmosphere around them, losing hope that there was enough magic to let them pick up where they'd left off so many years ago. *Please, God, let me do right by her*, he silently prayed.

"Of course I'm right!" she finally said.

Then why was she raising her voice in such a way? Daniel took a couple of steps toward her. "Lydia," he whispered. As he grew closer, he could see tears in her eyes. He took a chance and stretched his arms forward. "Lydia," he said again.

But she backed away.

"Leave me alone, Daniel." She swiped at one eye and held her chin high. "It's true that you are my children's uncle. I will respect that. For the children, and for Lena and Gideon. But I would prefer to keep company with you only when—when it's necessary."

All he could muster was "I'm sorry." Then he realized that the whole purpose of the mission had gotten lost somewhere. "What about Anna Marie? Is she all right?"

"*Ya.*" Lydia didn't elaborate, and her eyes were still fused with his.

Did she have more to say? Was she waiting on him to say something else?

"That's *gut*," he said finally.

Maybe now was the time. Maybe he should tell her the truth now, tell her why he'd left Lancaster County that Christmas Eve. But would it even matter? She said she'd forgiven him, but it sure didn't sound like it right now.

As he considered his options, Lydia walked toward him once again, and this time she cut him off at the knees.

"I never loved you the way I loved Elam," she said coolly and with the same smile on her face as before. Then she turned away, bent low, and slid beneath the branches.

Daniel listened to her rush across the grass and climb into her buggy. His feet stayed planted with the roots of the tree beneath him.

Hooves met with dirt, and with each *clippity-clop*, Lydia grew farther and farther away. Until it was quiet, eerily quiet, beneath the old oak tree.

Chapter Five

Lydia spooned dippy eggs onto Jacob and John's plates the next morning, so the boys could eat and get started on their morning chores. Evidently, Anna Marie had overslept. She knew breakfast was served promptly at five, and Lydia assumed her daughter was exhausted from her little trip last night. No excuse. There's a household to run and much to do in preparation for Thanksgiving in less than two weeks.

Lydia had hosted Thanksgiving since the first year she and Elam were married. Both her side of the family and Elam's would gather at her home again this year. She pulled the biscuits from the oven, put them on the table, and realized that there was no way to exclude Daniel from the festivities.

"Where's Anna Marie?" Jacob asked with a mouthful of eggs, trying to stifle a grin.

"I'm sure your sister is tired this morning." Lydia shot Jacob a look signifying that no more discussion was needed.

"Anna Marie's in trouble," John added with a twinkle in his bright blue eyes.

Lydia put her hands on her hips. "No one said anything about trouble. You mind your manners and eat your breakfast." She glanced toward Jacob. "Both of you. Those cows are ready for milking, and I have a very long list of things we need to do to get ready for Thanksgiving."

Lydia refilled John's glass with milk, then turned when she heard footsteps descending the stairs.

"Sorry I'm late." Anna Marie slid onto the wooden bench across from her brothers and bowed her head in silent prayer.

"*Ya*, and we know why." Jacob chuckled.

Anna Marie raised her head and cut her eyes in Jacob's direction. "You better be quiet."

"Stop it," Lydia said sternly. She served Anna Marie some eggs and then turned to Jacob and John. "Finish your breakfast. Quietly. You both have chores to tend to."

All the children ate silently, and Lydia contemplated the conversation she would have with Anna Marie after the boys left for school. There was a fine line between parenting Anna Marie and pushing her away, but Lydia knew she couldn't tolerate sneaking out of the house, no matter how sympathetic she was about her daughter's budding romance.

It was hard for Lydia to believe that Jacob would be sixteen in four years and also entering his *rumschpringe*. Thankfully, nine-year-old John had even longer to go before Lydia would have to watch her baby boy venture out to learn about the *Englisch* world.

She walked to the kitchen counter, placed her palms on the edge, and took a deep breath, wishing Daniel's face would stop creeping into her thoughts. It was a distraction that caused her a variety of emotions, none of which she wanted to feel. This morning, it was mostly guilt. It was as if her heart had been dipped in truth serum and was sending confessions to her brain about a love that had never died.

But I loved Elam.

"I'm done. I'll go start the washing." Anna Marie pushed her plate away. "Hopefully we have enough gasoline left to power the wringer."

Lydia nodded, but was mentally calculating. Today was Monday, wash day. No worship service yesterday, which meant they would attend church this coming Sunday, as was always the case—every other Sunday. Lydia cringed, realizing that Lena and Gideon were scheduled to host worship in their home this next weekend. She was sure Daniel would be attending, no matter who hosted, but it would seem even more intimate being at his childhood home.

The first time Lydia ever ate supper at Lena and Gideon's house, she was Daniel's guest, with no way to know that she would end up spending fifteen years alongside his brother at that very same table.

She recalled the first time Daniel asked her to a Sunday singing, when she was sixteen and just entering her *rumschpringe*. They were both working at the annual mud sale at the fire station in Penryn. The event was mostly run by Amish men and women. Plows, farm equipment, and large items were auctioned in the field next to the firehouse. Inside, the women auctioned quilts and household wares.

On that particular day, the auction had held up to its name. Heavy rain had doused the ground, and everyone's shoes were covered in mud. Lydia left the indoor auction to go find her father. Instead, she'd bumped into Daniel and Gideon. Her father-in-law to-be was bidding on a plow out in the open field. When Daniel saw her, he sloshed toward her in mud up to his ankles, smiling as he maneuvered his way through the crowd.

He'd already been in his running-around period for a year,

and Lydia recalled the smoothness of his voice on that day. "Wanna get out of here?" he'd asked.

She'd nodded. No words were really necessary. She'd seen the way Daniel stared at her during worship service. They sneaked away from the mud sale, walked down the paved street that ran in front of the fire station, and then cut down a gravel street that wound through the meadows, speckled with mostly *Englisch* farms. Lydia was sure they walked five miles that day. She had blisters when they returned to the auction site. They'd talked and talked, about anything and everything. She knew on that day that she would marry Daniel Smucker.

She sighed. Thanksgiving, then Daniel's baptism, worship every other Sunday, family visits, social gatherings . . . There was no way around it, Daniel was sure to become a permanent part of their lives. She'd need to harness any feelings that attempted to creep to the surface and focus on the things she had been tending to prior to his arrival—raising her children and running her household in a way that would make Elam proud.

And with that thought, she finished packing Jacob's and John's lunches.

"*Mamm*, we're out of gasoline for the washer." Anna Marie walked back into the kitchen, toting the red gasoline container they kept in the shed. "I'm going to take the buggy to *Mammi* and *Daadi*'s house to get some."

Lydia nodded. Her father-in-law always had plenty of gasoline on hand, and he always enjoyed a visit from one of the children.

Daniel. He would be there, of course. Lydia clamped her eyes tight, again fighting the visions of him.

"Anna Marie," she said before her daughter reached the front door.

"*Ya?*"

"We need to have a talk when you get back."

"I know, *Mamm*," Anna Marie said. "Thanks to my brothers, no doubt." She smiled slightly and then turned to leave.

Maybe it was Anna Marie's tone—calm, understanding, all-knowing—but Lydia had a sudden realization. Her baby was growing up.

~

Daniel had just finished helping his father milk the cows when he heard a buggy pulling up.

"That'd be Anna Marie," Gideon said to his son. "It's Monday. I reckon she's out of gas for the washing machine." He chuckled. "I think she does that on purpose as an excuse to come visit and avoid some of her chores. She's become such a regular on Mondays, your *mamm* usually bakes somethin' special for the girl to snack on when she gets here."

Daniel watched Anna Marie step out of the buggy. She looked a lot like her mother. Similar in height and frame, dark hair, deep brown eyes with a brightness and wonder all their own.

"I'm out of gas," Anna Marie called to her grandfather in such a way that Daniel knew immediately his father had been right—she ran out on purpose.

"Ain't that a surprise." Gideon grinned. He tipped his straw hat with his finger, walked toward the girl, and retrieved the empty can. "Get on into the house now and see what your *mammi*'s got cooked for ya."

Daniel started to follow his father across the yard, but Gideon turned and said, "Go spend some time with your niece. Get to know the girl." He pointed toward the farmhouse.

Daniel complied, but to himself he said, *I'm not so sure Anna Marie wants to get to know me.*

"I'm headed to town," his mother said when Daniel walked into the kitchen. "Daniel, sit down and have yourself a muffin with Anna Marie." She pointed to a chair across the table.

If Daniel didn't know better, he'd think that his parents had set up this whole scenario. He pulled out the chair and sat down.

When his mother left the room, Anna Marie eyed him with the same skepticism as before.

"Great muffins," he mumbled after he took a large bite and swallowed.

Anna Marie finished chewing and narrowed her eyes. "Why don't you have a *fraa* and *kinner*?"

Daniel shrugged. This was not a conversation he wanted to have with Lydia's daughter. "Just don't."

"Haven't you ever been *in lieb*?" Anna Marie's eyes began to sparkle, reflective of someone who was in love herself.

"*Ya*, I have been in love," he said.

"With who? Why didn't you marry her? Was she *Englisch*?"

Daniel cocked his head to one side. "You sure ask a lot of questions."

"I'm *in lieb*," she said breezily.

Daniel stifled a grin. "Really?" He reached for another muffin.

"*Ya*. We're going to be married next November." Anna Marie propped her elbows on the table and rested her chin in her hands.

Daniel wondered if Lydia had heard this exciting news. "And what does your *mamm* think about this?"

Anna Marie's expression soured. "She doesn't know yet." Her brows furrowed. "And please don't tell her."

Daniel shook his head. "No, I won't. That's your place." He paused. "Why the secrecy?"

"*Ach*, it's no secret. Amos just proposed last night, and I haven't had a chance to tell yet."

Her face lit up, much like Lydia's did when she was really happy—from what he remembered.

Daniel couldn't help but smile, knowing Amos had proposed under the old oak tree. He recalled his proposal to Lydia. While it wasn't under the oak tree, like their first kiss, it had been equally as romantic—a picnic on a spring day, wildflowers in full bloom, and enough love to sustain the two of them forever. At least, that had been the plan.

He and Lydia sat on the paisley quilt with the picnic lunch his mother had prepared, the bubbling creek only a few feet away. Blue skies and a gentle breeze, the best chicken salad he could remember eating, and Lydia—her eyes gazing into his.

Daniel returned to the present to find Anna Marie scoffing at him. "Are you listening?" she asked.

"Uh, sure." Daniel left the creek and the past and tried to focus on what his niece was saying, wondering how much he'd missed.

"Why, then?" Anna Marie leaned slightly forward and widened her questioning eyes.

"Why what?"

Anna Marie sighed. "I didn't think you were listening. I

asked you if you knew why *mei mamm* was crying after you left. Did you say something to upset her?"

Daniel pulled his eyes from hers and hung his head. "I certainly didn't mean to." He looked up to see Anna Marie growing less fond of him with each passing second, her eyes clawing at him like talons. Lydia's daughter was not going to be easy to win over. He wondered why the girl had already formed such a harsh opinion of him.

"I'm sorry I missed your *daed*'s funeral," he said. "I used to move around a lot, and my forwarded mail didn't make it to me in time." Daniel sighed, his heart filled with anguish. "I regret that more than you know."

But Anna Marie's expression didn't soften. She narrowed her eyes and pressed her lips together. Daniel reached for another muffin and tried to avoid her icy glare.

"What are you *really* doing here?" she finally asked.

Daniel took a bite of muffin, swallowed, and chose his words carefully. "I've spent enough time in the *Englisch* world to know that this is where I want to be. I miss my family."

"It took you eighteen years to realize that?"

Daniel leaned his head to one side and glared at her, wondering if the girl was always this disrespectful. "*Ya*," he said sternly. "It did."

Anna Marie rose from her chair, and it was then that Daniel noticed her right hand curled into a fist. She slowly opened her hand, and Daniel hoped she wasn't holding what he thought she was. *Couldn't be.*

She showed him her open hand. "Is this why you're back?"

Daniel took a deep breath and reached for the worn piece

of blue paper crumpled atop her flattened palm. His heart raced as he unfolded the note. There hadn't been much time, and he recalled how he had hurriedly scribbled the words. Seeing it again ripped open wounds that had never fully healed.

Dear Lydia,

> *I will love you until the day I die, but I can't stay here. The Englisch world is calling to me, and I can't live within the confines of our Old Order district. I hope that someday you can forgive me.*

Forever yours,
Daniel

"Where did you get this?" Daniel asked. *And why does Lydia still have it after all these years?* He wondered if he should be hopeful about this.

Anna Marie leaned down on both palms and looked Daniel in the eyes. "I hope that you have truly come back for the reasons you stated, that you miss your family and realize that you belong in the Amish community. Because if you have any hopes of rekindling a romance with *mei mamm*, you will be greatly disappointed. She loved my *daed* with all her heart and soul. He was her forever love. Not you."

And then she left without looking back.

Daniel stared at the note and wished that there was some way to change history, go back in time. He thought about how a split-second decision had changed the course of his life, and how he would forever live with its consequences.

Chapter Six

Lydia walked across the yard to join Anna Marie at the clothesline.

"This is the last load," her daughter said as she pinned up a pair of black socks.

Lydia scooped up a brown towel, grabbed two pins, and shivered. "Mighty cold out here."

"Not as cold as this morning when I took the buggy to *Daadi*'s *haus*. I plumb near froze."

Lydia twisted her mouth from side to side and debated how to approach the subject of Anna Marie's late-night outing. "I reckon it was even colder under the old oak tree last night," she said.

Anna Marie finished hanging another pair of black socks, then turned to face her mother. "Please don't be mad, *Mamm*. Not today. I promise I won't sneak out again." She grabbed both of Lydia's hands in hers and squeezed. "Amos asked me to marry him last night!"

"What? But I didn't even know the two of you were officially courting. Don't you think that's a bit quick?" But Lydia couldn't help but smile. Anna Marie was glowing, and she recognized the look.

"But I love him so much, *Mamm*. You know we've been going to the Sunday singings, and we spend all of our free time together. We want to get married next November!"

Relief washed over Lydia. They weren't going to have to plan a wedding within the next month or two, and both Anna

Marie and Amos would benefit from a year of courting, giving their relationship more time to mature. They would still only be seventeen when they married.

Lydia hugged Anna Marie and kissed her on the cheek. "It's *gut* to see you so happy." She pulled back and pointed a finger at her daughter. "But no more sneaking out of the house at night, Anna Marie. It worries me so. If your *daed* was here—"

"I won't, *Mamm*."

They were silent for a few moments as they pinned clothes to the line. Chilling winds blew through Lydia's black cape, and she could see Anna Marie shivering.

"One more towel," Lydia said. She clipped it to the line, then grabbed Anna Marie's hand. "Let's go sit by the fire."

"I talked with *Onkel* Daniel when I was at *Mammi* and *Daadi*'s," Anna Marie said when they walked inside.

Lydia closed the front door behind them and headed toward the fireplace. "I see." She tried to sound casual, but just the mention of Daniel's name caused her stomach to knot.

Anna Marie joined her mother in front of the hearth and warmed her palms. "I don't like him," she said as she scrunched her face in a most unbecoming way.

Lydia quickly turned toward her. "It's not proper to say such things." She wasn't sure what upset her more—the fact that Anna Marie would make such a comment, or the fact that it was directed at Daniel.

"Yes, ma'am."

"Let's get to putting these cookbooks together." Lydia walked to the table by the window where stacks of crisscrossed recipes were waiting to be organized and bound.

Anna Marie sat down at the table across from her. "Do you like him?" she asked. She lined the piles up in front of her and began to slip one page behind the other.

"Who?"

"*Onkel* Daniel."

Lydia took a deep breath and blew it out slowly. "He is your *daed*'s *bruder*. Of course I like him." She paused and then said, "Although, I don't really know him." The words stung with truth.

Anna Marie stopped working and twisted a strand of loose hair that slipped from the confines of her prayer covering. "Did you know him when you were young?" Her daughter's bottom lip quivered, and Lydia wondered what exactly Anna Marie and Daniel had talked about. Lydia clicked the pages on the table, smoothed the edges, and started inserting the binder into the square holes on the left margin.

"Of course I knew him. We all grew up together." Lydia sat up a little taller. Anna Marie was working again and handed her another stack ready to bind. "Why do you ask?"

Anna Marie shrugged. "He just seems very different from *Daed*."

"He spent many years in the *Englisch* world. I'm sure he'll come back around to our ways, since he's planning to be re-baptized the Sunday after Thanksgiving." Lydia knew that Daniel's shunning would be cast aside following his baptism, but she also knew that in *her* heart the shunning would continue.

"I bet he hurt a lot of people when he just up and left," Anna Marie said. "Especially—especially *Mammi* and *Daadi*."

"*Ya.* It was hard for them." Lydia didn't want to talk about this anymore. "What do you think about this cover your *aenti*

Miriam came up with? I like the wood-burning stove she drew and all the little details. Look at the smoke swirling up from the pot." She held the book up and faced it toward Anna Marie.

"I like it." Anna Marie looked up and smiled briefly.

"You finish up here," Lydia said. "I reckon I'll go brew us some hot cocoa. Your brothers will be home from school soon, and I'm sure they'd enjoy something warm in their tummies after a cold walk home."

Anna Marie nodded, but Lydia could tell her thoughts were somewhere else.

~

Daniel helped his father ready the house for Sunday worship. The sun was barely over the horizon when they carried the last of the benches from the barn into the house. His mother had been busy preparing food since before Daniel woke up, and the smell of freshly baked bread permeated the farmhouse.

"This should do it," Gideon said when the last bench was in place. "What else, Lena?" he hollered into the kitchen.

"That's all. I think we're ready." His mother walked into the den and touched Daniel's arm. "*Wunderbaar gut* to have you home for worship service."

Daniel smiled. His mother's joy warmed his soul, but regret still plagued his heart. Margaret had helped him learn to forgive himself through prayer, but true peace would come when he knew that Lydia's words of forgiveness were sincere. He hadn't seen any of her family all week, not since Anna Marie had sprung the note on him. He wondered if his niece said anything to Lydia about the letter. He suspected not.

Daniel felt the sting of the girl's words. *She loved my father with all her heart and soul. He was her forever love. Not you.*

As it should be, Daniel thought. But it didn't lessen the pain. He suddenly wondered if coming back here had been a mistake. Would it be simply a constant reminder of all he'd missed?

He could hear buggies pulling up outside and faint voices. He walked onto the front porch to greet visitors, many of whom he hadn't seen since he left the district. But when Lydia stepped from her buggy, smiled, and hugged his mother, Daniel closed his eyes and sighed.

"Hello, Daniel," she said politely when she walked up the porch steps. Then she turned to her sons. "Remember your *onkel* Daniel, boys?" She seemed intentionally formal.

Each son shook Daniel's hand. Anna Marie walked in behind the rest of them and crinkled her nose.

"Hello, Anna Marie." He tipped his straw hat in her direction.

She raised her chin a bit. "Hello." Then she scooted past him and into the kitchen.

~

Daniel's back started to ache about an hour into the service. It was going to take some time to adjust to the backless benches again, particularly during the three-hour church services.

As was customary, the men and boys sat on one side of the room, the women and girls on the other. From where Daniel was sitting, he couldn't see Lydia, but he could see Anna Marie, who took every opportunity to fire him a look that screamed, *You stay away from my mother.*

Sunday worship hadn't changed one bit in eighteen years,

and Daniel was glad he could still understand the service, spoken mostly in German. The temperature had dipped into the thirties, leaving it much too cold to eat outside. The men and boys sought seats throughout the downstairs, where tables had been placed. Women and young girls bustled around, serving meadow tea and placing applesauce, jams, and jellies on the tables. Daniel had missed the sweet tea leaves that grew wild in the meadows along the creeks in the area.

Lydia brushed past him, carrying two loaves of homemade bread. Their eyes locked, but she quickly looked away. Daniel joined his father at a table on the far side of the den.

He wasn't sure how or when, but he knew he needed to somehow find a quiet moment to speak with Lydia, to let her know that Anna Marie had found the note. It wasn't going to earn him any points, but Daniel felt Lydia needed to know.

It was almost two hours later before the large crowd disassembled. Daniel saw Lydia gathering up casserole dishes, and it looked like she was preparing to leave. She had avoided him all afternoon, refusing to even make eye contact again.

"Can I talk to you for a minute?" he whispered to her in the kitchen when no one was around.

She didn't look up, but continued gathering up miscellaneous kitchen items and placing them in a brown paper bag. "Talk," she said.

Daniel was hoping to talk somewhere quiet, away from everyone, but this might be his only chance. He touched her arm, and he could feel her body go stiff.

He found his way to her hand and slipped the note into her palm. "Anna Marie gave this to me."

Lydia kept her head down, unfolded the note, and appeared to be reading it over and over again. For several moments, he watched her trembling hand.

"I didn't tell her anything," he finally said. "I felt like it was your place to explain in your own way."

Her head twisted in his direction, her eyes blazing with anger and tears. "Explain to her? How do I do that, Daniel? What do I tell my daughter? That I loved you but ended up marrying her father when you abandoned me? Is that what I tell her?"

"Lydia—" Daniel touched her arm, but she pulled away.

"Haven't you caused me enough pain for one lifetime? Why did you come back here?"

Her eyes pleaded with him for some sort of relief from the pain she was feeling, and Daniel wanted nothing more in the world than to love her and take care of her for the rest of their lives. But seeing her like this, so distraught, hurting . . .

He knew he had made a mistake by coming back.

Lydia swiped at her eyes and waited for an answer.

"I missed this place, my family." He looked at the floor for a moment, and then back at her. "And I missed you. It was never my intention to hurt you a second time, Lydia."

She didn't bother to brush away the tear as it rolled down her cheek and dripped onto the wooden floor.

Daniel took a slow, deep breath, never taking his eyes from hers, and he spoke the words he thought she wanted to hear. "I won't stay, Lydia. I'll leave in the morning."

Chapter Seven

Lydia stuffed the note down in the bag with her casserole dishes, wooden spoons, and other items she had brought for dinner. Such an important piece of paper among such mundane items, she thought, as she dabbed at her eyes and turned toward Daniel.

"No. Don't go," she told him firmly. His expression lifted, and Lydia knew she needed to clarify her response. "It would be *baremlich* for your parents." She paused and, for the first time all day, gazed into his eyes.

"I'll be fine, Daniel. You and I were a long time ago, but I have to explain this to my daughter now. And I'm not looking forward to that." She shook her head. "I don't know how she found this. It was in my trinket box, in a drawer, underneath a bunch of other things, and—"

"The cedar trinket box I made for you?" He raised his brows.

Lydia let out a heavy sigh. "*Ya.*"

"I remember when I gave that to you."

"Let's don't do this. No traveling down memory lane. You are a part of this family, and as such, we will be together for a number of activities. It is taking me some time to get used to you being back, but we simply must accept what *was* and what *is.*"

He leaned forward, a bit too close for her. "Any chance that we can be friends?"

"I already told you, Daniel. I think it's best if we only keep company when necessary." She paused, but kept her eyes fused with his. "I married Elam, and I lived with him for fifteen years. We have three children. I am not the same young girl you—you proposed to so long ago."

"I think you are exactly the same, Lydia."

She chuckled. "Look closer, Daniel." She pointed to her face. "Do you see nineteen in this thirty-seven-year-old face? I think not." She was suddenly embarrassed, and she pulled her eyes from his and looked down.

"No, I don't see nineteen," he said as his face drew closer to hers. "But what I see is more beautiful than I even remember."

His tone was so tender, Lydia feared she might cry again.

"I'm just asking for a chance, Lydia," he said. "I'm the children's uncle, and I'd like to get to know them. And I'd like to get to know you again."

Lydia opened her mouth, but quickly clamped it shut.

"You were happy with Elam, weren't you?"

"Very happy. His death was devastating. I wasn't sure how I would go on without him . . ." She paused. "It's been hard for me and the children."

Pounding footsteps entered the kitchen. "Let's go, *Mamm*. Jacob and John are already in the buggy." Anna Marie stood poised like a snake, with fangs ready to puncture the air from Daniel's lungs.

Lydia picked up her bag and ignored her daughter's attitude. "We will see you on Thursday, Daniel. For Thanksgiving."

She didn't look back, and barely saw him nod as she followed Anna Marie out the back door of the kitchen. Anna Marie did enough head spinning for both of them, glancing over her shoulder several times, cutting her eyes in Daniel's direction.

"I'm going to go take these cookies I made to Amos," Anna Marie said later that afternoon.

"Not before you and I have a little talk." Lydia pointed to the stairway. "In my room, away from the boys."

"But I told Amos I would—"

"Now. March." Lydia gently tapped her foot and waited for Anna Marie to move toward the stairs.

"I know what this is about," she huffed.

Lydia didn't answer. She was busy trying to plan out some sort of explanation about the note. Ironically, she was hoping to soften Anna Marie's heart toward Daniel.

Anna Marie sat down on her mother's bed, and Lydia stood in front of her. She opened her hand and offered her daughter the note.

Anna Marie shook her head. "I've already read it."

"Anna Marie, I have had just about enough of your attitude. That tone of yours is about to get your mouth washed out with soap. I don't care how old you are." Lydia paced the room as she spoke. "Daniel and I had a courtship before I married your father. The relationship ended, and then I married your father. And that's all there is to that." She stopped and faced Anna Marie, and put her hands on her hips. "And another thing, young lady. What were you doing snooping through my things?"

"I wasn't snooping. I was looking for my black sweater, and I thought it might have been put in your drawer by mistake." She hung her head. "But then I saw the pretty box. I know I shouldn't have opened it, but . . ."

Lydia sat down on the bed next to Anna Marie and patted her on the leg. "All right."

After a few quiet moments, Anna Marie said, "He wants to court you now, doesn't he?"

"What makes you ask that?"

"I can tell by the way he looks at you."

Lydia twisted the ties on her apron and avoided the girl's inquisitive eyes. "That's nonsense," Lydia said after a few moments.

Anna Marie sighed. "*Mamm*, I am *in lieb*," she said smugly. "I recognize that look he gives you."

"*Ach*, Anna Marie, you're not old enough to recognize anything." Lydia shook her head, but then turned to Anna Marie, whose eyes shone with unshed tears. "I'm sorry," she added. "I keep forgetting that you are growing up."

"And getting married next year." Anna Marie held her chin high and folded her hands in her lap.

Lydia thought for a moment. "Anna Marie, I loved your father very much. But before him, it's true that I loved Daniel." She reached over and squeezed one of Anna Marie's hands. "But that was a long time ago. I'm sure you mistook any looks between us."

"*Gut!*" she said. "Because I don't like him!" And she bolted off the bed.

"Anna Marie!" Lydia hollered before her daughter reached the door. "Daniel is your *onkel*, and I will not have such talk from you. I expect you to treat him with the courtesy and respect that you would anyone else. Do you hear me, young lady?"

Anna Marie slowly turned around and faced Lydia. "Yes, ma'am."

"Now go check on your brothers and see if they've tended to the cows yet this afternoon."

When Anna Marie was out the door, Lydia unfolded the note in her hand and slowly read it again.

~

By Thanksgiving Day Lydia was a bundle of nerves, worrying about way more than the Good Lord would approve of.

Was the meal going to come together and would the turkey be juicy enough? Did she forget anything? Would Anna Marie mind her manners with Daniel? And—how was Daniel going to act?

"Jacob, more wood for the fire," Lydia instructed from the kitchen. "And John, I think your *Daadi* John and *Mammi* Mary are pulling in with *Aenti* Miriam. Go see if you can help them carry things into the house."

Jacob and John moved toward the door, and Lydia realized that she'd been barking a lot of orders at them the past couple of days. She'd been so preoccupied with Daniel's return and Thanksgiving preparations, she hadn't spent much time with her sons.

"John. Jacob."

The boys turned around.

"When you get done, I have one more chore for you."

John sighed, and Jacob twisted his mouth to one side.

Lydia smiled. "I need testers for my desserts. Is that something you boys might be interested in?"

"Before our meal?" John's eyes grew wide, and a grin stretched across his small face.

"*Ya*, I think so," Lydia said with a nod and wink.

Both boys scampered out the door.

Lydia's mother always brought more than was on her list. Lydia peeked out the window and wasn't surprised to see them coming up the walkway with their arms full. Her two brothers, John Jr. and Melvin, were pulling up with their families. Daniel and Elam's two sisters were also arriving with their spouses and children.

Mary Herschberger entered the kitchen, carrying two casserole dishes covered in foil. "Yams and a fruit salad." She placed the food on the kitchen cabinet, then walked to where Lydia was standing by the stove. "Lydia?"

"*Ya*."

Her mother wiped her hands on her black apron and pushed her eyeglasses up on her nose, ignoring the strands of gray hair that hung loose from beneath her prayer covering. She glanced around the room, then whispered, "Are you all right, dear?"

"I'm *gut*, *Mamm*."

Her mother's forehead creased with concern as she pressed her lips together.

"Really, *Mamm*," Lydia assured her. "I'm fine." Now if she could only convince herself she was all right.

"I know this must be *hatt* for you, having Daniel return."

Lydia loved Thanksgiving Day, and if nothing else, she was going to pretend things were all right. "That was a long time ago, *Mamm*."

Mary frowned a bit. "I know, dear. But I remember the way it was with you and Daniel."

So did Lydia. And those images kept assaulting her thoughts.

She kissed her mother on the cheek. "No worries today, *Mamm*. It's Thanksgiving."

Her father was less subtle when he entered the room. "So, I hear Daniel is back." John Herschberger looped his thumbs beneath his suspenders. Lydia quickly glanced around the room to see if anyone else had heard her father's remark. Only Miriam. Her sister scooted past her father, carrying two large bags. She smiled sympathetically in Lydia's direction.

"Shush, John. We all know he's back," Mary whispered as she rolled her eyes at her husband.

"Hi, *Daed*." Lydia hugged her father, then made her way to where Anna Marie was hovering over the sink.

Her daughter was peeling potatoes cheerfully, since Amos was coming for dinner. Lydia had always served the Thanksgiving meal at noon, and the Zook family planned to eat much later in the day.

Lydia glanced at the clock on the wall. Eleven fifteen. Everything was running smoothly.

Next to arrive was Lydia's sister Hannah, with her family, followed by her other sister, Rachel, and her group. Lydia poured the brewed tea from the pot into a pitcher and looked up to see Gideon, Lena, and Daniel standing nearby in the kitchen.

"*Ach*, hello. I didn't see you come in," she said to the three of them. She tried to avoid looking toward Daniel, but her eyes seemed to have a mind of their own.

"Gideon pulled up 'round the back of the house," Lena said. "Which is making it a mite hard to carry in all of my dishes."

"Anna Marie, I'll finish the potatoes," Lydia said. "You go

help *Daadi* and *Mammi* bring things in." Lydia took the knife from her hand.

"Let me," Daniel said when Anna Marie was out the door. "I seem to recall that you dislike peeling potatoes." He reached for the knife, but Lydia pulled away and slid the blade down one side of the potato.

"You've been in the *Englisch* world too long. You know that the men folk don't help with meal preparation," she said. "You best go busy yourself in the den."

"Suit yourself," he said. Then he picked up a peeled potato, inspected it, and placed it back in the colander. "You missed a spot."

Lydia looked up to see him wink before he turned and walked toward the den. That type of flirtatious behavior would get him nowhere. Even so, she felt herself blushing. Several men in the community had shown an interest in her over the past couple of years, but she couldn't recall any of them invoking a blush with such a simple gesture. And none of those potential suitors caused her heart rate to speed up the way it did when Daniel was in the room.

She picked up the potato and sliced off the leftover piece of skin. She recalled fussing to her mother every time she was asked to peel potatoes. *Hmm. Daniel remembered that.*

At straight up noon, everyone began to find a seat. Two tables were set up in the den, plus a small table for the young ones. Once everyone was settled, Lydia took a seat at the table in the kitchen. She was glad that Daniel had chosen to sit at a table in the den—but not so glad that he'd selected a seat near her father. Pop thought Lydia should have remarried by now, and she worried what thoughts her dad might be having concerning Daniel's return. Then she noticed Anna Marie by the window, and she realized that Amos hadn't shown up yet.

"I'm sure he'll be here, Anna Marie," Lydia said. "Come sit down so we can offer our blessings."

Anna Marie pried herself from the window and joined her mother at the kitchen table, along with Lena and Gideon and other family members. One seat was left for Amos.

But two hours later—after everyone had stuffed themselves with rhubarb pie, shoofly pie, banana pudding, and a variety of other desserts—Amos still hadn't arrived. Anna Marie had barely touched her food. Lydia knew how much she'd been looking forward to spending her first holiday with a boy, the one she intended to marry . . .

That was a concept still hard for Lydia to believe. Anna Marie seemed so young to her. Lydia knew that seventeen was an acceptable age for marriage, but it was still considered young by community standards. It saddened her to know that she would only have her daughter under her roof for one more year. Since weddings were always held in November or December, after the fall harvest, there'd be plenty of time to pick a date and prepare.

"Maybe his kin changed the time of their Thanksgiving meal," Lydia whispered to Anna Marie after everyone was gone. Everyone except for Daniel and his parents.

And Daniel didn't seem in a hurry to go anywhere. She scowled in his direction.

But what she saw next softened her mood. Jacob, John, and Daniel were huddled together, laughing and carrying on. Anna Marie might not have taken a fancy to Daniel, but clearly her sons had. Lydia had done her best to be both parents since Elam's death, but boys needed a male role model. They had her father and Gideon, but for the first time, she began to see something positive in Daniel's return to the community. Perhaps he would play catch with the boys or teach them things their father hadn't been able to before he passed.

"Come on with us, Anna Marie," Lena said. She retrieved her cape and bonnet from the rack by the door. "We'll run by the Zooks' place and make sure everything is all right over there."

Anna Marie's face lit up, and she rushed to her grandmother's side.

"You fellas come on too," Gideon said, much to Lydia's horror. "We'll dig out your Pop's old box of games."

Lydia knew how much the boys loved it when Gideon offered to play games with them, games that had belonged to their father when he was a boy.

"Gideon, they best stay home," Lydia blurted out, "with school and all tomorrow."

Jacob and John were already at the door. "Ain't no school the day after Thanksgiving, *Mamm*," John said. He scooted past his grandfather and out the door.

No, no, no. They can't all leave me here alone with Daniel.

But that's exactly what they did. Even Anna Marie didn't come protectively to her defense. She was too anxious to see Amos to worry herself about her mother's crisis.

Daniel was once again warming his hands by the fire. Everyone else was outside and loading into the buggy, except for Lena. It had taken her a little longer than the others to bundle for the weather. After she tied her black bonnet, she leaned over and hugged Lydia.

Then she whispered in her ear, "I love you, Lydia, like my own daughter. Please hear him out. It might make a difference to you." Then she pulled away, smiled, and walked out to the buggy.

It appeared Lydia didn't have a choice in the matter. She closed the door and turned to face Daniel.

He just shrugged, as if to say, *I had nothing to do with it.*

Lydia knew better.

Chapter Eight

Daniel watched as Lydia lit two lanterns and placed them on opposite sides of the den. After the door closed behind his parents, he was prepared for her to ask him to leave. But to his surprise, she didn't.

"It will be dark soon." She turned to face him. Her blank expression didn't offer any hints as to her thoughts about being coerced into this meeting. But one thing he remembered about her—the woman had an independent way of thinking and doing things. Daniel knew she was not happy at being set up.

He smiled slightly in her direction, afraid to say too much too soon, and waited—waited for her to tell him to get out.

She didn't return the smile, and her voice was monotone when she spoke. "Would you like some *kaffi*?"

"That sounds great. I mean *wunderbaar gut*." Again he smiled, but she just turned and walked toward the kitchen. Daniel followed her. "I'm surprised how much Pennsylvania *Deitsch* I remember."

Lydia poured two cups of coffee into white mugs, and Daniel noticed how she'd retained her youthful figure. Her black apron, tied snug atop her dark green dress, defined the smallness of her waist.

He sat down at one of the wooden chairs at her kitchen table and glanced around the room. Lydia owned more gadgets than his parents, who still did everything the old way. His mother still mashed potatoes with a hand masher and refused to buy a modern gas stove, but Daniel noticed a battery-operated mixer on the counter and a shiny white gas range next to the propane refrigerator in Lydia's kitchen. There was also a weather-alert radio at the end of the counter, also charged by battery.

"I was surprised to see that *mei mamm* still uses a woodstove to cook," he said. Lydia handed him the coffee and took a seat across from him at the kitchen table. He noticed a shift in her expression, from blank to fearful. Her coffee cup was in one hand, but she was grinding her thumb and forefinger fiercely with the other hand. "I would have thought that *Mamm* and *Daed* would have upgraded to something more modern. Something like what you have." He nodded toward Lydia's stove.

"They have talked about purchasing a gas range, but—" She stopped, locked her eyes with his. "But they haven't yet." Her eyes stayed fused with his, and her fingers were on overdrive.

She was so nervous and upset, Daniel wasn't sure this was the right time to tell her what he wanted to say. Perhaps he should just use this time to reconnect with her, hear about her life, her children—and Elam—see how all that went first.

"I told Anna Marie about us, about the note," Lydia finally said after a few moments of silence between them. She pulled her eyes from his and clutched her cup with both hands. She took a long sip, then kept a tight hold on the mug and lifted her eyes back to his. "She doesn't like you very much." She eased into a grin.

"It's nice to see you smile," he said. "And no, I don't seem to be Anna Marie's favorite person at the moment."

"That's understandable, I reckon. Now she knows her father wasn't my first true—" Her cheeks flushed, and she looked away. "She'll come around."

"But will you?" Daniel's pulse grew rapid as he waited for her to respond. She wasn't kneading her fingers together anymore, but her cheeks were still a rosy shade of pink, and her eyes reflected her unease.

Lydia sat taller and released her firm grip on the coffee cup. She folded her hands in front of her on the table, took a deep breath, and fused her eyes intently with his.

He waited for what seemed like an eternity.

"We will be friends," she said matter-of-factly. "You are the children's *onkel*, and I love Lena and Gideon as if they were my own parents. But . . ." She sat taller and lifted her chin a bit. "There can be no courtship between us."

"I never said anything about *courtship*." He couldn't help but smile at her presumption. Not that he didn't want exactly that.

"Well, I'm just—just making that clear." She paused, but held her head high and went on. "I was thinking earlier, when I saw you with Jacob and John, that perhaps it would be *gut* for you to be in the boys' lives."

"I'd like that," he said.

She was softening a little. During their first encounter, she'd made it quite clear that there would be no unnecessary socializing.

And he would settle for being her friend, although he didn't think it would ever be enough—for either of them. But one thing loomed over him, something equally as important to him as having her in his life.

"Lydia . . ." he began slowly. "I need to know if you have truly forgiven me in your heart. You said the words, but . . ."

She gazed at him with a faraway look in her eyes. Lydia had always been transparent, and he could tell she was about to tell a lie. An unintentional lie that she might not even recognize as such, but a fib just the same. "Yes, I forgive you."

He considered her response for a moment. "You said that awfully fast." Then added, "And I don't believe you."

"You think I would lie?"

"Not intentionally." Daniel looked her in the eye. "I think you *want* to forgive me, because you know it's what God wants you to do. But I think you are struggling to do so."

"Well, you're wrong," she huffed. "I do forgive you. I reckon you might give yourself a bit too much credit."

"Maybe," he said. Then he leaned his elbows on the table and leaned forward. "But I don't think so. We were in love, Lydia. It was real, and I've never gotten over it. I have missed you every single day, dreamed about you—and I know you felt it too. I think you still do."

She stood from the table. "Get out!"

He stood up and faced her from across the table. "Lydia, wait. I'm sorry. We don't have to talk about that, but there is something I need to tell you. Something about that night, Christmas Eve. Maybe you will understand—"

She rounded the corner of the kitchen into the den, and Daniel followed in time to see her yank the front door open. Flames flickered in the fireplace as a cold rush of wind swept into the room. "Please leave," she said.

"Lydia, just let me explain."

She refused to look in his direction and kept her chin held high. Daniel walked toward her and stood in the doorway as she reached for his coat on the rack by the door. She handed it to him without glancing his way. "Good-bye, Daniel."

"Lydia, please . . . let me tell you about the night I left."

Lydia closed her eyes and remembered what Lena had said. *Please hear him out. Listen to what Daniel has to say. It might make a difference to you.* She took a moment to silence the voices in her head and concentrated on the only voice that was important. She lowered her head and asked God for his guidance. Then she slowly opened her eyes and faced Daniel to see his eyes brimming with tenderness, begging her to reconsider. She pushed the door closed and motioned him to the couch in the den.

"*Danki*," he said.

Lydia flung his coat on the sofa and sat down in one of the rocking chairs facing it. She wasn't sure if she wanted to hear what Daniel had to say, or if it would make any difference. He'd given up on their love and left her. What more did she need to know? Besides, it was such a long time ago. Although, even all these years later, despite her marriage, the children, and her own belief that she had led the life she was meant to live, the raw hurt had resurfaced.

She wanted to forgive him. To understand. But those untapped emotions were bouncing around in a tight box of fear that gripped her, and she worried the lid might pop off any minute and expose what her heart screamed to her—that she'd always loved Daniel, and still did. And that thought made her feel like she was betraying Elam.

Lydia knew she needed to live righteously in the eyes of God, to forgive those who trespassed against her. *All this worry and guilt is a sin*, she thought. Daniel opened his mouth to talk, and Lydia made up her mind to forgive him and mean it, no matter what he had to say.

His expression seemed full of the life he'd led, in a world she knew nothing about. His brow furrowed, and the pain in his eyes was unmistakable. Whatever he was about to tell her, it was of great importance and discomfort to him.

"Go on, Daniel. I'm listening."

"Lydia, that night, on Christmas Eve—" He shook his head.

What in the world is he going to tell me? She realized she was literally holding her breath, and she forced herself to exhale. "It's all right," she said soothingly, as she would to anyone so tormented. And she hoped it would be—all right.

The sound of footsteps coming up the porch steps diverted their attention. No sooner did they both look in that direction than they heard a loud knock on the door.

Lydia rushed across the den and pulled the door open. "Amos! What are you doing here?"

He struggled to catch his breath. "Hello. I, uh—could I please talk to Anna Marie?"

Lydia scrutinized him for a moment, and then gently touched his elbow and pulled him over the threshold. She closed the door and glanced at her clock on the mantel. "Amos, Anna Marie was expecting you for dinner at noon. When you didn't show up, she left to spend the night with her *mammi* and *daadi*.

They said they were going to stop by your house on the way. Is everything all right?"

Amos's eyes jetted toward Daniel.

"This is Elam's brother, Daniel." Lydia nodded in Daniel's direction, but then quickly turned back to Amos, who was still struggling to catch his breath. "I didn't hear a buggy," she said. "Did you run over here? And where is your coat?"

Daniel stood up and approached Amos with an extended hand. "Nice to meet you, Amos."

"Everything is *gut*, no?" Lydia asked again.

"*Ya*. Everything is *gut*."

Lydia eyed him suspiciously and noticed Daniel wearing a similar expression.

"I just need to talk to Anna Marie." Amos sounded desperate. "It's important, and I need to find her, and—" The boy leaned over, put his hands on his knees, and seemed to be gasping for air. When he lifted his head up, his eyes were clouded with tears. "I have to find her," he repeated.

"Amos, what is wrong?" Lydia brought her hand to her chest. "Is someone hurt? Did something happen?"

Amos stood straight again. He glanced back and forth between Lydia and Daniel and seemed unsure whether to talk.

Lydia put her hands on her hips. "Amos Zook, you tell me right now what's the matter."

"I'm in trouble," he finally said. He looked down toward his shoes and shook his head. "I'm in a lot of trouble."

Chapter Nine

Daniel heard the anguish in Amos's voice. "What kind of trouble?" he asked.

"Yes, Amos, what kind of trouble?" Lydia echoed.

"I—I . . ." Amos shook his head, and his eyes darted back and forth between Daniel and Lydia. "I have to go." He turned to face the door, pulled on the knob, and bolted down the porch stairs into the yard.

Lydia was instantly behind him. "Amos! Amos, wait!"

Daniel joined her on the front porch and watched the boy sprint across the yard.

"What could possibly be so bad?" Lydia asked. "Amos!"

Then something inside of Daniel ignited. "I'll go after him."

He hurried down the steps, into the yard, and then broke into a run. When he reached the street, he stopped to listen. In the darkness he could hear something moving down the road to his right. Daniel ran, thankful for his time at the gym the past few months. He slowly began to close the gap between them. "Amos, stop!" he yelled.

But the boy didn't slow down, and Daniel wasn't sure how long he could keep up this pace. He pushed himself to run faster, stretching each stride to its fullest length.

Now he was within a few feet of Amos. "Stop!" *Please.*

Thankfully, the boy slowed his run to a light jog. Daniel

tried to catch his breath as he drew near Amos, who finally stopped in the middle of the road.

The boy turned to face him. "There's no need to come after me," he said, breathless himself. "I will handle *mei* troubles."

Daniel held his palm forward, signaling that he couldn't quite choke out any words yet.

"Please tell Anna Marie that I love her. I'll always love her," Amos announced with the authority of someone much older than himself. He took a step backward.

"Please don't take off again," Daniel mumbled. He stood up straight and drew in a breath, releasing it slowly.

"Why are you following me? You don't even know me."

"But I know Anna Marie," Daniel said, hoping to entice the boy to talk to him. "And if you love her as much as you say you do, you won't run away from whatever trouble you're in."

"I don't have a choice." Amos pulled off his straw hat and wiped sweat from his brow.

Daniel wondered how the boy had kept it on. He'd lost his own hat early into the chase.

"We always have a choice." A cool trickle of sweat ran down Daniel's spine, beneath his long-sleeved blue shirt. "It's freezing out here. Can we talk back at the house? Just give me a few minutes to talk to you."

Amos instantly shook his head. "I don't want to talk in front of Anna Marie's *mamm*," he said firmly.

"I understand. Maybe we can talk man-to-man on the walk back—*walk*, no running." He smiled, trying to lighten Amos's mood. "What do you have to lose? If you don't like what I have to say, you can take off again." Daniel chuckled. "Believe me, I don't have the energy to chase you."

Amos stewed a moment, then agreed. Slowly the story unfolded.

He and two other boys—*Englisch* boys—had walked into a convenience store to get a soda. One of the boys, Tommy, noticed that the store attendant had gone into the back storage room. Tommy opened the cooler, and instead of a soda, he grabbed two beers and stuffed them inside his coat. The other boy, Greg, also snatched two beers and hid them in his jacket. Amos didn't want to do it, but the others kept nagging at him, so Amos finally hid two beers in his coat too. None of them counted on the camera in the store feeding to the back room, where the man watched them steal the beers.

To make things worse, when the man confronted them, Tommy took off at a run. Greg followed, then Amos—who ran right into the police officer that the attendant had called. The other boys were caught shortly thereafter.

"I've never stolen anything in my life." Amos shook his head. "I broke one of the Ten Commandments."

Tommy's father was the first one to show up and post bond for his son. It took about an hour for Greg's father to arrive. With no way to get in touch with Amos's family, the judge had allowed Greg's dad to post the bond for Amos as well. And since all three boys were underage, they didn't have to spend the night behind bars.

But Amos was standing right next to the police officer when he left a message on the phone in the Zook barn: "Mr. Zook, I

BETH WISEMAN

have your son Amos at the jail. He has been charged with theft."

"I can just picture the look on Pop's face when he hears that message. I have shamed my family." Amos hung his head. "And Anna Marie."

Daniel looked at Amos. The boy was three years younger than Daniel had been when he left on Christmas Eve. Even though Amos's problems didn't compare to Daniel's, it was still a heavy burden for an Amish boy. There might be a trip to the woodshed and a harsh reprimand, but in the end, the boy's father would forgive him for his poor choice. It wasn't like Amos had assaulted anyone.

Daniel stopped in the road and pulled on the boy's arm, and they stood facing each other. "Amos, you have to keep this in perspective. You made a mistake. Your father will be disappointed in you, and Anna Marie might be too, but if she loves you as much as she seems to, then she will stick by you. If you run away, sometimes it's too hard to come back."

"But I went to jail on Thanksgiving Day!" Amos blasted. "It's a day for family and fellowship, and I spent it eating a peanut butter and jelly sandwich in a room that had a toilet in the corner." He shook his head. "It was *baremlich*."

Daniel started to say something, but Amos went on.

"And the police officer—he said I have to go to court! I reckon I'm going to have to pay money and—" He paused and shook his head. "I can't talk to *mei daed* about this."

"It takes a real man to face what he did. Amos, don't make a decision right now that could affect the rest of your life."

Daniel took a deep breath and pushed the past out of his head. "What is news in the community today will be forgotten in no time. Are you really willing to lose Anna Marie over this? Where would you go?"

"I don't know," Amos said. "I just wanted to see Anna Marie one last time before I left."

They took a few steps. Daniel's teeth were chattering, and he was anxious to get into Lydia's house where there was a fire going, but not too anxious to take the time to help this young boy see things in the right light.

"Before we get back to the house, I have a story to tell you. A story that might help you decide whether leaving is the right thing to do."

∾

Lydia heard footsteps and faint voices outside. She opened the front door and was relieved to see Amos with Daniel.

"Thank goodness you are all right." Lydia touched Amos's arm and then glanced at Daniel. "Both of you." She quickly looked away when his eyes met hers.

As she pushed the door closed, Daniel and Amos walked to the fireplace.

"I'm going to give Amos a ride home," Daniel said. He continued to warm his hands in front of the fire.

"*Gut*," Lydia said. "It's too cold out there for walking." She eyed Amos with curiosity.

"I need to go home and talk to *mei daed*," he humbly said to Lydia. Then he turned to Daniel, and appreciation swept across his face. "*Danki*, Daniel."

Daniel smiled affectionately at him. "You're welcome, Amos."

Lydia wanted to ask Amos why he was thanking Daniel, what the two had talked about. A little earlier she'd been afraid to hear what Daniel was going to tell her; now disappointment nipped at the fear. While they were gone, she'd tried to prepare herself for anything, dreaming up every possible scenario that could have happened on that long-ago Christmas Eve. *Did he leave because he found another love? Maybe an* Englischer? *Did he have some grand opportunity for success in the* Englisch *world that he couldn't pass up? Did he decide he didn't love me after all?*

Lydia said good-bye and hugged Amos at the front door. After the boy walked outside, Daniel turned back to her.

"I'd still like to have our talk," he said. "Could I come back over after I take Amos home?"

It was still early in the evening, and Lydia didn't think she'd sleep a wink without hearing what he had to say. "*Ya.* I'll brew a fresh pot of *kaffi.*"

Daniel slowly lifted his hand to her face and brushed away a strand of hair that had fallen from beneath her prayer covering. His finger lingered on her cheek. "I'll see you soon," he said softly.

"*Ya.*"

She watched him walk to the buggy, mechanically closed the door, and didn't move for a moment. All the fear she'd fought to harness suddenly returned with a vengeance. If his touch invoked this type of reaction, how in the world was she going to be around him on a regular basis without facing her true feelings? That she had always loved Daniel. And still did.

Chapter Ten

It was almost eight o'clock when Lydia heard horse hooves coming up the driveway. She stood from her chair at the kitchen table where she'd been putting cookbooks together to use up her nervous energy, wiped sweaty palms down the sides of her black apron, and headed to the front door. Her stomach churned as she turned the knob, then waited for Daniel to come across the grass and up the steps. Lydia swung the door wide, stepped aside, and motioned him in.

She usually went to bed at eight thirty. She considered mentioning that in case things didn't go well, but she didn't have to.

"I know it's getting close to your bedtime—and mine too," he said. "I'm getting back on *Mamm* and *Daed*'s schedule, so I promise not to keep you up too late."

"I made fresh *kaffi*," she said. "Warm yourself by the fire, and I'll bring us each a cup."

When Lydia walked back into the den, Daniel was sitting on the couch. She handed him one of the mugs she was carrying and wondered where to sit—at the far end of the sofa, or in one of the rocking chairs. She backed away from him, eased into the rocker, and pushed the chair into motion with her foot while clutching tightly to her coffee cup with both hands.

"Lydia—" Daniel locked eyes with her. "As much as I want you to forgive me for leaving you that Christmas Eve, by telling you what really happened, I run the risk of losing you yet again."

"You don't *have* me," she said.

Lydia could see pain in Daniel's eyes.

"You might be angry with me after I tell you this story, but it's only fair that you know the truth." He paused. "I just hope that Elam would agree with me."

"Elam?" Lydia's eyes widened, and her pulse picked up. "What does Elam have to do with anything that happened that night?"

"Do you remember when Elam came to your house on Christmas Eve and gave you the note I wrote?"

She shot him a look that nearly knocked him over.

"I guess you do." He diverted his eyes and rubbed his hands together. "Anyway. That morning, Elam and I went to pick up your Christmas present, something I'd made for you. I was having it professionally engraved at a shop in town, and—"

"What was it?" The words flew from her lips. She recalled the present she bought for Daniel that year—a fine set of woodworking tools that she had eventually given to Elam.

Daniel's eyes met with hers again. "A cedar chest."

Lydia gasped. "You made me a cedar chest?" A gift like that was certainly allowable in their community, but considered somewhat extravagant in comparison to the small presents that are routinely exchanged at Christmas.

"*Ya*, I did," Daniel said in a low voice.

Lydia remembered telling Daniel on their way home from one of the many Sunday singings how she longed to have a cedar chest to store heirlooms for their future. She'd told him, but she'd never expected him to make her one for Christmas.

But wait a minute. Daniel was picking up her Christmas present that very day . . . ?

"Daniel . . ."

His eyes reconnected with hers. "*Ya?*"

"If you were picking up my Christmas present on Christmas Eve morning, what changed by that afternoon to—" Her voice broke. "To make you decide you didn't love me enough to stay?"

"What? Is that what you think?" He scooted toward the edge of the couch and leaned forward. "I loved you enough," he said with a quiet but desperate firmness. "Enough to leave."

"That makes no sense." She set her cup on the table next to her, crossed her arms, and waited.

"Something happened before Elam and I were able to pick up the cedar chest." Daniel leaned back against the couch. "We decided to get a glass of homemade root beer and a whoopee pie from the Stoltzfus Bakery."

He seemed to be struggling with every word he spoke, which only added to Lydia's apprehension.

"After that we were strolling past the shops on Lincoln Highway, and then we cut through a back alley to go pick up the chest." Daniel clamped his eyes shut. "We heard sounds of a struggle," he finally said. "An *Englisch* boy had a girl pinned down on the ground, and—and he was doing unthinkable things to her. The girl looked about our age, maybe younger. An *Englisch* girl."

He shook his head, and anger swept across his face. "At first Elam and I kept walking. It wasn't our place to get involved, nor was it our way. But then the girl saw us, and she cried out to us for help. I can see her face as though it happened yesterday. She had blonde hair and a pink shirt. I can still remember the fear in her eyes, begging us to help her, as the boy held her down on the gravel."

Lydia cupped her hand to her mouth.

"There were shops that backed up to the alley, and a few houses farther down the way. I kept waiting for someone to come help her, but there was no one around but Elam and me. She kicked at the boy and tried to scream, but he slapped her across the face and told her to shut up." Daniel paused. "And then something in me just snapped."

Lydia had stopped rocking in the chair and sat immobilized with visions of that poor girl, but she didn't understand Daniel's comment. "Snapped?"

"*Ya*, I snapped—I just couldn't take it anymore. I told Elam to stay back. The boy—his name was Chad—swore at me and told me to be on my Amish way, that it was none of my concern. But I kept walking toward him. He was big too. Muscular. And about my height. I told him to let the girl up.

"Finally, I was standing right beside them." Daniel took a deep breath. "I could hear Elam calling my name. I took a step backward, but then that girl's eyes met with mine again, and I moved forward and told the boy to let her go—or else."

Lydia held her breath and tried to imagine Daniel, or anyone from their community, speaking in such a way.

"He let her go, jumped up, and within seconds my face went numb, and I could taste blood. I knew my nose was broken, but I wasn't sure if the blood was coming from my nose or my lip, which was on fire. I landed on my back, and when I was able to stand up and focus, I saw the girl running and screaming, but he went after her, grabbing the back of her collar and throwing her back on the ground.

"I couldn't imagine him hurting that girl any more than he

already had. Elam was yelling for us to go home, but instead I marched over to Chad, grabbed him by the shirt, and returned an equally sound blow to his face. Then I hit him again and again, until he went down and stayed down. When I looked up, the girl was gone, and two men were running toward us."

Lydia's mouth hung open. She knew that violence was wrong, but she still admired his chivalry. And in the back of her mind, she wondered, *What did this have to do with his leaving on Christmas Eve?*

"As it turns out," Daniel went on, "Chad told everyone I'd assaulted him while my brother stood and watched, egging me on. It would have been a pretty unbelievable story—two Amish boys involved in such a mess—but Chad looked much worse than I did, and he knew the policeman who showed up. Officer Turner. I remember the way the cop looked at me with such shock, but he handcuffed me just the same and hauled me to jail."

Lydia gasped as more fearful images swirled in her head. "What about the boy, Chad? He went to jail too, no?"

Daniel shook his head. "Not only did Chad know Officer Turner, but his father knew him too. He didn't spend even one minute behind bars. Only me."

"Where was the girl? Couldn't she explain what happened? And what about Elam? He saw everything." Lydia was wondering why Elam never told her this story.

"The girl was long gone, and Chad refused to admit that there was even a girl there. He stuck to his story that two Amish boys approached him in the alley, and that I beat him up." Daniel cringed. "I wasn't proud of my actions, by any means. Chad had a broken nose, like mine, but also two broken ribs. And always in the back of my mind was Pop. I'd shamed my family."

Lydia searched anxiously for the meaning behind his words. What was he trying to say?

"I just couldn't come back, Lydia. I was being charged with assault of another human being, something unheard-of in our community. I spent the night in a cell with four big, burly-looking men, and the jailer that night asked me repeatedly if I wanted to make a phone call. It wasn't until morning when I decided to call someone, an *Englisch* man I'd met a couple of months earlier; he was someone I trusted not to tell anyone. But it was Christmas Day. I had to wait until the day after Christmas for him to post bail and get me out. It was a *baremlich* two days."

Lydia finally understood. "You left our way of life—and me—because you couldn't face your father?"

"I know it sounds cowardly, Lydia, but I didn't want to shame my family like that. It seemed like I was always getting a lecture from Pop about not being able to hold my tongue, and this was much worse. But not a day went by that I didn't think about you and miss you."

She fought the tremble in her voice. "Did you not think to pen me a letter to explain all of this after you left?" Lydia brought her hand to her mouth as another realization hit her, one equally as bad, if not worse. "Elam knew all this." She rose from the chair and began to pace the room.

"Lydia, let me explain." Daniel stood up and walked toward her.

She held both arms straight out in front of her.

"He befriended me. I cried on Elam's shoulder." A tear

rolled down her cheek. "And all the while, he knew! He knew what happened. Elam let me wonder why you would leave me, repeatedly telling me that you just wanted to live in the *Englisch* world. How could he do that to me when he knew how much I was hurting?" Her eyes blazed. "Did the two of you keep in touch?"

Daniel stood before her, his own eyes clouding with emotion. "For a while. Until—until he began to court you."

He took a step toward her, and she backed up.

"I knew Elam was in love with you, and I knew he'd be a *gut* father to your children. I, on the other hand, had a court date to face, and I ended up being convicted of assault and spending six months in jail, so there was no coming back. I wanted you to have the life you deserved. I knew Elam could give you that."

"The life I deserved?" Lydia backed up farther until she bumped against the wall. She flattened her palms against the whitewash wall, steadied herself, and then brought one hand to her chest. "You and Elam got together and planned my future? Instead of telling me where you were and giving me a choice, you both just kept quiet, while my heart was breaking?"

All her wounds reopened. Her beloved Elam. How could he have lied to her? She'd been in such anguish, and he could have put an end to it. Instead he chose to pursue her for himself.

"I'm telling you all this, Lydia, for several reasons. First, it's the truth. Second, I want you to know that I never left because I didn't love you enough. And I knew Elam would treat you as you deserved to be treated. I, however, was a criminal."

"When did you write the note?" She choked out the words.

"Later that afternoon, when I realized I wouldn't be home

for Christmas Eve supper or Christmas Day. I sent a note to you and one to my parents."

"Elam wouldn't do this," she said. "I don't believe any of it!"

But deep inside, she knew it was the truth. If there had ever been a chance of her forgiving Daniel, it was gone. Now she would struggle with how to forgive her husband for his role in this convenient lie.

"Why did you come back?" Lydia felt like she'd been hit in the stomach. "Not only did you leave me all those years ago, but now you tell me this news of my husband, that he lied to me so that I would be his. All the while, my heart was breaking for you. It is unforgivable. All of it."

Daniel reached for her, but she pulled away. "Lydia, I don't want mistruths hanging over us. I have confessed my sins before God, and now I declare them to you."

Lydia clamped her lips together in an attempt to squelch her sobs. She wished Elam was here to explain all of this to her . . . to say that he would never withhold information about Daniel just to win a place in her heart for himself. *Please, God . . .*

When Daniel wrapped his arms around her, she buried her head in his chest and sobbed. He could have been anyone— anyone willing to hold her up. But he was Daniel, and to stay in his arms would cause her nothing but heartache. No matter how much she had loved him, staying righteous in God's eyes was now compounded by her inability to forgive not only Daniel, but her husband as well.

She pulled away from him and pointed toward the door.

Chapter Eleven

Lydia placed a poinsettia plant on either side of the fireplace, and the flowery red blooms invoked bittersweet memories. Elam had loved Christmastime. She placed colorfully wrapped presents in various places throughout the den, adding an air of celebration to the room. But inwardly she was having trouble finding the spirit of the season. She'd been praying for a reprieve from the grief that festered inside her, but it continued to gnaw away at her from the inside out. Amid all her troubles, she knew that forgiveness was the only thing that would free her soul to find the peace she so desperately longed for.

"*Mamm*, when are we leaving for *Onkel* Daniel's baptism?"

Lydia arched a questioning brow at Anna Marie's casual acceptance of her uncle, whom she'd been less than fond of so recently. "Soon," she said.

She hadn't seen Daniel since Thanksgiving, and three days later, her stomach still rolled every time she thought about what Daniel and Elam had done. But there was no way out of attending the baptism, which would be at Daniel's new home at the old Kauffman place. Lena and Gideon told her that he'd moved in the day after Thanksgiving. She said Daniel had spent his time in the *Englisch* world doing odd jobs, mostly carpentry. And according to her sister Miriam, who'd stopped by Daniel's house to deliver eggs on behalf of their parents, he was doing an amazing job restoring the place.

Lydia rounded up Jacob and John, motioned to Anna Marie that it was time to go, and they loaded in the buggy to head to Daniel's baptism.

∾

Lydia watched as the deacon ladled water from a bucket into the bishop's hand. Daniel sat with one hand over his face, to represent his submission and humility to the church. The bishop sprinkled Daniel's head three times, in the name of the Father, Son, and Holy Ghost, and then blessed him with a holy kiss.

It was such a sacred occasion, and despite the circumstances, Lydia was glad that Daniel received the sacrament of baptism after cleansing himself through prayer and confession, and that he had not accepted such a blessing without first being truthful with her, his parents, and the bishop.

But she couldn't seem to corral her emotions into one central part of her brain, where she might be able to process the information in a new way. Her thoughts were all over the place and filled with what-ifs. And it was that questioning of God's will that kept her up at night. If the events of that night had played out any differently, she wouldn't have Anna Marie, Jacob, or John, and she wouldn't have shared fifteen joy-filled years with Elam.

Every time she prayed for the strength of heart and mind to forgive both men, her heart wrapped itself in a self-preserving cocoon. She knew that for God to do his work, she would have to let down her barriers and allow herself to feel the pain, so his glory could help her move forward.

After Daniel's baptism, the women prepared chicken and

wafers for dinner in the kitchen, while the men found seats at one of the many tables set up throughout Daniel's house. Lydia had brought a tomato pie to the event. Elam's favorite. As usual, there was a vast variety of offerings, more than enough to feed the one hundred in attendance: three ham loaves, four meat loaves, succotash, cabbage casserole, several types of potatoes, and at least two dozen desserts. Chow-chow, jams, jellies, and ten loaves of homemade bread lined the countertop.

Lydia glanced at the clock on the hutch in the kitchen. Straight up noon, and she could feel her stomach growling.

She had to admit, Daniel had already done wonders with the old Kauffman place. After four generations raised families in the home, the house was retired two years ago, after the last generation was unable to have children and passed on. A niece, who already owned a home in the community, inherited the place, and the farmhouse had been in need of much repair.

Lydia breathed in the smell of freshly painted whitewashed walls and noticed new cabinets throughout the kitchen. Crisp green blinds were drawn halfway up on the windows, and festive garlands were draped across the windowsills, with tiny red bows attached. She poured brewed tea into a pitcher and handed it to Anna Marie, instructing her daughter to add sugar and begin serving the men.

Lydia picked up a bowl of pickled red beets and carried it into the den. Daniel was sitting with his father, the bishop, and two elders on the left side of the room. She veered to her right, where her own father was sitting, and put the bowl on the table.

Daniel's den was warm and cozy with a blazing fire in the

hearth, and Lydia noticed the beautiful mantel above the fireplace—simple, with no ornate carvings, but bold and eye-catching. She wondered if Daniel was responsible for the fine carpentry. He'd always had a knack for building things. She thought of the cedar chest and wondered, not for the first time, what had become of the forsaken gift.

She took her time walking back to the kitchen, wanting to soak in every detail of Daniel's home as the what-ifs stirred in her thoughts. What might their home have looked like if she had married Daniel? Did they have similar tastes? While most Old Order homes were simply decorated, each one still possessed character and individuality. She saw Christmas presents placed around the house and bright poinsettias on either side of the fireplace, just as they were in her own home. A green, leafy garland spiraled around the railing of the banister that led upstairs, trimmed with holly and with a large bow at the foot of the railing. Her stairway was also decorated with garland and bows, but she couldn't put her finger on why Daniel's trimmings looked better than hers.

She lingered in the den for a moment and pretended to be checking tea glasses for refills, but her eyes kept involuntarily shifting to the flight of stairs that ascended to Daniel's bedroom.

Does he keep a box of tissues by the bed? A pitcher of water? A flashlight? Does he read at night before he goes to sleep? What color is the quilt on his bed? Which side of the bed does he sleep on?

The questions pounded obsessively in her head. She glanced in his direction, and his blue eyes rose and clung to hers. She jumped when someone touched her arm.

"Are you all right, dear?" Lena asked.

"*Ya.*" Lydia faced Lena, but she could feel Daniel's eyes still on her.

"Daniel said that he told you of his trouble on Christmas Eve. I reckon that must have been difficult to hear." Lena's kind eyes shone with tenderness and sympathy.

"*Ya,*" she said again. "But it didn't make me feel differently about things, Lena, like you said it might. I feel worse. I feel like Elam betrayed me too, and he isn't even here to defend himself."

Lena nodded. "I understand. Both boys behaved badly. Daniel should have come to us instead of running away. We would have felt shame, but we would have gotten through it and had our son in the community." Lena's brows drew together in an agonized expression. "Elam did not act in a *gut* way either. He also should have told the truth. But my dear, sweet Lydia"— Lena's voiced sharpened—"it is not our place to question God's will, nor to pass judgment on others." She paused. "I remind myself of this when *mei* own hurt rises to the surface."

Lena was a wise woman, and Lydia had always been close to her. "I know you're right, Lena." She glanced back toward Daniel, who was busy stuffing a spoonful of food into his mouth and listening intently to something his father was saying. "I'm just trying to find my way through all of this."

Women scurried around them as they stood off to one corner, whispering.

Lena smiled. "You already know the way, my child. Now you must travel the path of least resistance and welcome forgiveness into your heart. Let God heal what pains you."

"*Mamm,* we need more butter bread," Anna Marie said as she brushed by Lydia and Lena.

Lena gave Lydia a quick pat on the arm. "I have bread warming in the oven. I'll go get it." She started to leave, then stopped. "Lydia, I am chilled to the bone, and I'm not about to shuffle around here in my long cape. Upstairs is a closet at the end of the hallway. I saw a sweater in there while I was helping Daniel clean the place up last week. Must have been left behind by one of the Kauffmans. Would you be a dear and get it for me?" She winked at Lydia and headed to the kitchen.

∽

Daniel watched Lydia going up the stairs. The thought of her that close to his bedroom sent tidal waves of longing and desire pulsing through his very being. He grew restless as he searched for an excuse to go upstairs. As Lydia disappeared out of sight, he pulled his eyes from the stairway and met his father's speculative gaze. Gideon's brows furrowed in Daniel's direction, and he feared a reprimand from his father for ogling Lydia in such a way.

But then Gideon's left brow edged upward mischievously. "Daniel, I reckon I've eaten more of this *gut* food than I should have, and it's left me with a bit of a bellyache. Could you fetch me something from your medicine cabinet?"

"Right away, Pop." Daniel's fork clanged against his plate as he hurriedly pushed back his chair. He saw the hint of a smile on his father's face, which Gideon quickly masked as he reached for a piece of butter bread.

Daniel tried to keep his anticipation in check as he walked up the stairs. He hadn't been alone with Lydia since Thanksgiving, the night she cried in his arms. Her hurt had speared through his own heart, leaving him with regret and despair.

He wondered why she had gone upstairs and where she might be. There was a bathroom downstairs for guests. He glanced through the open door on his left, and then a few steps farther, through another open door on his right. Lydia wasn't in either of the extra bedrooms, which meant she was either in the bathroom farther down the hall or in his bedroom at the end of the corridor. His pulse quickened when he passed by the bathroom and she wasn't in there.

He slowly stepped around the corner to his bedroom, and there she was—sitting on his bed, running her hand gracefully across the dark-blue quilt atop his bed. Rays of sunshine shone through the window and danced on the wooden floor. She didn't look up, but the old stairs and wooden slats down the hallway had crackled beneath his feet, announcing his coming.

"Which side of the bed do you sleep on?" she asked. Her hand continued to stroke the counterpane in a way that tantalized Daniel's senses.

"The side you're sitting on," he said with a shaky voice.

"Hmm—" She raised her eyes to his. "It would have never worked. I sleep on this side too." She patted a spot beside her on the bed.

Daniel nervously ran his hand through his freshly bobbed haircut. His sister had given him a proper trim yesterday in preparation for his baptism. "I would have gladly changed sides."

Hope was alive in his heart, and he feared she'd snatch it from him at any second. So he watched her, savored her, sitting on his bed in such a way. He expected her to get up and walk out of the room at any second. But instead, she slowly rose off the bed and began to wander around his room.

• BETH WISEMAN

"Do you read before you go to sleep?" She turned to face him, and her expression was that of a woman basking in the knowledge of her power over him.

"*Ya*," he answered, his feet rooted to the floor. Her movements were intoxicating to him.

"Hmm—" she said again as she continued walking lightly around his room. She scanned every single item in the small room as if her life depended on it.

Daniel felt utterly scrutinized.

She picked up the small battery-operated alarm clock that he kept on his bedside table. "I have this same alarm clock in my bedroom," she said. Then she gently put it back in its place and continued around the room.

He hoped her scent would linger in his bedroom long after she was gone.

"Lydia—" He was finally able to push his feet into the room and draw near her, expecting her to back away. "I'm so very sorry about everything."

She didn't move, and her lips curled slightly. "I know you are."

Did he hear her correctly? Was she coming around? His heart danced a jig of victory, and he moved closer to her. "Can we please spend some time together, get to know each other again?"

She allowed herself a long gaze around his room, and then turned back and faced him with deep longing in her eyes, which her words defied. "No," she said, her voice uncompromising, yet with a degree of warmth Daniel found confusing.

Daniel heard footsteps coming up the stairs and down the

hallway. He knew that his and Lydia's presence in his bedroom was inappropriate and would be frowned upon by anyone who found them here, but neither of them made a move to leave. They stood facing each other, longing in both their eyes, and neither moved until they heard Anna Marie's voice at the doorway.

Chapter Twelve

Lydia's delusional state of calm left her when she saw Anna Marie in the doorway. She'd assumed it would be Lena or Gideon, and she could have handled either of their reactions. But Anna Marie was another story. She braced herself for a harsh lashing from her daughter as she and Daniel stood side by side in the middle of his bedroom, looking like they'd been caught doing something they surely hadn't.

"Sarah and Miriam are looking for you," Anna Marie said with an air of unexpected composure, and even amusement. "I reckon they need your help serving dessert."

Lydia recalled the way Anna Marie had referred to Daniel as her uncle this morning, with a fondness in her voice. And now she seemed tolerant of Daniel and Lydia being alone in Daniel's bedroom together.

Lydia walked to where her daughter was standing in the doorway, and they both started down the hallway. Daniel followed.

When all three reached the bottom of the stairs, Lena gave Lydia a puzzled look. Lydia widened her eyes, mirroring her mother-in-law's expression.

"The sweater?" Lena asked.

"*Ach!* I forgot." Lydia twirled around to head back up the stairs, but Daniel gently touched her arm.

"I forgot to get something for Pop. I'll grab the sweater for

Mamm while I'm up there." He stepped past her and took the stairs two at a time. Lena merely shook her head and walked back to the kitchen.

Anna Marie stood before her. Lydia was having trouble reading her daughter's expression.

"Daniel and I went upstairs together—I mean not together," Lydia stumbled. "We went upstairs because we needed to—No, *ach*. What I mean is, we—well, I reckon I was coming for a sweater for *Mammi*, and Daniel was, uh . . ."

"And *Mammi*'s sweater was in Daniel's room, no?" Anna Marie smiled sagely at Lydia.

This was role reversal at its worst. And Lydia had done nothing wrong. Frustration swept over her in a blanket of confused thoughts, and she shrugged and said, "I have to go help Miriam and Sarah." She shook her head and stormed away, embarrassed that she was behaving like someone Anna Marie's age.

When she entered the kitchen, the cleanup process was underway. Several women were lined up at the sink, one washing dishes, another drying, and a third putting the dishes where they belonged in the cabinets. The young girls were hauling the dirty plates in from the other rooms and stacking them in a pile by the sink. It was almost too crowded for Lydia to maneuver through the room, and she wasn't sure where she was needed. Then she spotted Miriam and Sarah in the corner.

"What do you need help with?" Lydia glanced back and forth between her sister and her friend. Miriam wasn't much older than her own daughter. And Sarah was also considerably younger than Lydia. All of a sudden Lydia felt old and even more ridiculous about her behavior in Daniel's bedroom.

BETH WISEMAN

"We just wanted to make sure you were all right," Miriam said. She looked toward her shoes for a moment, her glasses slipping down her nose. She gave them a push upward, then raised her eyes back to face Lydia. "We saw Daniel go upstairs behind you."

Lydia hadn't said anything to Miriam about Daniel, but of course her sister knew. Everyone knew. But Lydia was touched by her concern. "I'm fine," Lydia assured her.

Sarah leaned her face closer to Lydia's. "You were up there for quite a while." Sarah arched her brows and grinned.

Lydia opened her mouth to tell Sarah that her presumptions were out of line, but then she recalled her behavior in the bedroom. Even though she hadn't done anything wrong, she knew her conduct was improper. But then she noticed something. *Sarah is grinning.*

It was so nice to see her friend smiling. Each time she'd been around Sarah recently, the sadness was evident in her eyes. The closer it came to the anniversary of her miscarriage, the more she seemed to revert inside herself. Perhaps Lydia's affairs of the heart were a distraction for her friend. Although she didn't feel comfortable discussing it in front of her sister.

"Miriam." They all turned to see Miram and Lydia's mother holding two brown bags. "Can you carry these to the buggy for me? This one is a mite too heavy for your old mother." She lifted the bag on her left hip up and pushed it toward Miriam.

"You're not old, *Mamm*," Miriam said. She took both bags and walked out the door.

Lydia was glad when her mother went back to the other side of the room.

Sarah's eyes were wide with anticipation, and although Lydia wasn't proud of the way she'd acted upstairs, if a few details would brighten Sarah's day, then so be it.

⁓

Daniel retrieved the sweater for *Mamm* from the hall closet and then grabbed a bottle of Tums from the medicine cabinet in the bathroom for *Daed*. He slipped into his bedroom and breathed in, but all he could smell was the aroma of food permeating up the stairs. He glanced around for any trace that Lydia had been there and saw the indent in his blue comforter where she'd sat. Why had she come to his room? And what might have happened if Anna Marie hadn't interrupted them?

Lydia had said she was not interested in getting reacquainted with him, but Daniel didn't care what she said—her eyes had brimmed with unspoken passion. There was still something between them. After seeing the expression on her face, the thought of reestablishing a relationship with her didn't seem so far-fetched as when he'd first arrived. He just hoped and prayed that she would give him an opportunity to make up for what he'd done and give him a chance to love her forever.

He edged down the stairs, and the last person he wanted to face was standing near the bottom step with her hands on her hips. The crowd was dispersing, and Daniel slid past Anna Marie, but not without her calling him back. "*Onkel* Daniel?"

It was strange to hear her call him uncle. He cringed and turned cautiously around. "*Ya?*"

"Can I talk to you for a minute?" Her voice didn't have the sharp edge to it that he'd gotten used to from Anna Marie.

"I need to tell everyone good-bye. Can you wait a few minutes?" he asked, halfway hoping she couldn't. He wasn't in the mood for whatever she had to say about catching him and Lydia upstairs together. They weren't children and didn't need a reprimand from a sixteen-year-old.

"*Ya*. I'll wait." Her voice was smooth and unbothered.

He nodded in her direction and then headed into the den to say his good-byes. It was about fifteen minutes later when he found Anna Marie sitting at the bottom of the stairs, apparently having not moved from that spot. The women, including Lydia, were gathered in the kitchen, chatting about the upcoming holidays, and he imagined his father and the few remaining men were in the barn, telling jokes. He walked over to where Anna Marie was sitting, and she stood up.

"What did you want to talk about?" He prepared for the worst.

"I just wanted to say *danki*," she said as she cast her eyes to her feet, which were twisting beneath her. Then she looked back up at him with glassy eyes. "Amos said you convinced him to stay and face his troubles. Otherwise, he might have left, and I would have died of heartbreak." Her voice rose as she spoke, and then she covered her face with her hands.

Daniel stifled a grin. Anna Marie was as dramatic as her mother at that age. "You're welcome," he said.

Anna Marie dropped her arms to her side and sighed. "The story you told him . . ." she began. "I know you changed the names and all, but I reckon I figured it all out." She cast her eyes downward again. "I'm sorry all that happened to you, but I can't be sorry *mei daed* is *mei daed*."

"Of course not," Daniel said quickly. "Everything that happens is God's will. I made my choices that night, and I have to live with them. Your *daed* was a *gut* man and very deserving of your *mamm*'s affections."

"But she loved you first," Anna Marie said. She seemed to be trying to accept the concept that her mother could love someone else before her father.

"I'd like to think so," he said. "We were courting before everything—before everything happened."

Anna Marie tapped her finger to her chin. "You know . . ." Her eyes twinkled with mischief. "Amos is coming over this evening, and we are all going to play games, make cookies, and welcome in the Christmas season properly." She paused with a grin. "You should come."

Daniel thought he might fall over. "Really?"

"*Ya.* Amos will be arriving at five o'clock. And *Mamm* is making a ham with honey drizzled on top." She smiled, and he knew it was a genuine invitation.

Daniel was starting to feel optimistic about the days ahead. If Anna Marie was coming around, it gave him hope that Lydia could too. "I'd love to," he said, then paused. "But we should probably ask your *mamm* about it."

Anna Marie wrinkled her nose. "She'd just say no. Do you really wanna risk it?" She folded her arms across her chest.

Daniel grinned at his new ally. "I guess you're right. I'll see you at five."

~

Lydia had chastised herself enough about her behavior in Daniel's bedroom, flirting with him in a way unsuitable for any woman, especially an Amish woman. She was ashamed to face him, and glad that tonight would be a quiet family night filled with baking cookies and playing games. Amos would be spending the evening and having supper with the family, and Lydia planned to put any thoughts about Daniel to rest for the night.

After devotions with her children in the early afternoon, Lydia spent the rest of the day with Jacob and John in the kitchen. At twelve, Jacob liked to pretend that he was too old to lick the beaters when Lydia made desserts. But when he heard the fun that his *mamm* and brother were having in the kitchen, he joined them. John's sweet little face was covered with cookie dough and icing when Jacob entered the kitchen, and her elder son couldn't resist. They laughed, sang songs, and acted silly all afternoon. Anna Marie had spent most of her afternoon in the sewing area upstairs, finishing a new burgundy dress to wear that evening.

By early evening Lydia's heart was as warm as her toasty kitchen, heated by a small woodstove in the corner. She didn't use the old appliance to cook, but it provided a cozy atmosphere on these chilly nights, and she was able to keep her supper casseroles warm on top of it while her potatoes and celery finished cooking on top of the range. She took a peek at her ham in the oven and was pleased to see a golden glaze forming on top. *Perfect.*

"Anna Marie, Amos is at the door," she hollered from the kitchen when she heard a knock on the door. She twisted her neck to see John in the den. "John, could you please put another log on the fire?"

Lydia checked her potatoes, dried her hands on her apron, then turned around to welcome Amos.

"Daniel!" she gasped. "What are you doing here?" She could feel a flush rising in her cheeks.

"I invited him." Anna Marie bounced into the room. "It's all right, no?"

Lydia's eyebrows rose at the same time her jaw dropped. She stood speechless, her eyes jetting back and forth between the two of them. Then someone else knocked at the door.

"Now, that would be Amos," Anna Marie said. She skipped to the door, leaving Lydia alone in the kitchen with Daniel.

"Lydia, I can go if—" Daniel hesitated. "If you really don't want me here."

I really don't want you here. She bit down hard on her lower lip but didn't say anything. As badly as she didn't want him in her home or in her heart, she was torn by conflicting emotions. But then he smiled, and Lydia reconsidered. "You might as well stay." She shrugged. "There's enough for everyone."

"Anna Marie seems to have softened toward me, and when she asked me to come for supper, I hated to say no." He said the words tentatively. "But if I make you uncomfortable, I'll go."

Ach. His arrogance! She was not going to let him get the best of her. "I'm not uncomfortable at all." She forced her lips into a curved, stiff smile.

"Hello, Daniel," Amos said. "It's *gut* to see you again."

Amos extended his hand to Daniel, and after they'd exchanged pleasantries, Anna Marie suggested the men go into the den and warm themselves by the fire while she helped her mother finish supper. She sounded very grown-up.

Lydia waited until she could hear Amos and Daniel chatting, and then she put her hands on her hips and faced off with her daughter. "What are you doing, inviting Daniel here?" she asked in a whisper.

The bell on the timer rang. Lydia blew out a breath and swirled around to remove the ham from the oven. She placed it on top of the range by the potatoes and celery, then turned back around and waited for Anna Marie to answer.

"He's in love with you," her daughter said smugly.

Lydia felt weak in the knees. "That's ridiculous. He doesn't even know me anymore." She rolled her eyes. "Why would you say such a thing?"

Anna Marie let out a heavy sigh as a smile filled her young face. "I know about these things."

Oh, my dear daughter, you have so much to learn. "I thought you didn't like him. What made you change your mind?"

"It's wrong for me to harbor such ill will. Such thoughts are not proper in God's eyes," Anna Marie said with conviction.

Lydia sat down at the kitchen table and motioned for Anna Marie to take a seat across from her. She leaned her head back to check on the men in the den and saw that Amos, Daniel, John, and Jacob had busied themselves with a board game in the middle of the floor. Lydia kept her voice low so as not to be heard above their chatter.

"I'm glad to hear you say that, Anna Marie. But I have told you before, there is no courtship between Daniel and me." She paused and narrowed her eyes. "Besides, you made it perfectly clear that you didn't want me to have anything to do with Daniel, outside of his being your *onkel.*"

Anna Marie rose from the table, leaned down, and kissed her mother on the cheek. "I've changed my mind."

Lydia sat dumbfounded.

Anna Marie stood tall, touched Lydia on the shoulder, and gazed lovingly into her mother's eyes. She smiled. "Don't worry, *Mamm*. I will tell you everything you need to know about courtship and love." She left to join the others in the den.

Lydia was amused by her daughter's overstated display of maturity, but for some reason Anna Marie's words lingered in her mind. Maybe she did have much to learn about love, since the only two men she had ever loved had betrayed her.

Chapter Thirteen

Lydia couldn't sleep. Two hours had passed since Daniel and Amos left, and the children were already in bed. She kept replaying the evening in her mind. So much laughter and talking. The sounds of family.

Jacob and John clearly adored their *onkel* Daniel, and now that Anna Marie had opened her heart to him, Lydia struggled for a reason not to see Daniel when he asked her to join him for supper on Saturday.

Now, lying in her bed—the bed she'd shared with Elam for fifteen years—she wondered if she'd made a mistake by accepting Daniel's invitation. It would seem like a date, although she made it clear to Daniel that it would be two friends catching up on the past eighteen years, and nothing more.

"Elam, how could you have not told me about what Daniel did?" Lydia whispered. She pulled the covers taut around her chin and fought the shiver in the room and in her heart. "You let me cry on your shoulder, and all the while you knew where he was." A tear trickled down her cheek, and she dabbed it with her quilt. For the first time in months, Lydia allowed herself a good, hard cry. She stifled her pitiful moans with her bedcovers and let it all out, in some sort of effort to release all the pain she felt.

When she was done, she felt drained, and the torment was still there—a future with Daniel that tempted her, and a past with Elam that had been built on lies. She closed her eyes, too exhausted to fight sleep.

It was around two o'clock in the morning when she rolled over in the bed to see Elam sleeping beside her. It was completely dark, but somehow Lydia could see his face, illuminated in a way that allowed her to see every feature, every laugh line, and the tiny scar above his eyebrow that he'd had since childhood. She was lucid enough to know she was dreaming, but the sight of him gazing back into her eyes was a moment she wanted to hold on to forever.

Hello, my love, he whispered tenderly. He cupped her cheek in his hand, the way he'd done a thousand times during their marriage. Lydia closed her eyes and basked in the feel of his touch. *I've missed you.*

She was afraid to move, scared to breathe, for fear she'd wake up and he'd be gone.

I know you have questions, Lydia.

She could hear the regret in his tone, but she didn't care about the past right now. His lie suddenly seemed tiny in comparison to the fifteen years they'd shared as husband and wife. She closed her eyes and placed her hand on top of his as he continued to cradle her cheek.

"Elam," she whispered. "I've missed you so much."

I'm sorry, Lydia. I'm sorry I didn't tell you about the night in the alley. Daniel begged me not to, but I should have told you anyway, given you a choice. It's just that—

"It doesn't matter, Elam. It just doesn't matter." She squeezed his hand, again fearing she'd wake up any second.

He smiled at her—so familiar, so real, so perfect—and

filled with memories only a husband and wife could appreciate. Her wedding day flashed before her, and then the births of all three of her children.

It might not matter to you at this very moment, Elam said soothingly, *but in the morning, the decision I made so long ago will creep into your thoughts again.*

"Are you really here?" she asked. Lydia didn't care about anything else. "Stay with me, Elam. Don't leave me again. Please," she begged. Tears began to well in eyes already swollen from the night before.

There, there. Elam swept a thumb gently across her face and wiped away a tear that had spilled over. *You know I can't stay.*

"Then I don't want to wake up." Her body began to tremble as she cried in desperation.

Elam pulled her into his arms and held her close. *Of course you do, Lydia. What about our children? Our daughter needs you now more than ever. She is at a difficult age, and will need much lieb and support from you.* He paused and pulled her closer. *And then there is Daniel.*

Lydia tensed. "I don't want to talk about him."

Elam leaned back and tilted Lydia's chin upward. He fused his eyes with hers. *God blessed me so by allowing me to be in the first half of your life. Consider letting Daniel into your heart for the second half.*

"No." She pulled her eyes from his and buried her head in the nook of his shoulder. "Stay with me, Elam."

You must forgive him, Lydia. Only then will you find the peace you need to move forward. He paused. *I carried a heavy weight on my shoulders, Lydia, by not telling you the truth while I could. My love for you was all-consuming, and I was afraid that if I told you Daniel was living nearby, that you'd go to him.* She felt his chest rise and fall beneath her. *And you would have. But I'm sorry I didn't give you that choice. Please forgive me.*

Lydia knew that she forgave him the minute she saw him lying next to her. They'd shared a wonderful life, and what she had learned seemed less important now. "I do forgive you, Elam."

Forgive Daniel too, Lydia. He's hurting.

"No." She could feel him slipping away. "No, Elam," she cried. "Please don't go."

I love you, Lydia. I'll always love you.

And then she woke up.

❧

Daniel was completely out of practice with dating. He'd done very little of it over the course of his life. He'd found out early on that there wasn't going to be anyone to replace the love he felt for Lydia, so he'd more or less given up trying, especially after Jenny died. Jenny was very special, and he'd loved her, but it was never the kind of love he felt for Lydia.

From the little bit he knew about courting, flowers were always a nice gesture. Lydia had made it quite clear that this was no date, but both of them knew otherwise. He chose a traditional bouquet of red roses, sprinkled with baby's breath and greenery.

He knocked on the door with the nervousness of a teenaged boy.

Anna Marie swung the door wide. "Flowers are always a *gut* idea," she whispered. "*Mamm* is in the kitchen."

Daniel walked into the den. He'd worn his best blue shirt and black pants, along with a black felt hat and long black coat. Lydia entered the room in a dark green dress and black apron, looking as beautiful as always, but something was different. The glow of her smile warmed him from across the room, and her eyes glistened with a peacefulness she didn't seem to have before. It had been almost a week since Daniel had last seen her.

"Hello." She sounded nervous as well, but there was a hint of excitement in her voice.

Daniel handed her the roses. "I hope you like roses. I remember that you like orchids, but the boutique in Paradise didn't have any, and—anyway, I—I hope you like these." He was having trouble keeping his voice steady, and it was bordering on embarrassing. "Not that this is a date or anything," he added.

"The flowers are lovely."

Lydia's entire demeanor had changed since he saw her on Sunday after his baptism. Perhaps she'd found true forgiveness in her heart after all.

"Let me go put these in some water." She walked to the kitchen while Anna Marie kept him company.

"Where will you be taking *Mamm*?" Anna Marie asked. She had a concerned expression on her face.

"I thought I'd take her to Paradiso. Does she like Italian food?" He honestly couldn't remember.

Anna Marie smiled with approval. "It's a quaint place, and *Mamm* will be pleased."

"I'm ready," Lydia said. She grabbed her cape and bonnet from the rack by the door.

"Make sure your brothers handle their chores this evening, Anna Marie. And remember to put price tags on the jellies to take to market." She finished tying the strings of her bonnet. "And Sarah will be by to pick up some cookbooks to deliver for me when she goes to Bird-in-Hand this week."

"It'll be fine, *Mamm*." Anna Marie folded her hands together in front her. Her eyes gleamed. "You two just go and have a *gut* time."

Daniel and Lydia's eyes met in mutual amusement at Anna Marie's grown-up comment. Lydia nodded at her daughter. Daniel didn't feel like Anna Marie was too far off base. He did feel like a kid out on his very first date.

Once they were in Daniel's buggy, he pulled the thick, brown blanket from the backseat and draped it around Lydia. He'd love for her to be sharing the blanket with him, but maybe on the way home.

"*Danki*." She turned to face him. Her eyes were filled with childlike enthusiasm that shone bright in the pale light of the moon. Yes. Something had definitely changed, and Daniel couldn't have been more pleased. He'd been praying hard that Lydia would give him another chance.

When they got to the restaurant, Daniel offered Lydia his hand to step down from the buggy. They fended off stares from the *Englisch* tourists when they walked in. It was easy to differentiate the locals from the visitors. The *Englisch* from this area didn't give the Amish a second glance. Daniel recalled how much the stares bothered him when he was growing up. But now he was with Lydia, and he wanted to scream to the world that he was home where he belonged. *So stare all you want.*

They'd barely finished their chicken parmesan when the waitress asked if they would be ordering dessert.

"Just *kaffi* for me," Lydia said.

Daniel nodded. "Two, please."

For the first time since he'd been back, his conversations with Lydia flowed effortlessly. He wasn't proud of the life he'd lived some of the time, but as he filled Lydia in about his past, she never judged him. Several times, when he felt particularly ashamed, her eyes had shone with more kindness and tenderness than he could remember from their youth, or deserved now. Lydia had always been kindhearted and loving, but this was different, and Daniel wondered if it was due to motherhood or if she had just matured into someone far grander than he could have imagined.

"Now you," Daniel said as they sipped their coffee. "I know you married Elam. And of course, you have three children. Tell me everything."

Daniel would be lying if he didn't admit that it stung a little to see her smile when she spoke about her life with Elam.

"It was a *gut* life with Elam," she said.

Her eyes drifted from his for a moment, and she shifted her weight in the chair. When her gaze returned to his, she seemed hesitant to continue. But Daniel nodded for her to go on.

"Elam was fortunate enough to be able to make a *gut* living working the fields. We always had a fine harvest. Since you left," she went on, "even more farmers are supplementing their income by holding jobs outside of our community. Many work in construction or building furniture. I don't know anyone who wouldn't prefer not to do this, but growing families, lack of land, the economy—well, it's just forced us out into the *Englisch* world more than we would like."

"What about you? I know you have your cookbooks and that you sell jams and jellies at market. But what else occupies your time?"

"*Ach!* You know the answer to that." A gentle laugh rippled through the air, and right before his eyes, she transformed into the bubbly nineteen-year-old love he'd left behind. "Up at four thirty. Breakfast at five. Then there are the cows to be milked, which Jacob and John take of, and Anna Marie and I tend to laundry, sewing, baking. . . ."

She was still talking, but Daniel was only halfway listening. He was lost in the moment—her smile, the sound of her voice, her laughter, and sheer joy about the life she'd lived so far.

After Daniel paid the bill, they left. Once on the road, it seemed much colder in the buggy, so Daniel turned on a small battery-operated heater he'd brought from home and turned the fan in Lydia's direction. She bundled herself in the blanket and thanked him. Daniel's teeth were chattering wildly, and his body shook from the cold. He recalled the way they used to sit close together and share the warmth of the blanket and each other. But she didn't offer to share, and he didn't ask.

It was nearing seven o'clock, but there was still time for one more trip down memory lane, if Lydia would agree.

The old oak tree.

Chapter Fourteen

Lydia was tempted by Daniel's offer. Stars twinkled in thick clusters overhead, and she knew it would be a magical night under the old tree, but she wasn't ready for that yet. She was still working on being friends with him, getting to know him again, and truly forgiving him. She was praying hard about it, and it was all coming together nicely, but friendship was all she had to offer him at this point, and the old oak tree would spark things within herself that she wasn't ready to face.

"It's been a *gut* night, Daniel, but I think you best take me home."

Lydia could see the disappointment in his eyes, but he nodded.

She tried to imagine what it must have been like for him eighteen years ago. A conviction that carried jail time, and then the start of a new and unfamiliar life. If he'd only trusted their love more, he'd have known that there was nothing they couldn't have endured together.

She recalled the way Daniel spoke of his past, with remorse over the choices he'd made. But she'd also watched his face light up when he spoke about the old woman, Margaret, who showed him the way back to the Lord. And he'd spoken fondly of a woman named Jenny, and Lydia could tell how much her death pained him. It was strange to hear him talk about caring for another woman in that way. But even with all the years gone by, she could still see her Daniel in every word he spoke, his movements, and even the way he scrunched his nose when he was trying not to laugh.

Elam's words in her dream echoed in her head. *God blessed me so by allowing me to be in the first half of your life. Consider letting Daniel into your heart for the second half. Forgive Daniel too, Lydia. He's hurting.*

Daniel turned his head her way and caught her eyes on him. "Are you all right?" he asked with such tenderness it caused her heart to flutter.

"*Ya,*" she whispered. She pulled her eyes away from his and sat quietly, lost in the moment. She couldn't help but wonder. *What if . . .*

~

Daniel pulled the buggy to a stop in front of Lydia's house. "Whoa, boy."

His pulse quickened as he helped her from the buggy, unsure what the proper protocol was. In his previous world, a simple kiss good night would solidify that the night went well and suggest that another date might be in order. But he was home, and this was Lydia. Doing things right had never been more important to him, and he felt his future hanging on this moment. He didn't want to scare her, but he'd never longed to take another woman into his arms the way he did right now.

At the door, she turned to face him. "*Danki* for supper, Daniel."

He searched her face and tried to read her expression. For a long moment, she gazed back. His heart pounded viciously against his chest, and he knew that he was going to kiss Lydia good night, the way he'd dreamed of for many years. He took a deep breath and leaned forward toward her.

In less time than it took for him to uproot his feet from their position, Lydia turned, opened the door, stepped through the threshold, and turned to face him. "Good night," she said abruptly. And the door slammed shut.

Daniel smiled. She might have closed the door on his intent to kiss her good night, but just the fact that she considered kissing him was enough to ensure he'd get a good night's sleep.

〜

For a moment, Lydia stared at the wooden door. He'd almost kissed her good night, and she'd almost allowed it. She drew in a deep breath, then turned to see Anna Marie standing behind her like a mother hen waiting for her little chick to return.

"Well?" Her daughter raised questioning brows. "How did it go?"

Lydia untied the strings on her bonnet and refused to make eye contact with Anna Marie. She was fearful her daughter might see into her heart, into the secret chamber where a woman stores her most intimate thoughts. But the corner of her mouth tweaked upward unconciously.

"*Ach*, it must have been *gut*," Anna Marie said smugly.

Lydia hung her bonnet on the rack by the door and untied the strings on her cape. "I am not discussing this with you, Anna Marie," she said firmly. Although she couldn't seem to control the grin that kept threatening to form on her face.

"Did he kiss you good night?" Her daughter's eyes widened with anticipation.

"Anna Marie!" She hung up her cape, then turned to face her daughter with her hands on her hips. "It's not appropriate for you to ask me such a question." She pulled off her gloves and walked to the fireplace.

Anna Marie was on her heels.

"He did, didn't he?" Anna Marie stood beside her in front of the hearth as Lydia warmed her palms. "He kissed you good night."

"As a matter of fact, no, he did not." Lydia narrowed her eyes in Anna Marie's direction. "Anna Marie, I'm glad that you are not harboring dislike toward your *onkel* anymore, but you need not be getting any silly notions in your head."

Much to Lydia's surprise, Anna Marie turned to face her, and her eyes were serious, her voice steady. "I just want you to be happy, *Mamm*."

Lydia sighed and grabbed Anna Marie's hands. "I know, Anna Marie."

"Pop is gone. And I know that you have a history, a past with Daniel." Anna Marie's forehead crinkled. "I didn't care for him much in the beginning because I feared he would try to take *Daed*'s place, and I wasn't sure if I was ready for that. But I will be marrying Amos next year, and Jacob and John need a father." Anna Marie looked hesitant to go on. "Daniel told Amos what happened the night he left you on Christmas Eve."

"What?" *That wasn't Daniel's place to do that*, Lydia thought as she waited for Anna Marie to go on.

"Oh, he changed the names, and he probably didn't tell him everything, but it wasn't hard for Amos to figure out that Daniel was talking about himself in the story. And he told Amos enough to keep Amos from making the same mistake he did."

Now Lydia understood why Anna Marie had changed her mind about Daniel.

"*Mamm?*"

"*Ya?*"

Anna Marie gazed lovingly into Lydia's eyes. "I'd really like to hear—to hear about you and Daniel, when you were young." Anna Marie looked toward her shoes.

Lydia thought hard for a moment. Wonderful memories floated to the surface of her mind. She lifted her daughter's chin and smiled. "You go brew us some *kaffi*. I want to go check on Jacob and John." She paused and studied Anna Marie for a moment, trying to really see her daughter as the woman she was becoming. "Then I will tell you about Daniel and me."

Anna Marie's expression lifted, and she bit her lip, then headed to the kitchen. Lydia went to check on her sons.

For the next two hours, Lydia and Anna Marie cuddled under a quilt on the couch in front of a toasty fire on the cold December night, and Lydia told her daughter all about her first true love. After all these years, she could still vividly recall every detail of the times she'd spent with Daniel—times that, until now, she'd kept secretly stored away in her heart, refusing to unlock her memories for fear of the pain that loomed there.

But as she shared these precious reflections with Anna Marie, Lydia realized that instead of fear and pain—something else was forming in its place and was growing with every word she spoke.

Hope.

Chapter Fifteen

Following a quiet day of rest and devotion on Sunday, Lydia awoke on Monday with a burst of energy she didn't remember having for a long time. She ran the broom along the wooden floor in the kitchen and recalled the conversation she'd had with her daughter on Saturday night, her spirit invigorated as she drew on memories from her past. And Anna Marie, a true romantic at heart, had hung on Lydia's every word with a sparkle in her eyes, often comparing her relationship with Amos to Lydia and Daniel's.

After the boys left for school, Miriam picked up Anna Marie for sisters day, a monthly affair that all the women in the community looked forward to. It was a time for sewing, quilting, baking, and any other project of the women's choosing. Mostly, it was a time for chatter—who was courting whom, upcoming baptisms, weddings being planned, etc.

Lydia declined the invitation this morning, but encouraged Anna Marie to attend. Lydia told her daughter she would take care of the Monday laundry chore. She preferred to be alone with her thoughts, which inevitably drifted to Daniel. She could still recall the way his eyes clung to hers last night, familiar and full of desire. He would have kissed her if she hadn't forced herself to turn away. She'd wanted nothing more than to press her lips to his and recapture a tiny bit of their youth, if only for a moment.

Lydia knew her walls of defense against Daniel were crumbling, leaving her heart exposed. She couldn't help but wonder if there was enough love in her heart to forgive Daniel. Again, she heard Elam's voice in her head. *You must forgive him, Lydia. Only then will you find the peace you need to move forward.*

During her morning devotions, she'd prayed extra hard for guidance. Perhaps the quiet voice in her head wasn't Elam.

Lydia cleared the last of the breakfast dishes. She was drying her hands on a kitchen towel when she heard a knock at the door.

"I'm looking for Mr. Smucker," a woman said when Lydia opened the door.

The *Englischer*, in a fancy brown coat and matching knee-length boots, towered over Lydia. "I'm—I'm sorry," Lydia stuttered, "but Mr. Smucker passed away about two years ago."

"Oh no." The woman hung her head. "I didn't know that. I was told I could find him here."

The woman's teeth were chattering, and Lydia wondered if she should invite her in. She didn't look like an *Englischer* from Lancaster County. Her sophisticated attire distinguished her somewhat from folks in the area; she looked like she was from a big city. Golden blonde hair fell loosely on top of her head, and loose tendrils blew against high cheekbones. Her eyes were heavily painted, but not in an unbecoming way. Diamond rings adorned both her hands, and her nails were long and manicured.

Lydia wasn't sure if it was the kindness in the woman's sapphire-colored eyes or blatant curiosity that compelled her to invite the *Englischer* in, but she eased to one side of the door. "Please come in out of the cold," she offered.

The woman bit down on her trembling lip and narrowed her eyes in deliberation. Then she slowly walked inside.

"Is there something I can help you with?" Lydia asked as she pushed the front door closed. "I am Mr. Smucker's wife." She sighed. "I mean, widow."

"I'm so sorry for your loss," the woman said. "He was a good man." Her eyes clouded with tears, and Lydia couldn't imagine how her husband knew this woman.

"But no, you can't help me," she went on. "I wanted to resolve some issues with Daniel, and now that's not possible."

"Daniel?" Lydia's eyes widened in surprise. "Daniel Smucker isn't dead."

"What?"

"I was married to *Elam* Smucker, who passed two years ago." Lydia wasn't sure if she felt relief or alarm at this new information. "You are looking for Elam's brother, Daniel, who lives down the way." She pointed to her north. "At the old Kauffman place."

"Thank you so much!" The *Englisch* woman wasted no time heading toward the door. "I'm so glad Daniel Smucker is alive. I've come a long way to find him, and——" With her hand on the doorknob, she turned around.

Again Lydia saw kindness in her eyes.

"I'm sorry about your husband, Elam." Her bright red lips formed into a tender smile. "But I am very thankful to have found Daniel. I just hope that he'll see me after all this time. I pray that he will."

She gave a quick wave and was gone.

Lydia's mind spun with bewilderment, and the zest in her

spirit plummeted. How naive she'd been. Daniel had lived among the *Englisch* for nearly two decades. It stood to reason that he would have ties from his past—beautiful ties. If that was the type of woman Daniel associated with in his former life, why in the world would he want anything to do with her?

She walked briskly to the bathroom and studied her plain face in the mirror. Tiny lines feathered from the corners of tired eyes, and her light brown lashes were sparse. The circles under her eyes were a shade darker this morning from staying up too late the night before. She leaned in closer to inspect lips that had lost their pinkish pucker and skin that no longer glowed with the benefit of youth.

She stood straight again and ran her hands along hips that had aided in the delivery of three children, and then she held her hands in front of her and spread her fingers wide. Short finger-nails rounded out long fingers, which wrinkled slightly beneath her knuckles as she stretched them to capacity, giving way to more creases across the top of her hand.

What am I doing? She lowered her chin. Vanity was wrong in the eyes of God. Lydia knew in her heart that such pride was a sin and that her appearance in no way represented the person beneath her plain look. And yet she couldn't help but compare herself to the beautiful woman who'd resurfaced from Daniel's past. Lydia felt her stomach sink. *Why would he choose me?*

Daniel slowed his horse as he eased under the covered bridge in Ronks and enjoyed a brief reprieve from the flurry of snow-flakes that had started earlier this morning. But even the bitter cold couldn't dampen his spirit. His heart was warm and his mind filled with thoughts of Lydia. Beautiful Lydia.

But for all her outer beauty, it was the woman inside with whom Daniel was in love. His Lydia. He was so happy knowing she hadn't changed a bit.

He headed up the Old Philadelphia Pike and made his way to the farmers' market in Bird-in-Hand. It was a shopping stop mostly for tourists, but Daniel wanted to pick up something special for Lydia. When they were kids, she'd said the bakery inside the market made the best molasses crinkle cookies. She had joked that she could never get her cookies to taste like the ones from the market.

Daniel suspected she had perfected the recipe after all these years, but he was going to buy her some of the cookies just the same.

~

Carol Stewart carried her red suitcase up to the second floor at Beiler's Bed and Breakfast—to the Rose Room, which lived up to its name with four walls painted a dusty pink color. She plopped her suitcase, coat, and purse onto the queen-sized bed, which was topped with a lovely white bedspread. Then she eased into one of the floral high-back chairs in the sitting area and pulled off her boots. She stretched her toes, leaned back, and blew out a sigh.

She'd stopped by Daniel Smucker's farm, but he wasn't home. She even waited for almost an hour to see if he would return. Her desperateness to see him was all consuming, and she was determined to somehow make things right. Perhaps after a short catnap, she'd try again. She was sleepy from her three-hour drive from New York City.

She thought back to the last time she saw Daniel, and the expression on his face when she left. He'd probably thought he would see her again. But she had run, the way she always ran when she couldn't face her troubles. She was through running now—from the memories of Daniel that haunted her, and mostly from herself. Her father was dead now, so nothing would prevent her from finding Daniel. She prayed that he could somehow forgive her.

Chapter Sixteen

Daniel passed by Lydia's house on his way home and was surprised to see her in the front yard, toting firewood. He stopped his buggy. Snow was falling and starting to accumulate. It was colder than cold outside. He jumped from the seat to give her a hand.

"Why aren't you at sisters day?" he asked as he crossed the front yard.

She shrugged and kept walking, bundled up in her heavy coat and gloves.

"Here, let me." Daniel caught up with her and scooped the two logs from her arms. She allowed it, but she looked more irritated than appreciative. He followed her into the house and set the wood on the rack near the fireplace.

"*Danki*," she said. She hung up her coat and took off her gloves, never once looking in his direction. This wasn't the same woman he'd said good-bye to on Saturday night.

"Lydia?"

"*Ya?*" She walked to the fireplace where Daniel was standing and suspended her gloves from two nails sticking out of the mantel. She placed her palms in front of the fire.

"Is everything all right? Why aren't you at sisters day?" he repeated.

"I just didn't feel like going," she said, then shrugged.

Daniel remembered the cookies he bought for her at market. "I'll be right back. I have something for you."

He returned a few moments later with a brown bag. "These are for you."

She opened the brown sack and pulled out one of the individually wrapped cookies, studied it, and put it back in the bag. The hint of a smile flickered across her face, but faded when she briefly glanced up at him. "*Danki.* I'll just go put these in the kitchen."

Maybe she didn't care for the cookies anymore. Daniel followed her.

"I remember how much you used to like these when we were kids. You said the best ones came from the farmers' market in Bird-in-Hand, so I picked you up some this morning."

She stowed the bag on the counter, not acknowledging what he'd just said. "There was a woman here looking for you this morning."

"Who was she?"

Lydia briskly moved past him, grabbed the broom, and began to sweep her kitchen floor. "I have no idea," she said sharply.

"An Amish woman?"

"No. *Englisch.* A very beautiful *Englisch* woman. She looked very big-city." She raked the broom harder across the floor.

Daniel crinkled his forehead and thought for a moment. "I can't imagine any *Englisch* woman looking for me here. What did she look like?"

"I told you. Very pretty."

Her voice was edgy, and it took him a moment to catch on.

"Hmm—" He rubbed his chin and watched the broom whipping across the wooden slats. "I know so many pretty women. I wonder which one it was."

"I'm sure I wouldn't know." Her face reddened.

Daniel stifled a grin. "Lydia, I'm playing with you. I don't know any pretty women who'd be looking for me. The only beautiful woman I'm interested in is standing in this kitchen."

She stopped sweeping and rattled off something in Pennsylvania *Deitsch*, so fast he couldn't understand what she said.

"Whoa, slow down."

"Daniel, it isn't proper for you to be here right now. I have chores to tend to." She started to run the broom over the floor again.

"Lydia, can you stop for a minute, please?" He cautiously moved toward her, and she propped the broom in the corner. She faced him, folded her arms across her chest, and bit her bottom lip.

"Are you mad at me because this woman showed up here, looking for me? I can't imagine who it is. Really."

"No, of course I'm not mad," she said. "I'm just very busy right now."

Daniel knew they'd taken a step backward. He didn't want to worsen things, but this hot and cold she played was irritating. He tipped his straw hat in her direction. "Then I'll let you get back to work." He didn't try to hide the cynicism in his voice.

Lydia walked him to the door. "*Danki* again for the cookies."

"You're welcome."

~

She closed the door, embarrassed by her childish behavior. But in addition to her struggle to forgive Daniel and move forward in their relationship, she needed to trust him. She'd done that once, and it hadn't served her well. She walked to the window and watched him walk to his buggy, feeling silly that she'd overreacted. He'd just opened the door to climb inside when a sleek, tan car pulled up behind his buggy.

Daniel closed the door and walked to the driver's window and leaned down. Lydia couldn't see who was in the car, since Daniel's body was blocking her view. She edged to her left, then to her right. Then she remembered seeing that same car earlier. Her recollection came about the time Daniel walked to the passenger side and climbed inside—with the elegant blonde-haired woman in the driver seat.

~

"Thank you for agreeing to have coffee with me," Carol said as Daniel fastened his seat belt.

He pushed back his straw hat, glanced briefly in her direction, and offered her the best half smile he could muster up. So many times he'd thought about what he might say to her if he had the chance.

"I'm going to Europe in a few days. When I heard you were back in Lancaster County, I felt compelled to find you before I leave."

Daniel could see why Lydia would think this woman was beautiful. Carol had delicate features and full lips. Her hair was golden, like a field of grain, and her blue eyes shone with a warmth Daniel hadn't expected. But in his mind she didn't compare to Lydia, whose beauty ran from the inside out.

Lydia's reaction flattered him, but it was worrisome. He knew she was already struggling to find a place for him in her life, and he didn't want this to cause a permanent setback. His attitude when he left probably didn't help things, but she didn't need to be so snippy. The fact that Carol was in Lancaster County shocked Daniel as much as it had Lydia. He had never expected to lay eyes on the woman again.

"Is this place okay?" Carol pointed to the Dutch bakery on the right.

"*Ya.* That's fine."

Daniel fought the resentment that he felt toward Carol and told himself that he would listen to her with an open mind and heart. He'd prayed for her, despite the pain she'd caused.

Although, looking at her now, she didn't seem to be the monster he'd made her out to be. Maybe she'd changed. As she pulled her car into the parking lot of the bakery, Daniel reckoned he was about to find out.

∼

It was later in the afternoon when Lydia took the buggy to Lena and Gideon's to pick up Anna Marie. Her daughter told her this morning that, after sisters day, she was going to go back to her grandparents' house for a while to work on a special quilt that she and Lena were making as a Christmas present for Sarah. It wasn't a full-sized quilt, but more of a lap cover. Lydia had seen the work in progress, and it was beautiful.

Everyone in the community adored Sarah and her husband, David, and the women also knew that Sarah was having a difficult time as the anniversary of her miscarriage approached. Lydia thought it was a lovely gesture for Anna Marie to want to make her something so special for Christmas.

"You've come a long way on this, Anna Marie." Lydia inspected the finely quilted squares bursting with every color in the rainbow. "And you've done a fine job."

"*Mammi* helped a lot, too," Anna Marie said as she tucked her chin.

Lena waved her off. "No, I reckon I just supervised." She pulled a pan from the oven. "Plain ol' sugar cookies, if anyone is interested." She placed the tray on her cooling rack.

"Your cookies are always *wunderbaar*, Lena." Lydia sat down at the kitchen table while Anna Marie stored the quilt back in Lena's sewing room upstairs. "How was sisters day?"

"It was a *gut* day." Lena put the last cookie on the rack and then joined Lydia at the table. "Why didn't you go?"

Lydia shrugged. "*Ach*, I don't know. I just had a lot to do around the house." She recalled her zesty spirit and how wonderful she'd felt this morning—before the *Englischer* showed up.

"You should have gone," Lena said. She winked at Lydia. "You know how chatty everyone gets. Maybe they wouldn't have talked so much about you if you'd have been there."

Lydia's eyes widened. "What? Why would the ladies be talking about me?"

"There was much speculation about you and Daniel." Lena's voice was hopeful, and Lydia hated to disappoint her.

"We went to supper. There's nothing to speculate about. Was my daughter listening to everyone chat about me?"

Lena folded her hands on the table and sat up a little taller. "Actually, it was Anna Marie who started the conversation. She's glad you and Daniel seemed to be getting along so well, and I think she's hoping—"

"It was just supper, Lena." Lydia knew who was doing most of the hoping. But she regretted her own snappy tone. "Sorry," she said, then bit her bottom lip.

A few awkward moments of silence ensued until Anna Marie came bouncing back into the kitchen, about the same time Lydia heard a buggy pulling up in the driveway.

"Gideon will want some hot cocoa," Lena said. She stood up, walked to the stove, and lit the gas burner. "He's comin' back from Leroy Blank's place. Leroy wanted him to see a woodworking project he has going on." Lena shook her head. "It's too cold to be goin' anywhere."

"Yum. Sugar cookies." Anna Marie snatched a cookie and leaned against the counter.

Lydia heard the front door close and footsteps nearing from the den. But it was Daniel who rounded the corner, not Gideon.

"Hi," he said. He took off his hat and coat, hung them on the rack. "This is a nice surprise."

Daniel and Lydia's eyes met, but she quickly looked away. There was an edge to Daniel's voice, and she wasn't sure he found her presence a nice surprise at all.

Lydia bolted up from the table. "Anna Marie, we must go home and start supper. Jacob and John will be getting hungry soon." She retrieved her heavy coat, gloves, and bonnet from the rack where she'd hung them when she first arrived.

"Hi, *Onkel* Daniel." Anna Marie smiled at Daniel.

"Come along, Anna Marie. Get your coat on." Lydia tied her bonnet. She kissed Lena quickly on the cheek. "See you soon."

"Lydia, can I talk with you for a minute before you go?" Daniel asked.

"Anna Marie, come with me." Lena practically dragged Anna Marie by the arm through the kitchen. "I have something upstairs to show you while your *mamm* and *Onkel* Daniel talk."

"No, Anna Marie, we have to go," Lydia said firmly.

Anna Marie frowned playfully, and then mouthed the word *Sorry* to her *mamm* as her *mammi* pulled her toward the stairs.

"What is it, Daniel?" Lydia asked. She was all bundled up and ready to go, and he was just standing there staring at her. "Hmm?"

"I wanted to explain about that woman. You seemed upset about her coming here. She came to talk to me about something that happened a long—"

"Stop." Lydia held her palm up. "Please, Daniel. There is no need for you to explain. I'm sure there are many women from your past."

"And apparently that bothers you a great deal." He looped his thumbs through his suspenders.

"*Ach!* It most certainly does not." *How dare he?* "You and I agreed to be friends, nothing more. I don't care about your romantic past, nor should you feel the need to tell me about it. It's most inappropriate."

Daniel was quickly on her heels. "You know that I want to be more than your friend, Lydia, but I'm willing to accept your terms. But you have the wrong idea about Carol. My relationship with her—"

"I don't want to hear." Lydia covered her ears with her hands and shook her head.

"Can you please quit interrupting me?" Daniel thrust his hands on his hips. "That's an irritating habit you have when you don't want to hear something."

Lydia wanted to be mad at him and show anger, but instead her eyes began to instantly fill with tears. "If I'm so *irritating*, then why don't you just leave me alone?"

Daniel sighed, then reached for her arm. She jerked away from him.

"I didn't mean to hurt your feelings, Lydia. That's the last thing I'd want to do."

She stormed across the den and yelled upstairs. "Anna Marie. Let's go!"

When Anna Marie hit the bottom stair, Lydia grabbed her daughter's hand and pulled her toward the front door.

"Why does everyone keep dragging me around?" Anna Marie asked. She glanced back and forth between Lydia and Lena.

Lydia didn't answer. As the door closed behind them, one thing was for sure. Lydia had used bad judgment when she'd decided to let her guard down with Daniel, and now she needed to force some distance between them and patch the tiny cracks in her heart.

Chapter Seventeen

Daniel knew that by forgiving Carol, he'd made peace with some of his past as well. She'd wept openly and said she couldn't move forward without knowing that Daniel forgave her. He knew the agony of seeking exoneration from someone. He didn't want to leave Carol in that lonely place where past regrets gnaw away at your soul, where peace is within your grasp but yanked away by your own guilt. Daniel was familiar with that place.

He'd like to think that he'd forgiven himself for the decision he'd made Christmas Eve, but occasionally he revisited that dark place where Carol had been. Maybe now she could find the kind of happiness that had evidently eluded them both.

Perhaps Lydia would find a way to open her heart to him. He'd settle for just her friendship, if that's all she could give him, but after their last conversation, he realized that even being friends was a challenge.

It was quiet in his house. Too quiet. Too much time to think. He carried the lantern upstairs and got into bed knowing sleep wouldn't be coming for a while. He knew of something he could do in the meantime. He tried to clear his thoughts so he could truly commune with God.

God's will is not to be questioned. It was a belief he'd carried with him into the *Englisch* world. Even though he'd lost his way for a while, in his heart he'd always known that to be true. If he hadn't made the decision to leave, there'd be no Anna

Marie, Jacob, or John. Elam might not have shared his life with someone as wonderful as Lydia.

He recalled the way Lydia's eyes iced over at the sight of him this afternoon. She'd just started to warm up to him when Carol showed up and put a glitch in things. If Lydia only knew. His heart had always belonged to her, even when she wasn't there to accept his love. He couldn't help but wonder if she'd thought about him over the years. Guilt washed over him for having such thoughts about another man's wife, particularly when that man was his own brother.

"I'm sorry, Elam," he whispered. "She was your wife."

He turned off the lantern, closed his eyes, and prayed for God to lead his thoughts in the right direction.

Over a week went by without Daniel and Lydia resolving their troubles, and Lena knew her son was suffering. She didn't know how to ease his pain, or Lydia's, for that matter. She served Daniel dippy eggs, buttermilk pancakes, bacon, and scrapple for breakfast on this cold December morning. His favorites, and it was worth her small effort to brighten his day.

"It will take time, Daniel," she said after Gideon went to tend to the animals. "Lydia needs time to adjust to you being here."

"I know, *Mamm*." Daniel moved his eggs around on the plate. "But it's been over a week now. Did you see how she avoided me at church service on Sunday?"

Lena sat down at the table across from her son. "Daniel." She chose her words carefully. "You know how much your *daed* and me love you, no?"

He nodded.

"But your coming home after all these years took some time for us to get used to. I reckon we'd buried you, so to speak. Eighteen years is a mighty long time, Daniel. And it took many years for us to heal after you left." She paused as her forehead creased with concern. "I tell you this, son, not to hurt you, but to make you realize that Lydia is dealing with things the best way she can. These are strange circumstances.

"Nothing would please your pop and me more than for you and Lydia to court. The children need a father, and I think it is what Elam would want. But such issues can't be forced. God has his own time frame, and he will guide your way. Just be patient."

∼

Lydia spread out the children's Christmas gifts on the floor in the den. With the boys at school and Anna Marie at market with Miriam, she wanted to take advantage of this time alone to wrap some gifts. She set Lena and Gideon's gifts to her right, in a pile next to the presents for her side of the family. None of the items she'd made or purchased were extravagant, but she had a little something for everyone—everyone except Daniel.

She picked up the battery-operated hand mixer she'd purchased for Lena and wondered if her mother-in-law would use it. It would make things so much easier on her, particularly since the natural doctor in town said she'd developed some arthritis in her hands. The herbs the doctor suggested weren't helping, and Lydia thought the ease of the portable food mixer might help her. For Gideon, she'd purchased a special blend of herbal tea that he enjoyed, and she planned to make him a batch of raisin puffs.

Lydia picked up the pink diary she'd purchased for Miriam, since she felt like her younger sister tended to keep her feelings inside. Inside the diary, she'd written Miriam a special inscription.

For her other two sisters, Hannah and Rachel, she'd selected simple black sweaters. Each of her brothers, John Jr. and Melvin, was receiving a fine pair of leather work gloves. And for her parents she'd bought a battery-operated weather warning system, like the one she kept in her kitchen. She thumbed through the rest of the presents and made sure she had small tokens for all of her nieces and nephews.

For her son John, Lydia had purchased a new winter coat and warm gloves. Her bookworm, Jacob, was getting a collection of books from an author he enjoyed. She'd struggled with what to get Anna Marie, but in the end she'd chosen the set of china she'd received from Lena and Gideon when she and Elam were married. It would mean more to Anna Marie than anything Lydia could have bought her, especially now that she was planning to start her life with Amos.

Yes. There was something for everyone but Daniel. What could she possibly get for Elam's brother, the children's *onkel*, the man for whom she harbored such mixed feelings? She recalled his interaction with the *Englisch* woman, the way he'd hopped into her car and left. *Where did they go? What did they talk about?* She couldn't help but wonder if Daniel regretted his decision to get rebaptized. Maybe the woman hoped to reunite with him.

She tried to push Daniel from her mind, but she could still

see the glow in his eyes when he handed her the molasses crinkle cookies. She'd shown little appreciation.

Lydia spread a roll of shiny red paper in front of her. She could feel the warmth of the fire behind her and wished some of that warmth would spill over into her heart and cast out the cold spots that lingered there.

Only ten days until Christmas. Lydia placed Miriam's boxed diary on the wrapping paper and folded it inward as she thought about what she could give Daniel for Christmas.

Daniel knew that Christmastime would be difficult for Lydia, so he'd stayed away from her for over a week. But tomorrow was Christmas Eve, and the entire family would be together. He took special care on this day to wrap Lydia's present. After he attached the bright red bow, he moved the gift to the far wall in his den. He glanced around the room at all the wrapped packages, and he knew he'd gone overboard. It just seemed there was so much to make up for.

Lydia's parents were hosting the worship service on Christmas Eve, and the community would have lots of time for visiting on Christmas Day and on Second Christmas, which was celebrated on the day following Christmas. Daniel knew that he and Lydia would be thrown together a lot over the holidays. He planned to give her all the space she needed, but he would continue to hope and pray that she would give him a chance. And hopefully he would find an opportunity to explain why Carol was here. It wasn't a subject he cared to talk about, with Lydia or anyone else, but Lydia had clearly gotten the wrong idea about her.

The weather forecast in the newspaper was calling for a foot of snow and blizzardlike conditions, starting the day after tomorrow, on Christmas Day. He pulled on his heavy black boots and prepared to ready his house for a storm. He worried how that would affect the community celebrations. Sarah and David Fisher were hosting a First Christmas celebration, along with several others in the district.

Surely Lydia would make sure any loose objects outside her house were secured, that shutters were fastened, and that food was in full supply in case they were shut in for a few days. How awful it would be if the weather kept everyone from enjoying the holidays with friends and family. He longed to go to her house to make sure she was prepared, but he knew she had the three children to help her.

Daniel pulled himself from his chair at the head of his kitchen table and headed outside to secure his belongings and tend to his animals. Tomorrow was Christmas Eve, and it would be a busy day.

Anna Marie snuggled into the brown blanket Amos gave her before they left on this buggy ride through the winding back roads of Paradise. A light snow was falling, and it was much too cold to be joyriding, but Anna Marie feared she might not see Amos over the holidays. He and his family would be spending Christmas Eve with relatives in another district, and she would be with her family at her grandparents' house. Then on Christmas Day, no one was sure how bad the weather would be and if it would be fit for travel. She and her family were planning to attend Sarah and David's gathering.

"I heard *mei daed* talkin' with *mei mamm*, and he said no one knows for sure when the storm is coming," Amos said.

"I hope it's not too bad to get out on Christmas Day," Anna Marie said as her house came into view. "It would be *baremlich* not to see you on Christmas." She smiled at her future husband. "Just think, we'll be married by this time next year. I'll be your *fraa*, Anna Marie Zook." A warm glow flowed through her, despite the chatter of her teeth.

"We best get you inside and warm," Amos said. He turned the buggy into her driveway.

"*Ach*, wait. Can you stop a minute? I want to grab the mail from the mailbox."

Amos pulled the buggy to a stop at the end of the long driveway, close enough to the mailbox that Anna Marie didn't even have to get out.

"I love being the first one to read the Christmas cards," she said. She thumbed through the stack of cards. "*Ach*, here's one from my cousin in Ohio!"

Three other cards were postmarked in Lancaster County, and she recognized all the names. But one piece of mail had unusual postage markings Lydia had never seen before. She held the letter-sized envelope up to show Amos. "What's this?"

Amos leaned toward her to get a better look. "That's a letter from overseas." He pointed to the postmark. "All the way from Europe. From France."

"It's addressed to *Mamm*." Anna Marie eyed the return address curiously. "I wonder who Carol Stewart is?"

Chapter Eighteen

Lydia kissed her boys good night and forced a smile. "I love you both very much." She closed the bedroom door and headed down the hallway. She could hear Anna Marie bathing.

During the short buggy ride home from worship service at her parents' house, Lydia and the children had sung songs, but she was having a terrible time getting into the spirit of the season. A permanent sorrow seemed to be weighing her down. Twice she'd caught Daniel staring at her from across the room during worship, his expression forlorn and pleading for some sort of response. She'd merely looked away.

She hadn't seen him in over a week, and she'd felt a hodgepodge of emotion when she saw him this evening. Glorious visions of past Christmases with Elam and the children danced in her mind. But those good memories were invaded by recollections of a Christmas Eve eighteen years ago.

Grief, despair, and an unquenchable longing mixed with hopelessness. She plopped herself down on the couch in front of the fireplace and hoped the warmth in the flames would thaw the ice surrounding her heart. She closed her eyes.

Please, God, help me release the bitterness in my heart and truly forgive Daniel. Help me to welcome this prodigal son back into my heart with forgiveness and love—the same way you so unconditionally welcome back your children. I pray that Daniel and I will find a good place to dwell, a peaceful place, in friendship or

whatever it is that you see fit for us. Help me to listen to the inner
voice that is you.

Lydia rested her head against the back of the couch, kept her
eyes closed, and tried to push aside all her other thoughts to make
room for the one voice she needed to hear. But when no revela-
tion came, she sighed, opened her eyes, and decided to thumb
through the Christmas cards Anna Marie brought in yesterday.

She smiled when she saw that her daughter had already
opened the cards. Anna Marie loved to be the first one to read
good tidings from friends and family. Her cousin Mary had written a lovely note inside her card, and Lydia tried to stay focused
on the blessed time of year as she read two more cards from
friends in the area. At the bottom of the pile was an unopened
envelope. Lydia's mouth dropped in dismay when she saw the
return address.

Why would Daniel's old girlfriend be writing a letter to me all
the way from France?

She twisted the envelope nervously in her hand. *This is the*
last thing I need right now. But she slid her finger along the seam
and unfolded the crisp white sheets of paper.

Dear Lydia,

My name is Carol Stewart. I am the woman who
showed up at your house looking for Daniel. I'm so glad to
have found him and feel particularly blessed that he spent
several hours talking with me.

Lydia took a deep breath and considered not reading any
further, but curiosity pushed her to continue.

We weren't far into the conversation before I realized that my actions many years ago greatly affected you. If I had done things differently, it certainly would have altered the course of your life.

Daniel tells me that you were married to his brother for many years and that you have three beautiful children. I am so sorry about the death of your husband. That must have been incredibly hard. I can't imagine.

Daniel and I talked a lot about God's will, in regard to everything that has happened, and it is through prayer and guidance that I decided to write you this letter. I suspect that Daniel has told you by now who I am, but on the off-chance he hasn't, I am a woman who has grown up with a lot of regret in her heart—regret that I ran from a crime scene eighteen years ago and allowed an innocent man to be convicted. Daniel went against all his beliefs to keep that horrible boy from hurting me more than he already had. But instead of going to court and explaining that to the judge, I disappeared and left Daniel to be prosecuted for a crime that Chad Witherspoon lied about. Chad's father hired a powerful attorney with a grudge against the Amish, and Daniel didn't stand a chance. And because of all this, I understand that Daniel felt like he could never return to his community—or to you.

I am so very sorry for my part in all of this. I have carried around the guilt over what I did for so long, and I prayed hard that Daniel would forgive me. It wasn't until Daniel and I talked that I realized my cowardly actions affected your life as well. It basically came down to Daniel's *word against Chad's, without me there to tell the police what really happened.*

You see, I knew Chad well. We had been dating, and I was trying to break up with him when he savagely attacked me. He told me he'd kill me before he let me leave him. I was afraid of him, his family, and their power. And the one thing Chad didn't know, and still doesn't know: I was pregnant. So I too ran from everything I knew to protect myself and my child.

When Daniel told me that he has spent his entire life loving you and unable to be with you, I knew I had to write you this letter. He said that you are struggling to forgive him for leaving on that Christmas Eve. I can understand that. But I hope that in some way this letter will inspire you to forgive Daniel the way he so unselfishly forgave me. His forgiveness freed my soul in a way that I couldn't comprehend. I was finally released from the guilt I'd felt for my entire adult life.

It is clear to me that Daniel loves you, has always loved you, and longs for a place in your heart. I think that he may be the best man that I have ever known, and any woman would be lucky to have him in her life.

May you have peace and be blessed this Christmas season.

In His name,
Carol Stewart

Lydia tried to control the tears streaming down her face, but through blurred eyes she watched the blue ink on the paper beginning to smudge. She swiped at her cheeks, dabbed the wet spots on Carol's letter, and placed the note back in the envelope. She could hear Anna Marie coming downstairs following her bath. Lydia quickly sat up taller and took a deep, cleansing breath.

Anna Marie strolled to the kitchen in her robe and slippers, then came back through the den carrying a glass of water. As she headed back to the stairs, she said, "Good night, *Mamm*."

She looked at Lydia and smiled—a smile that quickly faded. "*Mamm!* What's wrong? What happened?"

"I'm fine, I'm fine." Lydia sniffled, held her head high, and lifted herself off the couch. "I have to go somewhere. I won't be long."

"*Mamm*, it's late, dark, and cold. Can't it wait till morning?"

"*Ach!* I'll be right back." Lydia ran past her daughter, up the stairs to her bedroom. Suddenly, the package of socks she'd gotten Daniel for Christmas seemed incredibly wrong. She reached into her dresser and grabbed something she thought he might like much more. Clasping it within her palm, she ran back downstairs, found a small gift bag, and shoved the item inside before Anna Marie could see.

"I'm not going far." Lydia took her bonnet and heavy coat from the rack by the front door. "Daniel's house is right down the road." She smiled at her daughter, kissed her on the cheek, and walked out the door.

~

Daniel couldn't imagine who would be venturing out this time of night in the cold, but he was certain he heard a buggy turning into his driveway. He closed the book he was reading, placed it on the table by his couch, and picked up the lantern. He walked to the front window and watched the buggy come to a stop and a woman run toward the door. *Lydia?*

He flung the door wide, grabbed her by the arm, and pulled her into the house. "Are you crazy? What are you doing out this late by yourself? It's freezing outside."

He gently pulled her toward the fireplace. Her teeth were clicking together as she pulled off her gloves and warmed her hands in front of the hearth. She was holding a small, red gift bag in one hand. Her clothing was dusted with snow.

"Let me take your coat and bonnet." Daniel held out a hand and waited for her to shed the coat. With one hand she clung to the bag. With the other hand, shaky fingers fumbled with the strings on her bonnet. Daniel hung her wraps on a hook by the door, then turned to face her. "What is it, Lydia? Is it one of the children? Is something wrong?"

"Everything is fine. I just needed—" Her lids slipped down over big, brown eyes for a moment. Then she slowly looked back up and blinked her eyes into focus, eyes glassy with tears. She sniffled. "I just needed to give you your Christmas present." She pushed the bag toward him.

"What?" Daniel accepted the gift with one hand and rubbed his forehead with his other hand. "You came over this late to give me my Christmas present?"

She shrugged, but a smile lit up her face, and Daniel realized—something had changed again. This time, for the better.

"I hope you like it."

Daniel opened the bag, looked inside, and then worked to

control his emotions. He pulled out the red heart he'd given her the day he asked her to marry him. The small token fit in the palm of his hand, and Daniel gazed at the inscription. *My heart belongs to you.*

"Lydia . . . does this mean—"

She stepped forward, stared into his eyes, and said, "It means I love you. I've always loved you." She paused. "And I forgive you."

Daniel's legs threatened to give way beneath him. But as Lydia wrapped her arms around his waist and burrowed her head into his chest, he steadied himself and embraced her. "Oh, Lydia. My love. I've missed you."

"I've missed you too, Daniel."

He held her, and it took a lot to gently push her away, but he had a gift for her as well. "Lydia, I have a present for you too." He pointed to the large, oddly wrapped present to his right.

"Daniel—" she breathed. "Is that what I think it is?"

He was delighted when she walked to the present, squatted down, and pressed her hands against the massive structure. She twisted her head around and looked at him with eyes wide with excitement. "It is, isn't it?"

"Open it and see." Daniel walked to her side and squatted down beside her.

Lydia ripped the paper from the sides of the cedar chest and then stroked the wood gingerly. "Is it the same one?"

"I refinished the stain, but *ya,* it is."

She opened the chest. And there was the inscription.

To Lydia, from Daniel . . . I will love you forever.

A Change of Heart

To Carol Voelkel. Hold on to the dream, my writer-friend.
"Miracles happen to those who believe."

Chapter One

LEAH FOLDED HER ARMS ACROSS THE SPIRAL NOTEBOOK and held it close to her thumping chest. She was late for supper. Again.

She eased her way up the front porch steps of the farmhouse and peered through the screen door. Her family was already seated at the long wooden table in the kitchen. She sucked in a breath and prepared for her father's wrath. Supper was always at five o'clock, and preparations usually began an hour before that. Leah was expected to help.

Her eldest sister, Edna, cut her eyes in Leah's direction as Leah closed the screen door behind her. Mary Carol scowled at Leah, too, and blew out an exasperated sigh.

"Sorry I'm late." Leah tucked her chin but raised her eyes enough to catch a sympathetic gaze from her youngest sister, Kathleen. Leah forced a smile in Kathleen's direction.

"Wash for supper, Leah." Marian Petersheim didn't look at her daughter but instead glanced at her husband, a silent plea for mercy on her face.

"Yes, ma'am." Leah rushed upstairs, stored her notebook in the top drawer of her nightstand, and quickly washed her face and hands. She tucked loose strands of brown hair beneath her prayer covering, smoothed the wrinkles from her black apron, and walked briskly down the stairs.

She slid in beside Edna on the backless wooden bench and bowed her head in silent prayer as forks clanked against plates. When she was done, she reached for the chow-chow and spooned a small amount of the pickled vegetables onto her plate. She helped herself to a piece of her mother's baked chicken and then eyed her favorite casserole. Leah loved the way Kathleen prepared the green bean mixture with buttered Ritz cracker crumbs on top, but the casserole was on the other side of her father, and she wasn't about to ask him to pass it.

Daed didn't look up as he swallowed his last bite of chicken and reached for another piece on the platter to his right. The father of four teenaged girls—Edna, nineteen; Leah, eighteen; Mary Carol, seventeen; and Kathleen, sixteen—James Petersheim ran the household with steadfast rules and imparted strict punishment when those rules were disobeyed. Every one of the girls had been disciplined with a switch behind the woodshed at some point in her life. Leah wished she were still young enough for the switch. It would surely be better than what her father was about to unleash on her.

She pulled a piece of butter bread from the plate nearby and glanced toward him. Leah knew he would finish his meal before he scolded her for being late. She dabbed her forehead with her napkin, unsure if the sweat gathering on her brow was due to nervousness or the sweltering August heat.

"Abner's *mamm* is giving us her fine china as a wedding present," Edna said after an awkward moment of silence. Edna and Abner's wedding was scheduled for November, after the fall harvest, and Edna often updated the family about the upcoming nuptials during supper. "It belonged to his grandparents." Edna sat up a little straighter, and her emerald eyes shone.

"Wonderful news," their mother said. "I've seen Sarah's china, and it's lovely."

Leah waited for Mary Carol to chime in. Her wedding was scheduled to take place in December.

Leah recalled her father pointing his finger at her and Kathleen. "I reckon the two of you best not be thinkin' of marrying until at least next year," he'd teased after hearing Mary Carol's news two months ago—news that came on the heels of Edna's announcement only one week earlier.

Mary Carol smiled. "I have something to share too," she said, glancing back and forth between their mother and Edna. "Saul's parents are giving us twenty acres to build a new home. Until that time, we'll be living with his folks."

Here we go, Leah thought. Jealousy is a sin, but Mary Carol was translucent when it came to her feelings about Edna. And if Leah were honest with herself, she'd admit that she, too, had often been jealous of their oldest sister. Edna was the prettiest of all of them, with silky dark hair and stunning green eyes. She'd gotten her figure early, too, and all the boys took notice of Edna by the time she was fourteen. The other three Petersheim sisters were much plainer, with mousy brown hair and nondistinctive dark eyes, and without the curves Edna was blessed with. And Mary Carol battled a seemingly incurable case of acne, always trying some new potion the natural doctor suggested.

"That's very generous of Saul's family." Their mother nodded toward the green bean casserole. "Kathleen, could you please pass me the beans?"

Kathleen complied, putting Leah's favorite dish within reach. After her mother scooped a spoonful onto her plate, Leah helped herself.

"Abner and I will be livin' in the *daadi haus*, since his grandparents have both passed on. Then when Abner's brothers and sisters are grown, we'll move into the main house, and his parents will move to the *daadi haus*," Edna said.

"Our *haus* will be new." Mary Carol flashed her sister a smile.

"But we will be able to live in our *haus* right after we're married," Edna scoffed. "We don't have to wait for a home of our own, and—"

"Girls . . ." Their mother's voice carried a warning. "This is not a competition."

They all ate quietly for a few moments. Leah could hear their dog, Buddy, barking in the distance, presumably tormenting the cows. The golden retriever was still young and playful and often chased the large animals unmercifully around the pasture, nipping at their heels. Several cows voiced their objection, which only caused Buddy to bark louder.

"Aaron asked about you," Edna said sheepishly to Leah.

"Why?" Leah narrowed her eyes. Abner's brother ogled her enough during worship service every other week. Now he was conversation for suppertime?

Edna shrugged. "It's the second time he's asked how you are."

"*Ach.* You can tell him I'm mighty fine." Leah squared her shoulders and raised her chin, hoping that would put an end to the subject of Aaron Lantz. He was Edna's age, a year older than Leah. He was Abner's only brother, and Leah could smell a fix-up from a mile away. She'd had plenty of them lately. Just because Mary Carol was getting married before Leah didn't mean Leah would end up an old maid at eighteen.

Just the other day, Amanda Graber had stopped by to personally invite Leah to attend a Sunday singing coming up this weekend at her home, mentioning that Abram Zook might be there. *Abram Zook?* No, no, no.

Her own mother had invited Stephen Dienner for supper two Sundays ago. What was she thinking? Stephen was a good six inches shorter than Leah. While her mother insisted that it was only a friendly gesture, Leah suspected otherwise.

"Aaron is such a fine boy," her mother said. She smiled warmly in Leah's direction. "And very handsome too."

Leah swallowed a bite of bread. "You've always taught us that looks don't matter."

"That's true, Leah. But we're human," her mother answered. Then she glanced at their father—a tall man with sharp features and brilliant green eyes like Edna's. His beard barely reached the base of his neck and didn't have a single gray hair amid the thick whiskers. He was handsome, indeed.

Her mother refocused on Leah. "I hear Aaron attends the Sunday singings. Maybe you should go this Sunday."

Leah rolled her eyes and immediately wished she hadn't. Her father's expression blazed with annoyance at her display. She dropped her head. "Maybe," she whispered.

"Actually . . ." Edna cringed a bit. "He's coming over with Abner for a visit later."

"Why? Do you and Abner need a chaperone?" Leah pulled her mouth into a sour grin.

"No, we don't. I thought maybe—"

"You didn't *think*. I don't care anything about dating. I never want to get married! Everyone needs to stop—"

"Enough!" When their father's fist met with the table, everyone froze. Leah didn't even breathe. They all watched as he pulled himself to a standing position. He faced Leah with angry eyes, but far worse for Leah was the disappointment she could see beneath his icy gaze. "Leah will clean the supper dishes," he said after taking a deep breath and blowing it out slowly. "Every night this week."

"Yes, sir." Leah pulled her eyes from his and laid her fork across the remainder of her green bean casserole.

"I'll help you," Kathleen whispered to Leah when their father was gone.

"No. It's all right. I'll get it." Leah began to clear the dishes.

"You girls will learn not to behave in such a way during the supper hour." Their mother rose from the table and carried her plate to the sink. "Your *daed* works hard all day long, and he doesn't want to listen to your bickering during supper." She turned her attention to Leah. "Brew a fresh batch of tea for Abner—and Aaron."

After their mother headed upstairs, Mary Carol and Kathleen went outside to tend to the animals. Edna lagged behind.

"You know, you might like him," Edna said. She cleared the few dishes left on the table and put them next to the sink. "Like *Mamm* said, he's very handsome, and he seems to have taken a liking to you."

"He stares at me during worship service. But other than that, he doesn't even know me." Leah rinsed a plate and put it in the drying rack. "He was shy in school, barely talked to anyone."

Edna reached for a dish towel, then picked up a plate and started to dry it. "That was four or five years ago. He's quite talkative when I have supper with their family."

Leah sighed. She'd much rather spend her free time upstairs working in her notebook, not making small talk with Aaron Lantz. Her story was coming along nicely, and she was anxious to get back to work on it.

"You missed a spot." Edna handed the plate back to Leah and grabbed another one from the drain. "Leah . . ." She put the plate back in the water. "This one is still dirty too." Edna shook her head. "I'm going to go clean up before Abner gets here. Maybe you should clean up a bit too, no?"

Leah blew upward and cleared a wayward strand of hair from her face. "I'm fine, Edna."

Her sister shrugged and left the room.

Leah finished the dishes with dread in her heart. Why couldn't they all just let her be? Now she'd be spending the evening with Aaron, a young man she barely knew and didn't really care to know.

Chapter Two

MARIAN PULLED HER LONG WHITE NIGHTGOWN OVER HER head, then removed her prayer covering and allowed her wavy brown hair to fall almost to her waist. She folded the quilt on their bed to the bottom. It was much too hot for any covers . . . maybe just the light cotton sheet for tonight.

Rays of sunlight beamed through the window as the sun began its descent. It was too early for bed, but Marian wanted to give the young people some time to themselves. She was glad when James followed her upstairs after their evening devotions. As much as she'd like to read for a while, she suspected James wanted to talk—about Leah.

Marian sat down on the bed and applied some lotion to her parched hands, then smoothed it up her arms, the cool cream a welcome relief from the heat. She was still wringing her hands together when James walked into the bedroom, his dark hair and beard still damp, his eyes filled with tiredness and concern.

"I don't know what to do about Leah." He stood in the middle of the room in only his black breeches.

Marian eyed her husband of twenty-one years. His broad shoulders carried the weight of his burdens. It was a sin to worry so much; that was one area in which James could learn from Leah. Their carefree, spirited daughter tested the limits at times, but Leah seldom allowed her worries to press down on her for long.

James inhaled a long, slow breath, and muscles rippled across a chest reflective of many years of hard work. "It's not fair to the other *maed* when Leah shirks her responsibilities."

"*Ya,* I know, James." Marian patted a spot on the bed beside her. "Sit. And we will talk about it."

James sat down and turned to face her. He ran a hand through her hair and twisted a few strands within his fingers. "So soft," he whispered.

For a moment his eyes suggested that they not speak of Leah, but instead communicate with each other the way only a husband and wife can appreciate. But no sooner did the thought surface than Marian saw two deep lines of worry form on her husband's forehead.

"I don't like these stories she writes," he finally said. His eyes narrowed. "They are of no use to her. I don't understand why she tinkers with such nonsense."

"James . . ." Marian cupped his cheek, raked a hand through his hair. "It's not nonsense to her. She has an imagination. That's all."

Her husband sat taller and scowled. "It will do her no *gut,* this imagination of hers. These tales she pens are a waste of time, Marian." His eyes widened. "And did you hear her at supper? She doesn't even want to get wed." He hung his head. "No fella I know would want to marry her."

"James," Marian huffed. "That's a terrible thing to say about your *maedel.*"

He leaned back on his hands. "I worry that she will live with us the rest of our days." He grinned at Marian. "You, me, and Leah."

Marian chuckled, glad that he was making light of his worries. "No, James. She will not live with us forever. Leah is finding her way. You must give her time."

"She is eighteen. Of proper marrying age." He sat tall again and twisted to face Marian. "And what kind of *fraa* will Leah make?"

Marian shared her husband's concerns about Leah and thought about it often.

"She cannot cook. She does not sew well." James brought both hands to his forehead. "Leah has no hand for gardening, nor does she do a *gut* job cleaning *haus.* These are all things a fine Amish *fraa* must do. Instead, she writes fanciful stories that have no place in our world."

"Now, James. You know that there are several people in our community who are writers. A few of them have even sold stories to people who print such tales. And it is allowed by the bishop, as long as the stories are wholesome and in line with our beliefs."

"It is a waste of time and will not help Leah to find a *gut* husband."

Marian heard the clippity-clop of horse hooves. She stood up and walked to the window. Abner was pulling onto the dirt driveway leading up to the house, and Aaron was with him. "Maybe she and Aaron will come upon a friendship," Marian said. She twisted around and smiled at her husband.

James joined her at the window, and they both watched as Edna met the boys at the buggy. "Edna will be a fine *fraa*," James said. "And Mary Carol too. Even young Kathleen will make a *gut* wife."

Marian patted James on the arm. "Leah will make a home with someone when she's ready."

"Where is Leah?" James pressed his face close to the window and peered against the sun's bright rays.

"Hmm. I don't see her."

James grunted. "Probably writing in that notebook she takes everywhere. Maybe you best go tell her that company is here."

"There she is." Marian was relieved to see Leah slowly making her way across the yard toward Edna and the boys. "Everything will be fine, James."

James twisted his mouth to one side. "I hope so."

Aaron stepped out of the buggy, waved at Edna, and then fixed his eyes on the lovely Leah. She was taller than most of the women he knew, but Aaron still towered over her by several inches. Her soft brown eyes, always brimming with curiosity, met briefly with his. He loved the way her two tiny dimples were visible even when she wasn't smiling, a detail that softened her expression even when she was deep in thought.

He remembered when he saw her walk into the small schoolhouse on their first day of class, her eyes twinkling with wonder and awe. She asked more questions than any of the other students, and everyone wanted to be her friend. It stayed that way until their graduation from the eighth grade, but Aaron never seemed to be in her circle of friends, nor did she seem to notice him at the Sunday singings when they got older. But he wasn't the shy boy of his youth anymore.

If he took into account everything that he knew about Leah, he should not be considering a courtship, no matter how much she intrigued him. From what he'd heard from his sisters, the girl was flighty and irresponsible, couldn't cook, couldn't garden, couldn't even use a needle and thread successfully. Yet his heart skipped a beat at the mere mention of her name.

"I brewed a fresh batch of meadow tea," Edna said as she batted her eyes in Abner's direction. "Let's sit on the porch." She swung her arm in that direction.

"Hello, Leah." Aaron got into pace alongside her. "*Danki* for inviting me." He smiled with enough hopefulness for both of them, but Leah's eyes widened with surprise. She twisted her head in Edna's direction, and Aaron knew he wasn't supposed to see the scowl on her face. *Too late.*

"Sure," Leah said when she turned her face back to his. Her lips curled upward, but it was a sorry attempt to rectify her initial response.

Aaron glowered in his brother's direction. A guilty expression flashed across Abner's face as he moved his shoulders in a shrug of innocence. Aaron had wondered why Leah invited him over, since he'd been trying unsuccessfully to get her attention. Twice he'd offered to take her home after a Sunday singing, and she'd politely declined. During worship service, he was guilty of letting his mind drift and trying to make eye contact with her. Nothing.

He'd get hold of Abner later, but for now he'd have to make the best of things and try to convince Leah that he was worth her time.

Aaron was the last one to walk up the steps and onto the porch. Four high-back rockers were lined up across the wooden planks, a small table between each pair of chairs. Four glasses of tea were waiting for them.

"Help yourselves," Edna said. She slid into the rocker at the far end of the porch, and Abner sat down in the chair closest to her. Aaron waited until Leah eased her way into one of the seats before he got comfortable in the rocker next to hers. He removed his straw hat, placed it in his lap, and reached for a glass of tea. Beads of sweat trickled from his forehead as he gulped the cool beverage, and he could feel moisture on his shirt, particularly where his suspenders met with the blue cotton fabric.

He raised his eyes above the glass. The others were swigging their tea as well. This was the hottest summer Aaron could recall. Or maybe he just thought that every year when the scorching August heat settled in. Leah was gazing above the rim of her glass toward the pasture. A dozen cows grazed in the meadow as the sun began to set behind one of the crimson barns.

The Petersheim farm was one of the oldest homesteads in their district. Five generations had grown up in the two-hundred-year-old house with its two stories and wraparound porch. The tin roof was painted the same color as the red barns, and a fresh coat of white paint on the clapboard masked the structure's true age. Over six hundred acres surrounded the house; James Petersheim was one of the few farmers who didn't have to supplement his income by working as a carpenter or in another trade outside of the community.

Aaron set his glass down and wiped his forehead with the back of his hand.

"Leah, did you know that Aaron works with Abner at their father's furniture store?" Edna leaned forward in the chair.

This is a pitiful attempt at small talk, Aaron thought as he waited for Leah to respond. *Of course she knows.*

"*Ya,* I did know that." She glanced briefly at Aaron, forced a half smile, then pushed her bare feet against the porch, sending the rocker into motion and her dark purple dress flowing at her shins.

"Abner said you like to write stories," he said cautiously. The subject had come up at supper one night when Edna was a guest in their home. Both Edna and Abner seemed to think such a hobby was a waste of time, as did everyone else at the table, including Aaron. But when Leah's eyes began to twinkle, Aaron was glad he had brought it up.

"*Ya,* I do." She twisted slightly in her chair to face him and seemed to come alive as her whole face spread into a smile. "Do you write? Stories, books, or maybe poems?"

She looked so hopeful, but Aaron didn't have time for such silliness. "No, I don't." As soon as her expression went grim, he added, "But I like to read—whenever I have time."

Her response came quickly. "What do you read?"

"I, uh—I read the Bible, mostly."

She gave a nod of approval, then shifted her weight back to an upright position, as she'd been before he sparked her interest.

"We're going to take a walk," Edna said. She stood up from her chair and waited for Abner to do the same.

Aaron waited until they were out of earshot. "What do you write about?"

Her eyes narrowed skeptically, as if she didn't believe he was really interested. He was interested in anything that would help him get to know Leah better.

After a moment, she said, "The *Englisch.*"

"Huh?" *Surely that isn't allowed.* "You write stories about outsiders? Why?" He stared at her.

"Why do you find this so odd? They write about us all the time." She shook her head and sighed. "And most of the time, they don't get it right."

Aaron folded his arms across his chest and cocked his head to one side. "Then why do you think you can get it *right* about them? You don't know nothin' about living in the *Englisch* world."

"I know that many of them don't know God." Her voice was sad as she spoke. "I write about *Englisch* people who are trying to have a relationship with God. Maybe it will make a difference to someone someday, help them find their way to the Lord." She got a hint of mischief in her eyes. "And there's always a happy ending!"

Aaron had to admit, he was fascinated by her effort to help others find a way to the Lord through her tales, but it wasn't something they were taught to do. "The *Ordnung* doesn't teach us to minister to those outside of our community, Leah, if that's what you're trying to do with these books." He liked the way her name slid off his tongue. "I reckon it's not our place—Leah."

"Why?"

"It just ain't."

They sat quietly for a few moments, but Aaron still had questions. "Where do these stories of yours take place? In an Amish district or in the *Englisch* world?"

"In the *Englisch* world and in Amish communities. You don't have to be Amish to have a strong faith and a relationship with God." Her eyes glowed with a sense of strength and purpose, and while her efforts were misdirected, he'd never been more attracted to her. But had she forgotten the one thing that almost always divided them from outsiders?

"Leah, we believe that all things are of God's will. I don't think most of the *Englisch* share our faith, dedication, and interpretation of the Bible."

"They do in my stories when I'm done with them," she said smoothly. Then she winked at him and set his heart to fluttering.

"How many have you penned?"

"I'm working on my third. They aren't as long as full-sized books. I mostly write at night after Edna goes to sleep, by the light of a small flashlight. It takes a long time to write longhand. I know that some of the writers in our district have typewriters. Not electric, but I suspect it's still faster than using an ink pen and paper. Someday I hope to have one."

"It seems like it would be *hatt* to write about the *Englisch* ways."

"I'm still in my *rumschpringe*, so the rules are relaxed enough to allow me time in the city, just like you. I have two *Englisch* girlfriends that I meet for lunch, and they help me with things about their world that I don't understand."

"It's interesting. Your writing." Aaron rubbed his chin for a moment. He wanted to ask her if she'd be better off learning to cook, garden, and sew, but instead he said, "Who will read these books?"

She took a sip of her tea, then placed the glass back on the table and shrugged. "I don't know." Her eyes lost their sparkle for a moment. "Maybe my two friends. Clare and Donna. That's their names. I hope they'll read my stories someday. They are such dear friends, but they seem to struggle with their faith." She paused, and her eyes became hopeful. "Do you want to read one?"

His body became rigid as he straightened in the chair. *I reckon not.* Aaron could barely fit his chores and devotions into his day in time to get a decent night's sleep. Of course he didn't have time to read her ramblings. "I'd be honored to read one of your stories," he said.

Leah was instantly on her feet. "I'll give you the shortest one to start off with."

Thank You, Lord.

Wait. *Start off with?* Did she expect him to read all of them?

"This is wonderful." Her eyes gleamed as she spoke, and her

tiny dimples expanded as her face spread into a smile. "I'll be right back."

Aaron watched her dart into the house and wondered what he'd gotten himself into.

When she returned barely a minute later, he stifled a gasp as she handed him a stack of lined white paper bound by two rubber bands. It was almost two inches thick.

"No one has ever read anything I've written. This is my shortest story. About a hundred and twenty pages." She lifted her shoulders, dropped them, and grinned. "How long do you think it will take you to read it?"

What? Probably forever. "Ach, I reckon I could finish it by—"

"By the Sunday singing at the Grabers' this weekend?" Her voice bubbled with hope, but Aaron knew he'd have to disappoint her. It was already Wednesday.

"Maybe . . ." She drew out the word, and her eyes batted with mischief. "You could pick me up and we could go together, if you'd like. We could talk about the story on the way to the singing."

Aaron reminded himself that he wasn't the shy, bashful boy who'd watched Leah from afar during the school years. He'd just tell her that he was much too busy to fit her ramblings into his schedule. He had his work at the furniture store and his chores at home.

She flashed a smile in his direction.

"I—I think that sounds great, Leah," he said, then sighed.

It would be a long week. He hoped she was worth it.

Chapter Three

LEAH WAITED UNTIL SHE COULD HEAR EDNA SNORING in the other bed before she carefully opened the drawer to the nightstand in between them. She pulled out her notebook, pen, and flashlight, then propped her pillows behind her. Once she was comfortable, she pulled her legs toward her and rested the pad against her knees.

Edna would deny, up until her last dying breath, that she snored, but this time of year it seemed to be the worst. The natural doctor said she had allergies, and Edna took an herbal mixture to help with her condition, but it sure didn't help with her snoring.

She was glad Edna was sleeping. If she were awake, she'd just lecture Leah about how nonproductive her writing was, how she was never going to find a husband, and on and on. It wasn't that Leah didn't want a husband . . . she just didn't see what the rush was. She enjoyed her time to herself, and once she was married, there wouldn't be time for her writing. There was barely time now. Once she was married, she would have not only a husband but an entire household to take care of, and babies would follow. Leah looked forward to all those things. Just not quite yet.

She tried to ignore Edna's unsteady wheezing and focus on her story. She reread the last page she had written the night before, but she couldn't concentrate. Aaron Lantz's face kept popping into her head. He wasn't the quiet, timid boy she remembered from school, and even though she saw him at social gatherings these days, she'd never paid much attention to him before now. He seemed . . . nice. And not bad looking either. Leah knew she should be ashamed for taking advantage of him the way she had, blackmailing him into reading her story in exchange for a date to the Sunday singing.

Her heart thumped in her chest all of a sudden, and she began to feel a little panicked. What if he didn't like her story? And told her so. Or what if he lost it? It was the only copy she had. What if he mistook their date to the singing as more than just a casual get-together? She'd need to straighten this out with him tomorrow, make sure he understood that friendship was all she was interested in. And someone to read her stories. Screen them, so to speak.

She shook her head. Aaron would tell her that he liked what she wrote, whether he did or not, just because he was smitten with her. She should have picked someone else to test her work on. Aaron couldn't be objective if he liked her—in that way.

Leah had to admit, if she were in the market for courtship, she'd be flattered by the way he looked at her, the way his big blue eyes seemed to call out for her to notice him, give him a chance. His build was a pleasing attribute. Tall and muscular. His light brown hair was sun-streaked with sandy-red highlights, as if he didn't wear his hat a lot of the time. And it was cute the way his mouth had twitched on one side when he'd seemed to be nervous around her earlier.

Why all the thoughts about Aaron? She'd always thought he was handsome. Just rather . . . insignificant. She silently reprimanded herself for having such a thought, especially after he'd been so polite earlier.

Leah blew out a breath of frustration. Her thoughts about Aaron were keeping her from her writing, and her heroine in her story was starting to put her faith in God, and Leah wanted to elaborate on that. It was her favorite part of storytelling, when things started to lead up to a happy ending.

She put the pen to the paper and let her thoughts about Abigail Bennett flow.

Abby listened to the inner voice this time, a voice she'd heard before but never paid attention to, a whispering in her conscience that beckoned her to follow the path to salvation through Jesus Christ.

Leah stopped writing when Edna started to cough. She sure wished the doctor could give her sister something better to help her. It sounded like the air in Edna's lungs was mixed with tiny rocks that she was trying to clear from her airway by taking deep breaths and then forcing the mess out. Leah didn't understand how Edna could sleep through it, but she always did.

When Edna's snoring resumed, Leah was able to reconnect with Abigail. By the time she finished telling Abby's story, it was almost midnight. Four o'clock would come early in the morning, but it was worth it.

She smiled as she wrote out the words *The End*.

Midnight? Aaron shook his head as he turned off the lantern on his bedside table.

He hadn't meant to read Leah's story until that late, but as it turned out, he couldn't stop turning the pages. He was fascinated by the main characters, two girls, one *Englisch* and one Amish. Lauren and Rose had nothing in common but the friendship they shared, and Leah's storytelling was tender and compassionate as the girls struggled to be friends, even though their families were less than approving.

Rose was tall, like Leah. She had brown eyes, like Leah, and if Aaron didn't know better, he would have thought that Leah was writing about herself. Rose was strong in her faith and ministered to her friend, but she didn't seem interested in learning the skills necessary in an Old Order Amish community. There was one particular scene where Rose was skipping through a field on a cool spring day, her arms stretched out to her sides like she was flying. Cool blades of grass tickled her toes, and wispy wildflowers brushed her shins as she sang.

Running over. Running over. My cup is full and running over.
Since the Lord saved me, I'm as happy as can be. My cup is full
and running over.

It was a song they sang during Sunday singings, usually followed by a game of volleyball. Aaron pictured Leah as the one skipping and singing in the meadow, and it was a delightful picture in his head.

But what held Aaron's attention the most was the budding romance between Rose and a boy in her Amish community—Jesse. Aaron cringed and wondered what his friends would think if they knew he was reading a romance book. He'd sure never tell them about it. But in the story, Rose wanted Jesse to accept her for the free-spirited girl that she was, and Aaron couldn't help but speculate that this was the kind of mate Leah was looking for too.

Aaron was certainly intrigued by Leah, but his reservations ran deep about whether he could make a home with someone like her. When he watched Abner and Edna together, there was no doubt that Edna would make a fine wife. Several times she'd brought casseroles or snacks to complement the meal his mother prepared for them all, and everything Edna brought was delicious. She often commented about the clothes she'd sewn for her family. She also talked about what a fine cook her youngest sister, Kathleen, was, and how Mary Carol grew amazing vegetables in their garden. But when it came to Leah, she would take a deep breath. "Leah will find her way," she'd once said.

Aaron got comfortable atop the sheets and hoped for a breeze to blow through the open window in his room. The heat was stifling, but he knew sleep would come. Normally he didn't need to set the battery-operated alarm clock on his bedside table, since his body was programmed to wake up at four o'clock, but on this night he did.

⟨⟡⟩

Leah made it a point to be downstairs before her father. She helped Mary Carol, Kathleen, and her mother prepare dippy eggs, bacon, scrapple, and biscuits.

"Where's Edna?" Mary Carol asked as she stirred the eggs.

Leah yawned. "She was still sleeping when I got dressed."

Edna was always up early and helped with breakfast.

"She was coughing a lot during the night again," Leah said. She poured herself a glass of orange juice. "Can't the natural doctor give her something that helps her more?"

Mamm walked away from the skillet of sizzling bacon, pulled six forks from the drawer, and walked toward the table. "Maybe she needs to go for another visit with him and see about that."

Leah picked up a fork to flip the bacon as her mother placed the other forks on the table.

"I can finish that, Leah. Why don't you get the butter and jellies from the refrigerator?"

Leah sighed. Maybe if everyone would let her cook occasionally, she'd get better at it. But she was too tired to argue. She set the fork down on a paper towel on the counter, then moved toward the refrigerator.

As she placed a jar of rhubarb jelly on the table, she heard footsteps coming down the stairs.

"*Guder mariye*," *Daed* said. He entered the kitchen, kissed their mother on the cheek, and sat down at the head of the kitchen table.

"And good morning to you," Marian said. The girls all echoed the sentiment.

Leah wanted her father to be proud of her, the way he was of her sisters. "Kathleen, I'll be going with Aaron to the singing at the

Grabers' house this Sunday," she said as she set the butter on the table. "I was hoping you could show me how to make that Lazy Daisy Oatmeal Cake you make. I'd like to bring that." She glanced in her father's direction, pleased to see his eyes shining with approval.

"Uh, are you sure?" Kathleen asked. She pulled the biscuits from the oven and put them on the table. "I reckon that cake is a lot of work. Maybe you could take a lemon sponge pie instead?"

"Kathleen, I'm sure your sister can make the oatmeal cake," their father said. "You give her a hand." He reached for a biscuit, and it warmed Leah's heart when he smiled in her direction.

"*Ya, Daed,*" Kathleen said.

Her mother sat down in a chair at the other end of the table from their father. "Did—did you and Aaron get along well?"

Leah waited until Kathleen and Mary Carol were seated on the bench across from her before she answered. "He seems nice." She let her eyes veer in her father's direction.

He nodded his approval.

They all bowed their heads to pray, but *Daed* spoke up only a second or two into the blessing. "Where is Edna?"

"Sleeping," Leah answered. *But I'm here, on time, and I helped.*

Daed smoothed his beard with his hand. "Leah, go and check on your sister before we continue with the blessing. She is never late to breakfast."

Leah stood up from the table. "*Ya, Daed.*" *No one says anything bad about Edna being late for a meal.* She grabbed one of the lit lanterns on the kitchen hutch and marched up the stairs, thinking how she could have used an extra hour of sleep.

Their bedroom was the last one on the right, at the end of the hall. "Edna, get up!" she said before she pushed the door wide. "Breakfast is ready, and everyone is already . . ."

Leah froze for a moment. Her bare feet seemed rooted to the wooden slats on the floor as she looked at her sister lying in the bed.

"Edna?" Her eyes filled with tears as she slowly moved toward her sister in the bed. "Edna!"

She grabbed Edna's shoulders and shook her. "Edna! Wake up!" Edna's mouth was slightly parted, and her face was the color of ripe blueberries.

She's not breathing. Please, God, dear God in heaven. Help.

"Mamm! Daed! Mamm! Daed!"

There was a stampede of steps up the stairs. Her father was the first one to enter the room. "Mary Carol, go to the barn and call 9-1-1!"

Daed's mouth was quickly on top of Edna's, forcing air into her lungs, after he tilted her head back and pinched her nose. His hands were trembling, but he kept the breaths steady. Thank goodness her father had training in CPR when he was a volunteer at the local fire department years ago. Leah thanked God that he apparently still remembered his training.

Mary Carol jetted from the room to do as their father instructed. Kathleen was starting to cry, and Leah reached for her hand and squeezed it in hers. *Mamm*'s face was as white as the cotton sheet beneath Edna, and Leah didn't think her mother was breathing either. Her fingers were clamped tightly against her lips, and her eyes were wide and fearful.

Dear God, save her. Dear God, save her. Leah prayed like she'd never prayed before. *I promise not to be jealous of Edna ever again. Please, God, save her.*

"Daed!" Leah yelled. "Make her breathe!" Tears rolled down her cheeks as she watched her father trying to pump life into Edna. *"Daed!"* she yelled again.

I love you, Edna. I love you, Edna. Please wake up. God, wake her up.

Chapter Four

SIRENS SHRIEKED IN THE DISTANCE, INTENSIFYING THE fear in the room as their father continued his efforts to breathe life into Edna. But when Edna began to flail her arms about, their father backed away. Edna began to gasp for air, as if there were a shortage in the room. With each deep inhalation, a tiny bit of color came back to her face.

They'd all subconsciously moved closer to the bed, and *Daed* told them to step back. "Give her some room," he said, holding his hands outward.

Leah had seen her father angry, even frightened, but nothing like this. Even in the midst of a crisis, he always showed a level of calm. She recalled a fire in the kitchen a few years ago when a lantern got knocked over at suppertime and ignited a small rug by the sink. The fire had spread quickly and scared them all, but their father stayed reasonably calm as the old kitchen floor splintered and glowed. He hadn't hesitated but quickly retrieved the fire extinguisher and put out the fire.

They'd all had accidents as kids, and once their mother even fell down the porch steps carrying a casserole dish. She busted her knee up good, and Lydia had watched her father run from the fields when he was called. But again, he'd handled the situation calmly. But *Daed* looked anything but calm now, and Leah knew that Edna had been dead. Somehow she just knew. And their father had brought her back to life. Their father—and God. *Thank You, dear Lord.*

Sweat trickled from *Daed*'s wrinkled brow and poured over eyes that were wild with a mixture of terror and relief. The sirens grew louder, and Edna continued to cough and gasp, but she was breathing. Leah let the tears flow full force. *If anything had happened to Edna* . . .

Mamm clutched Edna's hand and seemed to take over where their father couldn't. "Edna, dear. Breathe slowly. Help is on the way."

Edna's eyes sought relief from their mother, but she continued to inhale and exhale, each breath crackling into the room with effort. Leah heard footsteps bolting up the steps, and within seconds two men dressed in navy blue entered the room. They brought in machines and gadgets Leah had never seen before, and they instructed everyone to move away from the bed. The first thing they did was put some sort of mask over Edna's face, and her breath clouded the clear plastic in shallow bursts.

The men didn't say much as they worked on Edna, but after about fifteen minutes they said that they were going to take her to the hospital in the ambulance, and that there was only room for one parent to ride along. All eyes were on their father, but it was *Mamm* who stepped forward.

"I am going," she said, standing taller. Then she reached for Edna's hand and squeezed it tightly within hers. Leah wanted to go so badly she could hardly stand it, but she could see that her father wanted to go equally as much, and they'd said there was only room for one anyway.

"I am going also." *Daed* stood taller and spoke with an authority that challenged the men in uniform. "She is my—my daughter." His voice broke as he spoke.

The two men in blue glanced at each other. Leah thought they could almost be twins, brothers at the least—both short and stocky with thick crops of unruly dark hair. And the shape of their eyes, more round then oval, was similar.

"I guess we can make room," one of the men said.

Leah recalled her trip to the movies with Clare and Donna a few months ago. Her father would have been furious, but she suspected her mother must have known she was indulging in the freedoms of her *rumschpringe* when she saw Leah leave in Clare's car that day. In the movie, there had been a scene where an ambulance picked up a sick girl, and the girl died on the way to the hospital. Leah closed her eyes and squelched the thought.

The men popped up a sort of portable bed right next to Edna's bed, and *Daed* helped them get Edna onto it and down the stairs. Once they reached the first floor, things happened quickly.

"We'll get word to you soon!" *Mamm* yelled as she and *Daed* followed Edna and the men across the yard. Her parents crawled into the back of the ambulance with one of the men, and the door slammed shut. The other man in blue scooted into the front seat. For what seemed like an eternity, the ambulance didn't move. Leah could feel her heart pounding in her chest.

After a while, the ambulance eased down the driveway and onto the main road. Thin beams of sunlight speared through gray skies as dawn approached, but thunderous rumblings from far away lent confusion as to what type of weather the day would bring.

The men didn't turn the sirens on. No swirly, colorful lights either. Leah presumed this to be a good thing. No sense of emergency.

"Edna will be all right, no?" Kathleen turned toward Leah. She blinked back tears and her lip trembled.

Leah reached for Kathleen's hand. "*Ya*. She was breathing on her own."

"But it sounded terrible, like she was choking, and her face was so blue," Mary Carol said, sniffling. "I've never seen anything like that."

Leah knew it was her job to reassure her younger sisters. "But her color started to return, and she was breathing. If it were that bad, they would have turned on the sirens."

Then Leah recalled why they didn't turn on the sirens in the movie.

The girl was dead.

Aaron picked at his eggs and stifled a yawn.

"Aaron, I got up at midnight to go to the bathroom, and I could see a light shining from beneath your door," Annie said. "What in the world were you doin' up at such an hour?"

He was too tired to deal with his sister this morning. She had a way of talking to him that he classified as clucking. Her tongue met with the roof of her mouth in an annoying manner.

"Reading." It was true, although he sure didn't want to elaborate—that he was reading to impress a girl.

"At that hour?" Mary chimed in. "What were you reading?"

"Nothing that would interest you," Aaron said, hoping to halt the inquisition. He stuffed a piece of biscuit in his mouth.

Annie and Mary shuffled around the kitchen with his mother while Aaron, his father, and his youngest sister, Mae, waited for breakfast to be served. Five-year-old Mae had already placed jams, jellies, and butter on the table, which was her only job for breakfast. Aaron suspected Mae had been a surprise, even though his parents denied it. But Abner was twenty, Aaron was nineteen, Annie, seventeen, and Mary, fifteen.

Aaron yawned. This time he didn't try to hide it. It just took too much effort. He reached for the bowl of applesauce to his right and scooped a generous helping onto a buttered biscuit. Then he piled eggs on top and took a big bite, thinking there was no better combination in the world than applesauce, egg, and buttered biscuit. Now if he could just have a cup of coffee, he might make it through the day. But his mother didn't believe in coffee. "We shouldn't need stimulants to get us through the day," she'd say.

Ridiculous. Other families in their district certainly enjoyed coffee. He'd asked his father about it once, and his father quickly said, "It was the only rule your mother said she wanted to enforce when we got married, and I choose to abide by it." Then *Daed* had smiled. "Coulda been a lot worse things to give up."

Aaron knew his father liked to sip wine in the barn from time to time and even enjoy a cigar occasionally. But on this morning, nothing sounded better to Aaron than a steaming cup of freshly brewed coffee. A mocha latte would certainly work. He'd had plenty of those in town. Maybe he could convince his father to stop at the bakery on the way to the furniture store this morning.

After two more buttered biscuits with egg and applesauce, Aaron excused himself to milk the cows. As he strolled out to the barn, he couldn't stop thinking about Leah and her story. He was anxious to see how the tale ended, but didn't see how he was going to stay up another night reading. Then he thought about having Leah by his side at the Sunday singing, and just the thought gave him a burst of energy comparable to that from any cup of coffee.

Leah, Mary Carol, and Kathleen tried to stay busy all morning, but when the storm finally rolled in midmorning with lightning that lit up the skies and thunder that shook the china cabinet, a sense of dread further settled over the girls.

"It's so dark outside," Kathleen said. She lit another lantern and took a seat at the kitchen table. Mary Carol was seated and chopping cucumbers into tiny cubes.

"What's that for?" Leah slid in beside Mary Carol and studied the cucumbers.

"A new recipe Kathleen is trying," her sister said, not looking up. Then she slammed the knife down on the table. "Why haven't we heard anything?"

"I don't know." Leah figured her parents would have sent word by now. She glanced at the clock on the wall. Ten thirty. "Everything must be okay, or *Mamm* and *Daed* would have sent someone to pick us up."

Kathleen twirled the string on her *kapp* with her finger, then jumped when another flash of light lit the room, followed by a clap of thunder that Leah could feel in her chest.

"Look! Lights!" Mary Carol jumped from the table and walked toward the kitchen door.

Leah and Kathleen followed her onto the porch where they were misted with cool rain blowing up under the rafters. Leah put her hand to her forehead and watched the car coming up the driveway. Another bolt of lightning caused them all to jump, but they stayed on the front porch and waited.

"I don't recognize the car," Kathleen said. "Do either of you?"

Mary Carol shook her head. Leah strained to see past the headlights glaring onto the porch. "It's one of those big truck-like things with a backseat."

"It's a Cadillac Escalade Hybrid," Kathleen finally said, relief in her voice. Not because she knew who was in the vehicle, but because she'd identified it.

Kathleen had a strange fixation with automobile makes and models. She even had a *Car and Driver* magazine hidden in her room. "Front engine, rear-wheel drive, and it will hold eight people. Zero to sixty miles per hour in 8.4 seconds."

Leah glared at her sister in disbelief. "Who cares!" she snapped. "It's not like you're ever going to have one."

Kathleen's lip turned under, and Leah shook her head and sighed. She was about to apologize, but then the car eased all the way into the driveway and cut the lights.

All three of them moved a little closer to the edge of the porch, peering through the downpour to see who it was. Hopefully, it was their parents with Edna. But Leah knew right away that it wasn't anyone from her family when she saw the brightly flowered umbrella pop from the open car door and a high-heeled brown boot step into the mud below.

Chapter Five

LEAH LOOKED AT HER SISTERS. "DO YOU KNOW WHO THAT IS?"

A plump woman trekked up the driveway on her tiptoes, balancing a bag on one hip and holding her umbrella with the other hand. *Daed* had recently added gravel to the dirt driveway, but it was still a sludgy mess from all the rain this morning, and the woman's fancy boots were sinking with each step she took.

"I've never seen her before." Kathleen arched her brows, then whispered, "She's rather old. She can barely walk in them shoes."

"I don't know her either," Mary Carol said. "Maybe she has word about Edna."

The woman stumbled toward them with a wide grin stretched across a wrinkled face painted with bright colors. Her eyelids were covered in dark blue, and her lashes were long and black. A rosy streak ran high along each cheekbone, and her lips were the color of cherries. Puffy gray hair topped her head in a loose twist.

Leah took in the women's floral print dress, which hung below her knees and didn't seem to go with her boots. She looked like a walking bouquet of mixed flowers from Mary Carol's garden, planted in those dark brown boots. And as the rain blew under her umbrella and slapped across her face, she merely licked those red lips and kept trudging. Leah bit her lip to keep from giggling. *Who is this Englisch woman?*

"Hello, hello!" she yelled as she neared the porch. The woman's presence was a light amid the gray skies and pouring rain. "Your sister is fine!" The stranger seemed as delighted by the news as Leah,

Kathleen, and Mary Carol, who turned to each other for a quick hug.

"Thank the Lord," Leah whispered. Then she pulled away and returned her attention to the woman coming slowly up the slippery porch steps. Leah took the bag from her hand, gave it to Kathleen, and gripped the woman's elbow to help her up the steps.

"Come into the *haus*. It's awful weather out here." Leah motioned toward the open screen door that led into the kitchen.

The woman placed her umbrella on the porch, then dripped her way into the kitchen. Mary Carol and Kathleen followed.

"Sit down. Tell us about Edna. Can I get you a cup of hot tea or *kaffi*?" Mary Carol moved toward the kitchen counter.

The woman raised her bottom lip and blew upward to clear a strand of wayward hair. Then she pointed to her feet. "I knew these boots were the right choice for today. I got these at a little shop by my house last year." She smiled at Leah, then at Kathleen. "They're sharp, aren't they?"

Kathleen's mouth hung open, but she nodded her head.

"*Ya*, they are," Leah said. "Edna is all right?"

"*Ach, ya*. Your sister is gonna be just fine. Asthma. That's what she's got. Your folks will be bringing her home this afternoon." The woman dabbed at droplets on her bright cheeks with a white handkerchief. "The Lord whispered in my ear that the weather was gonna be terrible. I listen when the Lord speaks. Do you?"

Leah nodded, but she knew her expression must be a mirror of Kathleen's—dumbfounded. "Do you speak the *Deitsch*?" Leah asked cautiously.

"Oh, sure." The woman waved her hand dismissively at Leah, then slid onto one of the wooden benches at the table.

Kathleen narrowed her gaze. "How could you know how to speak Pennsylvania *Deitsch*?"

Leah didn't care how she knew. She was just glad that Edna was coming home, and she found this stranger delightful.

BETH WISEMAN

The woman's eyes matched the shadow on her lids, and they grew wide as she spoke. "Why, it's not that much different from German."

Kathleen sat down across from the woman on the other bench. "You know German?"

Following a sigh, the woman said, "And French, and Italian, and Spanish, and . . ."

Leah was still standing as she listened to her rattle off several more. *Who are you?*

"I'm Leah," she said when the woman finished.

"Nice to meet you, Leah." She smiled with a warmth that Leah found contagious.

Kathleen was still scowling suspiciously. "I'm Kathleen. How do you know—"

"Oh! Kathleen is the name of my neighbor. Kathleen Fontenot. She's French." She paused and glanced at Mary Carol. "Honey, did you offer me a beverage earlier?"

"Yes, ma'am." Mary Carol stepped forward a bit. "What would you like, some tea or *kaffi*? Or we have lemonade or milk. And, um . . . I'm Mary Carol. And—and what is your name?"

The woman popped herself in the forehead with her hand. "My manners! I'm Ruth Ann Lantz. But you girls just call me Auntie Ruth. Everyone does." She smiled again, revealing a perfect set of white teeth.

Leah didn't think they could possibly be real. She glanced at Kathleen. Her sister's expression was still one of caution, but a smile tipped the corners of her mouth. Mary Carol stood by the counter and waited to see what Auntie Ruth wanted to drink.

"Um . . . something to drink?" Mary Carol offered again.

Auntie Ruth twisted her mouth from side to side. Then she looked hard at Mary Carol. "A nip of brandy would be nice."

The girls all looked at each other. Leah took the lead. "I—I don't believe we have any brandy."

The woman sat taller. "Sure you do. Look in that bag. I brought my own. Oh, and I brought a meat loaf, cooked celery, and a chocolate shoofly pie." She pointed to the bag. "It's all in there. My niece sent it when she heard her future daughter-in-law was in the hospital. All except for the brandy. I added that myself."

"Abner's *mamm*?" Leah was having trouble connecting this woman to Sarah Lantz.

"Well, not just Abner's. There's Aaron, Mary, Annie, and little Mae too. But yes, I'm Sarah's aunt, on her father's side."

Leah nodded toward Mary Carol to pour Auntie Ruth a glass of brandy, although she'd never heard of anyone partaking in such a thing at this time of day. *So this is Aaron's great-aunt?* Then Leah remembered. She'd heard about this woman from others in the community. The odd aunt who visited the Lantz family twice a year. She'd left the Old Order before being baptized, and she always stayed with Sarah and her family when she visited.

"Please thank Sarah for us, for sending the food. That was very thoughtful." Leah watched Mary Carol set the glass down in front of Auntie Ruth. She was glad that her sister only poured a small amount into the glass, since Ruth was driving. Ruth gulped it down in one swig. Then burped.

"Goodness me!" She chuckled, then said, "Well, they weren't sure early this morning just how long Edna would be in the hospital, and Sarah wanted to help."

Kathleen looked somewhat disturbed by Auntie Ruth, and Mary Carol just looked confused. Leah thought the woman was a welcome relief from the fear that had gripped them earlier in the day.

"So can you tell us more about Edna?" Leah took a seat in her father's chair at the head of the table. Mary Carol slid in beside Kathleen.

"Evidently she had an asthma attack. A bad enough one that it caused her to stop breathing." Ruth puckered her lips and nodded her head. "Your pop saved her life, I heard them say."

Thank You, Lord. "We appreciate you bringing this food to us in this miserable weather." Leah rested her elbows on the table, then cupped her cheeks with her hands. "Where do you live? Are you just visiting your relatives for a while?"

"Honey, do you think we could eat now? I get the cramps when I don't eat by eleven. The doctor says it's a gastric problem." She arched her eyes at Leah, as if she hadn't heard a thing she'd said.

"I'll get you something," Kathleen said. She rose from the table, but not before cutting her eyes in Leah's direction and making a funny face.

"I live in Florida," Ruth finally said. "I come up here a couple of times a year, and Sarah and her family visit me once a year as well."

Leah knew several families in their community who vacationed in Florida, but she'd never actually met anyone who lived there.

"Were you, um . . ." Mary Carol hesitated. "Shunned?"

"If I was, can I still eat here with you?"

None of them knew what to say. Of course they weren't going to ask her to leave.

Ruth burst out laughing. "Gotcha, didn't I?" Then she quickly turned serious. "No, my dears. I wasn't shunned. I chose to leave before my baptism, that's all."

"How long have you been visiting your kin?" Kathleen asked.

Ruth yawned. "Just got here this morning. Drove all the way by myself. When I got to Sarah's, they'd just received the news of your sister." She shook her head. "Abner was most distraught. I drove the boy straight to the hospital and waited with him until we knew Edna was out of harm's way."

Kathleen placed a plate in front of Ruth, filled with meat loaf and creamed celery from Sarah and some homemade bread Kathleen had made the day before.

"*Danki, danki.*" Ruth dived in.

All the girls looked back and forth at each other.

"How long will you be staying?" Leah stood up, retrieved a napkin from the counter, and pushed it across the table to Ruth, in case Ruth wanted to wipe the creamed celery from below her bottom lip. Evidently she did not.

Ruth chewed a bite of meat loaf, and Leah tapped her finger to her chin. "You have a, uh . . . bit of . . ."

"Oh my." Ruth swiped at the splotch of celery. "*Danki*, dear."

"Ruth, I was wondering . . . ," Kathleen began.

"Auntie Ruth, dear." Ruth smiled warmly in Kathleen's direction, then kept eating.

Kathleen grinned. "Is it true that your Cadillac can hit zero to sixty miles per hour in 8.4 seconds?"

Mary Carol rolled her eyes. "Kathleen, why does it matter? I don't understand your need to know these things."

"Honey," Ruth said, "I can hit seventy miles per hour in seven seconds on the open road."

At the way her sister's face lit up, Leah knew that Ruth had won Kathleen over.

"Oh, sure." Ruth sat up a little taller. "Now, I best be getting back to Sarah and the girls. Aaron went on to the furniture store with their father, but Abner chose to stay at the hospital. He was sure shook up about your sister. I'm glad she's going to be all right." She stood from the table and pushed the bench back with her leg.

Leah suddenly remembered her concerns about giving Aaron her story. "Ruth—I mean, Auntie Ruth, do you think you could drop me by the furniture store on your way? I'd take the buggy, but I'm not sure about this weather." It wasn't raining anymore, but the sky was still gray and threatening.

"Of course, dear." Ruth scuttled across the kitchen floor and reached for her umbrella.

Kathleen stood up and folded her arms across her chest. "Why do you need to go to the furniture store and get to ride in the car?"

"I have some business to take care of." Leah didn't owe Kathleen an explanation. "But I'll be home soon. Probably before *Mamm* and *Daed* get home with Edna."

Kathleen got in step beside Ruth. "You never did say how long you were staying. Maybe sometime I could ride in your car?"

Ruth pushed the screen door open and walked onto the porch, and the girls followed. Ruth's expression grew serious. "I don't know how long I'll be staying. It just depends on—on how things are handled." Then she narrowed her eyes at the three of them. "Till the good Lord tells me it's time to go, I reckon."

"What?" Then Leah remembered the brandy. "*Ach*, do you want your brandy to take with you?"

Ruth shook her head. "No, you girls keep it."

Mary Carol giggled, but Ruth didn't seem to notice.

"What do you mean, you'll be here until things are handled?" Leah grabbed her shoes from the porch, sat down in the rocker, and laced them up.

"Oh, honey. It's a secret. I surely can't tell you." Ruth's eyes widened, then she turned away from them and headed down the porch steps.

"I'll be back soon," Leah said as she followed Ruth to the car.

And I bet I'll know what Auntie Ruth's secret is.

Chapter Six

LEAH HAD BEEN IN PLENTY OF AUTOMOBILES OVER THE years, but she'd never experienced anything quite like riding with Auntie Ruth. The woman knew one speed—fast. As they peeled onto the highway, Leah double-checked her seat belt as Ruth sped over a well-known speed bump, causing Leah to bounce in her seat.

"Oops," Ruth said, then chuckled. "Didn't see that coming. So tell me, Leah. Are you sweet on my nephew, Aaron?"

Leah quickly turned toward her. "What? No. No, we're just friends." *And barely even that.*

"He sure seems sweet on *you*," she said, batting her long lashes. "When I arrived this morning, I heard him mention your name several times. And later, in private, he told me you like to write."

Leah was surprised Aaron had shared that news with his aunt. "*Ya*, I do. I love to write stories about people turning their lives to God."

"What a glorious feeling it is to know that you are a child of the Lord." Ruth zipped around the corner, even squealing the tires. "This car can take the curves," she boasted. "I'll have to take Kathleen for a ride sometime. She seemed awfully interested in my car."

Leah rolled her eyes. "*Ya*. She loves cars, and none of us knows why."

Ruth's lips curled at the corners, but only a little. "Sometimes we just can't understand what makes a person tick, now can we?" Ruth looked at Leah as if she was the keeper of more than just her own secret.

"I suppose not." Leah stared straight ahead, very alert. "So, you said you don't know how long you'll be staying?" She couldn't imagine what this charming, odd woman might be keeping as a secret.

"Till it's time for me to go," she repeated, then sighed.

They arrived at Lantz Furniture much too soon for Leah, and there really hadn't been an opportunity to question Ruth about her secret. Ruth screeched to a halt in front of the store.

"*Danki* for bringing me," Leah said.

"You're welcome. It was very nice to meet you and your sisters. I'll let you tell Aaron and his father about Edna. I'm going to head back to the house to let Sarah and the girls know she is going to be all right."

"Very nice to meet you too. We will see you again, no?"

"I hope so." Ruth smiled. "Take care, my child of God. Keep writing your stories. You never know who you might touch someday."

Leah climbed out of the car, then hesitated before she shut the door. She wanted to tell Ruth how she felt this strange connection to her, how she wanted to get back in the car and spend the day with her, but she simply said, "Good-bye, Auntie Ruth."

Aaron carried the wooden rocker to the back of the store, tucked it in the corner, and hung a Sold sign on it. Ms. Simpson said she'd be back this afternoon to pick it up. His father would be glad the rocker sold, along with three others this morning. Seemed to be a popular style with the *Englisch*. There was nothing fancy about the oak chair, but it was larger than most, and Abner had constructed the seat in such a way that a person's fanny seemed to nestle right in.

Aaron wiped the sweat from his brow and raised the window in the back of the store to allow a cross breeze, wishing he'd done that earlier. Then he headed back up to the front in time to hear the bell on the door chime and see Leah walk in.

"How's Edna? Abner's at the hospital, but we haven't heard anything." Aaron stopped in front of Leah, thrilled that she was the one to deliver any news, but also concerned about Edna.

"She's gonna be fine. She has asthma. *Mamm* and *Daed* will be bringing her home later this afternoon." She smiled, but only a little, as if forcing herself.

"That must have been a real scare for your family."

"*Ya.*" Leah's expression confirmed that it was. She avoided his eyes, hung her head slightly. "She was an awful shade of blue, and— and she wasn't breathing."

Aaron stepped a little closer and leaned down a bit. "But she's all right now, no?"

Leah took a deep breath. "Thank the Lord."

"*Ya.*" Aaron glanced past her and out the glass window of the shop and noticed that the designated buggy area was vacant. "How'd you get here?"

Then a large smile swept across her face, and those tiny dimples came into view. Aaron smiled along with her. He couldn't help it. She looked awful pretty in her green dress, and her face was aglow about something.

"Auntie Ruth brought me."

His mouth dropped open. "*My* Auntie Ruth?" *Oh no.* Auntie Ruth was as fine a woman as had ever lived, but she was a tad—off. Aaron wondered what sort of conversation Leah had with his great-aunt.

Leah grinned. "I liked her very much. She wanted me to let you and your *daed* know that Edna would be all right."

Aaron was confused. Why would his aunt bring Leah here and drop her off, instead of just coming to tell him and his father herself? He opened his mouth but was unsure how to phrase the question.

"I asked her to give me a ride to come see you, so she dropped me off and asked me to tell you about Edna."

Aaron looped his thumbs in his suspenders and tipped his straw hat a bit. "Really? And why did you want to come see me?" Perhaps he'd made a fair impression last night after all.

"I—I just wanted . . . I wanted to make sure that you understood that we wouldn't be courting if we went to the Grabers' Sunday singing together." She shrugged. "You know, it'd be more like—like going as friends."

Aaron mentally pulled her foot from his gut. "Of course it's only as friends. I reckon it's a mite silly for you to think otherwise." He folded his arms across his chest and stood taller.

"No. I didn't think otherwise," she quickly said. "I just didn't want *you* to think it was anything more than a friendly ride together. You know how sometimes people tend to assume that a boy and girl are dating when they attend a singing together."

"If you're so worried about it, why did you ask to go with me?" He realized right away that his voice revealed more anger than he would have liked.

"Well, I—I thought we would talk about my story." She batted her eyes at him and smiled. "Have you read any of it?" Then her face grew still. No smile, only questioning eyes. She bit her lip and waited.

"Maybe."

"You did, didn't you?" She actually bounced in her black leather shoes, and the dimples were back.

He couldn't help but grin. "*Ya*, I did." He recalled the romance between Rose and Jesse. "Jesse just told Rose that he loves her." Aaron hated it when he blushed. That was something women did, yet he could feel his cheeks taking on an embarrassing shade of pink. But he felt a tad better when he saw Leah's cheeks matching his in color. She looked toward the ground.

"That's one of my favorite parts." Then she looked up and smiled. "What else? Do you like it? Am I a good storyteller? Are there any parts you didn't like? And what about—"

"*Ach!*" He pointed a finger in her direction. "We are supposed to talk about this when I'm done." *Plus, if I tell you now, you might back out of our Sunday date, which isn't a date.*

She twisted her mouth to one side. "Aaron?"

"*Ya?*"

"You won't let anything happen to my story, will you? It's the only copy I have, and I've worked hard on it."

He spoke with tenderness. "No, Leah. I won't let anything happen to it."

"And you like it so far?" Her eyes begged him to say yes.

"*Ya. I do.*" *And I will finish it by Sunday so I can spend time with you.*

"*Ach, gut!*" She gave a little bounce again. "Then I will see you on Sunday."

Aaron nodded as she turned to leave. He was just about to get back to work when Leah spun around and faced him.

"Aaron?"

"*Ya?*" She walked back toward him, folded her hands across her chest, and pressed her lips together. "Did you know your Auntie Ruth has a secret?"

Aaron laughed out loud. "I reckon Auntie Ruth must have lots of secrets." He paused. "Why?"

Leah shrugged. "I don't know. She told my sisters and me that she has a secret. And that she'd be staying until things were handled. I just wondered what that meant."

Aaron scratched his forehead. "You can probably tell that Auntie Ruth is—is different. There ain't no tellin' what she might be talking about."

"She's very special. I can tell. I hope I get to see her again."

"She's special, all right." Aaron recalled the time Auntie Ruth told him where babies came from. At twelve, he was probably old enough to know, but it was the *way* she'd told him. "*Now, honey, here's how it works . . .*" Aaron cringed at the recollection. He was sure his parents would have doubled devotion time that entire year if they'd ever found out. But Auntie Ruth never meant any harm. She just had a funny way of doing things.

"How are you going to get home? It's a far piece if you plan to walk. But the weather is better, I reckon."

"*Ach*, I'm going to hold my thumb up and hitch a ride from the *Englisch*."

Aaron's eyes grew to the size of golf balls. "Leah! You can't do that. That's not safe for you——"

She doubled over, laughing, then looked back up at Aaron, dimples and all. "It was just a tease, Aaron. You're so serious. *Mei Englisch* friend Donna works at the bakery. She gets off work in about twenty minutes. I will *hitch* a ride with her. 'Bye now."

Leah waved and turned again to leave. Aaron shook his head. It was no wonder Leah took to Auntie Ruth so well. He suspected there was a tiny bit of Auntie Ruth in Leah.

❧

Donna pulled into the driveway and put the car in park. "Are you sure you don't want to meet me and Clare at the movies later? We can pick you up near the road, like we did last time."

"No. *Danki*, though." Leah looked at the large family buggy pulled up next to the spring buggies. "My parents are home from the hospital with my sister, and tonight would not be a *gut* night to get caught sneaking out."

"I'm glad everything is okay with Edna. And you'll be in your *rumschpringe* until you're married, so I feel sure we have *plenty* of time to go out another night."

Leah giggled at her friend's use of Pennsylvania *Deitsch*—and at her implication that Leah wouldn't be married for a long time. "You're still not saying it right," she teased. She opened the car door. "*Danki* again for the ride."

As she strolled up to the door, she looked into the sky at the sun set squarely between the house and the silo, amid skies that were still a bluish gray, and positioned in such a way that Leah knew she was late for supper. She bit her bottom lip and picked up the pace, not realizing so much time had gone by. But Donna had wanted to stop for a root beer before heading home, and then they'd talked for a while, and now she was late . . . again.

She cautiously opened the screen door that led into the kitchen, expecting to find everyone seated for supper. The smell of Kathleen's beef stew filled the kitchen, but no one was in sight. Leah tiptoed to the stove, lifted the lid, and dipped the spoon into the dark brown sauce, making sure to pick up a chunk of beef. She blew on it, then opened her mouth.

"Leah!" Her father's abrupt tone caused her to drop the spoon. She scurried to pick it up, scooping the lost load into her trembling hand.

"*Ya, Daed.* How's Edna? Is everyone upstairs? I'm sorry I'm late. I had to catch a ride in town."

Daed's face was as red as Auntie Ruth's lipstick. He walked toward her, his hand raised in such a way that she actually thought he might strike her. He pointed his finger in her face.

"Your sister spent the day in the hospital. You were not even here to welcome her home, to make sure she's all right." He stood rigid, his eyes ablaze. "It is bad enough that you continue to test my will by being late to the meals and do not partake in your share of the chores around this *haus*." He pulled off his straw hat, raked a hand through his hair, and sighed. "There will be no more story writing. No more sneaking out for movies and fun times with your *Englisch* friends."

Leah's eyes widened. Who had told him?

"Your *mamm* and me are not *dumm*. Do you not think we know that you are sneaking out some nights? We have always looked the other way during our daughters' *rumschpringes*. But no more." He stomped his foot. "Edna will have to stay in bed for a while, and then

BETH WISEMAN

she will be on a light chore schedule. You will do her sewing and mending. You will help Mary Carol with the garden. You will learn to cook from Kathleen. These things you will do to become a proper Amish woman."

"*Ya, Daed.*" Leah hung her head, and a tear ran down her cheek. She hated being such a disappointment to him, but she wasn't good at all these things he spoke of. *And no more writing?*

Her father drew in a deep breath and blew it out slowly. "*Mei maedel*, you are eighteen years old. A grown woman of marrying age. Do you want to live with your *mamm* and me forever?" He shook his head, then looked at Leah's tearstained face. "You are punished to the *haus* until I say otherwise."

"But for how long?" She stared into his cold eyes.

"Until I see fit." He pointed to the stairs. "Best go check on your sister. And dry your tears. Edna has had a hard day today."

Leah didn't say anything as she brushed past him. Then she turned slowly around. "*Daed?*"

He widened his eyes but didn't say anything.

"What about the Sunday singing that Aaron Lantz invited me to this weekend?"

"I will get word to Aaron that you will not be able to attend."

"But—"

"Leah!"

She turned and ran up the stairs, and despite her father's instructions, the tears fell full force.

Chapter Seven

MARIAN SCOOTED NEXT TO HER HUSBAND IN THE BED. She snuggled up close to him and laid her head on his shoulder. He wrapped an arm around her but kept reading his book—a book about raising daughters. Marian smiled.

"You do know that book is written by an *Englisch* man, no?"

James pulled his gold-rimmed reading glasses off and closed the book. "*Englisch* or Amish, I am finding that these daughters can be difficult to rear, no matter what. This man's words calm me. Makes me feel like I am not alone with our troubles."

"James, dear. We have four beautiful daughters, all in their *rumschpringes*. What did you expect when they reached this age? Do you not remember when I was in my running-around period?" She winked playfully at him. "Things will be challenging. But they are all *gut* girls." Then she nudged him with her shoulder. "Even Leah."

Her husband grunted. "I love all *mei* daughters. I just want Leah to do as she should."

"James, you cannot make Leah into someone she is not. As I've told you before, Leah will find her way."

He turned to face her and lifted his brows. "When?"

Marian chuckled. "Well, I don't know exactly when, but she will."

James settled himself atop the covers and pulled her close.

"Don't you think that maybe you were a bit hard on Leah? Punishing her to the *haus*—indefinitely."

"Maybe if she is here more, and not writing those silly stories and running with her *Englisch* friends, she will learn to do the things a *gut* Amish woman should. I am doing Leah a favor."

Marian cuddled closer to her husband. "It's such a shame that she won't be able to go with Aaron Lantz to the singing on Sunday." She paused. "He seems like such a nice boy."

"I'm not bending my rules." Her husband sat up taller in the bed.

Marian tenderly ran her finger down his arm. "Are you sure?"

James finally grinned. "I know what you are doing, my love. And it won't work." But he wrapped her in his arms just the same.

Later that evening, Leah sat down on the edge of Edna's bed and clutched her sister's hand. "I was so scared, Edna. I'm sorry I wasn't here when you got home."

"Leah," Edna said tenderly. "I told you when you brought me supper earlier, I have no worries about that." She paused. "How did *Daed* act during supper?"

"He didn't say much to me. He did ask me to hem his new pair of breeches."

"That's an easy task." Edna propped herself taller against her pillow and reached for the inhaler the doctor had given her.

"Does that help?"

"*Ya*, it does." Edna put the inhaler to her mouth and breathed in the medication, then said, "There's no need for all this fuss over me. I feel well enough to resume my chores tomorrow."

"Edna! You just got out of the hospital. At least give it a few days. I can handle your sewing and other chores." Leah released her sister's hand, then lowered the flame on the lantern that sat between them on the nightstand. She climbed into her own bed. "*Daed* said I'm not allowed to write my stories anymore."

Edna sighed. "I know you enjoy doing that, Leah, but is it really necessary?"

"To me it is." She kicked her quilt to the foot of the bed. "And I won't be able to go to the singing with Aaron on Sunday."

Edna twisted to face her. "*Ya*, Abner told me that the two of you were supposed to go together, and I must ask, why? You never seemed interested in Aaron."

Leah shrugged. "He's okay. I'm just not in the market for courting. I know you and Mary Carol are ready to get married, but I'm not yet."

Edna's face brightened. "It's a wonderful feeling to be in love, Leah. You'll see someday."

Leah thought for a moment. "I write about finding the Lord in my books, but I also write about finding love."

"Maybe when you fall in love, your writing will be even better." Edna smiled, then took another whiff from the inhaler. "I'm tired, Leah." She eased herself down in the bed. "But it won't bother me if you want to leave the lantern on and write."

"Actually, I'm tired too." Leah turned the knob on the lantern until the flame was extinguished, then lay down. Thankfully, there was a bit of a breeze blowing through the window screen, but it was still dreadfully hot.

"Leah."

"*Ya?*"

"Maybe if you are on best behavior for the next few days, *Daed* will rethink his decision and let you go to the singing."

"Do you think?"

"If you work really hard to please him, he might. For starters, don't be late for meals."

"How can I be late if I'm not allowed to go anywhere?"

Edna chuckled. "True. Good night, Leah."

"Good night."

Leah lay there for a few minutes, and despite how tired she felt, her thoughts were all over the place. "Edna, are you asleep?"

"Almost."

"Did you meet Abner and Aaron's Auntie Ruth?" Leah smiled as she recalled the high-speed car ride earlier in the afternoon.

Edna giggled. "*Ya.* I guess you met her too. I heard her say that she was going to go report to my sisters that I was doing fine. Isn't she a funny *Englisch* woman?"

"She seemed a bit odd, but I liked her." Leah recalled the way Auntie Ruth told her that perhaps her stories would touch someone someday. She couldn't imagine who at this point. She'd hoped that maybe Clare or Donna might be inspired by her stories to put more faith in God and His will, but she wasn't sure when she would even see her *Englisch* friends again. Surely her father would ease up on her.

They were quiet for a few minutes, then Edna started to cough badly. Leah bolted up in the bed. "Edna, are you okay?"

"Leah, I'm fine," she said in a hacking voice. "I just have to keep using this inhaler. I have an infection, and it worsened this asthma that I didn't even know I had."

Edna coughed, inhaled from the tube, and coughed some more. Leah recalled Edna's bluish color this morning. She closed her eyes. She felt like she couldn't pray enough for Edna, so she offered up yet another prayer for her sister before she dozed off.

❧

The next morning, Leah made sure she got up extra early. Everyone seemed shocked, and almost afraid, when they walked into the kitchen to find Leah finishing breakfast. Nothing fancy. Scrambled eggs, sausage, and toast.

"*Ach*, I can take over from here," Kathleen said as she joined Leah by the stove and reached for the spatula.

Leah jerked it away. "It's almost ready. The sausage is keeping warm in the oven, and I'm almost done with these eggs."

"What's that smell?" Mary Carol entered the kitchen, pinching her nose.

Leah put one hand on her hip and stirred the eggs with the other. "I burned the toast, but only a little."

"It's black!" Mary Carol eyed the plate of toast on the kitchen table. "I'm not eating that."

"You will all eat what your sister cooked." *Daed* walked into the kitchen carrying a copy of the *Die Botschaft* tucked under his arm. He put the newspaper on the counter and sat down at the head of the table. "Your *mamm* is upstairs with Edna, and she said to begin without her. She will eat upstairs with Edna in a while."

Leah poured the eggs into a bowl, unsure why they looked different from usual. Then she took the bowl of eggs and the plate of sausage and placed both on the table. She took a seat beside Mary Carol and across from Kathleen.

"Let us pray," their father said. They all bowed their heads.

Since no one seemed particularly hungry this morning, Leah went first and spooned eggs onto her plate, snatched a piece of sausage, and helped herself to a piece of toast.

"Where're the jams and jellies?" Mary Carol scanned the table. "We're gonna need them," she added under her breath. She slowly reached for a piece of toast.

Leah cut her eyes at Mary Carol. "I'll get them." She rose from the table and returned with a jar of rhubarb jam and a jar of apple butter. Once she was seated again, she took a bite of the eggs. They weren't so bad. An odd texture, maybe.

She glanced around the table at the others.

"How long did you cook these eggs, Leah?" Mary Carol's mouth twisted with displeasure.

"The eggs are fine," *Daed* said with authority. He glanced at Leah with a slight smile.

That was all she needed from him. It was a start, and she was tired of being such a disappointment to him.

"May I be excused? I want to get started on Edna's sewing chores." Leah didn't think she could finish the meal. Her sisters would have to figure out their own way to avoid eating her cooking. *Maybe I'll be better at sewing.*

Daed nodded.

Leah left the kitchen, walked through the den, and headed up the stairs. She met her mother midway. "How's Edna?"

"She seems better this morning." Her mother paused. "What's that smell?"

Leah sighed. "I fixed breakfast."

Her mother's eyes widened. "*Ach.* That's nice, dear."

"I'm going to go hem *Daed*'s breeches. Maybe I'll be better at that." She scooted past her mother.

"Leah?"

She spun around and saw her mother coming back up the stairs. "*Ya?*"

"Keep making a *gut* effort, and I will try to convince your father to let you go to the singing on Sunday."

Leah smiled. "*Danki, Mamm.*" She knew she'd be more than ready to get out of the house by Sunday. And she was very eager to hear what Aaron thought about the rest of her story.

She headed upstairs to start on the sewing chores. First she'd hem her father's pants, then see what else was in the pile. She would plan on cooking for the next couple of days too. Surely that would win her some points.

Or maybe not.

Chapter Eight

JAMES EYED THE MENU AT PARADISO. HE DIDN'T TAKE
Marian out to eat often, but a Saturday night in town, eating some fine
Italian food, was just what he and Marian needed. Leah had insisted
on cooking the meals all day on Friday, and he'd suffered through
breakfast and lunch today. At Paradiso the food was always good.

"What's the occasion?" Marian grinned as she spread her napkin
on her lap and picked up her menu.

"I reckon you know exactly what the occasion is."

"Yet you left Edna, Mary Carol, and Kathleen to fend for themselves, no?"

James decided on lasagna and closed his menu. "Kathleen made
a batch of corn chowder while Leah was helping Mary Carol in the
garden. She stashed it in the back of the refrigerator, in case Leah's
meat loaf was not *gut*." He paused, tilted his head to one side. "How
can you mess up meat loaf, though?"

"She's trying so *hatt* to please you, James. And I think her ham
loaf last night would have been all right if she hadn't gotten her
teaspoons and tablespoons mixed up." Marian sighed. "I failed with
Leah, I reckon. I've tried to teach her everything she needs to know
about being a *gut* Amish *fraa*, but I must have done something
wrong."

"You didn't fail, Marian. Leah has never been interested in cooking, sewing, gardening, or cleaning. And now, at eighteen, she's
trying to master these skills?" He shook his head. "She is only doing
this so that I might change my mind and let her go to the singing."

Marian pressed her lips together, raised her chin, and opened her eyes wide. It was the look she wore when she was about to confront him about something. "Maybe you should let her go, James."

He knew she was right. A boy was interested in Leah, and he certainly didn't want to hinder progress. "I don't know . . ."

"I know the girls in the Lantz family. They have all been around Leah enough to know that she does not excel at certain things. I'm sure they've told Aaron that, and if he is still interested in her—perhaps you should reconsider her punishment, even if just for one night."

James nodded at the approaching waitress, then waited for Marian to order before he ordered his lasagna. Maybe Leah just needed the right boy to motivate her to learn the skills necessary to become a good wife. "I reckon one night would be all right."

Marian's face lit up, and James was suddenly anxious to get home. His wife still caused his heart to skip a beat when she looked at him a certain way. After twenty-one years of marriage, he was as in love with her as the first day he saw her on the playground at school. Her brown eyes still sparkled with youthful enthusiasm when she was pleased, the same way they did the day that James offered her a piece of chewing gum in the fourth grade.

"I think that is a *gut* decision," she said with a wink.

Sunday morning, Leah wasn't surprised to see Kathleen, Mary Carol, *Mamm*, and even Edna making breakfast before she got downstairs. And they were up earlier than usual to do so.

"I know my cooking stinks." She sighed. "I'll get the jellies and such and put them on the table. Hard to mess that up." She shuffled toward the refrigerator, her head hanging low. She'd really tried. How hard could it be to scramble eggs?

"Leah," her mother said tenderly. "No worries. You will find something you excel at. And your cooking was fine."

"It is a sin to lie, *Mamm*." She placed the jams on the table, then thrust one hand on her hip. "I know that I got confused about the measurements with the ham loaf Friday night. And I know my meat loaf was heavy on the salt. But eggs? I should be able to do that." She stomped her foot a bit. "I put the oil in with the eggs just like I've seen Kathleen do a hundred times."

They all turned to face her, expressions blank.

Then Kathleen exclaimed, "That's for cakes, Leah! I mix the oil in with the eggs when I'm making cakes, not when I'm just scrambling the eggs." She shook her head and laughed.

"That explains it," Mary Carol said.

"Explains what?" *Daed* entered the kitchen.

But no one answered him. Instead, laughter erupted throughout the kitchen as all eyes landed on his pant hems. One leg was hemmed much higher than the other.

"Leah," Edna said, "is that the pair of pants you hemmed for *Daed?*"

Leah didn't answer. She glanced back and forth between her sisters. Even her mother was chuckling. Their laughter echoed in Leah's head as she ran out of the room.

She heard Edna calling after her, but she didn't turn around. Then she heard her mother say that no one was making fun of her. But they were. All of them. If they knew how hard she'd really tried, they wouldn't be laughing. She threw herself facedown on her bed.

"We should all be ashamed of ourselves," Marian said. She dried her hands on her apron. "I'll go to her."

James cut in front of her path. "No. I will do it."

He wasn't even to the top of the stairs when he heard Leah crying. He slowly pushed open her bedroom door. She bolted upright and swiped at her tears.

"I'm sorry, *Daed.*" She buried her face in her hands. "I tried. I really did. I even tried to help Mary Carol in the garden, but she said I wasn't picking the vegetables the right way. I'm not *gut* at any of this."

James didn't like to see Marian or any of the girls cry. And he was responsible for her pain. He sat down on Edna's bed, across from Leah. "Leah," he said tenderly, "the reason you are not *gut* with these skills is because you don't practice them enough. If you practice—"

"That's not true, *Daed.* I've tried on and off for years to be a better Amish woman. It just doesn't come naturally to me, and I don't know why."

I don't know why either. James stroked his beard and thought for a moment. "What do you want to do with your life, Leah? If these things that are necessary to become an Amish *fraa* don't interest you, what does?"

James knew the answer, but he'd been praying for some guidance where Leah was concerned. Maybe she could explain her writing to him in a way that he could understand, tell him why such a silly thing was so important to her and seemed to distract her from more important things. It would serve her no purpose in their community, especially as a woman doing so. Women had certain responsibilities within the district. His daughter knew this.

Leah sniffled. "I'm eighteen years old. I know that I need to work on my home skills, and I will continue to do so." She sat up taller.

James grimaced as he thought about more experimental meals, but he was the one who had forced this issue. *Why doesn't she mention her writing?* "Is there something else you'd rather do, Leah? If so, tell me about it. Help me to understand."

She looked at her feet. "No. Nothing. I will work harder to do better with my chores."

A sense of despair settled over James. This was what he'd always wanted to hear from her, but he knew that she was stifling her dreams to say what he wanted to hear.

"I know you have been working *hatt*, Leah. I have decided to allow you to attend the singing tonight at the Grabers'." He paused. "But your punishment is only on hold for tonight. Edna still needs to take things slowly until her infection is better, and I'd like to see you helping out more for the next couple weeks. No lunches with your *Englisch* friends or traveling to town. Then we will speak of this matter again."

"*Danki, Daed.*"

James left his daughter's room and knew he should feel victorious. Leah was finally coming around. But something just wasn't right in his heart.

Chapter Nine

AARON PUT LEAH'S THICK STACK OF PAPERS IN A PAPER bag and headed down the stairs. He slowed as he hit the den and listened for voices. Nothing. Maybe his sisters had already left for the singing. He wasn't eager for anyone to know he'd been reading Leah's book. He'd finished it last night and had to admit he was impressed.

His parents were in their room, and Abner was already on his way to the Petersheims' for a visit, since Edna didn't feel up to attending the singing. A clean getaway. Aaron tucked the bag under his arm and shuffled across the den to the front door. He'd already readied his horse and courting buggy earlier in the day. He pushed the screen door open and darted down the stairs.

"Where ya goin' in such a hurry?"

Auntie Ruth. He'd forgotten about her. Aaron spun around. "To pick up Leah and take her to the singing, and I'm running late." Which was true.

She stood up from the rocker on the porch, dressed in orange and red plaid breeches and a bright red blouse. Her toenails were painted a bright red and matched her long fingernails and the color on her lips.

You'd think that while she was here, she'd try to blend in just a little.

As she walked toward him, her eyes focused on his bag. "What's that? Aaron Lantz, you aren't trying to sneak alcohol into that singing, are ya?" She shook her head. "That stuff's bad for you."

Aaron glanced at the small glass in her hand half full of a dark liquid. "No, Auntie Ruth. It's not alcohol. It's—something of Leah's."

She toddled toward him. Aaron sighed, knowing he was going to be even later, and that was not a good way to start the evening. He loved Auntie Ruth, but he didn't have time for silly chitchat right now. She put one hand on her hip. "You read her book, huh?"

"What?"

"That's what's in that bag, isn't it?" Auntie Ruth took a sip from her glass, smudging it with red around the rim.

Aaron sighed.

"Don't worry. I won't tell. But was it any good?"

"Auntie Ruth, *ya*, it was *gut*. Now I have to go. I'm already late." Aaron started walking backward toward his buggy. "We'll talk later."

Ruth nodded, took another sip. Since she'd arrived, Aaron had seen her having an alcoholic drink every day, sometimes in the morning, sometimes in the evening. She'd never done that when she'd visited before, or when they visited her in Florida.

He turned around and hurried to the buggy. He set the bag down on the seat, then climbed in. He grabbed the reins and was getting ready to back his horse up, when he thought of something. Auntie Ruth was still standing barefoot in the front yard.

"Why did you tell Leah you have a secret?"

She raised her eyebrows. "Because I do." She took a few steps toward him. "Want me to tell you what it is?"

Aaron couldn't even begin to speculate what type of secret she might be keeping. This was the same woman who came to visit three years ago carting three baby ferrets with her. *Mamm* refused to let the "rats," as she called them, stay in the house. Another time, a few years before that, Ruth had shown up riding a big black motorcycle, wearing black leather pants and a matching jacket. There was just never any reckoning about what might be on Auntie Ruth's mind.

"If you want to tell me." Aaron began to back up the buggy as Ruth drew near. "But you don't have to," he added, hoping to be on his way.

But she kept walking until she was right beside the buggy, so Aaron stopped.

"I suppose it's best that you know." Ruth took a deep breath and let it out slowly. "I will be passin' on to the other side, to be with my heavenly Father soon." She raised her chin high. "Yes, Aaron. I'm going to drop dead shortly."

Aaron's mouth hung open. This was the most nonsense he'd ever heard from her, and he wondered why she'd make up such a thing. "Auntie Ruth," he finally said, "that's the craziest notion I've ever heard. What in the world would make you say somethin' like that? Are you sick?" He looked again at the glass in her hand.

"It's just my time, dear Aaron." She made the sign of the cross, took another sip of her drink, then pointed a crooked finger toward the sky. "I'll be goin' home soon."

He did not have time for her silliness. "Auntie Ruth, we'll talk about this later, but I reckon you ain't gonna drop dead any time soon."

"But I am, Aaron." She pressed her lips firmly together and blinked her eyes a few times. "I might drop dead right over there, amid the wildflowers in the pasture." She waved her free hand toward the wide-open field. "Wouldn't that be lovely? Taking my last breath in God's plush landscaping." Her eyes grew wide. "I think you best not tell anyone, though."

Aaron shook his head. He'd tell his mother about this as soon as possible.

Leah was starting to think Aaron had changed his mind. Mary Carol and Kathleen had left fifteen minutes ago, and Abner arrived to visit Edna shortly after that. The singing started at eight o'clock and only lasted about an hour and a half.

Leah pushed the rocker on the porch into motion. She could hear

Edna and Abner talking and laughing with her parents in the kitchen. If Aaron was trying to be fashionably late, as Clare and Donna would say, he was bordering on making her mad.

Then she heard the shuffling of horse hooves and saw him pull into the driveway. She pushed herself up from the rocker and padded down the porch steps and into the yard, blocking her eyes from the setting sun.

She waited until he stopped beside her, then cupped her hands on her hips. "You're late, Aaron Lantz."

"Sorry. It was Auntie Ruth. She was telling me a crazy story, and her ramblin' held me up." He reached onto his seat and offered her a brown paper bag. "Here's your book. I read the whole thing."

Leah accepted it. "Did you like it?"

"*Ya*, I really did."

She could tell by the way he said it that he meant it. Leah couldn't wait to talk about it with him on the way to the singing. But first she wanted to put it safely away. "I'll be right back. I just want to go put this in the house." She held up her index finger. "One minute."

She skipped back into the house and entered through the den to avoid her family in the kitchen. Then she bolted upstairs. She set the bag on her bed and reached for her other completed story inside the drawer. Leah pounded the papers on her nightstand in an effort to straighten them somewhat. She pulled the first book from the bag and tucked it safely in the drawer, then put the other book inside the bag. She slammed the door shut and ran down the hall, taking the stairs two at a time, then dashed through the den.

Aaron watched her coming toward him in her dark blue dress and smiled. Until he saw what she was carrying. *No, no, no.* He'd enjoyed Leah's story, but he needed sleep. He couldn't keep this up every night.

"Since you liked it, I thought you might want to read the second one I wrote." She pushed it toward him.

He forced a smile and accepted it, then stepped out of the buggy and offered her his hand. She latched on, and Aaron helped her into his courting buggy. He knew good and well that they weren't dating, yet he was about to have to read another book.

"I think it's better than the first, but it's much longer," she added.

Aaron slid in beside her, then took a peek inside the bag. He eyed the thick stack of paper but didn't say anything.

Leah waited until they pulled onto the two-lane road that wound through the back roads of Paradise. "So, what was your most favorite part?"

"The end." His meaning was twofold. When he had finished the last page, he'd assumed his sleep schedule would return to normal. But he decided to give her the other meaning within his answer. "Everyone is happy at the end of the book." *Particularly Rose and Jesse.*

Leah broke into a wide smile. "Wait until you read this next one!" She folded her hands in her lap and kept grinning.

Aaron eased his horse into a gentle gallop as he thought about all the sleepless nights ahead of him. "And when will we be talkin' about this next book? On the way to another singing?"

"Why, Aaron Lantz, you make this sound like a trade-off."

"I'm not the one who invited you to the singing. You invited me, no?"

"True. But I'm not sure when I will be able to go out again." She paused as her expression soured. "I have to help out more with the chores at home."

"Until Edna is better?" He was wondering how long that would be, and if she was just saying that as an excuse not to go anywhere with him.

Leah sighed. "I don't know. *Mei daed* said he would like to see me become a better cook, gardener, seamstress, and all the other things that go into making a *gut*..." She slanted her eyes in his direction, then turned and faced forward again. "... a *gut fraa.*"

Aaron chuckled, then realized from the look on her face that he shouldn't have.

"What's so funny?" She'd twisted in her seat to face him.

"Nothing." He tried to sound convincing.

"Oh, I'm sure you've heard from your sisters that I'm not very *gut* at quilting. We've been at many quilting parties together. And I don't cook very well either. It's just that . . ." She pressed her lips together and frowned for a moment. "I could be happy eating a sandwich, and it doesn't really bother me if the house isn't all that clean. I'd rather be writing my stories. I really believe that they might help someone someday." She shrugged. "Maybe not, though."

Aaron was thinking about her story, the way she intertwined the Lord's goodness with her characters' quest for spiritual guidance. "Do all your books help someone find their way to God? And is there always a romance?" She must believe in true love or she wouldn't write about it.

Leah smiled. "Not always a romance, but always a happy ending."

They were quiet for a few moments. The sun was bearing down on the horizon, and Leah looked to her left at the old Bontrager place.

"It's a shame about that place." She nodded toward the rundown homestead. The front porch on the old home was tilted, the paint was peeling, and weeds had taken over the property. "I heard some man and his son used to live there, but they just up and left one day, and no one knows where they went or why."

"*Ya.* That's what I heard too." He paused, straining to see the house as the skies began to darken. "Maybe someone will buy the old place and fix it up."

Aaron could see the Grabers' farm up ahead, along with dozens of buggies parked out front.

"What else did you like about my story?" she asked, as if sensing she didn't have much time to pump him for information.

"It seemed like you were writing about—" Aaron wasn't sure if he should be this honest.

"About what?"

"About yourself." He guided his buggy onto the Grabers' driveway.

"What? Rose isn't anything like me. She's actually a *gut* cook, tends her garden, and even sews clothes for her niece."

Aaron slowed his horse with a "whoa." Once they were stopped, he turned toward her. "Rose is full of life, and she has a big heart. She wants to help others, and she's—she's beautiful, inside and out." He was so far out on a limb, he wanted to jump. But then Leah gave him a smile that sent his pulse racing.

"*Danki*, Aaron."

"Why, Leah Petersheim, I think you're blushing, no?" He stepped out of the buggy and offered Leah his hand, which she accepted as she stepped from the buggy.

Leah opened her mouth to say something, but the sound of feet shuffling across the yard caused them both to turn toward the movement.

Aaron recognized the person heading their way.

Oh no.

Chapter Ten

LEAH WATCHED HANNAH BEILER SWINGING HER HIPS toward them. In a world that discouraged vanity and pride, Hannah seemed to have a hardy abundance of both. Propane lights hung from the trees in the Grabers' front yard, and Leah could see several people gathered around a picnic table filled with food. But the closer Hannah got, all Leah could see was Hannah's pearly white, straight smile. Leah ran her tongue over her own teeth, and it wasn't a straight sweep.

"Hello, Aaron," Hannah said cheerfully. Then through those clenched straight teeth, she turned to Leah. "Hello, Leah."

"Hi, Hannah." Aaron gently touched Leah's arm and coaxed her to his side, nudging her to walk with him up the cobblestone steps that led to the Grabers' front yard. It was an obvious attempt to avoid Hannah, and Leah silently scorned herself for the wrongful and confusing feeling of pride that swept over her. This wasn't a date with Aaron, anyway. She'd made that quite clear.

She saw Rebecca Miller standing in the front yard with some other girls. Ben Weaver was standing off to one side with two young men, and Leah smiled. Everyone knew Ben was in love with Rebecca, and he was never far away from her. But ever since Rebecca's twin sister, Lizzie, died five years ago, Rebecca just hadn't been the same. She was a few years older then Leah, but Leah could remember when Rebecca was much more outgoing. Leah had always heard that twins shared a special bond.

"Hi, Rebecca." She eased from Aaron's side and walked toward Rebecca, who smiled slightly. They began to chitchat about the food spread out before them: a variety of dips and chips, several desserts—and Kathleen's Lazy Daisy Oatmeal Cake. After the events at breakfast that morning, Leah had lost herself outside, worked in the garden, brushed and fed the horses, and did anything that would keep her away from everyone. She'd forgotten that she'd asked Kathleen to help her make the oatmeal cake. *Probably best,* she thought, remembering the scrambled eggs.

As Leah chatted with Rebecca, she saw Hannah cozying up to Aaron, laughing and carrying on. *That's my date.* Two other girls joined the conversation, and Leah excused herself and walked toward Aaron and Hannah.

"*Ach,* Aaron, you're so nice to say that," Leah heard Hannah say. She turned toward Leah. "Aaron was just saying how much he always enjoys my tomato pies. It's his favorite kind of pie." She swiveled back to face Aaron and pointed toward the table. "You better get yourself a piece before it's all gone. What's your baking specialty, Leah?" Hannah raised an eyebrow and smiled.

Hannah Beiler knew good and well that Leah wasn't much of a baker. Leah recalled the quilting party last month where she showed up with a cheesecake, at her mother's insistence. It really didn't taste so bad, but her mother told her later that perhaps crushed pineapple was not the best choice for a topping. "Strawberries, cherries, or blueberries, Leah," *Mamm* had said.

"Too many to choose from," Leah responded with a shrug. Then she turned to Aaron. "I'm going to go in and say hello to Amanda and her mother."

"I'll come with you." Aaron eased to Leah's side once again, and before she turned to walk toward the house, Leah told Hannah, with a smile, "See you in a bit."

Hannah's face fell flat, and she forced a grin.

"*Danki* for saving me," Aaron whispered as they walked side by side to the front porch.

Leah glanced in his direction. "Saving you from what?"

"Hannah attaches herself to my hip every time I'm around her, and I have no interest in her in that way."

Leah faced forward again. "She's very pretty."

Aaron shrugged. "I hadn't noticed." Then he smiled at Leah in a way that caused her to instantly recall what he had said to her before they arrived, when he compared her to Rose in her story. Rose, he said, was beautiful on the inside and outside.

"Hmm," she mumbled.

Aaron opened the screen door for Leah and followed her into the Grabers' kitchen where Amanda was scurrying around with her mother. At twenty-four, Amanda was the oldest of seven brothers and sisters. She wasn't particularly social, and Leah didn't know her all that well. But Amanda had made a special point of taking a large helping of Leah's pineapple-topped cheesecake at the quilting party last month, then told everyone it was the best cheesecake she'd ever had.

It was an untruth, but Leah had found it so endearing that she longed to know Amanda better.

"Can I help you with anything?" Leah walked to Amanda's side while Aaron stood in the kitchen full of women, looking rather lost.

"Leah, hello." Amanda wiped her hands on her black apron and smiled. "No, you two go enjoy yourselves. We're just finishing up a few things in here, and we'll be right out."

Leah nodded and turned to go back outside. Aaron followed, but when the screen door closed behind them, he gently grabbed her arm. "Please don't lead me back over there to Hannah."

"But she makes your favorite kind of pie." She didn't try to hide her cynical tone.

"Very funny."

After everyone stuffed themselves silly with food, they sang several songs in four-part harmony—something not allowed during worship service. Then some of the guests began to leave, while others started a late-night game of volleyball. The Grabers' outside lights lit the space well, and a full moon shone on the area. Aaron had joined some of the other young men near the barn, and Leah was outside watching the volleyball game and pretending to be interested in the conversation around her about an upcoming tea party. *Thank goodness I'm punished to the house and won't have to attend.*

Hannah, who was hosting the tea party, rattled on about the foods she would be preparing. Leah glanced at Rebecca, who was eyeing Ben on the volleyball court. She hoped a courtship could develop between those two. They'd arrived at the singing separately, but that didn't necessarily mean anything.

After all, she had arrived with Aaron, and there was certainly no courtship going on there. But she had to admit that it had bothered her when Hannah tried to get cozy with him earlier.

Leah saw Aaron walking toward them from the barn, and she wondered if he was ready to head home. Maybe if she got home early enough, she'd be able to do a little writing before she went to sleep.

Aaron strolled across the yard toward Leah. He was ready to go and hoped Leah would be too. It was going to be another long night of reading. Another long *week.* He couldn't help but wonder what his reward would be for reading another book, since that seemed to be how Leah worked. For now, he'd take what he could get, in an attempt to spend more time with her and get to know her better.

"Hello, ladies," he said as he approached Leah, Rebecca, Hannah, and two of Amanda's sisters. He stopped near Leah. "I was wondering if you might be ready to go?"

Leah nodded with a yawn. "*Ya,* I think so."

There was no mistaking Hannah's disappointment. Hannah

had a striking appearance, and she was known in the community as a good catch for any young man. On several occasions, Aaron's mother had mentioned what a fine wife Hannah would make. And Aaron knew she was right. She just wasn't the person for him.

They said their good-byes, and Aaron offered Leah his hand and helped her into his buggy. The feel of her hand cradled in his sent a tingle up his spine. He looked up at the thick clusters of stars that dotted the clear skies above them and decided to take a chance.

"Why are we going this way?" Leah asked when Aaron turned left instead of right out of the Grabers' driveway.

"It's such a beautiful night, I thought we'd take the long way. Is that okay? I reckon we really didn't talk much about your book, and I know that was the *deal*." He smiled in her direction to let her know he was just fine with the arrangement.

"I—I had a *gut* time." She seemed hesitant with her comment, but her lips curved into a cautious smile. "So I guess it was a fine *deal*."

"So when would you like to get together again and hear my thoughts on this latest book?"

"Hmm. I don't know. There is the issue with *mei daed*." She turned to face him, and in the moonlight he could see a twinkle in her eye. "But maybe if I work really hard on my chores, and if Edna continues to feel better, then maybe he'll let me go do something. But, Aaron . . ."

"*Ya?*"

"I was thinkin' . . . I reckon it was *hatt* for you to read my book so fast, like you did. Probably too much to ask."

"Not at all. I enjoyed it." Aaron knew he was willing to read the other one equally as fast if it meant he'd get to see her again. "What about a picnic Saturday after I get off work, if your *daed* will allow it? I only work until eleven that morning." She seemed hesitant, so he added, "I'll have the book finished by then. We could talk about it and have some lunch."

Aaron knew that at some point he was going to need Leah to

want to spend time with him without having to bribe her. But for now, he'd take however much of her time he could get, and with whatever strings attached.

"I guess I could ask *Daed* if it would be all right."

Aaron smiled at the thought of sitting quietly with Leah somewhere and having a picnic. It seemed much more intimate than a Sunday singing. "That sounds *gut*. I'll have *mei mamm* make us a picnic lunch."

Leah giggled. "Aaron Lantz, do you think I'm not able to prepare us a lunch?"

"No, of course not," he immediately responded.

"I am quite capable of making chicken salad sandwiches and some side items for a picnic, and I wouldn't want your *mamm* to have to do that." She laughed again. "Unless you're scared?" Her mouth spread into a wide smile, and her eyes gleamed from the light of the moon.

"I'm a *little* scared," he teased back, loving the sound of her laughter. "But I'm willing to take the chance, I reckon."

"I'll have Edna get word to Abner by Saturday, whether or not I can go."

Aaron smiled. Then he kept up his end of the bargain for the rest of the way home, as he recalled some of his favorite parts of Leah's book.

Chapter Eleven

MARIAN STRIPPED THE SHEETS FROM THE BED AS JAMES fastened his suspenders. Monday was wash day, and she wanted to get the sheets downstairs and into the pile.

"I think it's lovely that you are letting Leah go on the picnic with Aaron on Saturday." She turned in his direction and winked. "Sometimes there is cause to bend the rules a bit, no?"

James sighed. "How can I not? A boy is actually interested in Leah, and it's for sure that he knows she is lacking in skills. I'm sure his sisters have told him of this."

"Maybe all that's not important to Aaron. Maybe he just likes Leah for the person she is." Marian scooped the sheets into her arms. "Besides, Leah has been trying harder lately, helping more around the house."

James sat down on the bare mattress pad. "But this trying harder cannot be just to gain her freedoms. It should be a way of life. Edna is much better, but I would still like to see Leah stay around the house and work on her skills. This exception is for Saturday only."

"Did you see the way Aaron looked at Leah during worship service yesterday? It was very sweet. He really seems to like her a lot."

James looked toward the ceiling and folded his hands together. "*Danki*, Lord." He turned toward Marian and smiled. "I was worrying the girl might live with us forever."

There was a knock at the bedroom door. "*Mamm?*"

"Come in, Leah." Marian bunched the sheets up and balanced them on her hip.

Leah pushed the door open and came in. "*Daed*, I made your lunch. It's in your pail on the kitchen counter."

Marian smiled at James. "Isn't that nice, James? That's a chore I won't have to do this morning." She turned to her daughter. "*Danki*, Leah."

Leah hesitated near the door. "*Daed*, I was wondering . . ."

"What is it, Leah?" James finished tying his shoes and stood up.

"I was wondering if I could meet Clare and Donna for lunch today in town? I haven't seen them in——"

"No." James folded his arms across his chest. "I am allowing you to go to your picnic on Saturday, but that is all for now. You are making great strides, Leah, with your household chores, and I would like to see continued improvement. I waited much too long to enforce these rules. Your sisters can't be expected to do more than their share."

"But I've been doing my share, plus more," Leah argued.

"Edna is not one hundred percent yet, and I'd like you to keep doing what you are doing."

"But, *Daed*——"

"Leah, that's enough," Marian said. "Be grateful that your *daed* is allowing you to go with Aaron on Saturday."

"Yes, ma'am."

When the door closed behind Leah, Marian asked her husband, "How long are you going to keep this up, James?"

"Until it becomes natural for Leah to pull her share of the load around here, instead of coming in late for every meal, not helping with preparations, laundry, gardening, and other chores. And until she realizes there is no place or time in her life for these fanciful stories of hers. I am pleased with what I see, and I would like to make sure these are habits she will keep up with."

Marian kissed her husband on the cheek. "I'm going to go take these to her. She said she would start up the wringer and get the clothes washed today." Marian grinned. "In the past, Leah has made herself scarce on Mondays. I know she dislikes doing the clothes, yet she offered this morning."

James twisted his mouth to one side. "It wonders me what the girl has prepared me for lunch. After I tend to the fields, I plan to touch up the red paint on both the barns in the far pasture. If it doesn't make wet later in the day, that's my plan." James scratched his forehead and sighed. "That's a lot of work for a man to do on an empty stomach."

Marian smiled. "I will have you an afternoon snack, as usual. So, James Petersheim, you won't starve today if it is something not of your liking."

Her husband grumbled as he walked out the door. Marian followed along behind him, toting the sheets, hopeful that Leah would stay on course.

Aaron waited until he was able to catch his mother alone Monday morning.

"*Mamm?*"

"*Ya*, Aaron." She pulled a loaf of bread from the oven and placed it on a rack by the stove. "Your *daed* and Abner are already milking the cows."

"I'm heading out there, but there's something I wanted to talk to you about first."

Sarah Lantz pulled the kitchen mitt from her hand and placed it on the counter, then wiped a trail of sweat from her cheek. "I try to use this oven in the earliest part of the day, but yet this August heat is still unbearable." She looked up at Aaron. "What is it, dear?"

Aaron glanced over his shoulder and into the den. Seeing it was all clear, he asked, "Where's Auntie Ruth?"

"I imagine she's still sleeping. You know your aunt doesn't rise as early as we do."

BETH WISEMAN

Aaron didn't figure there was much he could tell his mother that would surprise her about Auntie Ruth, but Aaron had continued to be bothered about Auntie Ruth's comments.

"Did you know that Auntie Ruth thinks she is going to die soon?"

His mother scrunched her face. "What? Why would she think that? She's not sick, that I know of."

Aaron shrugged. "I don't know, *Mamm*. She said that she is going to drop dead soon." Aaron paused. "Do you think she's done gone crazy?"

Sarah patted her forehead with a napkin and took a deep breath. "I never know what to think about your Auntie Ruth." His mother took a seat at the kitchen table. "I remember when I was a girl, Auntie Ruth wasn't much different than she is now. Except she's slowed down with age." She smiled and shook her head. "Do you know that Auntie Ruth came for a visit once when I was twelve or fourteen, and she announced to the entire family that she was going to join a convent and become a nun?"

Aaron knew he needed to get out to the barn and help his *daed* and Abner, but he'd never heard this story. He sat down across from his mother. "A nun?"

Sarah laughed. "*Ya*. Of course, she changed her mind later, but I remember the look on everyone's face when she made the announcement." She paused. "Auntie Ruth is a spiritual person, but I reckon she is confused sometimes about her relationship with God. She often thinks God is *telling* her things."

"But doesn't God tell us all things—that little voice inside of us when we listen?"

"I suppose so. But, well . . . it's different with Auntie Ruth. Another time when I was young, she told me that God told her that He didn't approve of me dating a boy outside of our district." She smiled. "I don't think it was so much that God didn't approve, but that my parents and Auntie Ruth didn't approve." She shrugged. "That boy was your father, and all is *gut*."

"I'll go on to the barn. I just wanted you to know what she said."

"I wouldn't give it too much concern, Aaron. I love Auntie Ruth, but we all know she is a little—different."

⟋⟍

By Saturday, Leah was more than ready to go on a picnic—with anyone.

She packed the chicken salad sandwiches she'd made, along with some chips, sweet pickles, and two pieces of apple pie that Kathleen made the day before. She added two paper plates and some napkins, then closed the wooden lid on top.

"Leah?" Her mother walked to where Leah was standing at the kitchen counter, then placed a hand on her arm. "Your *daed* said that your chicken salad is quite *gut* and that he very much appreciates the way you have been making him lunch this week." She paused, grimacing a bit. "But he was wondering if, perhaps, you could make him something different next week."

Leah smiled. "I guess I finally mastered something in the kitchen, and I went a little overboard."

"Did you make chicken salad sandwiches for your picnic with Aaron today?"

"*Ya*, I did. I also made a tomato pie, *Mamm*, but it didn't come out right." Leah pointed to the pie on the kitchen counter, with one slice missing. "I tried it, and it doesn't taste anything like yours and Kathleen's. It tastes—grainy. So I snatched two pieces of apple pie that Kathleen made, instead."

Her mother picked up the pie and inspected it. "It looks fine, Leah."

"Taste it." Leah pulled a fork from the drawer and handed it to her mother. Then she watched her mother's face wince with displeasure. "See, I told you. It's not right at all."

"Leah, you are to *sprinkle* basil, parsley flakes, thyme leaves, oregano, onion powder, a little brown sugar, and some salt and pepper over the tomatoes. How much of the herbs did you sprinkle? Particularly, how much pepper?" Marian placed the pie back on the counter.

"Until it covered the tomatoes."

Her mother dismissed the subject with a wave of her hand. "We will work on this another time. For today, I'm sure Aaron will be very pleased with your chicken salad."

"Tomato pie is Aaron's favorite. I wish it had turned out." She stared at the pie and thought about the extra time she put in this morning to make it. *I could have been working on my story.*

"Are—are you and Aaron possibly starting a courtship?" Her mother's voice sounded hopeful but hesitant. Rightly so.

"No. We're just friends." Leah shrugged. "He's nice enough, I reckon."

Marian smiled. "He is certainly handsome."

"I miss Clare and Donna, *Mamm*. I hope *Daed* will let me have lunch with them soon."

"Your sister is much better, and you've been taking on your share of the household chores. I'm sure your father will come around soon." She paused. "But, Leah, he will expect you to continue doing your share of the work around here even after he releases you from your punishment."

Leah knew this to be true. And while she'd mastered chicken salad, she'd messed up everything else she'd tried to cook. Edna had resumed the sewing tasks, since Leah couldn't seem to sew a straight line or even hem a pair of breeches. Mary Carol practically forbade Leah to help her in the garden ever since she'd accidentally pulled up her sister's herbs, mistaking them for weeds. And Kathleen loved to do the cooking, so Leah didn't see why everyone was so insistent that she learn how.

"I just wish there was something for me to do that I'm more—

more suited to." She turned and faced her mother. "Like writing my stories, *Mamm*. I think that maybe someday they will touch someone, help them to find the Lord, or maybe—"

"Leah, these tales you weave . . . it is a fine hobby. But it does not prepare you to be a proper *fraa* some day. What will you feed your husband and children? Will you not have your own garden? Will your home not be clean and well tended? What about clothes for your husband and children? Have you thought about all these things and how important these skills are in our community?"

"*Ya, Mamm*. I guess so." Leah sighed. "But if I have to do all these things, I'd rather not get married."

"Leah. Now, don't say that. You know you don't mean it."

"*Ya*, I do! When I get married—a long time from now—my husband will have to allow me time to write my stories and live on chicken salad sandwiches."

Her mother hung her head, but when she looked up, she was smiling. "Leah, you will find your way."

Leah had heard her mother and Edna both say that before. Didn't they understand? *This is my way.*

"I think I hear Aaron pulling up," her mother said as she glanced out the open window in the kitchen. "Go, and have a *gut* time."

Leah picked up the picnic basket, kissed her mother on the cheek, and headed out the door.

Chapter Twelve

AARON RECALLED HIS CONVERSATION IN THE BARN WITH Abner that morning. "You better hope that Edna or one of the other girls prepared your picnic lunch." Then his brother had laughed.

He watched Leah toting the picnic basket out to his buggy, and he really didn't care what was in it. The sunlight danced across her angelic face, and there was, as always, a bounce in her step. When she smiled, Aaron could see her dimples, even from across the yard.

"I made chicken salad," she said proudly. She handed him the picnic basket. He placed it on the storage rack on the back of his courting buggy, then helped her in.

"I tried to make you a tomato pie, but . . ." She shrugged, then smoothed the wrinkles from her apron and folded her hands on her lap. "It just didn't taste like it was supposed to."

Aaron was touched that she would attempt to make him a tomato pie. He let his mind drift and pictured himself and Leah as a married couple. What would he eat? Even as the thought crossed his mind, Aaron knew he was going to do everything in his power to win her over. He gave his horse a flick of the reins.

"I love chicken salad." He smiled.

After a few moments of silence, she asked, "So what did you think about my second story? Did you like it as much as the first?"

Aaron had already pondered his situation. If he gave up all his sleep, finished the book, then met her today, they'd have no reason to meet again—unless she gave him yet another book to read, and he knew he couldn't keep this up. "I haven't finished it, Leah."

The disappointment registered on her face instantly.

"But I will." He smiled. *As soon as we spend enough time together for you to get to know me.*

"It's all right," she said as she turned toward him. "I know you probably need sleep. *Mei daed* has me doing all these chores I never used to do, and I am finding less and less time to write my books. I'm too tired at night." Her face twisted into a scowl. "And I don't like that."

"I guess you'll write your stories if it's important enough to you." Aaron carefully crossed Lincoln Highway. As they passed the Gordonville Bookstore, he said, "Maybe your books will be in that store someday."

"*Ach!* Wouldn't that be something?" Her dimples puckered inward. "So many *Englisch* tourists visit that store. They'd buy my book and maybe somehow find their way to the Lord. If I helped one person seek out God, wouldn't that be wonderful?"

Aaron couldn't understand why that was so important to her, especially since ministering was not their way. But the thought seemed to thrill her so much, he didn't want to spoil the moment. "*Ya,* I suppose it would be wonderful."

"How far did you get? In the book?"

"The fourth chapter. Amos and Annie are, uh . . ." Suddenly he felt awkward. "They're on the picnic."

It was her story, so obviously she knew that Amos and Annie shared their first kiss while they were at the picnic. Aaron found his eyes drawn instantly to Leah's lips. He quickly looked away.

"Oh." Her cheeks flushed as she stared straight ahead. "That's a very *gut* part of the story."

"Do they fall in *lieb?*" Now Aaron was blushing.

Leah turned toward him and pointed a finger in his direction. "No, no, no. I can't tell you."

Aaron chuckled. "Aw, come on . . ."

She folded her hands in her lap, then swiveled to face him. "What do you think?"

"I think that if all your stories have happy endings, then I reckon they fall in *lieb*." Aaron turned onto an unnamed dirt road that led to what he believed would be the perfect picnic spot. He'd spent his lunch hour this past week trying to find the ideal spot to take Leah. Somewhere shady, hidden away, and romantic. And he'd found that perfect place at his cousin's farm.

"Where are we going?" she asked, neither confirming nor denying that the characters in her book did indeed fall in love.

"My cousin's place. Leroy and his family are in Ohio, and I know he won't mind if we have a picnic by his pond."

The unpaved road narrowed, and trees arched overhead in a picturesque display, blocking the bright sun as they neared the long driveway that led to his cousin's farm. Aaron pulled into the gravel entrance and followed it almost up to the farmhouse, then veered to their left across the pasture.

"The wildflowers here are beautiful!" Leah eyed the stretch of meadow leading down to the pond.

Aaron knew this would be the perfect place. He pointed toward the water, surrounded by tall greenery, and toward a patch of trees off to the side of a wooden deck that stretched across the pond. "I was thinkin' that under those trees would be a *gut* spot. At least we'll have some shade." He ran his sleeve across his forehead. "Maybe it's too hot for a picnic. I'll be ready for some lemonade or tea." He pulled the buggy to a stop as close to one of the trees as he could, then jumped down and secured his horse. When he turned back to offer Leah a hand down, her face was puckered into a frown. He thought it was kind of cute the way her dimples showed even when she frowned. "What's wrong?"

She latched onto his hand and hopped down. "I forgot to bring anything to drink. And I didn't bring a blanket or anything to sit on."

Aaron recalled Abner telling him about the picnic he went on with Edna, complete with wet towels for cleanup afterward. He smiled. "It's no problem. I'll just walk up to the house and get us something to drink and something to sit on."

"Sorry." She shrugged.

"While I'm gone, would you fill this up and give ol' Pete a drink from the pond?" He handed her a metal bucket from the back. "It's so hot, I reckon he could use a drink."

"*Ya*, of course." She took the bucket and started to walk toward the pond.

"Don't fall in while I'm gone," he teased. "Back shortly."

Leah swung the small bucket all the way to the pond, leaned down, and dipped it into the water. Then she set it down, cupped her hands, and pooled some of the water up to her face. It wasn't cool water or fit for her to drink, but it was wet and felt good against her hot skin.

She carried the water back to the horse and offered it to him. "Pete, you're thirsty, no?"

After the horse emptied the bucket, Leah returned it to the storage rack behind the buggy, then eyed the wildflowers—orange, yellow, and pink buds nestled among towering green stems. She found a thick cluster of pink blooms in the middle of the meadow and lay down, thankful to God for the beauty that surrounded her. It felt good to be away from the house, out in the middle of the field, with only the cows voicing an occasional hello. She crossed her ankles and propped her hands behind her head. A breeze rustled through the flowers, and she thought about Rose in her story, how she loved the flowery meadows. Maybe Aaron was right. Maybe she did write some of her own personality into Rose's character.

She breathed in the moment. *Thank You, Lord, for this beautiful land You've given us, that calms us and nourishes us.* She propped herself up on her elbows, opened her eyes, and peered toward the house. She could see the front door still open, so she figured Aaron must be rounding up a blanket and something to drink. *I can't believe I forgot the lemonade.*

Leah glanced to her left. All was quiet, except for two brown cows grazing in the next pasture. Leah lay back down and closed her eyes.

                                        ᘒᘓᘒ

Aaron made his way across the front yard after locating a blanket and filling a thermos with lemonade, thankful his cousin didn't feel the need to lock his farmhouse door.

Aaron knew Leroy wouldn't mind the intrusion, especially if there was a young woman involved. He was always encouraging Aaron to find a wife and didn't understand his fascination with Leah. "She doesn't seem like the marrying kind to me," Leroy had said.

Aaron squinted and scanned the pond area, but he didn't see Leah. He draped the cumbersome brown blanket over his shoulder, got a good grip on the lemonade, and picked up his pace. *Where is she?*

Sunlight poured down from clear blue skies, and if it had been about twenty degrees cooler, it would have been a perfect day for a picnic. But he'd endure the heat for a chance to spend time with Leah. He tipped his straw hat back to have a better look across the meadow filled with colorful wildflowers, and as he left the yard and entered the pasture, he spotted her lying amid green leafy foliage topped with orange, yellow, and pink blooms. She looked like an angel, with her arms stretched high above her head, her dark blue dress in clear contrast against the colors around her.

Aaron smiled. *Only Leah would do something like this*, he thought as he neared her. He expected her to stand up at any moment, stretch her arms out, and gracefully waltz through the meadow, as Rose had done in her story. It was a perfect moment, watching her like this.

"I got the lemonade!" he hollered as he got within a few yards of her. "And a blanket."

No response. Aaron stopped a few feet away from her, his feet rooted to the ground.

"Leah!"

She didn't move, and suddenly Leah didn't look so angelic, and the soft swishing of the tall grass amid the flowers seemed eerie and sent a chill through him. He thought about Edna and how she'd been rushed to the hospital, barely able to breathe. Auntie Ruth's words had lingered in his mind all week too. *I might drop dead right over there, amidst the wildflowers in the pasture.*

Aaron dropped the blanket and the thermos, and his hat flew off as he dashed toward her, fell down in the grass beside her, and pulled her forcefully into his arms.

"Leah!"

She screamed, piercing his eardrum. "Aaron Lantz, let go of me! What in the world are you doing?"

Chapter Thirteen

LEAH FOUGHT TO WRIGGLE OUT OF AARON'S STRONG arms, pushing her hands into his chest and putting some distance between them, but one arm still cradled the small of her back, and an unfamiliar sensation swept over her. She stared into eyes wild with—with something.

"Aaron Lantz, what are you doing?" She shoved him back, stumbled to her feet, and brushed the powdery flower residue from her dress. "It wonders me if maybe you're not crazy!"

Aaron rose to his feet, put his hands on his hips, and stared into her eyes. "I thought you were . . ." He took a deep breath.

"Thought I was what?" She couldn't help but smile at how distraught he looked, for reasons she didn't understand. "I love this time of year, when all the wildflowers are in bloom. And I feel close to God when I lie on His precious earth. What in the world came over you?" She glanced over his shoulder. "Would that be our lemonade and blanket back there?" Leah was starting to question whether this picnic was a good idea.

Aaron pulled off his hat and wiped his forehead with his sleeve, something he did too much of. Didn't the man own a handkerchief? Then, without warning, he latched onto her hand and pulled her along beside him.

"I'll explain later. Let's go have our picnic."

His hand was strong, and although she was surprised by his aggressiveness, she didn't feel compelled to pull from his grasp. When they reached the blanket and the toppled thermos of lemonade, Aaron let go of her hand and picked up the thermos. He twisted off the attached cup and poured her a cup of lemonade.

"Here," he said, handing it to her. Then he chuckled.

Leah swigged the entire cupful and handed it back to him. "What's so funny?"

Aaron shook his head. "My crazy Auntie Ruth."

"Huh?"

He poured himself some lemonade and swigged it down in one gulp, then reattached the cup to the thermos. He picked up the blanket and swung it over his shoulder. "I'll explain later. Let's go spread this underneath the trees by the pond. I'm starving. What about you?"

"I reckon I'm a little hungry," she said as she cut her eyes in his direction. But as they walked toward the cluster of trees near the pond, Leah couldn't seem to shake the feel of his arms wrapped tightly around her earlier. She'd never been that close to a boy. And Aaron was hardly a boy. Discreetly, she allowed her eyes to dart in his direction and took in his tall stance, the way his blue shirt almost looked too small as his muscles rippled beneath it, the confident way he walked. Despite the scorching heat, a shiver ran down her spine. *What is happening to me?*

Aaron spread the blanket beneath the trees and motioned for her to sit. Then he walked to the buggy and retrieved the picnic basket. After he placed it on the blanket next to the thermos of lemonade, he sat down beside her.

"Do you want to tell me what all that nonsense was about?" Leah used her most demanding voice, even though she was secretly wishing they could replay the entire scene.

"Can we eat first?" Even his smile now sent a wave of something unfamiliar streaming through her veins.

She sat up taller, folded her hands in her lap. "I'm not sure I can eat until you tell me exactly what caused your strange behavior."

Aaron opened one of the wooden flaps on the top of the picnic basket, closed one eye, and playfully squinted into the basket. "Please, can't we eat first?"

Leah shook her head and shrugged. "I reckon so." She pushed his hand out of the way and pulled out two paper plates, then placed a sandwich on each plate, along with some chips and a sweet pickle. "I have apple pie too."

"I'm impressed." He grinned before taking a large bite of the chicken salad.

"Don't be. Kathleen made the pie." Leah picked up her sandwich, started to take a bite, then stopped, noticing that Aaron had already eaten half of his sandwich. "You've probably heard that I'm not exactly a very *gut* cook."

He swallowed, then grinned. "*Ya*, I've heard that." He paused. "Not much of a seamstress or gardener, either. That's what I'm told."

Leah slammed her sandwich down on the paper plate. "Then why did you even want to come here with me on this picnic? I'm sure *Hannah* could have prepared you a much better lunch." Leah regretted the statement the minute she said it.

Aaron ignored the comment. "I'm startin' to think that everyone's not been real truthful with me about your cooking. This is the best chicken salad I've ever had. And I mean that."

Leah took another bite of her sandwich, chewed, then swallowed. She smiled. "It really is good, isn't it?"

Aaron nodded.

When they'd finished, Leah pulled out the two pieces of apple pie and handed one to Aaron. "Compliments of Kathleen," she said. "Sorry my tomato pie didn't turn out."

"Not everyone can make tomato pie like Hannah." He grinned, then raised the piece of pie to his mouth and took a big bite.

Leah felt her face reddening. *Oh, you just wait. I will be making you a tomato pie—better than Hannah's.*

"I reckon not," she responded curtly. "Now, tell me why you assaulted me in the field."

Aaron held up one finger, indicating that she wait. He finished chewing, then slowly licked a pie crumb from his mouth. Leah watched his tongue slide across his bottom lip, and her pulse quickened. She put a hand to her chest, as if that might slow her heart rate.

"Let's finish eating first," he finally said.

When they were done and everything was loaded back into the picnic basket, Aaron stretched out on the blanket, leaned back on his elbows, and crossed his ankles. Leah sat Indian-style beside him, arms folded across her chest, facing him.

"Well?"

Aaron sighed, and his mouth twitched on one side. "I know it's gonna sound dumb, but I thought—well, I thought maybe something was wrong with you."

"What?"

He shook his head. "Auntie Ruth, who is a little nuts, told me a few days ago that she thinks she's gonna die soon, and that she hopes it's in a field full of wildflowers. And when I saw you there, you weren't moving, and I guess that was on my mind, and—and, I don't know. It just made me fearful for a minute."

Leah laughed out loud. "You thought I was *dead?*"

"I told you. It was dumb."

Then Leah gasped. "*Ach!* Is something wrong with Auntie Ruth?"

Aaron shook his head. "No, she ain't sick or nothing. She's just—just off in the head sometimes."

She smiled again. "You thought I was dead."

Tongue in cheek, Aaron sat there quietly for a moment. "*Ya.* As dumb as it sounds, I guess I did for a minute." Then his expression turned serious. "It ain't funny, Leah."

Leah stifled her grin, both amused and touched by his chivalry. "Okay," she said.

They were both quiet for a few moments.

BETH WISEMAN

"I like Auntie Ruth. Tell me all about her," Leah said after a while.

᠎

For the next hour, Aaron filled Leah in about Auntie Ruth—everything from the ferrets and motorcycle to her almost joining a convent. They'd both laughed, and eventually Leah had gotten comfortable on the blanket, resting her head on her hand as she lay on her side and faced him. Aaron wanted to hold her hand, but it had taken her this long just to seem relaxed and comfortable.

"Well, I just love her," she said, when Aaron took a break from telling stories. "She is an odd *Englisch* person, for sure. But I wish I could spend more time with her while she's here."

Aaron's mind began to work on ways to make that happen. It couldn't be a quilting, sisters' day, tea party, or other event for only the ladies. He wanted to assure himself another day in Leah's company.

"Auntie Ruth loves to go eat pizza at Paradiso. Maybe we can take her there for supper one night?"

Leah laughed. "Or maybe she can take us in that fancy car of hers?" Her eyes twinkled. "Even if her driving is a little scary."

Aaron chuckled, thrilled at the opportunity to spend more time with Leah. Even if it did mean they'd have Auntie Ruth in tow.

They decided on Wednesday night. Leah said she'd have to clear it with her father, since she'd been doing extra chores since Edna got sick, but Aaron was hopeful that James Petersheim would give his permission. They spent the next two hours talking about Leah's books, and Aaron loved the way her face glowed when she described her characters. He relished the warm sensation he had when he was in her presence.

Chapter Fourteen

JAMES WATCHED MARIAN STOMP ACROSS THE FRONT YARD and toward the barn, her expression familiar. Those beautiful lips of hers were pinched together and curved into a frown. She was about to scold him for something, and James strained his mind to think what he might have done to irritate her.

He finished washing his hands at the pump outside the barn, flung them a few times in the hot air, then wiped them on his pants. "And what brings *mei* lovely *fraa* out to the barn when it's nearly suppertime?" He raised his eyebrows and grinned, hoping to lighten her mood.

Marian stopped in front of him and planted her hands on her hips. "James Petersheim, you cannot punish Leah to the house when it suits you, then allow her to go out with Aaron. She just told me that you said she could go out with Aaron and his aunt tonight." She pulled off her black sunglasses and stared him down. "It ain't right to keep the girl from her other friends but agree to let her spend time with Aaron."

James tugged on his beard for a moment. "She likes to run with those *Englisch* girls, and when she ain't doin' that, she's writing those stories. I like it better when she's here working, like she's supposed to be. She's been slacking with her chores again, and you know that."

"Yet you allow her to go out with Aaron?"

James hung his head slightly, then looked back up at her. "That boy might be Leah's only chance for marriage. How can I say no?"

Her look softened, but not much. "James . . ." She shook her head. "Finish up out here. Kathleen has supper ready."

Screeching tires pulled their attention to the Cadillac turning onto the driveway, and they both watched the automobile come barreling down the drive as if there was some sort of emergency. The car pulled to a halt with a jerk.

"That looks like Aaron in the front seat," Marian said. "I reckon that big-haired woman driving is Ruth?"

James shrugged as he and Marian waited for their visitors to exit the vehicle.

"Hello, hello!" The woman was dressed most peculiarly, and James recognized her right away as she crossed the yard and came toward them, waving.

He cautiously waved a hand in her direction. She was wearing bright pink breeches that hit her about midcalf, and her blouse sported more colors than a full rainbow. She had on big gold fancy rings and loud dangly bracelets to match.

Ruth.

"James and Marian, how *gut* to see you both!" She thrust her hand at James, and he hesitantly took hold, thinking it just didn't sound right for her to be using the Dutch. "Been a long time. I didn't see you at the hospital. That nurse wouldn't let us in the back where you were with Edna. And I don't think I saw you during my last couple of visits. So *gut* to be here." She finally released his hand and offered Marian the same forceful handshake.

James saw Aaron shuffling up behind her, his face red as fire. *Poor boy.* He needn't be embarrassed for his aunt.

Aaron extended his hand to James. "Hello, sir."

James shook hands with the young man he hoped to be his future son-in-law. He was sure praying about it. "Leah's inside, Aaron. I reckon she'll be out any minute." He glanced at the car. "Pretty sure she heard ya comin'."

"Isn't it dandy that these two young people invited me to Paradiso for supper?" She nudged James, enough to cause him to lose his footing. "Not sure why they want me around." She chuckled.

Normally James might have found her comment offensive, but it was Ruth. He'd known Ruth since he was a boy. She had already converted to *Englisch* by the time James was born, but she was always at family gatherings and continued to make her trips to Lancaster County.

"I'm sure the three of you will have a lovely time," Marian said.

James could tell by his wife's expression that she was surprised to see Ruth accompanying the young people to supper, and so was he. "Are you enjoyin' your visit, Ruth?" James glanced toward the house but saw no Leah. *Leave it to that girl to be late for her own funeral someday.*

Ruth puckered her red lips into a circle, sucked in an abnormal amount of air, and then blew it out extra slow. "For as much time as I have left," she said, her brows drawing together.

"What . . ." James scratched his forehead.

"There's Leah!" Aaron yelled over James. He grabbed his aunt by the arm. "Let's go, Auntie Ruth." He pulled her toward the car. "Nice to see you both." Aaron tipped his hat in James and Marian's direction.

James nodded as Aaron opened the car door for his aunt, then walked around to open the front door for Leah. "I'll sit in the back," he told Leah, who giggled.

"You think it's safer back there, no?" James heard his daughter say to Aaron, who smiled. They were clearly getting along, and James knew he'd made the right decision to allow Leah to spend time with Aaron, with or without his nutty aunt.

James and Marian watched Ruth maneuver the car down the driveway in the same fashion as she'd arrived, and James could see heads bobbing.

"Do you think they're all right in a car with her?" Marian clutched his arm. "That woman has never been quite right."

James smiled. "I think they'll be just fine."

BETH WISEMAN

Leah braced her hands against the dash when Auntie Ruth pulled into the parking spot at the restaurant. She twisted her head around and grinned at Aaron. This was great fun already, and they'd only just arrived. Not much was said on the short drive to the restaurant. Auntie Ruth mostly sang to the radio and danced in her seat.

Paradiso was her parents' favorite place to go on the rare occasion that they ventured to town for supper. Leah had only been here twice, so this was a treat on several levels. A good meal. Some time with Auntie Ruth. And she had to admit she was looking forward to being around Aaron. But the bonus was that she'd gotten word to Donna and Clare that she would be here.

Leah knew to clip a note to the mailbox when she needed a message to reach one of her *Englisch* friends, and Charles the mailman would deliver it. Usually it was just a note requesting a car ride, but the system worked just as well for something like this. She grabbed the plastic bag she'd brought with her and reached for the handle on the car door just as Aaron pulled it open for her.

"Whatcha got there?" He eyed the plastic bag, and his expression took on a hint of worry. "Leah, I haven't finished the second book yet."

Leah rolled her eyes but grinned. "It's not for *you*."

"I can smell manicotti!" Auntie Ruth slammed her car door, threw a big pink purse over her shoulder, and headed toward the entrance, where Leah and Aaron met up with her. "Do you eat manicotti, honey?" She clutched Leah's arm, and before Leah had a chance to respond, Ruth said, "You must. It's the best here."

Leah nodded, since the way Ruth advised her about the manicotti seemed a matter of life or death. The only Italian food Leah had ever heard of was pizza.

Aaron pulled the door open for the two of them. A Seat Yourself sign met them in the entrance, and Ruth made her way down the middle aisle of the restaurant, lined with booths on both sides and tables in the middle. It probably wouldn't be considered fancy to the *Englisch*, but Leah thought it was very nice. There were colorful placemats on the tables, and televisions in opposite corners of the room. The patrons were mostly *Englisch*, but Leah noticed two Amish families dining to her left.

They'd only taken a few steps when Leah saw Donna and Clare in a booth against the wall to her right. *You made it!* Ruth passed by the girls, but Leah stopped at the booth, whispering to Aaron that she would join them in a minute. Ruth chose a table for four in the middle aisle.

"We got your note!" Donna said. "Where've you been? I left a message on the phone in your barn, but I didn't hear back. Is everything okay?" Donna moved over to make room for Leah to sit beside her.

Leah put the plastic bag on the table and eased in beside her friend. "*Ya*, everything is all right. But *mei daed* has made me stay around the house since Edna got sick." Leah briefly filled them in about Edna's asthma.

"Who's the Amish hottie over there?" Clare nodded toward Aaron. "He's a babe. Are you two dating?"

"No. We're just friends. *Daed* allows me to go out with him because I think he's hoping we'll start to court, but you know how I feel about that. Too soon to be tied down."

Clare cocked her head to one side and gazed at Aaron. "I don't know, Leah. I think I'd have to give it a try. He's too cute not to."

Leah looked toward Aaron, who was chatting with Ruth. Then she turned her attention back to Clare, who was still mesmerized by Aaron. "I reckon he's not bad looking." The image of Aaron's arms around her waist in the pasture flashed in Leah's mind.

"Is he nice?" Donna sat up a little taller and eyed Aaron. "And who is that with you guys?"

"*Ya*, he's nice. We're friends. But that's all." She paused and pulled the stack of handwritten papers from the bag. "And that's his Aunt Ruth. She's visiting from Florida." She slid the story sideways until it was in front of Donna. "This is the book I was telling you about."

"Oh." Donna eyed the title. "*A Walk in My Shoes*. Sounds nice."

"It's about an Amish girl and her *Englisch* friend, and there's also a love story." Leah smiled. "But the best part is the way that the *Englisch* girl finds her way to the Lord, and how her life changes when that happens." Leah couldn't wait for her friends to read the book. "Aaron read it, and he seemed to really like it."

"*He* read it?" Clare's eyes grew wide.

"*Ya*, why do you look so shocked?" Leah rested her elbow on the table and supported her chin.

"Oh, I don't know. He just doesn't look like the reading type." Clare shrugged. "He just looks more—more the manly type."

"He said he loved the book. And I think both of you will too." She glanced back and forth between the two of them. "I can't wait for us to be able to talk about what you think after you read it. I think there are so many messages, messages that God wanted me to put in the book. It just felt so right to put the story into words, and—"

"Okay. Sure." Donna put the book back into the plastic bag and pushed it to the edge of the table, next to the wall. "I'll read it first."

"I better go to my table." Leah gently touched Donna's hand. "I've missed you both. Hopefully, it won't be long until *mei daed* will not be so strict with me. I'd love to meet you for a movie soon."

"Call us," Clare said. "We've missed you too."

Leah excused herself, stood up, and joined Aaron and Ruth. "I'm sorry. Those are two of my dear friends that I haven't seen in a while." She sat down in the chair in between Aaron and Ruth. Her eyes drifted in Aaron's direction, and she saw his mouth twitch a bit. *He's nervous.* Leah felt a little nervous herself, all of a sudden, as their eyes met and held for a moment.

"Manicotti for everyone!" Auntie Ruth bellowed when the waitress walked up.

"Auntie Ruth, don't you think we should give Leah time to look at the menu? She might not want manicotti." Aaron looked up at the waitress and smiled.

And Leah found it bothersome the way the *Englisch* waitress smiled back at Aaron, her light-colored hair draping down around her shoulders and framing her bright blue eyes. Leah suddenly felt even plainer than usual. *Stop looking at her.*

Leah silently scolded herself for allowing such feelings of jealousy into her mind. And it had been happening a lot lately.

"Mani—manicotti—is fine for me." She could feel a flush in her cheeks. "Did I say that right?" She turned toward Ruth, who was gathering up all their menus.

"Yep. You did. Here, hon." Ruth handed the menus to the pretty girl who couldn't seem to take her eyes off of Aaron. "Three teas too." Ruth leaned toward the waitress. "That's all, dear."

"Sorry," Aaron said to Leah. Then he turned to Ruth. "Auntie Ruth, you didn't even give Leah a chance to pick something."

Ruth puckered her red lips as her eyes widened. "Now, Aaron Lantz, why in the world would Leah want to order something else when the manicotti is the best thing on the menu?" She shook her head and turned toward Leah. "Honey, you wouldn't have wanted to do that, now would you?" She leaned back in her chair and folded her arms across her large chest. "I mean, think about it . . . Aaron and I would be having the manicotti, and you would have settled for something not nearly as good. Wouldn't have been right."

"I might have chosen something besides the manicotti too," Aaron mumbled.

Auntie Ruth didn't seem to hear him. She pulled her big pink bag from where it hung on the back of her chair and slammed it down on the table.

"Now, prepare yourselves, young people." Ruth leaned in closer and in a whisper said, "I have something to show you."

Chapter Fifteen

AARON BRACED HIMSELF FOR WHATEVER RUTH WAS ABOUT to show them, and wondered if using her as an excuse to see Leah was really going to be worth it. No telling what she might pull out of that bag of hers.

He glanced at Leah. Her smile stretched across her face, and somehow Aaron knew that whatever it was, Leah wouldn't be offended or embarrassed. She seemed in awe of Aaron's crazy aunt.

Ruth eased her hand into the bag and, as if to build tension, glanced back and forth between Aaron and Leah. "Are you ready?" She batted long black eyelashes at them. Then she took a deep breath and pulled her hand from the bag with a jerk.

Aaron thought he might fall out of his chair. He put a hand across his eyes and shook his head. But when he heard Leah giggle, he spread his fingers and viewed the object again.

"Ain't this the darnedest thing?" Ruth held up a stuffed pink cat as long as her arm. "I found this little critter at a shop in town. If you push this button, he sings and dances up a storm." Ruth fumbled around the back of the pink cat.

"Auntie Ruth, don't push that button." Aaron pulled his hand from his eyes and glared at her with enough of a warning that Ruth stopped her search for the switch.

"Well, all right." Ruth shrugged and stuffed the cat back into her oversized pink bag. "I'll show it to you later, Leah, when Mister Stuffy Pants isn't around."

Leah put one hand to her mouth, clearly holding back a giggle.

The manicotti arrived a few minutes later, and it was good, as

Ruth had predicted. For the next forty-five minutes, Leah hung on Ruth's every word as she detailed her travels and odd adventures. Aaron didn't think Leah had ever looked more beautiful. Twice she'd looked at him with a twinkle in her eye and smiled.

"Now, I reckon I best get to the ladies' room before we get back on the road." Ruth pushed her chair back.

"Me too," Leah said. "Be right back."

As Leah followed Ruth to the women's restroom, Aaron smiled. The two women were different in so many ways, but both had a spirited way of looking at life. He took a sip of his tea and thought about how he might be able to set up another date with Leah . . . without referring to it as a date, of course.

Paradiso was clearing out, but Leah's two friends were still in the booth nearby. He could hear them chatting quietly, and he didn't mean to eavesdrop, but when he heard Leah's name mentioned, he couldn't help but tune in. He smiled when he heard one of the girls say what a sweet person Leah was.

"But I wish she wouldn't force all this religious stuff on us," Aaron heard the other girl say. "I mean, she's fun to hang out with when she's not preaching. And now she wants us to read her Amish book? I don't think so."

But it's not an Amish book. It's about love, kindness, special friendships, and a relationship with the Lord.

"I agree. Leah is nice enough, but I'm not buying into all this religious junk."

Aaron cut his eyes briefly in their direction, long enough to see them stepping away from the booth and heading to the exit door.

Leah's book.

They'd left it in the plastic bag, pushed up against the wall, as if it weren't anything special at all. *It's her only copy, and it's very special.*

Aaron acted quickly. He grabbed the bag filled with handwritten lined white pages—words Leah had toiled over until a

BETH WISEMAN

perfect tale of love and God's blessings had spilled onto the pages. He scurried back to his seat, and he could hear Ruth's voice around the corner.

His urge to protect Leah overwhelmed him. *It's a good book.* He stood up, leaned over, and stuffed the plastic bag as far down in Ruth's giant bag as he could get it, amid items he was sure he didn't want to see. Aaron threw himself back into his chair right before the two women entered the room.

"I just love your aunt," Leah whispered when she sat down. "She's delightful."

"You're delightful." It just slipped out, and Aaron silently blasted himself for being so forward. But Leah's dimples shone with approval.

James peered out his bedroom window, straining to see into the darkness.

"Are you spying on our *maedel?*" Marian wrapped her arms around his waist and leaned her head around him to see. "They were gone for a good bit."

"*Ya.*" James watched Aaron walk Leah to the door, but once they hit the porch, James could no longer see them from the upstairs window. The car headlights lit up the front yard, and James thought about what an entertaining supper it must have been with Ruth.

"Perhaps they are becoming more than friends, no?" Marian pulled away from him and moved toward the bed. James followed her, rubbed his beard, and waited for his wife to pull back the covers.

He grinned. "I hope so."

James turned on the small battery-operated fan on his night table and sat down on the bed. He stretched his legs atop the covers, crossed his ankles, and yawned. Marian dimmed the lantern and snuggled up next to him, kissed him on the cheek, and then moved to her side of the bed. They both bowed their heads in silent prayer.

James thanked the Lord for the many blessings in his life, and once he was done with his usual prayers, he added a special request.

Please, dear Father, help Leah to master the skills necessary for her to be a gut fraa. *Help her to realize her place and to stop wasting her time with these silly stories she writes. Guide her, Lord, and help her to be a responsible young Amish woman. In Jesus' name, I pray.*

"Good night, my love." Marian extinguished the lantern.

James locked his hands behind his head and faced the small fan, the gentle breeze a small relief from the stifling heat. "Good night."

∽∾∿

Aaron climbed into the front seat with Ruth after he walked Leah to the door. There was an awkward but wonderful moment when Leah's eyes had fused with his in a way that made him think that they were becoming more than just friends.

"So did you ask her out again?" Ruth peeled down the driveway.

"*Ya,* I did. Worship service is at our *haus* this Sunday. I asked her if she'd like to take a buggy ride to Bird-in-Hand after the meal." He paused, checked his seat belt, and grabbed the dash as Ruth rounded the corner.

"She's a fine girl. Spunky." Ruth turned toward Aaron. He wished she'd keep her eyes on the road. "But Aaron, Leah isn't your ordinary Amish girl. As a matter of fact, I'm not seeing where you two have much in common." She stared straight ahead again. "You're rather boring compared to her."

"What?" Aaron twisted in his seat to face her. "How can you say that to me?"

Ruth shrugged. "I love ya, Aaron." She hesitated. "Actually, you're my favorite, but don't tell the others. Anyway, you just strike me as the kind of young man who is gonna want a woman to cook for ya, sew, tend to your house, and be, well—traditional." Ruth chuckled. "I didn't have to spend much time with Leah to realize that she ain't real traditional. And I've heard your sisters speak of her. When they heard we were all going out to supper, I heard Annie telling Mary that the two of you weren't a very good match."

How dare they? "Leah and I would make a fine match." Aaron sat taller and looped his thumbs in his suspenders. "And I'm not boring."

"Maybe that was a bad choice of words. But you ain't spunky like she is. And there's nothing wrong with that."

"It's one of the things I like about Leah, her free spirit."

Ruth pulled into the Lantz driveway. "From what she said tonight, I don't think that father of hers encourages that free spirit. And Leah don't strike me as someone who's gonna be tamed into something she's not."

Aaron thought about what Ruth was saying, surprised at how much sense his aunt was trying to make, even if she was wrong about him. "I wouldn't try to change her, Auntie Ruth."

Ruth turned the car off and grabbed her big pink bag, then Aaron remembered.

"*Ach*, Auntie Ruth. I stuffed something in your purse when you were in the bathroom with Leah."

She pushed open her car door, draped one foot out the door, but turned to look at him, her nose crinkling with displeasure. "Like the silverware, or what?"

Aaron grunted. "No." He pointed to her purse. "There's a plastic bag filled with papers. It's one of Leah's stories. Her *Englisch* friends left it on the table at Paradiso. I'll give it to her on Sunday, but I didn't want to make the night bad by telling her that her friends left something so important behind."

Ruth dug around to the bottom of the bag and pulled out the plastic bag. "I thought this purse felt heavier." She glanced at Aaron. "Have you read this?"

"*Ya*. It's *gut*."

They sat quietly in the dark for a moment. "Think Leah would mind if I read it?"

Aaron shrugged. "She seems to want people to read it. I reckon it'd be all right."

Ruth put the bag back in her purse, then groaned as she lifted herself to a standing position. Aaron eased out of his seat, and they both closed the car doors and began walking toward the house.

"I'll read it tonight. I might be dead tomorrow or the next day."

"Why do you keep saying things like that, Auntie Ruth?" Aaron shook his head, then latched onto her arm as she walked up the porch steps. He thought about Leah lying in the meadow and how ridiculously he'd acted.

He reached for the matches on the shelf inside the kitchen door, pulled the lantern from the same place, and lit it. He held it out so Auntie Ruth could see her way into the kitchen.

She dropped the big purse on the kitchen table, put her hands on her hips, and stared hard at Aaron. "I say it because it's the truth."

Chapter Sixteen

LEAH TIED THE STRINGS ON HER *KAPP* AND RUSHED DOWN-
stairs for Sunday breakfast. She was late for the second time this
week. Everyone was seated at the table, already eating, when she
walked in. Her father didn't look up, but everyone else did.

"Why didn't you wake me up?" she whispered between clenched
teeth when she slid onto the bench beside Edna.

"I shouldn't have to." Edna didn't whisper, and Leah cut her
eyes at her sister.

"That's enough," their mother warned.

Leah was looking forward to spending time with Aaron after
worship service, for reasons that surprised her. She wasn't sure what
the point was. Aaron clearly wanted more than just friendship, and
Leah wasn't ready for that. But every time Leah thought about him,
a strange feeling overtook her.

"*Daed?*" Leah knew this wasn't the best time to approach her
father about her plans with Aaron, but once breakfast was over,
there would be morning chores, then they'd all be off to church
service.

Her father looked up.

"Aaron asked me to go for a ride to Bird-in-Hand after worship
service today. Would that be all right?"

Edna slammed her fork down on her plate, and Leah saw her
draw in a breath and press her lips together. Leah watched her father
warn Edna with his eyes. A first that she could recall.

Mary Carol and Kathleen glanced up but stayed quiet, as did
their mother.

"I reckon it will be all right," *Daed* said as he reached for a piece of bacon.

Leah fought the urge to send grumpy Edna a smug grin. "*Danki, Daed.*"

Ever since she'd started spending time with Aaron, her father didn't seem to mind what she did or didn't do around the house. She didn't mean to be late for breakfast, she'd just stayed up too late working on her book. She thought about Donna and Clare, and she couldn't wait to see what her friends thought about her story, and whether it would help the girls have a better understanding of God and how a relationship with Him would change their lives.

Ruth flipped open her big red suitcase, the one she'd purchased at the market in Tuscany. She recalled the big burly man trying to get her to pay the sticker price. *He didn't know who he was dealing with.*

It had been six months since she'd attended an Amish worship service, which was during her last visit to Paradise. She pulled out her favorite red dress with large white polka dots and glanced at her red straw hat hanging on the bedpost. *Perfect.*

As she dressed, she cursed herself for staying up almost all night to finish young Leah's story. The girl had a gift. That was for sure. But she couldn't help wonder how much this community would try to mold her into something she was not, and whether they would ever encourage her writing. Ruth thought about how difficult it was when she left the Old Order at eighteen, choosing not to seek baptism into the faith. She'd never let on to anyone, but many times she'd regretted her decision. She hoped Leah wouldn't make the same mistake. Ruth could tell that the girl had a spirit like a wild stallion, not to be harnessed. If her family would give her a little room outside the box within which they all lived, Ruth believed Leah could grow and thrive in this community. Back in Ruth's day there was no bending of the rules; an Amish girl was expected to perform a certain way, no questions asked.

But at this time in her life, so near to death, Ruth wanted to be in this peaceful place with family. *I'll be home soon, Lord.*

She pulled her hat over her gray hair, wound tightly atop her head, and covered her lips with a bright red color to match her ensemble. She looked in the small mirror hanging from a chain on the far wall. It was important to look her best each and every day. *When I go, I'm going out in style.*

She grabbed her big pink purse from the night before, dumped all the contents into an equally large red bag, then grabbed Leah's story from the dresser and stuffed it inside her purse.

Aaron helped Abner take down the removable walls that separated the den and dining room to make room for the hundred or so people who would be attending worship service at the Lantz house this morning. Every eight to nine months, it was their turn to host worship. It was the only time the walls came down, unless they were hosting a Sunday singing, which they did about twice a year.

Aaron was anxious to see Leah, but something was chewing at his insides, and he couldn't seem to shake it. *I am not boring.*

Auntie Ruth's words kept ringing in his mind, and Aaron had thought about this for half the night, until sleep finally came at around midnight. He decided that he might be a tad set in his ways. He also appreciated a schedule and enjoyed the structure in his life. But boring? *I think not.*

Then why couldn't he get the comment out of his head?

"Hurry, boys. People are starting to arrive." His mother slammed her hands on her hips and glanced at the clock on the wall. "It's almost eight o'clock, and you still don't have those walls down." She turned to head back into the kitchen, and Aaron could hear her barking orders at

Annie and Mary. He shook his head. *Now there is a person who lives a structured life,* he thought. Sarah Lantz had everything organized to perfection all the time, and she was always on schedule—with everything.

Aaron listened to his mother's voice rise a little as she told Mary that the bread in the oven must be pulled out right when the timer dinged, not a minute afterward. All of a sudden, he wondered if his mother ever did anything just for fun. Even when his father took a break to read a book, *Mamm* was always tending to something on her schedule. She never seemed to do anything that wasn't preplanned. *Am I like that?*

Aaron searched his mind for some wild, adventurous thing he'd done lately—or ever. Failing that, he tried to recall the last time he'd done something out of the ordinary or veered from his schedule. *I read Leah's book.*

He saw Leah through the window then, walking across the front yard with her family, and he determined that today would be the day he was going to show Leah Petersheim that he was anything but boring, and he would prove his aunt was wrong.

Worship service lasted three hours, as usual, with the men on one side of the room, the women on the other, and the bishop and deacons in the middle. Leah sat with her mother and sisters, and Ruth had chosen a seat next to her. She could hear Ruth's stomach growling—loudly.

"This is one thing I don't miss," Ruth whispered to Leah. "Three hours of worship on these backless benches every other Sunday."

Leah nodded, stifled a giggle. She felt sure that everyone around them heard Ruth's comment. Ruth sat a little taller in her red and white polka dot dress and matching hat and shoes. Leah had thought her mother's eyes were going to pop out of her head when she saw Ruth come downstairs earlier, making a proud grand entrance. Most everyone there knew Ruth, and it shouldn't have been a shock to anyone, but eyes bulged at the sight of her just the same.

"I hope we have ham loaf," Ruth whispered to Leah.

Leah nodded again, then looked across the room. She found Aaron, who was shaking his head but smiling. Perhaps Ruth's voice was carrying more than Leah thought.

She thought about the ride she'd be taking with Aaron after the Sunday meal and realized that she'd been looking forward to it ever since they'd all dined at Paradiso on Wednesday.

"Praise be to God!" Ruth stood up immediately after Bishop Ebersol closed the worship service in prayer.

Leah wasn't sure if Ruth meant the comment as actual praise to God in response to Bishop Ebersol's recitations or as relief that the service was over. Either way, the bishop glowered at Ruth.

She didn't seem to notice. "Let's eat," she said as she pushed ahead of the others toward the kitchen.

Following the meal, some of the older folks headed home, but a lot of the men gathered in the barn to tell jokes, and the women chatted in the kitchen and den. Rebecca Miller was organizing a volleyball game, and Leah smiled when she saw Ben standing nearby.

Leah was playing a game of croquet with a couple of the younger children when Aaron approached her from behind. She jumped when he poked her slightly in the back. "Ready to get out of here?"

She turned around. His lip was twitching, and she wondered what he was nervous about. But Leah was nervous, too, for some reason. Maybe it was the way his voice sounded when he asked her if she was ready to leave, or maybe it was the way he was looking at her. Something seemed different.

"Okay." She handed her croquet mallet to one of the children. "Let me go put my shoes on and tell *Mamm* I'm leaving."

A few minutes later Aaron flicked the reins and guided his horse down the driveway, and Leah was glad to be in the courting buggy, with no top, the wind in her face. She pushed back sweaty strands of hair that had fallen from beneath her prayer covering.

"I can't wait for fall. I know it's busy with the harvest and all.

But this heat is terrible." Leah jumped a bit when Aaron settled against his seat and dropped one hand right beside hers on the seat. As his finger brushed against hers, she wondered if he was trying to hold her hand. She lifted her hand, then folded both hands in her lap. She kept her head straight but cut her eyes downward to see his hand still sitting there, seeming even closer to her.

"*Ach.* I almost forgot." Aaron lifted his hand from the seat, reached behind him, and pulled out a bundle of roses wrapped in green tissue paper. He handed them to her and smiled. "These are for you. They're from Annie's garden. "

Leah felt the color rush to her cheeks. She'd never had a boy give her flowers before. She'd never been on an actual date before, and this was certainly a date if there were flowers involved. "*Danki,*" she said sheepishly. She glanced up at him and forced a smile as she tried to decide how she felt about this.

Aaron kept the horse at a steady gait down the winding roads toward Bird-in-Hand, and Leah gazed at meadows covered with wildflowers that seemed to connect one Amish homestead to the next. Clapboard houses, mostly white. Outbuildings, roaming cattle, silos, and a sense of home. Leah had seen enough television in town to know that there was nowhere in the world she'd rather live. Some of her Amish friends talked of leaving as soon as they could gather enough money, choosing not to seek baptism into the community. It was a decision Leah didn't understand.

She glanced at Aaron. He sat tall in his seat, like a towering spruce, and his profile was sharp and confident as he flicked the reins and picked up the pace. This was not the quiet boy from their school days, but a man who caused her heart to flutter in an unexpected way.

When his eyes met with hers, Leah knew something was happening between them, whether it was a part of her plan or not.

Chapter Seventeen

JAMES WAITED ON THE FRONT PORCH FOR MARIAN AND the girls to gather up the dishes they'd brought to the Lantzes' for the Sunday meal. What a good day it was. A fine worship service, a wonderful meal, and plenty of good company. He waved as several buggies pulled out to head for home, as he was hoping to do soon. The heavy meal had settled on him, and he was ready to relax at his own home before bedtime, perhaps take in the sunset from the front porch. Tomorrow would be a busy day, but Sundays were a day of rest, and that was exactly how James planned to spend the remainder of this one.

The screen door slammed, and James turned to see Ruth joining him on the porch, toting a plastic bag. She'd shed her bright red shoes, and as she walked barefoot toward him, still dressed in the red polka dot dress, he couldn't help but smile. She didn't smile back.

"This is for you." She thrust the plastic bag at him, almost hitting him in the stomach. "Read it. Think about it. Pray about it."

"What?" James peeked into the bag. Dozens, or hundreds, of notebook-sized papers were bound with three rubber bands. "What is this?" He flipped through the pages for a moment, then looked up at Ruth.

"Leah has a gift from the Lord, James. Don't keep the girl from being who she really is by stifling her dreams." Ruth waved her hand in the air. "There's plenty of women around here who can cook, clean, tend gardens, and the like—but I don't know any who have the ability to touch another person through words on a page like your Leah. She is special, James. And someone is gonna read this book and be changed by it."

"This is Leah's?" He looked in the bag again. "Why are you giving it to me?"

Ruth grinned. "'Cause I think you're gonna be the first one to be changed by it." She slapped him on the arm. "Now, go store that in your buggy. No need to mention this to the others, but you take yourself home and you read that girl's story. Quit trying to mold her into something she ain't. She has a far greater purpose."

Then she actually gave James a little push on the shoulder. He just wanted her to go away, so he marched to the buggy, stashed the bag under the seat, and stalled a bit until he saw her go back inside. *Glad she's not my aunt.*

It wasn't long before Marian, Edna, Mary Carol, and Kathleen joined him, and they all squeezed into the buggy. Without Leah in between him and Marian, the ride was much more comfortable, even though his daughters were somewhat cramped in the back. But it was a short ride, and the entire way he thought about what Ruth said and about the bag under his seat.

Leah flung her hands into the air and held her head back, the wind whipping her cheeks into a rosy shade of pink, and Aaron didn't think he'd ever seen a more beautiful vision. Her brown dress brought out the color of her eyes, which flickered like gold in the sunlight. He picked up the pace even more, until his horse was in a comfortable gallop.

"I love to go fast!" She dropped her hands and turned toward him, and Aaron smiled in her direction. "I hardly ever get to drive our buggy. We have two, the family-sized covered buggy and the spring buggy. But if *Mamm* and *Daed* aren't using one, Edna gets the first chance to travel in it. Since she's the oldest and all."

Aaron slowed the horse to a trot, glad that he was fortunate enough to own a topless buggy. Unlike a spring buggy, which wasn't enclosed and held four comfortably, his courting buggy only had one seat—just room enough for two. A cozy arrangement for those of dating age. "You wanna drive?"

"*Ya!*" She twisted toward him. "I sure do!"

"Whoa, boy," he said, bringing the buggy to a complete stop. "There aren't too many cars on this road, but watch that curve up ahead in front of the Miller place. Sometimes the *Englisch* come barreling around that corner in their cars."

"I will."

Aaron walked around to the other side of the buggy, and Leah slid over to his side and picked up the reins. He was just getting ready to give her some simple instructions when she whistled and slapped the horse into action. Aaron grabbed his hat just as it began to lift off his head. He pushed it down tighter around his forehead as Leah brought the horse to a faster run than he had a few moments ago.

I hope this wasn't a mistake. She seems fearless.

But as he watched her slow the horse and ease around the sharp corner, his heart rate returned to normal. Then she picked it up again, and they flew down a long stretch of wide-open road. Her smile was eager and alive, and Aaron slid an arm around her shoulder. She slowed down almost instantly, and the perk in her mood seemed to deflate. Aaron pulled his arm back, realizing he'd gone too far.

"That's enough for me," she said. She brought the buggy to a halt and wasted no time jumping from the seat. Aaron exited his side and met her up front where she was rubbing Pete's snout. "He's tired. We probably ran him too hard."

Aaron knew that wasn't what caused her to jump out of his buggy.

"Why are we going to Bird-in-Hand?" She tilted her head to one side, still stroking the horse. "It's mostly for tourists."

Aaron shrugged. "Just somethin' to do. We can go anywhere you want."

He saw her take a deep breath, and she avoided his eyes when she spoke. "Maybe back to your cousin's pond. It's pretty there."

And private. "Sure. We can go there." It wasn't in his plan. He'd wanted to buy her something at the market in Bird-in-Hand, sip root beer at the small stand on the way there, and make sure she knew he wasn't boring. But this was a far greater plan.

Less than five minutes later, Aaron parked the buggy, and he and Leah walked down to the water's edge. He followed her out onto the pier. She pulled off her black leather shoes and socks, sat down, and dangled her feet in the water below. Aaron followed her lead, careful not to sit too close to her.

"Remember when we were younger, how everyone used to go to the river? The girls would all sit on the bank and watch all you boys swim." She turned toward him with an expression of fond recollections.

"*Ya.*" Aaron remembered that he was always looking at Leah to see if she was watching him when he took his turn on the tire swing. "Those were fun times."

They sat quietly for a few moments.

"I can't wait to hear what Donna and Clare think of my book," she said out of the clear blue.

Aaron took a deep breath, knowing he was about to kill the mood and the moment.

"Leah, I need to tell you something about that."

"What?" She was still splashing her feet in the water, but she looked up.

"Your *Englisch* friends left the book on the table, and I picked it up, and——"

"What?" Her feet grew still in the water, and her eyes searched his.

"I'm sure they didn't mean to. I saw them leave, and they must have just——"

"But that's my only copy. What if you hadn't picked it up?"

Aaron didn't have the heart to tell her what he'd overheard the girls saying. He wanted so badly to take her in his arms, comfort her, and tell her that those girls were not the ones meant to read her book. They weren't ready.

She bolted upright. "Where's the book now?"

"I didn't want to upset you that night, so I stuffed it into Auntie Ruth's purse. I meant to bring it to you, but I forgot to get it back." He paused. "*Ach*, and I hope it's okay, but Auntie Ruth asked if she could read it."

This brightened her face. "Really?"

"*Ya*. Is that all right?"

"*Ya. Ya.* I can't wait to hear what she thinks of it."

"I'm sure that Donna and Clare want to read it too." It was a lie, and Aaron wished he hadn't said it, but he felt compelled to make her happy.

She shook her head, then turned to him and smiled. "Maybe they just aren't ready."

He smiled back at her, and then without warning, she cut her foot to the side and splashed water all over him. "You were sweating like our pig!" she said, laughing.

Aaron wiped the water from his face, cut his eyes in her direction, and then returned the gesture, covering her with water. "You looked pretty sweaty yourself!"

She screamed when the cool water doused her, and immediately kicked water back at him. "Take that, Aaron Lantz!"

Laughter erupted from way down deep. Aaron wasn't sure what came over him, but he suddenly grabbed her around the waist and threw her in.

Leah bobbed up, soaking wet, bobbed back under again, then bobbed up, gasped for air, and said, "I can't swim!"

Aaron's heart leaped from his chest as he jumped into the water to rescue her. He wrapped his arms around her, pulled her close to him, and then stood up in the four feet of water. Leah stood up then, too, laughing so hard she could hardly speak. "Gotcha!"

But Aaron still had his arms tightly around her waist. "Who's got who?"

She stopped laughing, and fear stretched across her face as her eyes met with his. He could feel her trembling. The honorable thing to do would have been to let her go and help her out of the water and back onto the pier. Instead he pulled her closer and kissed her gently on the lips. Then he kissed her again, and this time she closed her eyes and kissed him back.

"Leah," he whispered. He pushed a strand of wet hair from her cheek and attempted to tuck it back beneath her wet prayer covering. "I've wanted to do that for a long time."

"Aaron, I—I—" She pushed away from him. "I'd make a terrible choice for courtship." She crinkled her face as if she'd bitten into something sour.

He stepped closer to her in the water and gently put his hands on her waist and turned her so that her back was against the pier. She was still trembling. With ease, he lifted her up and onto the pier. He stayed in the water facing her. "Is this the part where you're gonna tell me what a terrible cook you are, and how you can't sew?"

She hung her head, then looked back up at him. "Not only is it true, it doesn't even bother me much that I can't do these things. I'd rather be writing and doing things that matter to me."

Aaron grabbed his straw hat, floating nearby. Then he lifted himself onto the pier. He set the wet hat down beside him, pushed back his soaked hair, and turned to face her. "Why don't we just see how it goes?"

Leah nodded. "Okay." Then she pointed a finger in his direction. "But don't say I didn't warn you. I'll never be one of those women who cooks and cleans and waits on a man constantly, without any other outside interests, and I also will not—"

Aaron kissed her again, and she stopped talking and fell willingly into his arms.

Chapter Eighteen

MARIAN CLIMBED INTO BED BESIDE JAMES, BUT HE DIDN'T even look up.

"Leah is home. She said she had a wonderful time with Aaron. *Gut* news, no?"

James nodded. "*Ya.*"

Marian reached for her lotion on the bedside table and lit her own lantern on her side of the bed. "Leah's clothes were damp and wrinkled, like maybe they'd been swimming, but I didn't ask."

Her husband still didn't look up.

"James, you've been reading all afternoon. Are you still trying to learn from the *Englisch* author how to rear daughters?"

James had Leah's note pages propped up against the book he'd been reading, so it was no wonder Marian thought he was reading the *Englisch* author. He veered the book in Marian's direction so that she could see the stack of notebook paper resting against it. "No, I am reading Leah's book."

Marian's eyes grew large. "Leah's book?" She scooted closer to him and pushed back his arm so she could see better. "Where did you get that? Does she know you're reading it?"

James pulled off his glasses and rubbed his eyes. "I don't know. Ruth gave it to me."

"Ruth? What was she doing with it?"

He raised his shoulders, dropped them slowly. "I reckon I don't know. She said she thought I should read it, though."

They sat quietly for a moment.

"Is it *gut*? The book," Marian finally asked.

James swallowed back the lump in his throat. "*Ya*," he whispered. Then he wrapped an arm around his wife, pulled her closer. "Listen to this." James put his glasses on and read a page from Leah's book.

Rose thought about her relationship with God, and she couldn't imagine herself alone and without faith—like Lauren. She sat down beside her Englisch friend and prayed for guidance, for a way to open Lauren's heart to the Lord and His Son, Jesus. As she silently prayed, she thought about her father and what he might do in a situation such as this. Rose's father was the wisest man she knew, often strict with his daughters, but Rose had never doubted his love for her, or his faith in God. And he had a way of knowing what to do in a crisis.

Rose recalled the time when her father's brother died, Rose's only uncle. It was the only time she'd ever seen her father cry, and despite all of their grief, he'd reminded his daughters that God's will often causes us pain that we cannot understand, but that to question His will is to question all things in life and our purpose on this earth. "We each have a purpose," her father had said. "Mei brother's purpose has been fulfilled."

James took a deep breath, glanced at Marian.

"She's talking about you." Marian stroked his arm tenderly. "And David."

James thought back to when his brother's horse—an animal fresh off the track with no road experience—bolted out onto Lincoln Highway and into oncoming traffic. He nodded, then went on.

But this was a different kind of crisis. No one had died, yet a part of Lauren seemed to be dying on the inside. Her father was a loving man, but he thought Lauren should follow in his footsteps by running the family business. But Lauren had her own dreams, dreams her father couldn't understand.

BETH WISEMAN

"My father says my dreams are nonsense, and that playing music will never make me a fine living, like taking over his business will," Lauren said. "How can I make my father understand that he can't make me into something I'm not?" She looked at Rose. "I want to make my father proud of me, but I also want to live my own life."

James pulled off his glasses again and leaned his head against the headboard.

"James." Marian leaned her head on his shoulder, then kissed his cheek. "She is also talking about you here." Marian reached for the book on her husband's lap. "Here, let me."

James lifted his hand so Marian could take Leah's loose pages. He closed the *Englisch* book and placed it on his bedside table. Marian straightened Leah's pages, pulled her knees up, and propped their daughter's words in front of her. James kept his head resting against the headboard as his wife read.

Rose smiled at her friend, then latched onto her hand. "Let me tell you about Jesus. He is a personal friend of mine, and I'd like to introduce you to Him." Rose proceeded to tell Lauren about Jesus and His Father, and she prayed constantly that God's words would flow from her and into her friend's heart. When Lauren began to weep, Rose knew that the Holy Spirit was settling around her friend, and she thanked God continually. In the back of her mind, though, she kept wondering if her own father would be proud of her.

James felt a tear roll down his cheek.

His wife set Leah's book aside and kissed away his tear. "My darling James."

"I've been praying for the wrong things, Marian." He took a deep breath and gathered himself, embarrassed for Marian to see him like this. He'd only cried once in his entire life—when David died—and yet his daughter's words were having a profound effect on him. "I've prayed each night for God to rid Leah of these silly stories, not once considering that His will *is* being done." He turned toward Marian. "Perhaps this story of hers will change a life somehow."

Marian smiled. "Maybe it just did."

When Aaron took Leah home, he kissed her yet again, and the feel of her lips against his stayed with him all the way home. What a wonderful day it had been. After their swim, they'd spent hours talking, and Aaron knew that someday he was going to make Leah his wife.

He wasn't surprised to see the Petersheim spring buggy at his house when he pulled up. When he dropped Leah at home, she'd commented that Edna had probably taken the buggy and gone back to see Abner. The closer it got to the wedding, the more inseparable Abner and Edna were.

Aaron tended to his horse, then walked up to the house, a newfound bounce in his step. He smiled. He might have to eat a lot of chicken salad for the rest of his life, but he was willing to do that to be with Leah.

When he hit the porch, he heard voices. Edna and Abner were evidently in the den. Aaron heard his name and paused.

"Leah is only using Aaron. You do know that, right?" Edna's voice coursed through him.

"What do you mean?" Abner asked.

Aaron inched closer to the door, careful to stay out of sight, then leaned his ear toward the door.

"*Daed* won't let her go out and do anything because she shirks all her responsibilities at home. She's late to meals all the time, and she just doesn't do her share," Edna said. "She helped a little bit when I got sick, but then she just slipped back to her old ways."

"How is that using Aaron?"

"*Daed* wants so badly for Leah to find a husband, he's not about to tell her she can't go out with him. She only goes because it's her ticket to freedom."

Aaron's chest tightened.

"She threw a fit that first night when I said Aaron was coming over. She's never had an interest in him. I think it's just wrong the way she is using him to get out of the house, because I think Aaron really likes her."

"*Ya*, he does," Abner said. "But are you sure about this?"

"Sure am." Edna paused again. "Remember the other night when Aaron and your aunt picked up Leah to go to Paradiso?"

"*Ya.*"

"Well, she'd already sent word by way of the postman for her *Englisch* friends to meet her there. *Daed* didn't want her spending time with them until she was doing her share around the house."

Aaron's stomach began to churn. *How stupid I've been.*

But then he thought about the afternoon they'd just shared, the kisses, the playfulness, the long talk. *No. This couldn't be true.*

"I don't want to see Aaron get hurt, that's all," Edna went on. "Leah has said over and over that she doesn't want to get married. At least, not any time soon. And Aaron seems ready to settle down."

Aaron had heard enough. He walked in the door, said hello, and marched up the stairs, but he did overhear Edna say one more thing before he hit the second floor.

"Uh-oh. Do you think he heard me?"

The next morning Leah beat everyone downstairs, started breakfast, and bounced around the kitchen, humming. And she had the strangest urge to attempt another tomato pie.

She busied herself all morning with the day's chores. After she finished the laundry, she worked on other things to help her sisters. She even took another stab at hemming a pair of pants for her father. She'd stayed up working on her latest story, but something was different. Leah didn't feel like she *had* to help out—she wanted to.

She wondered if this new attitude was what caused her tomato pie to turn out perfectly. She couldn't wait to take it to Aaron. Maybe he would kiss her again. Her stomach somersaulted at the thought.

"*Mamm*, can I take the buggy to town?" It was nearing two o'clock, and Aaron had mentioned yesterday that he would be leaving work at two o'clock to go home and start readying the fields for the fall harvest. She wanted to catch him at the furniture shop and give him the pie.

Her mother folded two kitchen towels and placed them in a drawer before turning around to face Leah. "I reckon it will be all right with your *daed*." Marian glanced at the pie. "Did you make this, Leah? Did it turn out this time?"

"I made it for Aaron, and it turned out perfectly," she said proudly.

"Hmm. I thought you didn't like to cook."

Leah shrugged. "I'm not good at it, but something about Aaron makes me want to try harder."

Her mother nodded. "Ah, I see."

"I'm going to go ready the buggy."

Chapter Nineteen

LEAH PULLED UP AT THE FURNITURE STORE AND PARKED the buggy in a designated space. She carefully retrieved the tomato pie. She'd never felt as proud of anything she'd done in the kitchen as she did this pie. Again she wondered if Aaron would kiss her. She wondered if Aaron's father and Abner were here or if they'd already left to tend to the fields.

The bell chimed when she walked in. She spotted Aaron right away. He was so tall, his head rose higher than the shelves on one side of the store; it looked like his hat was just bouncing along the aisle. When he rounded the corner, Aaron tipped his hat back, but he didn't look as happy to see her as she'd hoped.

"Hi. I brought you this." Leah handed him the pie, then bounced on her toes a few times, beaming from ear to ear. "I made this all by myself. Tomato pie."

"*Danki.*" Aaron set the pie down on the counter next to a sales log and a cup full of pens. "You didn't have to do that."

"I—I wanted to," she said as he turned his back to her and walked around the counter to the other side. "Do you want to try a piece now?"

Aaron lowered his head and began writing numbers on the log. "I can't right now, Leah. I'm busy."

She glanced around the shop. "But there's no one here."

He looked up from the log he'd been focused on. "I still have things to do. I have responsibilities around here. *Daed* and Abner have already left to go work in the fields."

"So we're alone." It was much too bold a statement, and she wished right away that she hadn't spoken the words aloud.

"*Ya.*" Aaron picked up a box on the counter, walked to a shelf, and started unloading the items inside.

Leah's pulse quickened. What was going on? She walked to where he was squatting on the ground.

"Aaron, are you angry with me about something?"

He looked up at her, but his smile seemed hard, his eyes cold. "No. Why?"

"You—you just seem, I don't know . . . different."

"I'm just busy," he said with a shrug.

Leah waited a few moments to see if he'd finish what he was doing and resume the conversation, but he stayed quiet. She took a deep breath.

"Do you want to go on another picnic Saturday? I'm sure *mei daed* would let me, and—"

"I'm sure he would," Aaron grumbled.

"What?"

"Nothing, Leah." He stood, picked up the empty box, and walked back to the counter. "I'm sorry. I can't go on a picnic Saturday."

"Working in the fields?" Any bounce Leah had had in her step earlier was completely gone.

"Uh, *ya.* I have to work in the fields."

You're lying. "Well, Sunday there isn't any church service. Maybe we—"

"I'll let you know when I'm not busy anymore."

He turned and walked to the back of the building, and Leah wished she'd never allowed herself to feel anything at all for Aaron Lantz. She should have stayed focused on writing her stories, something that made her feel good.

As her bottom lip began to quiver, she ran out the door.

Aaron walked to the front of the store and watched Leah through the large glass pane in the front of the shop. When she swiped at teary

BETH WISEMAN

eyes, he whispered her name. He wanted to go to her, but what was the point? She probably forced herself to make the pie as an excuse to bring it to him, which got her out of the house for the day to go do whatever she really wanted to do.

He pulled his hat off and raked a hand through his hair, then blew out an exasperated sigh. He should have known better than to pursue Leah. He didn't want to live on chicken salad the rest of his life anyway. Aaron glanced at the pie. Or tomato pie.

But the ache in his heart defied his thoughts as he watched her drive her buggy out of the parking lot.

❧❦

Leah allowed herself a good cry on the way home. Aaron's face kept flashing before her—his cold expression, the glassy stare. Not the same person as yesterday. She thought about how hard she'd worked to get the tomato pie just right and how good it felt to make the pie for him.

To make matters worse, she stopped at the bakery where Donna worked and asked her about leaving the book at Paradiso. She'd hoped her friend would apologize for being so careless, but Donna didn't seem to think it was of much importance. She just shrugged and said she didn't have time to read. Leah left the bakery with hurt feelings, wondering if her father had been right about the dangers of spending too much time with those unequally yoked.

Her thoughts drifted back to Aaron. If she hadn't allowed herself to get close to him, she wouldn't know what she was missing. In the stories she wrote, she could control every little detail and ensure a happy ending. Not the case in real life. She'd had a change of heart about her life and the possibility of something more with Aaron. What a mistake.

She crossed Lincoln Highway and headed toward home. On the way she passed Aaron's cousin's farm, and she could see the pond and the pier from the road. Memories of the playful time they'd had, their kisses, and their long talks swirled in her head, and anger began to build. Why would Aaron give her flowers and treat her with such kindness yesterday, only to turn on her today?

Leah pulled into her driveway, parked the buggy, then sat in a rocker on the front porch. She wasn't ready to see anyone just yet. She kicked off her shoes, pulled off her socks, then pushed the chair into motion. Her father was on the plow behind the mules, getting the fields ready for harvest, and she knew he'd be heading this way for supper soon. Leah could hear her mother and Kathleen scurrying around in the kitchen.

Sighing, she leaned her head back against the back of the rocker and fought the urge to cry again. She didn't even feel like writing. Anger tugged at her even more. Not only had Aaron played with her emotions, but now she wasn't even inclined to work on her stories. *Daed* would be happy about that.

Supper was one of those meals where Edna and Mary Carol dominated the conversation with talk of their upcoming weddings, which only added to Leah's state of mind.

"Leah, I'd like to talk to you." *Daed* wiped his mouth with his napkin, and Leah's sisters all searched their father's face right along with Leah.

"Okay," she responded, then sighed. *What did I do now?* She finished off her tea, then rose from the table when her father did. She followed him onto the front porch, thinking it must be something really bad if he didn't want to scold her in front of everyone else.

"Let's take a walk." *Daed* walked down the porch steps, and Leah joined him.

"*Daed*, I got up extra early to do my chores. I didn't leave to go see Aaron until after everything was done. *Mamm* said she thought you wouldn't mind."

His face was solemn, his mouth drawn into a frown. "I know, Leah." He looped his thumbs in his suspenders and kept his eyes toward the ground in front of him.

Leah's heart was beating out of her chest. She couldn't recall her father ever asking her to take a walk with him before. They passed the barn and went to Mary Carol's garden, where there was a bench underneath a shade tree. Leah could smell the wisteria growing along the barbed wire fence off to her right, the sweet fragrance doing little to calm her nerves. A gentle breeze swept across her face.

This was one of her favorite places to write her stories. From this spot, she could see across the meadow to where the cows were grazing near the pond, and butterflies seemed to enjoy this place as much as she. She scanned the wide-open fields as the feel of the plush grass wrapped around her toes.

Daed sat down and motioned for Leah to do the same. He took a deep breath, then turned to face her. "I read your book."

"What?"

"The one with Rose and the girl Lauren."

"But how did you—"

"Ruth brought it to me. She said she'd read it, and she thought I should read it too." He raised his brows. "And I did."

Leah's chest hurt from the pressure. His expression was impossible to read, and while he didn't look angry, the wrinkles in his forehead had grown more defined as he spoke.

He pulled off his hat and set it on his lap, then wiped the sweat from his brow. "You have a gift, Leah," he began.

She felt the pressure in her chest lift just a little.

"And for me not to encourage you to use that gift as a way to reach those in search of the Lord . . ." He shook his head. "I reckon it would be wrong."

Leah tried to absorb what he was saying.

"It's not normally our way to minister to others, but after readin' your story, it seems to me that the Lord is working through you, and to keep you from doing His work would be a sin." He looked away from her and stared at the ground, twirling his hat in his hands. "You have my blessing to pen your tales, as long as you keep up with your share of the chores around the *haus*." He faced her again, sighed, and said, "I reckon everyone ain't meant to be a perfect cook, seamstress, and housekeeper. But if you plan to keep seeing that boy, you might want to at least work on those things just a little." He grinned.

Her father's words had lifted her up so much that she'd momentarily forgotten about Aaron. Afraid of crying, she just nodded.

He stood up, put his hat on, and started to walk away. Leah sat there. She needed to think.

"Leah?"

She looked up when she heard her name. Her father was looking back at her.

"I love you."

He turned around and hurried across the yard before Leah could say anything. James Petersheim was a man of few words, and he had never spoken those three words directly to Leah.

It was impossible to choke back the tears.

Chapter Twenty

ALMOST TWO WEEKS PASSED, AND NOT ONLY HAD LEAH not seen Aaron, but she hadn't worked on her latest story at all. Her father had given his blessing, so she didn't have to hide it anymore, and yet—her heart was filled with sadness and the words didn't seem to come. She chopped the weeds around the garden with the weed eater, and it sputtered a little. Probably running out of gas.

"Leah!" Mary Carol's snappy tone pulled her from her musings. She let the weed eater idle.

"What?"

Mary Carol threw her hands on her hips, scowled, then pointed to the ground. "Those are not weeds! Those are greens that *were* almost ready to pick. Move that machine away from my garden."

"Sorry." Leah rolled her eyes, moved to the bench under the tree, and whacked away at the weeds climbing up the legs of the seat.

How could he have kissed me? And more than once.

Leah wasn't sure whom she was angrier with, Aaron or herself, for stepping outside the safe pages of her books and into a real-life situation . . . one that had left her heartbroken.

She jumped when someone poked her on the back. This time she cut the motor on the weed eater.

"This was clipped to the mailbox." Kathleen pushed an envelope in Leah's direction.

Leah set the machine down, wiped her face with her apron, then accepted the envelope. "Who's it from?"

Kathleen shrugged. "How would I know?" She took off across the grass toward the house, and Leah plopped herself down on the bench, the shade a welcome relief from the glaring sun.

Edna used to do the weed eating, until she found out about her asthma, so they'd switched some chores around. Leah swiped her brow, thinking she'd gotten the bad end of the deal. Edna was inside, sitting at the table in front of the fan, chopping vegetables to make chow-chow.

Leah peeled back the flap on the envelope and pulled out a small sheet of red paper. In black ink it read:

Leah,
  Please meet me at our place tomorrow at noon. There is much to be said, and I miss you.

Her heart fluttered.

Then she read the next sentence:

Can you please bring lunch?
Kindest regards, Aaron

Leah stared in disbelief at the letter. *Is he crazy?*

First of all, she didn't know that they had a *place*. Secondly, the nerve of him!

"Who's the note from?" Mary Carol was toting a garden hoe as she approached.

Leah stood up and stomped her foot. "It's from Aaron Lantz! And can you believe that he wrote me this note?" She showed the red piece of paper to Mary Carol. "The nerve of him to ask me to bring lunch. He barely talked to me the last time I saw him." Leah shrugged. "Well, I reckon I'm not going." She folded her arms across her chest.

Mary Carol burst out laughing.

"What's so funny?"

Her sister struggled to catch her breath. "I've just never seen you like this about a boy."

BETH WISEMAN

"Like what?"

Mary Carol handed the letter back to Leah and grinned. "So smitten. You really like Aaron."

"Well, I thought I did. Then he just turned very—cold. I can't imagine why he wants to meet." She scrunched her face up, but then couldn't help but grin. "Maybe he just loves my chicken salad and tomato pie."

"Somehow I doubt that's it." Mary Carol turned, walked back to her garden, and yelled over her shoulder, "I think you should go!"

"I'm not going!"

The next morning, Leah pulled her tomato pie from the oven, wrapped it in foil, and added it to the picnic basket, along with two chicken salad sandwiches and some chow-chow that Edna and Kathleen made the night before. She glanced at the clock hanging on the wall in the kitchen. Eleven thirty. She was going to have to ride her foot scooter to meet Aaron, since today was *Mamm*'s day to go to market. Leah didn't want to prepare the larger family buggy just to go down the road a mile.

As she toted the picnic basket outside, she felt torn about Aaron's note. As glad as she was that he wanted to see her, why the sudden change? And she couldn't get past how bold he was being about asking her to bring lunch. Irritation and a sense of excitement swirled together as she placed their lunch inside the metal basket on the front of the scooter.

She kicked herself into motion, and just as she was rounding the corner from her driveway to the road, she saw her father plowing the fields to her right. He waved, and Leah returned the gesture, balancing herself on the foot scooter with one hand. Things were different between them now, and Leah thanked God for that blessing each day. *Daed* seemed to see her in a new light, accepting her for the person she was as opposed to who he thought she should be.

Warm wind blew in her face as she scooted past the abandoned Bontrager place.

Leah slowed her pace on the scooter as she turned the corner and neared the Lapp farm. Aaron was already there. His courting buggy was parked near the house, and she could see him leaning against the buggy with his ankles crossed and—

Are those flowers he's holding?

She squinted against the sun's glare to have a better look. Sure enough, he was toting a bouquet of flowers in his right hand. She felt a tad guilty about balking over lunch.

As she pulled into the driveway, she could see that they were roses, again wrapped in green tissue. Her heart flipped as she neared him and slowed to a stop.

"These are for you." Aaron offered her the roses. "I've missed you, Leah."

Leah accepted the flowers but avoided his eyes. "*Danki.*" She didn't move from the scooter, unsure what to say or do.

"I see you brought lunch." Aaron nodded toward the picnic basket. "That was nice."

You told me to. She tried to push back her bitterness about that, since he'd shown up with flowers and said he'd missed her. "Chicken salad and tomato pie." She lifted the basket out of the tray and gently set the flowers inside.

"I brought a blanket. Do you want to go back to our spot under the tree by the pond?"

"I reckon." Leah forced a smile. He seemed genuinely glad to see her, but she still wondered what had caused him to change his mind. They started walking toward the pond, and Aaron took the basket from her. He had the blanket draped across his shoulder and a thermos in one hand.

"I remembered to bring tea this time," she said as she eyed the silver thermos.

"We'll have plenty to drink then." He smiled.

BETH WISEMAN

Leah's head was filled with recollections of their last time here, especially of his tender kisses. But she was leery of him now. If he'd turned on her so suddenly before . . .

When they got to the pond, Aaron spread the blanket underneath the tree and set the picnic basket and thermos in a far corner. He motioned for her to sit down.

Leah folded her legs sideways beneath her and fingered the intricate stitching on the blue and yellow quilt, with weaving vines of greenery connecting the bright flowers. Aaron sat down beside her, too close. His leg brushed against hers and sent a ripple through her. She edged back and took a deep breath.

"I finished your second book," he said. "Like the first one, it was great."

She smiled. "*Danki.*"

"Auntie Ruth said she gave your first story to your *daed* and suggested he read it." Aaron scowled. "I told her I wasn't sure if that was such a *gut* idea."

"Actually, it turned out to be a very *gut* idea. *Daed* read it and decided that my stories were inspired by God, and he encouraged me to keep writing."

"Leah, that's great." Aaron reached for her hand, but she pulled away. She wasn't interested in talking about her book, her father, or anything else but why they were here.

"You said there were things to be said, Aaron. What things?" She sat up a little taller and held her head high.

"Huh? *I* said?" His mouth twitched slightly to one side, and he tilted his head.

"In your note to me, you said—"

"What? What note?"

Leah raised her brows. "The note you pinned to my mailbox, of course."

Aaron rubbed his chin. "Leah, I didn't pin any note to your mailbox."

Leah had on her working apron, and since she'd read the note again that morning, she realized it was still in her pocket. She pulled it out and shoved it in his direction.

She waited while he seemed to read the note over and over again, shaking his head. "Leah, I didn't write this." He looked up at her, his eyes filled with confusion.

"What? Of course you did!" She jumped up from the blanket, put her hands on her hips, and stared down at him. "Then what are you doing here?"

Aaron lifted himself up, reached into his own pocket, and retrieved a red piece of paper just like the one Leah had just handed him. "Because *you* pinned a note on my mailbox."

"I did no such thing!" She grabbed the note from his hand.

Aaron,
    Please meet me at our place tomorrow at noon. There is much to be said, and I miss you.
    It would be lovely if you could bring me flowers.
Kindest regards, Leah

Leah handed him the note back as if it were poison. "I can assure you, I did not write that." She brought her hand to her chest. "What *must* you have thought, to think that I would ask you to bring me flowers?"

Aaron shrugged, grinning. "I reckon it seemed strange, but . . ."

They both stood quietly for a few moments.

"I can think of only one person who would do this," Aaron said.

Leah snapped her finger. "And her favorite color is red!"

They grew quiet again, both lost in amused thought.

"I wasn't even sure what you meant by *our place*." Leah giggled.

"I wasn't sure either." Aaron looped his thumbs in his suspenders. "And just so you know, I wouldn't have asked you to bring lunch."

Leah's face soured, and she cut her eyes at him. "Because of my cooking?"

"No, no. Because it's just, well . . . rude."

"Looks like we have lunch, and I have flowers, and . . ." Leah folded her arms across her chest. "Why would Auntie Ruth do this?"

Aaron's mouth twitched slightly to one side, and he avoided her eyes. "I reckon it's because I've been mopin' around a bit lately. At least that's what Auntie Ruth said." He looked up at Leah. "She knew I missed you."

Leah didn't understand at all. "But you are the one who didn't want to spend time with me anymore." She turned away from him. "I feel silly even being here now."

Aaron walked up behind her, so close she could feel his breath against her neck. "I've always wanted to spend time with you, Leah. I just didn't want to be your excuse to get out of the house if you weren't feeling the same thing I was feeling."

She spun around, putting their faces only inches apart, and her recollections of shared kisses danced in her mind. "What? Why would you say that?"

"I overheard Edna telling Abner that the only reason you were spending time with me was because your *daed* wouldn't let you out of the house. I reckon it didn't seem right. I almost didn't come today."

Leah looked down. "Oh no. That's not true, Aaron." She glanced up again. "It must have seemed that way, but I love—love spending time with you."

"That's *gut* to know." Aaron backed away a little, his mouth twitching slightly. "Wanna eat?"

"I guess so."

He reached for her hand, and together they sat down on the blanket. Leah opened the picnic basket and handed Aaron a sandwich, but before they took their first bite, their attention was drawn to the road. Dirt flew from beneath the horse's hooves as Abner rounded the corner and came barreling onto the driveway, going much too fast and yelling Aaron's name.

They stood up, abandoning the picnic, and Leah followed Aaron across the field. His quick walk turned to a run, and Leah broke into a jog behind him.

"What's wrong?" Aaron tried to catch his breath.

Abner climbed out of the buggy and put his hand on his brother's shoulder. "It's Auntie Ruth." Abner's forehead creased with sorrow as he spoke. "She's gone, Aaron. Passed in her sleep while she was taking a nap. We need you at home."

Chapter Twenty-one

BISHOP EBERSOL GRANTED PERMISSION FOR AUNTIE RUTH to be buried in the Amish cemetery, even though she wasn't a member of the Old Order. Aaron's parents explained that Ruth didn't have any other family, and since Ruth was Amish by birth, the bishop had agreed. An autopsy was waived because Aaron's mother found Ruth's medical records in her suitcase, along with all of her affairs neatly in order. She'd had chronic heart disease.

Leah looked for Aaron amid the crowd of people in attendance at the funeral. She recalled the way his bottom lip had trembled when he drove her home after hearing the news three days ago. He'd hurriedly kissed her on the cheek when he dropped her off, and Leah suspected he was anxious to be away from her to experience his emotions. Leah had cried when Abner told them the news, but Aaron had clamped his lips tight and merely nodded. Leah hadn't seen him again until now.

She scanned the Lantzes' den, surprised at how many people in the community were in attendance to pay their respects to Ruth. But as she overheard various conversations going on around her, she realized that Ruth had touched a lot of people.

"Remember when the Miller family suffered such tragedy when young Lizzie died four years ago?" she heard Amanda Graber's mother say to her husband. "Ruth stood guard outside the gate and kept those pesky reporters away."

Katharine Graber paused. "She certainly had a good heart."

Leah walked across the room as people began to take their seats. Rebecca Miller was standing in a corner talking to Ben. Leah knew funerals were tough for Rebecca and her entire family. She was glad Ben was nearby, but Leah wondered if those two would ever become a couple. Rebecca seemed to be lost inside herself and kept most everyone at a distance. Particularly Ben. Leah reminded herself to say an extra prayer for Rebecca tonight.

"Did you know that Ruth helped to deliver you?" Leah's mother whispered to her as they took their seats.

Leah didn't know, and she turned toward her mother. "Really?"

"*Ya.* The midwife had taken ill, and Ruth filled in like she'd delivered a baby a hundred times." Her mother smiled. "Turned out, you were her first."

The room grew quiet, and Leah found Aaron sitting on the far side of the room with the men. Her heart hurt when she saw him hastily swipe at his eyes, and she wanted to run to him, hold him, comfort him.

During the two-hour funeral, many voiced their respect for Ruth, but the focus was on admonition for the living, as was the Old Order Amish way.

Following the service, they all made their way to the buggies, and the caravan accompanied Ruth to her final resting place where a hand-dug grave awaited. Her modest tombstone had been prepared, plain like the others in the cemetery.

When the bishop closed the outdoor part of the service, Leah knew that Aaron would stay behind to help close Ruth's grave, so she left with her family to go back to the Lantz house where a meal would be served.

It was nearly two hours later when Aaron and Leah finally found some quiet time to talk, around the back side of the barn. Once they were alone and out of sight, Aaron wrapped his arms around Leah and kissed her tenderly on the cheek.

B E T H   W I S E M A N

"I've been wanting to do that all day."

Leah burrowed her head against Aaron's shoulder and basked in the feel of his arms, a place that felt safe and somehow . . . right. He gently eased away from her and reached into his pocket. He pulled out a red piece of paper, just like the one their notes had been written on.

"*Mamm* gave me this when I got home from our picnic." Aaron handed Leah the note. "She was—she was writing us . . ." Aaron's voice broke. "Auntie Ruth was writing a letter to you and me just before she died."

Leah gasped. "What? Why?"

"Read it." Aaron swallowed hard.

Leah unfolded the crumpled red piece of paper, took a deep breath, and read silently.

My dear Aaron and Leah,

I'm getting ready to lie down for a nap this wonderful after-noon. The birds are chirping, and it's a beautiful day outside. But, Aaron, I ate your mother's peas, and you know what those do to me. Got a bellyache. Feels like I swallowed a watermelon. Do her peas do that to you?

Leah smiled. Auntie Ruth wrote just like she lived. A maze of thoughts that somehow made sense.

Anyways, Leah and Aaron, I have you two on my mind this fine day. I'm sure you done figured out that it's your old auntie who set the two of you up. Sneaky, ain't I? But you two kids belong together. And all this moping around is a waste of God's precious time that He allows us on this earth. Yes, Leah—I hear from Edna and Abner that you've been doing your share of moping around your house too.

Leah didn't look up, but she could feel herself blushing.

Do you know that right now there are two redbirds sitting on
my windowsill? They're lovely. I think they're a couple. I can tell
these things.
So I hope my little plan brought the two of you together, as
that was my intention. I'm tired now. Very tired. So I'll close.
Sending you both a big hug. Aaron, you're my favorite, but
don't tell the others.
Love, Auntie Ruth

Leah folded the letter up and handed it back to Aaron. She
blinked back tears as she gazed into his eyes. "Aaron . . . ," she
whispered.

He kissed her again, this time on the lips, and Leah wanted nothing more than to stay in his arms forever.

Marian walked toward her husband. Most of the funeral attendees
had left, and James was sitting alone at a picnic table in the Lantzes'
yard with his head in his hands. She sat down beside him.

"I saw you talking to Aaron earlier." She put her hand on his leg.
"It looked like a serious talk."

"*Ya.* It was." James shook his head, turned toward Marian. "He
wants to marry our Leah in the fall. *This* fall."

Marian jumped, then reached for James's hand. "*Ach!* James!
That's wonderful! This is what we've been hoping, that Leah would
find a *gut* mate and wed."

"*Ya, ya.* I know." James sighed. "But *three* weddings? We will have
Edna's, Mary Carol's, and Leah's weddings all within two months of
one another."

She squeezed her husband's hand. "It will be fine, James." Then
she nudged him playfully. "Think how quiet it will be around our
house."

He smiled. "*Ya.* I reckon so."

They sat quietly for a few moments. Marian was thankful for the slightly cooler temperatures, but the sun was bright as she raised her hand to her forehead and looked across the yard.

"Uh-oh," she said. Then she nudged James again and pointed toward a couple over by the barn.

"No, no, no." James shook his head as his face twisted in disbelief. "Not Kathleen too! Go over there and tell them not to be gettin' any notions in their heads!"

Marian laughed aloud. "Now, James," she warned, "you wouldn't want me to do that."

"She's only sixteen," he mumbled.

"*Ya.* It's young for marriage, but I was only sixteen when I married you." She laid her head on his shoulder, and they watched their youngest daughter grinning and talking with Mark Huyard.

Marian glanced to the porch where Mary Carol, Saul, Edna, and Abner were all sitting. Then she spotted Leah and Aaron chatting beneath an oak tree near the barn.

Marian wrapped her hands around James's arms and squeezed. "We're very blessed to have such wonderful daughters."

He twisted his head, kissed her lightly on the lips, and smiled. "*Ya.* We are."

Marian closed her eyes and silently thanked God for all she'd been blessed with. Not only for her four daughters, but for the wonderful man sitting next to her, whom she was just as in love with today as the day they married.

Aaron latched onto Leah's hand and helped her up from their spot beneath the oak tree. "I have something else for you." He motioned toward the double doors that led into the barn.

"Yesterday I went to town for *Mamm* to run some errands, and this was in the window of a little shop off Lincoln Highway." Aaron pushed the barn door open with his shoulder and coaxed her inside. He pointed to a workbench against the wall.

Leah gasped. "That's for me?" She dropped his hand and hurried to the bench, toward the typewriter sitting on top of it.

"It's old. I think it's an antique. And not electric, of course. But you said you wanted one."

Leah caressed the black machine, surprised at what good shape it was in.

"It works too." Aaron rolled the piece of paper that was already inserted upward. He eased her aside and began to type. *I love you.*

Leah bit her bottom lip, blinked hard, and turned to face him.

He kissed her gently on the lips, lingering there for what seemed like an eternity. Then he pulled back, cupped her cheeks in his hands, and said, "Leah, you're never gonna be a traditional Amish *fraa*, and I'll probably have to live on chicken salad and tomato pie for the rest of my life . . . but I've loved you since I saw you the first day of school." He paused, took in a deep breath.

Leah could feel her heart pounding against her chest.

"I love your stories. I love the person you are. I just love—I just love you."

"Oh, Aaron." Leah wrapped her arms around him. Then she pulled away and looked deeply into his eyes. "I'll try to learn how to make something besides chicken salad and tomato pie."

"Love me, Leah." He kissed her again.

"I do."

Healing Hearts

To my sisters—Laurie, Valarie, Melody, and Dawn

Chapter One

LEVINA LAPP PEERED THROUGH HER KITCHEN WINDOW, past the red begonias on the sill, across the plush green grass that tickled her toes earlier in the day, to the end of her driveway. Her husband of thirty-one years stepped out of a yellow taxi, closed the door, and headed up the driveway toward his home. A home he hadn't stepped foot in for almost a year.

As Naaman approached, toting the same dingy red suitcase he'd left with last summer, he walked with a limp. Levina knew from his last letter that he'd injured himself during a barn raising while he was visiting cousins in Ohio. He'd downplayed his ten-foot fall, but Levina knew her husband well enough to recognize the pain in his expression as he eased his way up the concrete drive, taking each step slowly and deliberately.

"I'm going to visit Levi," he'd said eleven months ago. But they both knew that his trip was more than a visit. It was a reevaluation of their lives. At least for Naaman it was. Levina was an unwilling participant in his venture, with little more than a brief consultation before he abandoned their marriage in pursuit of . . . what? She had no idea.

When the youngest of their five children married, she and Naaman were left alone. "Empty nesters," as the *Englisch* called it. It took a grand total of nine weeks before the silent life they led lured Naaman out the door and away from Lancaster County—away from their home and everything they'd ever known.

Now he was back, heading up the driveway, after asking if he could come home and work to heal their marriage.

Lavina smoothed the wrinkles from her dark blue dress and tried to calm her rapid heartbeat as Naaman struggled up the porch steps. She pulled the door open just as he was about to knock, which seemed strange yet respectful.

"Hello, Naaman." Levina held the door wide so he could enter. He was barely over the threshold when he set his suitcase down and pulled her into a hug.

"I've missed you." Naaman clung to her tightly, but Levina eased away and forced a smile.

Her husband looked exactly the same as he always had. Levina wondered how that could be, since she'd examined herself in the mirror just this morning and studied the tiny lines that feathered from the corners of her eyes—evidence that she'd recently celebrated her forty-ninth birthday. Her brown hair had more streaks of gray these days as well.

Naaman's beard was longer than it used to be, but he didn't have a speck of gray in his dark hair or in his beard. His face was weathered by sun and hard work, but the tiny age lines about his mouth and eyes seemed the same as when he'd left.

"I made lunch. Nothing fancy. I'm afraid I haven't cooked much lately." She stepped away from him. "I've been eating at Yoder's Pantry, since cooking for one just—" She shrugged, hearing self-pity in her comment. "Anyway, I made some chicken salad, and everything is on the table." Levina motioned toward the bowl of chicken salad, bread, pickled red beets, and snitz pie in the middle of the table.

"It looks *gut*, Levina." Naaman smiled as he eyed the offerings, and Levina took time to inspect him further.

His shoes looked new, but the clothes he wore could have been the same ones he'd left in—black trousers, a dark blue shirt, suspenders, straw hat. Of course, he still towered over her, but his shoulders looked broader. Or maybe they just seemed that way.

"Sit down. I'll pour you some meadow tea." Levina moved

BETH WISEMAN

toward the refrigerator as Naaman took his seat at the head of the wooden table. She glanced over her shoulder to see him wipe sweat from his forehead. It was unseasonably hot for May.

"*Danki,*" he said when she placed the glass of iced tea in front of him.

She slid onto one of the backless benches to Naaman's right. They bowed their heads in silent prayer, then she waited until he made his sandwich before she scooped chicken salad onto a slice of bread.

"You've lost weight," he said after swallowing his first bite.

"Maybe a little." She took a bite of her sandwich and thought about all the laborious tasks she'd done around the farm since Naaman had left. Even with the children coming over to help, she had done much more physical labor than she was used to. It was no wonder she'd lost weight.

"Things will be easier on you now."

Naaman spoke without looking at her, but Levina heard the regret in his tone.

"Your trip from Ohio was *gut*, no?" Levina picked at her red beets with her fork and hoped the small-talk phase of Naaman's return wouldn't last long.

"*Ya*. It was a long bus ride, but uneventful." He looked up and smiled. "I'm just glad to be home." Naaman made himself another sandwich. "Mary couldn't make chicken salad like you do."

Levina forced another smile. He obviously intended the comment as a compliment. She fought the urge to scream, *Well, you wouldn't have been eating Levi's frau's cooking if you hadn't deserted your family here!*

Naaman ate a hearty helping of everything on the table, including two large slices of snitz pie. When he was done, he stood from the table and picked up his suitcase. "Guess I'll go unpack?" He waited, brows raised.

Levina nodded an acknowledgment and watched him walk

across the den toward their bedroom. She started picking up the plates from the table and turned on the water in the sink. She ran her hand under the cool flow, waiting for it to get hot, then changed her mind and turned the faucet off. She made her way across the den.

When she reached the bedroom, Naaman had already opened his suitcase and was putting his clothes in the dresser. She stiffened as a strange sense of intrusion engulfed her.

He pressed his undergarments into the second drawer, where they'd always been, and turned to face her. "Everything looks different in here." He glanced around the room, clearly noticing the new quilt on the bed, rug on the floor, and a vase full of freshly cut flowers. She'd never put flowers in their bedroom before.

"*Ya*. I spruced it up a bit." Levina bit her bottom lip and wondered if she should tell Naaman about the other things that had changed while he was gone. She should probably warn him before tomorrow when the children would arrive for a visit, but his presence at home—and in their bedroom—was enough to conquer for today. Tomorrow's problems would arrive soon enough.

LEVINA HEADED BACK TO THE KITCHEN, AND NAAMAN FINished unpacking his suitcase. He planned to spend the rest of his life making things up to his wife. *What kind of man abandons his family for almost a year?*

He sat down on the bed and ran his hand along the green ivy tendrils that connected tiny blue and yellow flowers. Naaman wondered how long ago Levina had swapped the old quilt for the new one. Did the new quilt represent a new beginning for his homecoming, or had she replaced it the minute he left, representing a new beginning for herself?

Not a fair thought, he knew. Levina was never included in the decision-making when he left for Ohio.

BETH WISEMAN

He pulled off his hat and ran a hand through his hair, then gave a heavy sigh. Faith and prayer had taught him not to shoulder the burdens of the past, but his choice to leave his wife and home had been a mistake. Once he'd been gone for a while and realized the bad choice he'd made, he hadn't known how to get back home where he belonged.

Yet here he was. In his home, in his bedroom, with his wife cleaning the dinner dishes on the other side of the house as if nothing had changed.

But Naaman knew that everything had changed, and despite Levina's politeness, he could see resentment in her eyes, feel it in her touch, even hear it in her voice. He was here in person, but the road back to his wife had yet to be traveled.

Tomorrow he would see his children for the first time in eleven months. He'd written all five of them, and he knew which ones were less than accepting about his return—his two oldest children, Rosemary and Adam. Rosemary's third child was born while Naaman was away, and she'd let him know how she felt about that. And Adam had actually said he thought Naaman should be shunned for what he'd done.

He and Levina had raised their children in accordance with the *Ordnung*, so Adam was right to have that opinion, but even the bishop, who had written Naaman several times, had held out hope that Naaman would come home prior to such a drastic action.

Somehow he would find a way to make things right again.

LEVINA DRESSED FOR BED IN THE BATHROOM. NAAMAN HAD bathed first, after working in the barn all afternoon, and he was lying in their bed reading the Bible. Levina ran a brush through her hair. Although it was streaked with gray, she was pleased that it was still full and silky like it was in her youth.

She recalled the first time Naaman saw her with her hair to her waist and without her *kapp* on—their wedding night. Tonight some of those same anxious feelings swept through her, a combination of longing and fear. It was different, though. Thirty-one years ago she was an eighteen-year-old girl who feared the unknown and hoped to please her husband. Now her fear was that she would never trust him the way she once had.

"Levina, are you all right in there?"

She stopped brushing and sighed. "*Ya*, I'm fine." She began applying lotion to her hands, eyed her toothbrush, and realized that she didn't need to brush her teeth a second time. There was nothing left to do except go to bed. She couldn't stall forever.

Naaman closed the Bible when she walked in. He sat taller in the bed, already tucked beneath the covers. Only the lantern on his bedside table was illuminated, but she could see his features clearly. His extraordinary blue eyes brimmed with tenderness and passion as they roamed the length of her body, a muscle quivering at his jaw.

Levina thought about all the times she'd dreamed of this moment, when Naaman would come home and love her the way a husband loves his wife. She ran her hands down the sides of her white gown, then she looked toward the wooden floor. She took a deep breath and looked back up at him.

"*Mei lieb* . . . you look as beautiful as the day I married you."

Levina wanted to run to him, but her lack of trust and confusion melded together and she just stood there. How could he come back into her life after all this time and act as if nothing had changed? She'd slept alone for almost a year, wondering if she would spend the rest of her life without her husband by her side. Now here he was, all tucked in and waiting for her to resume their life together as husband and wife.

She took a slow pensive step backward, then two more, as the hopeful light in Naaman's eyes began to fade.

Chapter Two

LEVINA BLINKED HER EYES A FEW TIMES BEFORE SHE REALized that she was in Tillie's old room. She rolled onto her side and pulled the pink and white quilt up around her neck. Day was breaking, and tiny rays of sunlight shone through the window and onto the foot of the bed. Outside, the rooster crowed good morning and the far-off moo of a cow reminded her that she needed to get up and milk. Then she remembered that Naaman was home to handle that chore.

She threw back the covers, then sat on the edge of the bed and rubbed the sleep from her eyes as she recalled how long she'd lain in bed last night before sleep finally won out. Today would be a hard day for all of them, but Levina quickly set to praying that it would be a blessed day filled with forgiveness.

Please, Lord, help the children to see their father for the truly wonderful man he is and not just for his actions this past year. Help them to remember that all things are of Your will, even if we don't always understand Your plan for us at the time. May You bless this day with Your grace and be with us during these trying times.

Levina knew that she needed to heed this prayer as well, to remember the many years Naaman had been a wonderful husband and doting father to their children. She stood up and walked to the closed door of Tillie's room, then slowly pulled it open. She was surprised to smell bacon. Thirty-one years of marriage, and she'd never known Naaman to cook breakfast. She wasn't even sure he knew how.

She scurried across the hall and eased the door open. The room was empty, the bed made. Levina breathed a sigh of relief as she walked to the row of pegs on the wall. She pulled down a dark green dress and quickly slipped out of her nightgown, glancing twice over her shoulder as she did so. It wasn't until she turned back around that she saw a piece of paper on the middle of the bed.

Slowly she eased toward the note and picked it up, then she squinted as she tried to focus. After finding her reading glasses on the nightstand, she read:

MEI DEAREST LEVINA,

I LOVE YOU MORE TODAY THAN I DID YESTERDAY, AND LESS THAN I WILL TOMORROW.

YOUR LOVING HUSBAND, NAAMAN

Levina pushed her glasses up on her nose and read the note again, recalling how Naaman always used to tell her that. She pressed the note to her chest and tried to remember the last time he had said those words.

Her pulse quickened as she crept across the den and into the kitchen, expecting to find him preparing breakfast—or trying to—but the room was empty. However, the table was set and a serving plate of bacon, scrambled eggs, and toast awaited her. He'd set the rhubarb jelly right next to her plate, knowing it was her favorite. In the middle of the table was a glass vase filled with tiger lilies from their flower bed.

She walked to the window and saw Naaman walking into the barn, then she turned back to face the table. She sat down and filled her plate with bacon that was burnt to a crisp, overcooked eggs, and toast that was blackened on both sides. She'd sneak the leftovers to their Irish setter, Hitch, when she was done.

She picked up a piece of bacon with her fingers. As she bit into it, most of it crumbled in her hand, but she thought about what a

BETH WISEMAN

lovely gesture this breakfast was. She took a few more bites, just to get her through until lunch, then scraped the rest onto a paper plate for Hitch.

After the dog enjoyed the leftovers and the kitchen was clean, Levina headed to the barn. Orange met with the green fields in the distance as the sun climbed upward, and fresh dew slipped between her toes as she strolled across the grass. She pulled the door open and saw that Naaman had just finished milking the cows. Her garden clogs were just inside the barn door, so she eased her feet into the shoes and took a couple of slow steps toward him.

"Where's Lou-Lou?" He looked up at her as he wiped his hands on his breeches.

Levina walked closer then sighed. "She died last month. I reckon I don't know what happened." Levina recalled the day she found the old cow on her side. "Maybe old age?"

"Remember when we named her?"

Levina smiled. "*Ya*. It was Tillie who called her that when she was young, and it just stuck."

They were quiet for a few moments, then Naaman walked to his workbench and ran a hand gingerly along the top. "I've missed building furniture."

"*Danki* for breakfast, Naaman. And for the flowers—and the note." She bit her lip for a moment, not wanting to hurt his feelings. "But you didn't have to make breakfast. You know I've always done that."

Naaman hung his head, then looked back up. "It was terrible."

"*Nee, nee* . . . it's not that. I just always—"

He chuckled. "No, Levina. It was awful. I ate as much as I could, and I reckon I hated to even set the table for you, but I thought you might eat a little."

Levina brought her hand to her mouth.

"I see you laughing." He pointed a playful finger at her.

"You never could cook, Naaman." She looked away. "But it was a very nice thing to do."

Naaman walked closer, until he was right in front of her. "I'm going to make things up to you, Levina, if it's the last thing I do."

"If you cook for us, it might *be* the last thing you do." She folded her arms across her chest but grinned.

Naaman got a look in his eye that she remembered from times past, a twinkle that always came before he said something very sweet. "I *will* make it up to you."

She inched one eyebrow upward. "See to it that you do." Then she spun around and walked out of the barn.

NAAMAN WATCHED HER WALK TO THE HOUSE. IF HE DIDN'T know better, he'd think she was the same spunky, playful woman he'd married over three decades ago. He couldn't recall the last time they'd joked like that, or done much of anything that didn't revolve around hard work and the children. Even though their lives had always included prayer, strong faith, and fellowship, the intimacy between husband and wife had eluded them for a long time.

Naaman thought about his time in Ohio. There'd been no pressure to do much of anything. He'd helped his cousin Levi with chores around the farm, but there was no worry about pleasing anyone else, and he had lots of time to himself.

Levi and Mary had two sons still living at home, both in their *rumschpringe*. The couple were going through some of the same things Naaman and Levina had experienced when their children were going through their running-around period. Levi was particularly perturbed when sixteen-year-old Ben sneaked into the house late one night, smelling of beer.

Naaman recalled a night like that with Adam. But once all of their *kinner* were out of the house, there was no one to focus on. Only Levina. And he didn't know her anymore.

He spent the rest of the morning working in the barn, clearing the cobwebs from his workbench and reorganizing his tools and supplies. Not much was out of order, but it felt good to shuffle around among his own things. Levina brought a ham and cheese sandwich out to the barn when he didn't come in for dinner, but she didn't stay. In the afternoon, he repaired a section of fence between the house and the west field.

It was midafternoon when he crossed the yard and headed toward the house. He noticed that there was a fresh coat of white paint on the hundred-year-old structure. He wondered which one of his sons had painted the house while he was away—or had they worked together? There were also two new rocking chairs on the front porch and a variety of potted plants that weren't there when he left last summer. He eased his way up the porch steps then into the house. He could hear Levina humming in the kitchen, something he never remembered hearing her do before.

She jumped when he walked into the kitchen. "*Ach*, I didn't hear you come in." She went back to chopping potatoes.

Naaman ran his hand the length of his beard and watched her, although the humming had stopped. "I missed you in our bed last night."

Levina stopped chopping, but she kept her back to him as she spoke. "Did you miss me in your bed for the past eleven months?"

Ouch. "*Ya*, I did." It was the truth. He hadn't slept well while he was away. Nearly every night he'd reached across the bed to drape an arm across Levina, but always awoke to an empty bed to match his empty heart.

Neither of them spoke for a few minutes.

Naaman sat down at the kitchen table. "When will all the *kinner* be here?"

"Around five. In time for supper."

He glanced at the clock on the kitchen wall. Three thirty. "I reckon I'll go bathe before they arrive." He paused when she didn't say anything. "I'm really lookin' forward to seeing everyone, especially Rosemary's new little one." His heart hurt as he thought about his grandchild being born in his absence. He mentally calculated— Adam had four children, Jonathan had three, and Rosemary had given birth to . . . his tenth grandchild—a baby girl they'd named Leah. Soon his two youngest daughters, Freda and Tillie, would be adding to that number, he reckoned. "It will be *gut* for us all to be together," he added as he stood up from the table.

"I laid out some fresh towels for you, ones that came off the line today." Levina poured the chopped potatoes from the cutting board into a pot on the stove.

"*Danki.*"

Levina knew how much he liked towels fresh from the line. It was a nice gesture for her to put some out for him. But not uncommon, he realized, wondering if he'd made a point to thank her in the past.

LEVINA ADDED WATER TO THE POT OF POTATOES, LIT THE GAS burner, then checked on the pot roast in the oven.

She turned around, leaned against the counter, and sighed. Perhaps she should have told Naaman that they wouldn't *all* be together today. Levina had pleaded with Adam, but he wouldn't budge.

"He is not *mei daed*," Adam had said firmly.

When Levina tried to remind her son about forgiveness, Adam said his father should have thought about his actions before he abandoned his family. "I have shunned him."

"You can't make that decision, Adam," she'd told him. "That is for the bishop and elders to decide."

But Adam had refused to listen.

Chapter Three

ROSEMARY WAITED FOR GLENN TO BRING THE BUGGY TO A stop in front of her brother's house.

"I just want to try one more time to talk Adam into coming." She glanced over her shoulder to check on Leah in the infant carrier and Sarah and Marie on either side of the baby. "I'll be right back."

Adam met her on the front porch. "Save your breath, Rosemary." He folded his arms across his chest and scowled. "I'm not going."

"Adam, are you sure?"

Her brother dropped his hands to his sides. "I don't want to be around him." He paused, then refolded his arms. "What about you? I thought you weren't going to speak to *Daed*. What happened to that?"

Rosemary sighed. "I know, I know." She pressed her lips together for a moment. "I'm still angry at him, Adam. But he's our father, and—and I guess I am also doing this for *Mamm*." She pointed a finger at him. "And for our *kinner*. They have a right to have a relationship with their *daadi*."

"My *kinner* will be just fine without him in their lives. He should've thought about everything he could lose when he abandoned his family."

"What does Hannah think about this?"

"*Mei frau* will support my decision." Adam gave a taut jerk of his head.

"What about forgiveness, Adam?"

Adams's eyes widened. "Have *you* forgiven him, Rosemary?"

She tucked her chin. "I'm trying."

"He wasn't even here for little Leah's birth."

Rosemary faced off with her brother. "Okay, Adam. I can see this is going nowhere. I just wanted to try one more time." She turned her back and headed down the porch steps.

"Rosemary?"

She spun around. "*Ya?*"

"Tell *Mamm* I'm sorry."

Rosemary stared at her brother for a moment. "I will."

As she headed back to her family, Rosemary's heart was filled with conflicting emotions. Naaman Lapp was their father, and he'd always been a good one until a year ago. She'd always respected him more than any other man in the world—now she struggled to understand him and hoped she could hold her tongue today.

NAAMAN WALKED INTO THE KITCHEN WEARING HIS BLACK Sunday vest over a burgundy-colored shirt Levina had never seen before. Levina didn't think he'd ever looked more handsome, but she could tell by the way the muscle in his jaw was working that he was nervous.

"You look very nice." She placed a tray of pickles on the table. "The *kinner* should be here any minute." She took a deep breath then sighed. "Naaman . . ."

He walked closer, raised a brow.

"Adam won't be here today." She bit her bottom lip. "Nor will Hannah and the children." She held her breath and waited for his response.

Naaman swallowed hard. "I guess it will take time for Adam to forgive me."

"I think so." Levina forced a smile, then turned to stir her green beans on the stove.

"What about you, Levina? Have you forgiven me?"

She turned to face him, and for a brief instant she almost went to him. His forlorn expression begged for a hug. "*Ya*, Naaman. I forgave you a long time ago."

"Because our faith requires it?" He hung his head slightly for a moment, then fearfully looked up at her.

Levina thought about easing his suffering, but she didn't want to lie. "*Ya*," she said softly. She took a deep breath, then went back to setting the table. A few moments later she heard the clippity-clop of hooves coming up the driveway.

Naaman walked to the window. "It looks like Freda and Jake." He paused, leaning his face closer to the glass. "And I think that's Tillie and Rufus behind them."

"You will be surprised when you see Tillie. Since she's been married, she's lost a lot of weight." Levina put a pitcher of iced tea in the middle of the table, then she brushed back a loose strand of hair that had fallen forward. "Tillie always loved to garden, and now that she has her own garden to tend to, along with her own house to take care of, she has trimmed up."

"I always thought she was perfect the way she was." Naaman turned briefly toward Levina and smiled.

"Tillie has always been a beautiful girl, but that extra weight she was carrying wasn't good for her. She'll have an easier pregnancy when the time comes, and that has nothing to do with vanity or pride."

Their youngest daughter had been the only one of their children to struggle with extra pounds, and Levina could tell that Tillie felt better about herself since she'd lost some weight. She walked toward the door when she heard footsteps on the porch. Naaman was quickly at her side, and her husband took a deep breath before he pulled the door open.

"Hello, *Daed*." Freda leaned forward and gave her father a hug.

Levina breathed a sigh of relief. To her surprise, Naaman eased away from Freda and embraced Jake in a hug as well.

Tillie came bouncing in behind her sister and brother-in-law and practically jumped into Naaman's arms. *"Daed!"* Her eyes filled with tears. "I missed you." She squeezed Naaman even tighter around the neck.

For Tillie, forgiveness had always come easily.

"You're squeezing him to death." Tillie's husband, Rufus, tapped his wife on the shoulder, and Tillie let go of her father so Rufus could shake his hand—but Naaman also pulled Rufus into a hug.

Levina tried to rest easier, knowing that two of her five children were accepting of and grateful for their father's return. She could see through the opened screen door that Rosemary was coming across the yard toting baby Leah. Glenn trailed behind her with their eight-year-old twins, Sarah and Marie.

"Hello, *Daed*." Rosemary's smile was bleak and tight-lipped. Her arms were full, carrying Leah and the diaper bag, and Levina instantly wondered if she had planned it that way. Her husband's hands were free.

"So this is little Leah." Naaman leaned down and eyed his newest granddaughter. "Four months old, no?"

Rosemary cut her eyes toward Levina, then looked back at Naaman. *"Ya."* She moved away from her father, even though he was still leaning down and looking at Leah, and kissed Levina on the cheek. "Where's Jonathan?"

"He's not here yet." Levina nudged Rosemary toward the den, out of earshot of the others. "Did you stop by Adam's?"

"Ya." Rosemary sighed. "He's not coming, *Mamm*. He said he's sorry."

Levina let out a heavy sigh as she searched Rosemary's eyes. Rosemary had just turned thirty last month, and she and her husband recently celebrated their tenth wedding anniversary. Levina loved her children equally, but she was closest to Rosemary. She would continue to pray that Rosemary would soften where her father was concerned.

"Well, I'm glad you're here." Levina smiled as she reached for Leah. "Let me hold that precious bundle."

"She spit up on the way here." Rosemary handed the baby to her mother. "I reckon because Glenn was driving so fast." She rolled her eyes but smiled.

"Well, she won't spit up on her *mammi*, will you, Leah?" Levina touched the tip of her finger to Leah's nose, then realized how quiet it was in the other room. She carried Leah back into the kitchen and took a peek out the window. "The meal is ready, if you want to sit down at the table. I see Jonathan and Becky pulling into the driveway."

Levina watched Naaman walk to the door, still limping. She knew that Jonathan was glad his father had returned, and she expected a warm reunion between the two, but as he embraced his father in a hug, she let out another sigh of relief. Becky and their three young children all greeted Naaman with a hug as well.

"Rosemary, there's a fold-up table in the den for your girls and Jonathan's three." Levina pointed toward the other room as everyone began to take their seats at her table in the kitchen, which would hold all ten adults. "And the playpen is folded against the wall in there, if you want to lay Leah in it while you eat."

Naaman took a seat at the head of the table, and Levina recalled the many meals she'd shared with her children while he was away. Yet he just took his seat as if not a day had passed . . . She closed her eyes for a moment. *Please, Lord. I don't want to hold a grudge.*

Levina was the last to sit, and everyone bowed their heads in prayer.

She opened her eyes and saw Jonathan scooping mashed potatoes on his plate. She narrowed her eyes in his direction.

"What?" His brows lifted beneath his sun-streaked bangs. "I said my blessings *fast*." He grinned. "I'm starving, *Mamm*."

As they all filled their plates, light conversation ensued. Jonathan talked about how much he enjoyed his new responsibilities at the furniture store where he'd worked for nearly six months. Naaman couldn't comment, since he didn't know what Jonathan had done before his promotion. Freda reported that her friend Rebecca, who was new to the area, was finally out of the hospital after surgery to remove a tumor in her stomach. Everyone at the table offered thanks and praise about the news. Naaman nodded, although he'd never met Freda's friend.

Tillie patiently waited to talk about her job at Yoder's Pantry, where she'd worked part-time for the past few months. Levina was glad to see Tillie directing her comments to Naaman.

"*Daed*, you and *Mamm* will have to come eat lunch together there. *Mamm* comes sometimes. They have the best pretzels in the world! And my friend Abby goes there a lot, too, for lunch. Remember Abby Kauffman, *Daed*? She married Joseph Lambert, right after he came home and was baptized."

Tillie's round little cheeks lifted above dimples that Levina was sure God made special just for Tillie. Her smile had always been contagious, and when she started talking, her hands became animated and her bubbly zest for life could lift anyone's spirits.

"*Mamm* and I helped teach Abby to cook. Abby's *mamm* passed a long time ago, so she'd never really learned how."

Levina was glad to see Naaman smiling.

"Anyway, I also love to talk to all the *Englisch* people when they come in." Tillie giggled. "They ask so many questions about our way of life, and I like telling them about our faith." She sat up taller. "*Mamm*, guess who came in yesterday?"

Levina swallowed a bite of beans. "Who?"

Tillie brought both hands to her chest and took a deep breath.

"Bishop Ebersol." She paused, pressing her lips together. "And guess what he said?"

"Just tell us, Tillie." Jonathan chuckled, shaking his head. "I reckon everything is such a big deal to you."

"He said that my bread pudding was the best he'd ever eaten. What about that?" A smile filled Tillie's face. Then she almost bounced in her seat. "And Mr. Princeton came into Yoder's last week too!"

Naaman cleared his throat. "And who is Mr. Princeton?"

"He's the *Englisch* man who owns the Pantry along with Martha and John Yoder. That's why we can have electricity, since an *Englisch* person is part owner." Tillie reached across her husband for the salt.

Levina stifled a grin. Tillie's husband, Rufus, was the quietest fellow she'd ever met. But his eyes lit up every time Tillie spoke.

Tillie went on for at least another ten minutes, filling her father in about every new family who had moved in, those who had left, and who was courting whom. With sadness in her eyes, she told him about the old widow who lived around the corner. "Sarah Dienner passed, too, *Daed*. Went in her sleep, they say. Her son is comin' to put the place up for sale, and—"

"Why don't you let *Daed* talk?" Rosemary interrupted. "I'm sure we'd all like to hear what he did in Ohio."

Levina drew in a deep breath as she watched Rosemary fold her arms across her chest.

"Well, *Daed*?" Rosemary arched her brows. "Tell us. Tell us all about Middlefield."

"Rosemary . . ." Levina said in a warning tone. No matter what, Naaman was still Rosemary's father.

"What, *Mamm*?" Rosemary shrugged. "So, *Daed* . . . tell us. What was so wonderful about Middlefield, Ohio, that it would cause you to abandon your family for almost a year?"

Chapter Four

NAAMAN GLANCED AT LEVINA, WHOSE CHEEKS WERE FIERY red at their daughter's persistence. They didn't raise their children to be so outspoken, but Naaman knew he owed his family some answers. He had just been hoping it wouldn't have to be tonight.

"Rosemary, let's don't do this right now."

Levina's voice was firm, but Naaman saw the raw hurt in Rosemary's eyes. It was hard for him to believe that his eldest daughter was thirty years old. He didn't recall a gray hair on her head when he left; now he saw a thread of silver that had escaped the confines of her *kapp*.

Where had the time gone? He knew his family thought a year of that time had gone to waste. *Had it?*

"It's all right, Levina." He smiled slightly at his wife, then faced off with Rosemary. "I left here to find myself." It was a lame answer, and Naaman regretted it instantly.

"When did you get *lost?*" Rosemary's bottom lip was trembling as she spoke.

Naaman had never heard his daughter use that tone with him.

"Rosemary, I don't think this is the time . . ." Levina stood from the table and began to clear the dishes.

"No, *Mamm.* We'd all like to know. Wouldn't we?" Rosemary glanced around the table.

No one spoke or even gave a nod. Jonathan stared at his plate. Freda and Tillie looked across the table at each other and didn't move.

"I guess I got lost a long time ago, Rosemary," Naaman said with a forced calmness in his voice. He wondered if they could hear the sadness, mixed with anger . . . mostly at himself.

"And now you're found?" Rosemary's eyes filled with tears as she spoke. "Do you know how hard it was for *Mamm* while you were away? All the chores here, the way people talk, and—"

"Stop it." Levina stomped her foot.

In all his years, Naaman had never seen her do that.

"This is your father's *haus*, Rosemary. I will not have you disrespect him in this way." She nodded her head toward the den and lowered her voice. "And not in front of the children either."

One thing Naaman didn't need was Levina defending him. He felt like a stranger at his own table. He was still the head of the family, the decision maker, the one they'd all counted on for most of their lives. But he didn't have one logical thought that could make them understand the choice he'd made eleven months ago. He didn't understand it himself.

A heaviness settled around his heart as he stood from the table and watched Rosemary dab at a tear. Her husband placed his hand on top of hers and gave her a gentle pat. Glenn was a good man. A good husband and father. Naaman used to think of himself that way.

He looked around the table at his family, then swallowed hard. "I am sorry to *mei* family. I don't have a *gut* reason for being away." He turned to Levina. "Your *mamm* is a wonderful *frau*." Naaman looked at each one of his children around the table. "And the Lord blessed me far more than I deserve with each of you." He paused and took a breath. "Excuse me, please."

LEVINA WAITED UNTIL NAAMAN HAD CLOSED THE SCREEN door behind him and was down the porch steps before she addressed their children.

"Your father is a *gut* man, and he is still the head of this household." She held up one finger when Rosemary opened her mouth to speak. "And it wonders me how you can speak to him with disrespect, Rosemary." Levina shook her head. "I won't have it."

Rosemary dabbed at her eyes with her napkin and sniffled. "I'm sorry, *Mamm*. It's just that we all watched how you suffered while he was gone, and now he's back as if nothing happened. I just don't understand it."

Levina wanted to blurt out that she didn't understand it either, but as much as she wanted to kick Naaman in the shins for what he'd done, her desire to shelter him from hurt far outweighed her own anger. *He is still my husband, and I love him.*

"But he's back." Tillie's eyes twinkled as she spoke softly to her sister. "Let's just be happy and thankful about that."

Rosemary stood up. "*Mamm*, supper was *gut*, but I think we should go." She walked to the den, and Levina could hear her telling Sarah and Marie to finish their milk.

Freda started helping Levina clear the table. "Give her time, *Mamm*. Rosemary will come around. So will Adam." At twenty-three, Freda had always possessed a maturity beyond her years.

Levina smiled. "I hope you're right."

Her three sons-in-law and Jonathan all headed outside. Levina hoped they would join Naaman in the barn, where he often went after a meal. Rosemary was gathering up her children, and Levina suspected she would be rounding up her husband as well.

Levina washed dishes as Tillie dried, and Freda gathered up jams, jellies, and other items to be stored in the refrigerator. Rosemary entered the kitchen holding Leah in one arm and the infant carrier in the other. The twins were right behind her.

"*Mamm*, can we go out to the barn?" Sarah looked up at Rosemary with her big brown eyes, and Levina smiled to herself, remembering how Rosemary used to give Levina the same look when she wanted something.

"I guess so. But we'll be leaving soon."

Rosemary waited until her girls were halfway across the yard before she spoke. "It's just hard for me to watch *Daed* sitting at the head of the table." She put the carrier in the middle of the table, then carefully laid her sleeping baby in it. "I'm trying to forgive him. I really am." She grabbed an empty pot from the stove and leaned around Levina to put it into the dishwater. "I just don't understand. Glenn would never do anything like that."

Levina felt her muscles tense as she turned to face her oldest daughter. "You don't know what anyone will do, Rosemary."

Tillie placed a dry plate in the cabinet then shrugged. "I read in a magazine that when people get old, they go through a midlife crisis." She paused, tilting her head to one side. "Maybe that's what happened to *Daed*."

"Tillie, where do you read such things?" Levina shook her head. *Old?*

"At the doctor's office. They have all kinds of magazines." Tillie raised her brows and grinned.

"What were you at the doctor for?" Levina stopped washing and turned to face her youngest daughter.

Tillie let out a heavy sigh. "I thought I might be in the family way." She frowned as she reached for another plate. "But I'm not."

"It'll happen, Tillie," Freda said. "I'm older than you and still waiting."

"The Lord will bless you both with *kinner* soon enough, I reckon." Levina drained the water from the sink, wiped the counter with the dishrag, then dried her hands. She walked to little Leah. "Such a blessing." She leaned down and kissed her newest grandchild on the head, then sat down at the kitchen table. She waited for all her girls to sit down.

"I know this is *hatt* for all of you, but we must try not to question God's will." Levina spoke the words her daughters expected, words they all knew were in accordance with the *Ordnung* by which they'd all been raised. But in her heart Levina knew that she'd been questioning God's will from the moment Naaman walked out the door last year. "You all know that your father is a *gut* man."

"I know that, *Mamm.*" Rosemary brought both hands to her forehead. "I'm just so disappointed in him."

Leah started to fuss, so Freda picked her up. "I'm disappointed in him, too, Rosemary. But I love him, no matter what."

"So do I," Rosemary huffed. "I'm not saying I don't love him."

"*Mamm?*" Tillie propped her elbows on the table and held her chin with her hands. "Why do you think *Daed* left in the first place?"

Levina took a deep breath. "*Mei dochders,* your father only came home yesterday. We haven't had much time to talk." She focused on Rosemary. "But I reckon sometimes people grow apart, for reasons we aren't quite sure of. Now your *daed* and I have to find our way back to each other."

Rosemary grunted, then stood from the table. "*Daed* got lost, got found, and now you both have to find your way back to each other. That's a lot of lost and found."

"Stop it, Rosemary," Freda said sharply.

Tillie just smiled. "For *all* have sinned, and come short of the glory of God."

"I know, Tillie," Rosemary said with a heavy sigh. "Just give me some time." Then she looked at Levina and shook her head. "I don't know about Adam though, *Mamm.* He doesn't even like to talk about *Daed.* He gets really angry."

Levina nodded, but her mother's instinct told Levina that something else was bothering Adam. Yes, he was angry at his father . . . but Levina had noticed some things about Adam that perhaps the other children had not.

Chapter Five

ADAM TOOK A BITE OF HIS MEAT LOAF AND WONDERED IF HIS mother had prepared a pot roast for supper. He loved Hannah's cooking, and the meat loaf was wonderful, but there was nothing quite like his mother's pot roast. He pictured Rosemary, Jonathan, Freda, and Tillie sitting around his parents' kitchen table, with their spouses and children, and regret pierced his heart. Then he envisioned his father sitting at the head of the table, and he scowled.

"Is something wrong with the meat loaf?" Hannah wiped mashed potatoes from Anna Mae's chin.

"No. It's *gut*. Like always." Adam smiled, then glanced around at his own family. Seven-year-old Ben and six-year-old Abner sat side by side, and four-year-old Katherine was in a booster chair across from them. Two-year-old Anna Mae was in a high chair next to Hannah. *I have a beautiful family. I would never leave them.*

"Can we be excused?" Ben set his fork on his plate, then rubbed his eyes.

Adam knew he'd worked his young boys hard today. While Adam plowed the fields, he'd left a long list of chores for Ben and Abner—clean the horse stalls, wash the buggy, and ready up the barn in preparation for worship service this Sunday. It was a tall order for such young lads, but Adam believed in hard work—something instilled in him by his own father. He grimaced again.

"*Ya.* You can both be excused following prayer."

They all bowed their heads, except for Anna Mae. When they were done, Adam took a bite of mashed potatoes and watched his boys get up from the table and head toward the den. "Boys?"

Ben and Abner turned around.

"*Ya, Daed?*" Ben said.

"You are *hatt* workers. You did a *gut* job today."

Both boys' faces lit up before they scooted off to take baths.

"That was nice, Adam. I'm glad you recognize the boys' hard work." Hannah helped Katherine from the booster chair and gently wiped her chin. Then she lifted Anna Mae from the high chair after also dabbing her face with a napkin. "Katherine, take Anna Mae's hand, and the two of you go into the den and look at your picture books while I clean the kitchen."

Adam wiped his own mouth and watched Hannah start to clear the dishes. He thought about his mother, and again he pictured the scene unfolding at his childhood home. Everyone there but him, he supposed. He wondered if his father headed to the barn after the meal, the way he'd always done. Did Jonathan and his brothers-in-law go? Did they tell jokes or talk about the day's events? Was everything back to normal, as if their father hadn't forsaken his family for almost a year?

"Your head is full with thoughts," Hannah said as she reached in front of him to take his plate. "Do you wish that we had gone to your father's homecoming supper?"

"No." Adam leaned back in his chair and looped his thumbs beneath his suspenders. "I don't have a father anymore."

Hannah let out a heavy sigh. "You don't mean that, Adam." She turned to put the plate in the sink.

"*Ya*. I do. What kind of a man leaves his family like that?"

Hannah turned around as the sink filled with water. "Why don't you ask him and find out?"

Adam stared long and hard at his wife of ten years. When did she start using such a tone with him? "I will not."

BETH WISEMAN

Hannah shrugged. "I reckon it will be your loss. Your *daed* is a *gut* man, and without talking to him, you don't know why he left." She spun around and began washing the dishes.

"Why are you defending him?" Adam heard the anger in his voice as he spoke. "What if it had been me? What if I had left you and the *kinner* and just taken off?"

Hannah spun around, clamped her jaw tight, and stared him down with brown eyes flecked with gold in the light of the propane lamp nearby. As the sun descended, a hazy orange glow filled the room. But even in the dim light, Adam saw the distinct hardening of his wife's eyes.

"I hope that will never happen," she finally said.

"Of course it will never happen." Adam looked away from her, shoved his chair back from the table, and stood up. "I'm going to go close up the barn for the night."

Hannah shrugged, then turned back around and started washing dishes again.

"Why do you do that?"

"Do what?" She didn't turn around.

"Shrug. You always do that. You shrug your shoulders at me when you don't agree with something." Adam folded his arms across his chest and waited for her to answer, but instead . . . she shrugged. He could feel his face turning red as he turned and headed out the door.

Lucky Daed. *He got a break from all this.*

LEVINA AND NAAMAN SAID GOOD-BYE TO THEIR CHILDREN and grandchildren, then sat down in the rocking chairs on the front porch.

"I missed these sunsets." Naaman didn't look at her, but instead seemed far away as they watched gray clouds pushing the sun toward freshly planted fields in the distance—crops planted by her sons and sons-in-law only a few weeks earlier.

Levina kicked her rocker into motion. "There's a storm coming. We'll need to close all the windows soon."

Naaman didn't say anything but continued to stare into the twilight.

"I'm sorry about Rosemary, Naaman. She will need time to make room in her heart for you again." Levina decided not to mention anything about Adam.

"Don't apologize for Rosemary, Levina. I reckon all the *kinner* have a right to be angry with me." He shifted his weight to face her, then stirred uneasily in his chair. "Have you made room in your heart for me, Levina?"

They'd been avoiding the conversation that Levina knew they had to have. She took a deep breath and let it out slowly. "I reckon you've always been in my heart, Naaman. But . . ."

Naaman's blue eyes searched her face. "But what?"

"I–I don't understand." Levina swallowed hard and sat up taller, determined to stay strong as she asked the next question. "Was there someone else? Another woman in Middlefield?"

Naaman's mouth dropped open briefly, then he clamped it shut as his eyes darkened with emotion. He twisted in his chair to face her. "Levina . . ." He spoke in a broken whisper. "Never. There has never been anyone but you." He hung his head. "I'm sorry you have to ask that."

"Then why? Why, Naaman?" Levina's voice rose an octave as she spoke, and she suddenly wished she could take back the question. Fear and anxiety knotted inside her, and she wasn't sure she was prepared to hear his answer. She tucked her chin and held her breath.

"I guess I needed to find—"

"Don't you dare say that you needed to find yourself!" She interrupted him with reckless anger. "You can give that answer to your children, but I am your *frau*, Naaman. What did I do to cause you to leave our home, our life?" She covered her face with her hands and prayed she wouldn't cry, but even though she bit her lip until it throbbed like her pulse, a tear still spilled.

When she pulled her hands away, Naaman was in front of her on one knee, just as he had been when he proposed to her thirty-one years ago. He reached for her hand, pulled it to his mouth, and kissed it gently. His touch was more tender than Levina could recall. "I'm sorry, Levina."

She eased her hand from his. "Then explain to me, Naaman. I need to understand if we are going to move forward, because right now I–I don't trust you."

"I don't blame you for not trusting me, Levina." He spoke softly, but his voice was filled with steadfast determination. "But I promise you that I will spend the rest of my life making it up to you."

Levina drew in a deep breath, then let it out slowly. "Then tell me why you left."

He gazed into her eyes. "I think you know why I left, and to be honest—I'm not sure it pained you as much as you are letting on."

"How can you say that?" Levina bolted from the chair and scooted around him to stand on the edge of the porch. She stared into the gray skies. The crescent moon was suspended in the sky—off balance, the way Naaman's comment had left her feeling. She turned to face him and asked again, "How can you say that?"

Naaman opened his mouth to speak, but Levina held up one finger, something she often did with her children when she didn't want to hear what they had to say. "While you were away, do you have any idea what I went through? Not just the chores and hardships of running this farm, but the people . . ." She paused. "Even in our community, the people still talk. I was humiliated."

Naaman walked closer to her, his eyes filled with sorrow. "I will not deny that what I did was wrong." He tilted his head to one side and stared at her in a way she didn't recognize, a far-off, burning gaze that seemed to drill a hole all the way to her soul. "But let me ask you something . . ." He stroked his dark beard, not taking his eyes from her. "Didn't you ever think about it? Just once? Didn't you ever wonder what else was out there? Weren't you ever tempted to get away, to get to know the woman you are, to experience more than we've ever known here?" He latched onto her shoulders. "Levina, be honest. Tell me that you have never fantasized about just going out on your own to—"

She jerked from his grasp. "Never! Not once, Naaman. I would never dream of leaving our children or grandchildren. I'd have never left you to experience some late-in-life *rumschpringe*!"

"Really?" His doubtful blue eyes bored into hers.

Levina stepped away from him. "Don't do this, Naaman. Don't you try to justify your selfish actions by accusing me of having the same deceitful thoughts."

He held his palms up. "Okay. I'm sorry."

"I don't even know you!"

The truth filled the space around them, and Levina felt suffocated by the honesty that hung in the air. Such things shouldn't be discussed, and yet she knew that she and Naaman were crossing over into undiscovered territory—foreign terrain that left her unsteady on her feet.

Naaman eased closer, his eyes probing hers as if his intensity could unlock the secret place in her heart where all thoughts—good and bad—were stored. Slowly he reached up and brushed away a strand of hair that had fallen from beneath her *kapp*. His eyes never left hers as he leaned closer and brushed his lips to hers, sending a wave of emotion and excitement pulsing through her body as if she were a teenage girl once more.

"Then let's get to know each other again," he said softly before he kissed her again.

Levina couldn't remember the last time his kiss had left her weak in the knees.

Chapter Six

NAAMAN WOKE UP WHEN A THUNDERCLAP SHOOK THE WINdows of the farmhouse. As he'd done for the past year, he reached over to drape an arm across Levina, only to find that he was alone in the bed.

He rolled from his side to his back, then locked his hands behind his head and watched the flashes of lightning brightening the room, only to have it go dark again. He closed his eyes and thought about his kiss with Levina last night. He couldn't remember the last time he'd felt such passion, such desire. But she'd quickly halted his efforts and made a firm commitment to sleep in Tillie's room. "For now," she'd said.

Another bolt of lightning shook the rafters. Naaman thought about all the storms Levina must have weathered alone in the house—thunderstorms had always frightened her. *What was I thinking to leave her?*

He crossed his ankles beneath the quilt, and the intimate moment between him and his wife replayed over and over in his mind. He'd offered to sleep in Tillie's room or one of the other bedrooms, but Levina insisted that he sleep in their bed since it was the largest bed in the house.

He uncrossed his ankles and straightened his left leg, then bent it at the knee, then put it down again and decided that there was no good position to stop the throbbing in his hip caused by his recent fall. The doctor said the hip was badly bruised and that only time would heal it, but the nagging pain only reminded him of Middlefield, which ultimately led to another self-lashing about what he'd done.

Dear heavenly Father, he prayed, *I may never understand what drove me to leave my family, but I pray that I am back on the right course and that my* frau *and* kinner *will accept me back into their hearts and forgive me for my selfishness.*

Another boom halted his prayer midway. It sounded like lightning hit a tree. He eased his legs over the side of the bed, then put on his black pants. The boards creaked beneath his bare feet as he tiptoed out of the bedroom and across the hallway. He could see a light coming from Tillie's room, and he slowly pushed the door open.

Levina was sitting up in the bed in her white nightgown, with her legs pulled to her chest. The lantern on her bedside table glowed, and stark fear glittered in her eyes.

"Levina, are you all right?" He took a hesitant step into Tillie's room, and a flash of light illuminated Levina's beautiful face as she smiled and her fear seemed to fade.

"*Ya.*" She crinkled her nose and frowned. "You know how I get scared when it's stormy outside." Another roar of thunder sent Levina's hands to her ears as she clamped her eyes closed.

Naaman walked to the side of the bed and hesitated, and instead walked to the rocking chair in the corner. He sat down and stared at his wife. He didn't think he'd ever wanted anything so badly in his life—just to hold her in his arms.

"Naaman, what are you doing?" She sat taller and narrowed her brows.

"Sleep, Levina." He spoke in a whisper. "I will stay here with you."

Levina pushed back long waves of hair from her face and shook her head. "That's silly. You don't have to do that. Go back to your bed, Naaman."

She spoke with authority, as if she were speaking to one of the children, but when another flash of lightning lit up the room, she was instantly transformed into a small child herself, scrunching her face up as she waited for the roar.

Naaman stood up and walked to the edge of the bed. "Levina, let me sit with you until you fall asleep."

"Go to your room, Naaman." She lowered her chin and looked up at him playfully. "Now."

Naaman winked at her. "You sure?"

"*Ya*. Now go." She shooed him with her hand.

He couldn't take his eyes from her, though. "You're so beautiful, Levina." He felt like a schoolboy with a crush on the prettiest girl in the eighth grade. Levina Beiler—she'd been his crush before he made her his wife.

They shared a smile, but Naaman saw the tremble in her lips. Fear of the storm? Fear of him? He wasn't sure. "Good night."

A few hours later Naaman awoke to the smell of bacon. Once he'd fallen back asleep, sometime after midnight, he'd slept uninterrupted. He sat up in bed, stretched his arms high, and then thanked the Lord for bringing him home where he belonged. He rubbed his eyes, stood up, and turned to make the bed. As he pulled the white cotton sheet taut on his side of the bed, he noticed the sheet tossed back on the other side, along with the quilt. Had he strayed that far over in the king-size bed? He never did that.

After running his hand the length of his beard a few times, he walked around to the other side of the bed. He picked up Levina's pillow and brought it to his face, then breathed in the smell of his wife, and again . . . he thanked God for the blessings of this new day.

LEVINA FELT GIDDY AS A SCHOOLGIRL AS SHE PULLED THE last piece of bacon from the skillet. It was an emotion that terrified and exhilarated her at the same time.

"*Guder mariye*, Levina."

Something about Naaman's suave tone made her think he knew she'd crawled into bed with him last night. She'd been ever so careful to stay far on her side, and she'd been quiet as she could be. Today would be a busy day, and she wanted to be fresh and alert. Curling up in the bed with Naaman provided a sense of familiarity and safety that she'd gone without for so long, and she'd slept peacefully the rest of the night. When morning came she'd sneaked downstairs before he ever knew she was there—or so she'd thought.

"*Guder mariye,* "she said without turning around. She held her breath, waiting to see if he would say anything.

He sat down in his chair at the kitchen table. "Sleep well?"

Levina twisted her mouth to one side as she tried to decipher his tone of voice—still suave and a little too smug. "*Ya*, I slept very well, *danki*." She carried the plate of bacon and a bowl of eggs to the table. "And you? How did you sleep?"

Naaman folded his arms across a dark green shirt, a silly grin on his face. "Soundly. I don't think I woke up once."

Levina placed a basket of biscuits in the middle of the table and eased into her chair. She nodded, avoiding his eyes. "*Gut, gut.* Glad you slept well."

They both bowed their heads in prayer.

"What are your plans for today?" Naaman buttered a biscuit as he spoke.

"I go to market on Friday mornings, and then I have lunch at Yoder's Pantry."

Naaman's brow shot upward. "Where Tillie works?"

"*Ya.*" Levina kept her head down as she scooped scrambled eggs onto her plate. She knew Naaman was waiting for an invitation, but she wasn't sure she wanted him to go with her to market—in public—until after he had his meeting with Bishop Ebersol. She thanked God every day that the bishop had not urged that Naaman be shunned.

She looked up to find him staring at her.

"Everything all right with breakfast?" Levina took a bite of her eggs.

"*Ya.* Much better than what I cooked for you." He kept staring at her, so she finally gave in.

"Do you—um—do you want to go to market with me, then to eat at Yoder's Pantry?"

"Sure."

Levina forced a smile, not sure of anything these days.

They ate quietly, and when they were done, she decided to broach two subjects that she wasn't looking forward to.

"You do remember that Bishop Ebersol will be here tomorrow at two o'clock, no?"

Naaman nodded. "*Ya,* I remember." His face clouded.

"And do you remember that worship service is at Adam's house on Sunday?"

Naaman's mouth took on an unpleasant twist as he chewed. After he swallowed, he rubbed his forehead with one hand. "I'm not sure I'm welcome there."

"It is worship service for our community, and you are in our community. Of course you're welcome." Levina gave a sharp nod.

"We will see."

"Are you thinking about not going?"

Naaman leaned back against the back of his chair. "Adam needs time, and I don't want to force myself on him."

Levina tapped her finger to her chin for a moment. "Naaman, you'll just need to trust me about this, but I think you need to force yourself on Adam. Something is going on with our oldest son."

Chapter Seven

NAAMAN PARKED THE BUGGY OUTSIDE OF YODER'S PANTRY as Levina scanned the parking lot. There were four other buggies tethered nearby, but it was impossible to distinguish between them. She dreaded walking in with Naaman, not knowing who she might bump into. Equally alarming was that Naaman latched onto her hand as they walked through the entrance. He knew that members of their community frowned upon public affection. She wiggled free of his grasp and frowned at him before they walked in, but he just shrugged—and with that childish grin on his face again.

"*Mamm! Daed!*" Tillie rushed to the front door right away. "Give me one minute, and I'll put you in our best seat by the window that faces away from the highway." Tillie bounced once on her toes and lifted her shoulders. "I'm so glad you're here!"

"That's *mei maedel*," Naaman said with a smile after Tillie skipped away.

"I hope she always keeps her childlike qualities." Levina folded her hands in front of her—just in case Naaman got any ideas—and scanned the restaurant. "Oh no," she whispered.

"What?" Naaman leaned closer.

"Eve Fisher is here, and she's a busybody."

"I know that I did not hear *mei gut frau* call someone a busybody." Naaman grinned.

"Shh. Keep your voice down, Naaman." Levina held her head high as she scanned the rows of jams and jellies on the shelf to her

324

right. She picked up a jar of rhubarb jam. "You know, Ellie Chupp makes a lot of these jams and jellies. She's dating Chris Miller—did I tell you he came back to the church? Tillie expects they'll get married this November."

She put the jar of jam back on the shelf and thumbed through various cookbooks, sundries, and of course, the large pretzels that Yoder's Pantry was famous for, each individually wrapped and tempting those who were on their way in or out.

Naaman was spinning a rack of books by the door. "Look at all these books with Amish women on the cover."

His puzzled expression caused Levina to giggle for a moment. Then she shrugged. "Lots of women in our community read these books. Who doesn't enjoy a good love story?" She blushed and grabbed the books from Naaman. After she placed them back on the rack, she turned her attention to those dining.

She hoped to avoid Eve Fisher . . . although she reckoned she should probably get used to the stares and the questions. Everyone would eventually welcome Naaman back into the community, but folks were human, and Levina knew there would be some uncomfortable moments.

"I have your table all ready!" Tillie was carting two menus, and her contagious smile warmed Levina's heart.

She hoped and prayed that Tillie would be in the family way soon. Levina wished that for both her daughters. Freda and her husband had been trying a bit longer to have a baby, but it was starting to feel like a race between the two sisters. Levina hoped that neither of them was disappointed. She recalled how easily she had become pregnant with Rosemary, Adam, and Jonathan, but it took a little longer to become pregnant with Freda. And Tillie was somewhat of a surprise. Levina had been doubtful that she could have more children, due to complications during Freda's birth. She would remind both Freda and Tillie that all things happen on God's time frame.

Once they were seated, Levina knew there was no way to avoid Eve, who was sitting only one table over. Tillie brought them each a glass of sweet tea and promised to return shortly. Seconds later Eve rose from her chair and headed their way.

"Hello, Levina." She smiled warmly at Levina, then turned to Naaman. "And welcome back, Naaman."

Eve, like Levina, was nearing the age of fifty—but for reasons Levina couldn't grasp, the woman didn't look a day over thirty. She reminded herself that physical appearance didn't matter, while also realizing that she should have given some thought about how she was going to respond to comments about Naaman's return. "Hello, Eve."

Naaman tipped his head in Eve's direction, and Levina saw the muscle in his jaw tense.

"Is this your first time here, Naaman?" Eve smiled. "I've seen Levina in here many times, but I don't reckon many men come in for lunch. They are mostly working in the fields."

Levina could feel her blood starting to boil. Naaman could run circles around most men in this community when it came to hard work, and she wasn't about to let Eve Fisher suggest that he wasn't a hard worker.

"Our fields are planted, and Naaman didn't get much sleep last night, so I'm treating him to lunch out." She raised her chin a bit and smiled at Eve, but when Eve's eyes widened, Levina figured she'd better clarify her statement. "When it makes wet and thunders so much, I get nervous and can't sleep. Naaman was tending to me, making sure I wasn't afraid."

"I see." Eve bit her lip and raised her brow. "Well, I best be goin' back to my table. Nice to see you both. I suppose we'll see you on Sunday for worship at Adam's *haus*."

"*Ya*. See you then." Levina gave a quick wave as Eve left.

"You don't like her much, no?" Naaman took a sip of his tea but kept his eyes on Levina.

"Naaman, why would you say such a thing? I have no bad feelings for Eve." Levina pressed her lips together, then took a deep breath. *I will pray hard tonight.*

Tillie came bouncing back to the table with her friend Abby. "*Daed*, remember Abby Kauffman? Only she's Abby Lambert now!"

Naaman extended his hand to Abby. "*Ya*, I do. Solomon's girl. Nice to see you."

Abby shook Naaman's hand, then turned to Levina. "*Danki* for letting me spend so much time at your *haus*."

"We're always glad to have you, Abigail. I enjoy it when Tillie brings you over and we all cook together."

Abby turned to Tillie. "I guess I better get back to Anna." She pointed toward a nearby table where she was dining with a friend.

Levina nodded, then she and Naaman each ordered the special—chicken and dumplings with a side of corn.

"Great choice!" Tillie waved to another patron across the room. "I'll be back soon."

After a few moments, Naaman leaned his head to one side and gazed long and hard at Levina. She thought she knew what was on his mind, but he surprised her.

"You mentioned that something is goin' on with Adam. What do you mean?"

Levina wasn't sure where to start. "I think there might be problems with him and Hannah. He won't talk to me when I ask him if everything is all right, and Rosemary tried to talk to him too. He insists nothing is wrong, but, Naaman . . ." She paused. "Something *is* wrong, whether it has to do with Hannah or not."

Naaman didn't seem interested in looking Levina square in the eye anymore. He seemed to be looking everywhere but at her. "It saddens me to hear that." He looked up when he heard someone scooting toward them. Tillie placed large platters in front of them. "Healthy portions."

"*Ya*, the servings are always generous here." Levina smiled at her daughter. "*Danki*, Tillie."

Her baby girl folded her hands together as her eyes brightened. "I'm so glad the two of you are here—together."

Then Naaman did the unexpected. He reached across the table and latched onto Levina's hand, then spoke with touching sincerity. "I'm glad to be home."

Levina's eyes drifted to her left. Eve was straining her neck in their direction. It shouldn't matter, but she wanted Eve—and the world—to know that everything was going to be all right with her and Naaman. It was wrong, and Levina knew that her choices were judged only by God, but when she looked up and saw a tear roll down Tillie's face, she swallowed back her own emotions.

"I'm glad you're home, too, *Daed*." Tillie leaned over and kissed her father on the cheek before she turned to leave.

Levina watched him struggling to keep his own emotions from becoming a public display. She gave his hand a squeeze. Her heart was filled with love for her husband and hope for the future, but she couldn't seem to conquer the distrust that threatened to destroy the moment and the future.

Would she always worry that he would leave again? How was she going to get past her own insecurities and move forward with the one man she'd always loved . . . but who had betrayed their union?

She started to pull her hand away but Naaman recaptured it. "I will earn your trust, Levina. And I will never leave you again. Not ever."

Dear Lord, help me to believe him. And trust him.

Chapter Eight

LARRY DOZIER PULLED HIS RENTAL CAR INTO BEILER'S BED-and-Breakfast and wished he'd had time to change out of his sheriff's uniform before leaving Middlefield. Cops made people nervous, and the last thing he wanted to do was draw attention to himself. As he walked to the small office on the side of the B & B, he heard the sound of a buggy coming up the drive that ran parallel to the large brick establishment.

Buggies and Amish folks were nothing new to him since he lived right outside of Middlefield, one of the largest Amish settlements in Ohio. He'd noticed during his drive from the airport that Amish folks in these parts drove gray buggies instead of black, and he found it downright frightening that signs lined the main highway stating *Watch for Aggressive Drivers*. And where were the speed limit signs? He scratched his chin and wondered if he was the only one who noticed this. He'd never been to Paradise, Pennsylvania, before.

He walked from the back parking area, rounded the corner, and saw a sign on the door—*Office and Dining Area*. He entered the room and found an Amish woman tidying up behind a counter that boasted a large coffeepot, cups, sugar, creamer, and a tray of cookies. There were several small tables in the room covered with white tablecloths, each with two chairs tucked close. He breathed in the aroma of freshly baked goods that permeated the space around him. This is where he would be having breakfast for the next few mornings, or however long it took to find Naaman Lapp.

"Good afternoon." Larry walked to the counter and set his suitcase down. "I have a reservation for Larry Dozier."

"*Ya, ya.* I have your key right here." The young woman reached into her apron pocket and handed Larry a key. "You're in the Rose Room. It's on the third floor."

Larry took the key and noticed that the white covering on her head was different from those worn by the Amish women in Middlefield. "Thank you." He picked up his suitcase. "Did you say the third floor?"

"*Ya.* It was the only room we had left when you called yesterday to make a reservation."

Larry nodded and wondered if his knee would hold out up three flights of stairs.

"And, Mr. Dozier, breakfast is served between seven o'clock and nine o'clock. It's buffet-style, so just come when you're ready."

He was heading for the stairs when the woman called his name again. He twisted to face her. "Yes?"

"When you called yesterday, you weren't sure how long you would be staying. Do you know yet?"

Larry saw her eyeing him up and down. She was probably wondering what he was doing in town, although he didn't owe her any explanation. It was Friday afternoon, and Larry figured he would be in town at least until Monday or Tuesday. Tomorrow he had to find a quilt for Patsy and pick up a few other touristy items his wife had requested. Sunday, he wouldn't bother Naaman and his family. He had enough respect for the Amish folks not to intrude on a Sunday. "Plan on my staying through Monday night. If that changes, I'll let you know."

"That sounds fine. I just wanted to make sure you wouldn't be needing the room into the following weekend. We usually book up on the weekends."

"I imagine my business here will be taken care of by then."

AFTER HIS TRIP WITH LEVINA TO MARKET AND LUNCH AT Yoder's Pantry, Naaman spent the rest of the day doing a list of odd jobs. He replaced the loose doorknob in the bathroom with one they'd bought that morning, carried a heavy box of books downstairs that Tillie wanted, and replaced a broken pane of glass in Jonathan's old room. Levina had told her older grandchildren not to play baseball so close to the house. She smiled to herself as she recalled the first time that Adam put a baseball through one of the windows. It wasn't the last time either.

For supper, she heated up some cream of carrot soup she had in the freezer and served it to Naaman with warmed butter bread. She and Naaman shared devotional time, followed by a small slice of German apple cake she had made earlier in the day. It all seemed very normal and familiar. Until bedtime.

Levina tried to focus on the gardening magazine she'd picked up in town, but her eyes were heavy and she kept having to adjust the lantern brighter and brighter to see. She pushed up her reading glasses on her nose and stifled a yawn.

"Levina, why don't you go to bed?" Naaman removed his own reading glasses and closed the book he was reading. "And let me sleep in Tillie's room tonight."

She yawned, then looked at her husband. "No, I will sleep in Tillie's room. It's no bother." She pulled her gaze from him and recalled the way she'd curled up in the bed with him the night before, quiet as she could be and careful not to get too close. She'd longed for the protectiveness of his arms around her, but until she was sure that she could trust him, she wouldn't slip back into her wifely role . . . even though her heart danced with excitement at the thought of Naaman loving her in that way.

Levina buried her head back in the magazine, but the words on the page blurred as she tried to recall the last time that she and Naaman were intimate. She couldn't remember. Were they too busy? Too tired? Or just uninterested? Levina could feel Naaman watching her intently, and even though she feared it would weaken her resolve, she looked up at him. The tenderness of his kiss lingered in her mind, and her desire to be held by her husband almost overrode her anxiety about trusting him again. But she forced herself to look away from his gaze, his eyes filled with tenderness and passion that she longed to share with him.

Such silliness. These were not proper thoughts for a middle-aged woman. *I'm a grandma, for goodness' sake.*

"Levina?"

"Ya?" Her heart raced. She recognized the suggestive tone of his voice, even though it had been a mighty long time since she'd heard it.

Naaman's brow furrowed. He opened his mouth to say something, clamped it shut, then opened and shut it again. Finally he drew in a deep breath and blew it out slowly. "I reckon I will bathe and go to bed."

"Good night." *And thank the Lord.*

Sharing a bed with Naaman was not a decision she could make casually, even though he was her husband. He betrayed their marriage vows the day he left for Middlefield, and she wasn't ready to let down her guard just yet. What if he decided that he didn't want to be here? Chose to leave again? Could her heart withstand another blow? For now, she wanted to keep a safe distance from him. But as she watched him walk across the den and down the hallway, there was nothing she wanted more than to follow him to their bedroom and fall into his arms.

AFTER HIS BATH, NAAMAN CLIMBED INTO BED, AGAIN FEEL-ing guilty that Levina was across the hall in Tillie's old bed. It seemed wrong for her not to be in her own bed, but Naaman knew it would take time for his wife to trust him again. For the thousandth time he pondered why he'd ever left Lancaster County in the first place.

When he stretched his memory to that time in his life, he could recall the tightness in his chest, the sense of suffocation, doubt about everything in his life, and the pressure to flee all he'd ever known. He pulled the covers to his waist and watched rays of light from the lantern flickering on the ceiling above.

Naaman thought about Paul Zook. He remembered when his friend left his wife and family to go live among the *Englisch* over twenty years ago. Paul never came back, and Naaman didn't think he would ever understand Paul's decision. For Naaman, it had never been about living in the *Englisch* world. That didn't interest him. When he left for Ohio, it was supposed to be for a few weeks, just to clear his head, though he didn't tell Levina that. He just said he was going to visit his cousins, and he didn't elaborate much. He was pretty sure Levina knew it would be an extended stay.

What kind of man am I? Being back with Levina and around the children made him question his actions even more. With each day he was consumed with trying to forgive himself and yet make it up to his family. His burdens seemed heavier than before he left. It had been a selfish move, and he knew it. He'd spent his entire life doing everything he was supposed to do—provided for his family, raised his children according to the *Ordnung*, been an upstanding member of the community. And he'd been a good husband to Levina. *So why?*

His chest tightened when he thought about his visit with Bishop Ebersol tomorrow. It was a meeting he couldn't avoid, but shame filled him. It would be hard to look the bishop in the eyes and explain his choices when Naaman didn't even understand them himself. He reached for the bottle of aspirin on his bedside table and popped two pills into his mouth, followed by a swig of water, and wondered if his hip was ever going to feel normal again. Then he let out a heavy sigh and settled into his pillow.

Dear Lord, help me to be a better man.

Naaman went through a long list of prayers, thanking God for all he'd been blessed with, but in the end, he repeated what consumed him the most. *Please, Lord, help me to be a better man.*

When the door to the bedroom suddenly swung wide, Naaman didn't think he'd ever seen such beauty. Levina stood in the doorway, her silky hair to her waist, wearing a long white gown that reached almost to the floor. In her bare feet she edged forward slowly into the room. Naaman sat up in the bed.

"Levina, are you all right?" He turned the lantern on his nightstand up a bit to see her better, which illuminated her face enough for Naaman to study her expression. Her brown eyes were flat and unreadable as stone, but Naaman could still see the unspoken pain she'd been burdened with since he arrived. He swung his legs over the side of the bed, grimacing as his hip popped with the movement. "What is it?"

She was a few feet from the bed when Naaman stood up. Her eyes shone brighter as she stepped into the pale light from the lantern, and a twinkle of moonlight spilled into the room. Had she come back to their marital bed, deciding to resume her role as his wife? Naaman tried to decipher the faraway look in her eyes. Was she longing for him the way he desired to be with her?

He took a step toward her, and with a slow and steady hand he reached up and ran a hand through her hair. "You look beautiful, Levina."

She didn't move as Naaman cupped her cheek. He leaned closer to kiss her, but she backed away, and there was undeniable pain in her eyes. Naaman braced himself for whatever she was about to say.

"Naaman?" She bit her bottom lip as tears filled her eyes.

"What is it, *mei leib?*" He stepped toward her, but she moved back farther, so he stood and waited, watching her eyes shift from remote and mysterious to sharp and assessing.

"I know I asked you this before, but I–I need to be sure that there wasn't someone else." She paused. "In Ohio. Are you telling me the truth, Naaman? If there was another woman, you must tell me."

Naaman's stomach sank as he ran a hand through his hair.

Chapter Nine

LEVINA HELD HER BREATH AS SHE WATCHED HIS EXPRES-
sion. Before he said a word, she already knew the answer.

"No, Levina."

It was the first time she had ever seen her husband's eyes fill
with tears.

"I'm sorry that you didn't believe me the first time you asked."

Levina let out a slow sigh. "I'm sorry, too, but I just needed
to ask again."

Naaman wrapped his arms around her, and she returned the
hug. But as his embrace grew more intense, she pulled slowly
away.

"I've missed you, Levina." He pushed back a strand of hair
that had fallen forward across her cheek.

"I've missed you, too, Naaman, but . . ." She hung her head,
but it was only a few seconds later when Naaman cupped her chin
and gently raised her eyes back to his.

"But you don't trust me, no? You're worried I will leave
again."

Levina nodded. "I'm sorry, Naaman. I need time." She
paused and took another deep breath. His blue eyes pierced the
short distance between them. "In some ways, Naaman, I know
you better than any other human being in the world." She smiled.
"I know that your jaw quivers when you're nervous. I know that
strawberries make you sick to your stomach. Your feet are more
ticklish than anyone I've ever known, even the children. You listen

to more than just the weather on your radio in the barn . . . . mostly country and western music. Your favorite color is yellow."

She paused again when she felt his hands on her arms. "You're a *gut* father to our children. You're smart about things many men in our community are not. Math, for example. And you never tire of a *gut* joke." Levina lowered her head for a moment as Naaman rubbed her arms, then she looked back up and watched the play of emotions on his face, seemingly unaware of where she was going with all this. "But, Naaman . . ."

"What is it, Levina?"

She stepped away from him, walked to the window, and gazed into the moonlit yard. "In some ways, Naaman . . . I feel like I don't know you at all." She turned slowly around. "And I don't know when that happened." Her heart sank as she spoke aloud the words that had previously been private thoughts.

Naaman walked around to the other side of the bed and sat down. Levina sat beside him. They were quiet for several moments, then Naaman spoke.

"Then let's get to know each other again."

Levina felt a combination of relief and sadness as she realized that Naaman felt the same way she did. She shrugged. "I don't know how to move forward, Naaman, when I felt such betrayal." She twisted to face him. "How can I trust that you won't tire of your life here again and just leave?"

"I didn't tire of my life, Levina."

"Then please try to explain it to me."

Naaman rolled his head around on his neck, and Levina suspected it was the same knot above his shoulder blades that flared up from time to time. In the past she would work the soreness out by rubbing his neck in the evenings. But on this night she sat still and waited.

"I don't have an explanation, other than what I've already told you."

Levina stood up and turned to face him. "Well, I hope you have some sort of explanation for Bishop Ebersol tomorrow. Maybe there is something you can tell him that you can't tell me, no?"

Naaman stood up. "When I figure out why I acted the way I did, Levina, you will be the first to know."

Levina folded her arms across her chest, blew out a huff of exasperation, then turned to leave. She wasn't to the door yet when Naaman called her name. She spun around, frustration in her voice. "*Ya?*"

"Would you like to go on a picnic with me down by the creek, after my visit with Bishop Ebersol tomorrow? Then we could drive to Bird-in-Hand and eat ice cream at that place you like."

Levina scrunched her brows. "Naaman, we haven't done that since we were kids, and—"

He walked closer to her. "*Ya*, I know." He smiled. "Our *kinner* are grown. It's just the two of us. Let's be kids together again."

Levina recalled times long since past, the picnics, trips to get ice cream, swims in the creek. "You're not going to prepare the meal, are you?" Her features became more animated as she spoke.

"If you want me to, I will."

She chuckled. "I think not." She tapped her foot a few times. "Hmm. All right, Naaman. I will make us a light early supper to eat. We will have a—a date tomorrow after your visit with Bishop Ebersol."

"I'll look forward to it."

"Fine." Levina left the room, but as she made her way across the hall, a smile filled her face. She was looking forward to her date with Naaman too.

NAAMAN BUSIED HIMSELF ALL THE NEXT DAY, FOLLOWING A heavy breakfast to hold him over until their picnic later in the afternoon. He made repairs to the barn that were long overdue and even managed to get a new coat of white paint on one side. But as two o'clock approached, his stomach began to churn with anxiety. Bishop Ebersol was the toughest bishop their community had ever had, and Naaman was expecting harsh words. At least he had his date with Levina to look forward to.

It seemed odd to call it a date. But it was exciting to think of it that way. Naaman was going to court his wife, make her see him for the man he'd always been, the man she fell in love with—and, he hoped, make her forget and forgive the man he'd been the past year . . . a man who had fallen into selfish temptation. God was all-forgiving, but Naaman needed Levina to forgive him too. And Naaman needed to forgive himself.

Then there was the issue of Adam. He would see his son tomorrow at church service. If he thought too much about that, his stomach roiled with worry. So, one worry at a time. He walked into the den in time to hear a buggy coming up the drive.

"Naaman, I'm going to go visit Freda for a little bit while you visit with Bishop Ebersol. I'll excuse myself after saying hello to him, then I'll be back around three."

Naaman grinned. "Sure you don't want to stay?"

She chuckled. "*Ach*, no. You are on your own, *mei lieb*."

Naaman couldn't remember the last time Levina had referred to him with such affection. It sounded nice, and for a brief moment the soothing tone of her voice calmed his nerves.

They both waited for Bishop Ebersol to ease his way up the porch steps, holding steady to the railing. He was a tall man in his seventies with a gray beard that ran the length of his chest. His brows were always slanted inward, giving him the appearance of always being angry. But despite his intimidating looks and strict rulings within the district, Naaman had always thought him to be fair. In Naaman's case, he'd probably been more than fair, since he hadn't recommended a shunning.

"Hello, Bishop Ebersol." Levina opened the screen door for the bishop and stepped to the side. "I will let you and Naaman visit." She turned to Naaman. "There's a pitcher of iced sweet tea on the table, Naaman, and I've laid out some gingersnaps."

"*Danki*, Levina." Bishop Ebersol removed his hat to reveal a sparse supply of gray locks underneath. "This won't take long."

Naaman's chest tightened as he wondered if the expected length of the visit was good or bad for him. He motioned for the bishop to take a seat on the couch.

"Can I get you some tea and gingersnaps?"

Bishop Ebersol sat down. "No. Emma made me a snack before I came."

No stalling. He was going to get right to the point. Naaman sat down in the rocker across from the bishop.

"Don't look so nervous, Naaman." Bishop Ebersol narrowed his eyes even further, so his words did little to calm Naaman's nerves. "Is there anything that you would like to tell me about your—your visit with your cousins?"

"It was a bad decision." Naaman pressed his lips together. "And it won't happen again."

Bishop Ebersol chuckled, something Naaman didn't think he'd ever heard from the man. "You sound like my grandchildren when you say that. You didn't just break a curfew or tell a tiny lie, Naaman." Bishop Ebersol raised his big bushy brows. "You took off on a late-in-life *rumschpringe* of sorts, even if it wasn't to live among the *Englisch*. Am I correct?"

Naaman sighed. "I reckon so. And I regret it."

"Why?"

"Why do I regret it?" Naaman scowled. Wasn't it obvious? "It—it was wrong. I hurt my family."

Bishop Ebersol stroked his gray beard. "And what did you learn while you were gone, my friend?"

Naaman was surprised by the bishop's compassionate tone.

He'd expected far worse, and it could still be forthcoming, but for now Naaman pondered exactly what he did learn while he was away. *Lord, please tell me there was a lesson in my actions.*

"Bishop, I reckon I learned that we can't run from our problems." He held his head in his hands for a moment, then looked back up to see the bishop waiting. "I was just as lonely in Middlefield as I was here in Lancaster County, and all the same things still plagued me. And added to that, I missed Levina and my children."

The bishop's eyes narrowed suspiciously. "Why did you stay gone so long?"

"The longer I was gone, the harder it became to return." Naaman sighed. "I don't know."

Bishop Ebersol actually grinned. "I hope you gave Levina better reasons than you are giving me."

Naaman forced a smile. "I don't think I have given her *gut* reasons at all, Bishop. I just don't understand myself, or why I did what I did."

"You might not understand the purpose of your trip for a long time, Naaman. Maybe not ever, or until you go before God in heaven. But we must remember—everything is God's will. It was His will for you to take that journey, and you must stop questioning it and move forth with your life, learning and growing in His glory."

"Why didn't you seek a shunning, Bishop Ebersol?"

The bishop let out a heavy sigh. "I think back to your wedding day, Naaman. I was a deacon back then. But I still remember the way you looked at Levina when you said your vows. And you've continued to look at her that same way. You've been a *gut* father to your children and an upstanding member of our community." He smiled slightly. "I had faith in you, that you would come back." He frowned a bit. "Although I didn't think it would take you almost a year."

Naaman nodded. "I've prayed about this every day since I left and every day since I've returned. It was so many things, Bishop Ebersol." Naaman paused, unsure whether to go on. "But it just seemed like Levina and me raised our *kinner*, worked hard, prayed, and tried to be *gut* members of the community, but I reckon somewhere along the way we just stopped talking. I mean, *really* talking. I didn't notice it as much until all the *kinner* were moved out. Then it just seemed—lonely." Naaman shook his head. "I didn't know *mei frau* anymore."

"And we know that all things work together for good to them that love God, to them who are the called according to his purpose."

Naaman thought for a moment about the Scripture reading. "Bishop Ebersol, I do know that all things are of God's will, but I don't know how there can be any purpose for my leaving my family."

"As I said, Naaman . . . the Lord always has a plan." Bishop Ebersol raised his hat to the top of his head. "So, what is your plan, Naaman?"

Naaman stroked his beard. "I reckon it will sound strange, but Levina and I are going on a date later. In a way, I guess we are getting to know each other all over again."

Bishop Ebersol stood up, and Naaman did so also. "I think that is a *gut* idea, Naaman." He extended his hand to Naaman. "Welcome home."

"*Danki* for coming by." Naaman walked the bishop to the door, and the elderly man was almost to the end of the porch when he turned around, a twinkle in his eye and a grin on his face.

"I've been married fifty-seven years, Naaman. I'm not sure we ever completely know or understand the womenfolk. Keep that in mind as you move forward." He headed down the steps, holding tightly to the rail for support.

Naaman waved as the bishop steered his buggy away, and he wondered why he'd feared the man all these years. He could think more about their conversation later. Right now, he wanted to clean up a bit before his date with his wife.

BETH WISEMAN

Chapter Ten

LEVINA FINISHED HEMMING A DRESS FOR FREDA WHILE
Freda sewed buttons on a shirt she'd made for Jake. She glanced
at the clock.

"Here you go." She handed the finished product to Freda. "I
guess I best be on my way."

Freda set her own project down on the kitchen table where she
and Levina were working and sipping iced tea. "It just seems weird
for you and *Daed* to date. I mean, he is your husband, and you live
together, and . . ." Freda shrugged. "That's not normal, *Mamm*."

Levina smiled. "Define 'normal' for me, *dochder*."

"Well, I reckon it's not being courted by your own husband."
Freda crinkled her nose and scowled. "I can't imagine you and
Daed out on a date. I mean, what will you do?" Freda waved her
hand in the air frantically. "Never mind. I don't want to know."

"Freda!" Levina stood up. "You're talking nonsense. It will be
nice to spend some time with your father away from work, our
haus, and"—she grinned at her daughter—"all of our *kinner*."

"Is *Daed* going to worship service at Adam's house tomorrow?"

"*Ya.* We will both be there. And if you speak with your *bruder*,
you remind him that I expect him to be respectful of his father no
matter his personal feelings."

Freda nodded then frowned. "You're so forgiving, *Mamm*. I just
don't know if I could be that way if Jake had done what *Daed* did."

"Of course you could. That's the way you were raised, Freda.
And especially where your family is concerned, it shouldn't even

be an issue." Levina raised her chin, driven to live by her own words. "Besides, you will understand more as you grow in your marriage. Now I need to go." She gave Freda a quick hug.

Freda sighed. "Have fun on your *date*."

"I plan to." Levina winked at her daughter, which produced a slight roll of the eyes from Freda. Levina didn't care. She had a date to go home and get ready for.

NAAMAN PULLED OUT SOME AFTERSHAVE HE'D BOUGHT years ago. He couldn't even remember why he'd bought it. It certainly went against his ways, but he slathered some on his cheeks and neck just the same.

He'd just tucked a clean blue shirt into his black pants and pulled up his suspenders when he heard Levina pulling into the driveway. He headed down the stairs feeling a bit giddy.

"I just want to freshen up a little," Levina said as he met her at the bottom of the stairs. Then she grinned. "Naaman Lapp, is that cologne you're wearing?"

"Just for you, *mei lieb*." He tried to play it off casually, even though he could feel his face reddening. But when Levina smiled, he was glad he'd chosen to splash on the spicy fragrance.

"I'll be down in a minute." She brushed past him on the stairs. "I've already prepared our picnic lunch," she said from the top of the stairs. "You can grab it from the refrigerator."

Naaman walked to the kitchen, opened the refrigerator, and pulled out a wicker basket with a flat lid that opened in opposite directions. It barely fit on the bottom shelf. He closed the door, then set the basket on the kitchen table and took a peek inside. Two sandwiches, a container that looked like it might be potato salad, a jar of pickles, two slices of pie, a thermos, and . . .

Naaman reached around the food and pulled out a piece of

pink paper that was tucked between the pie and the jar of pickles. Warmth filled his heart as he read the familiar note that was over thirty years old.

MY DEAREST NAAMAN,

YOU ARE THE MAN I WANT TO SPEND THE REST OF MY LIFE WITH. OUR WEDDING IS ONLY TWO WEEKS AWAY, AND I CAN'T WAIT TO BE YOUR FRAU! OUR LOVE IS BLESSED BY GOD, AND I KNOW THAT A LIFETIME OF HAPPINESS AWAITS US! WE WILL HAVE LOTS OF KINNER TO FILL OUR HOME. AND WE WILL GROW OLD TOGETHER! I LOVE YOU SO MUCH. YOU ARE MY EVERYTHING. MY NAAMAN. FOREVER.

YOUR LOVING BRIDE TO BE, LEVINA

Naaman swallowed hard as his eyes dropped to the bottom of the page where Levina had written a more recent note.

YOU ARE STILL MY NAAMAN. THE MAN I FELL IN LOVE WITH. THE MAN I WANT TO SPEND THE REST OF MY LIFE WITH AND GROW OLD WITH. YOU HAVE ALWAYS BEEN, AND ALWAYS WILL BE . . . MY NAAMAN.

LOVINGLY YOURS, LEVINA

Naaman gritted his teeth in frustration with himself. "I will make everything up to you, Levina. *Everything.*"

"I know you will."

Naaman jumped as he spun around to see Levina standing in the den, dressed in a dark green dress, black apron, and perfectly ironed *kapp*. In his mind's eye, she looked exactly the same as the day he proposed, on a picnic down by the creek.

"You look beautiful." He let out a sigh and wondered how he could have ever left her for so long.

"And you smell *gut.*" She walked into the kitchen grinning, then stopped when she saw him holding the note. "*Ach*, you found it. I was going to give it to you later." She dropped her gaze and bit her bottom lip, and a blush filled her cheeks.

Naaman waited until she looked back up at him. "I remember finding this on the seat of my courting buggy. Where did you find it?"

"It's been in the hope chest."

"The cedar chest I made you for our one-year anniversary, the one at the foot of our bed?"

"*Ya.*"

Naaman grinned. "What else have you got in that chest?"

"All kinds of things. If you redeem yourself, perhaps I will show you."

Levina was full of playfulness and smiles, and Naaman didn't think he'd ever wanted to please anyone more than he wanted to please her on this blessed day.

He picked up the picnic basket and held his arm out. Levina latched on above his elbow, and together they headed out the door.

LARRY CAREFULLY STUFFED THE QUILT INTO THE BACK OF the rental car alongside some other trinkets Patsy had requested. He sure hoped she liked it. It was the closest thing to the picture she'd sent with him that he could find, a mixture of blues, yellows, and light greens—which Patsy said would accent their blue carpet nicely.

There were plenty of quilts handmade by the Amish in Middlefield, but Patsy had to have one from Lancaster County. So now she did, and Larry had paid a pretty penny for it—almost eight hundred dollars. But his girl was worth it. He smiled as he pictured the way her green eyes would light up when she saw it.

He started the car and headed back to the B & B. He really could have saved this trip until early on Monday, but Patsy's folks were coming to town and that seemed as good a reason as any to start his trip early. It gave him time to shop for his wife and have a little downtime before he caught up with Naaman Lapp. Tomorrow he planned to sleep in, catch the late Mass at the Catholic church he saw down the road, and then take in the ball game on television. Maybe just lie around in his socks and boxers, munching on popcorn and drinking a beer. He didn't usually drink, but something about a man in his socks and boxers, snacking on popcorn—it seemed to call for a brew in one hand. A special occasion of sorts. That was how he planned to spend his Sunday.

Larry parked in the back of Beiler's Bed-and-Breakfast in the designated parking area. He eyed the three flights of stairs going to his room. The Rose Room. He shook his head. It was a frilly room for ladies, but it would serve his purpose while he was here. As long as it had a television, which it did, he was in good shape. Now if he could just manage the stairs with these bad knees.

As he gathered up his purchases, he recalled the breakfast he'd had that morning. Best breakfast he'd ever had, though he'd never tell Patsy that. After thirty-five years of marriage, probably best to let her believe hers was the best breakfast on the planet. But the owner, a woman named Barbie, laid out a fine meal—French toast, bacon, fresh fruit, sausage patties, homemade bread, and the best raspberry yogurt that had ever crossed his lips. Amazing stuff. Larry had followed the woman's suggestion and poured fresh granola on top. He made a mental note to see if he could purchase some of that to take to Patsy.

The owner, Barbie, wasn't an Amish woman, like the woman who had checked him in. But that morning, when Larry heard Barbie talking to four couples at a nearby table, he couldn't help but ask her how she knew so much about the Amish. She seemed to know things the average Joe wouldn't. Turned out she had grown up Amish—Beachy Amish, she called it. Evidently it was a less conservative form of Amish, similar to the Mennonites.

It hadn't seemed the right time to ask her about Naaman Lapp. Since the Amish didn't have phones and didn't drive cars, it was a little difficult to get an address. He could have done it before he left Middlefield if he'd taken the time, but he was in a hurry to avoid the in-laws. Another thing he wouldn't mention to his wife.

He hobbled up the stairs with Patsy's gifts, hoping they would all fit in his suitcase for the trip home. By the time he reached the third floor, he was as winded as a ninety-year-old man, not the fifty-five-year-old he was.

Need more exercise.

Larry knew he needed to get back to the gym, but the closer he got to retirement, the more he seemed to forego exercise and enjoy foods that should probably be forbidden at his age. Patsy kept him on a fairly strict diet, low in carbohydrates and cholesterol. He'd never cheated on his wife except when it came to food, indulging in his favorites behind her back.

This was his last road trip prior to his retirement. Once he found Naaman Lapp, he was done. And this thing with Naaman was different. It was personal.

Chapter Eleven

LEVINA WAITED FOR NAAMAN TO SPREAD THE BLANKET BY
the water's edge.

"How's this?" He placed the picnic basket in the middle of
the red-and-blue-checked quilt and motioned for her to sit down.

"It's perfect." She was almost certain that this was the exact
spot where he'd proposed to her over thirty-one years ago.
Coincidence? She didn't think so.

She pulled her black sweater around her. There was a nip in
the air, but the sun shone brightly, and it truly was the perfect day.

"Are you cold?" he asked, sitting down beside her.

"*Nee.* I'm fine. This is a lovely spot. Is it . . ."

Naaman smiled. "*Ya*, it is."

Levina pulled out two paper plates and two napkins, then she
retrieved all the lunch goodies she'd brought. "That was a long
time ago," she said softly. "I was an eighteen-year-old girl." She
smiled. "You proposed the day after your twentieth birthday."

"*Ya.*" Naaman watched her spoon some potato salad onto his
plate.

Levina thought about how he had missed their thirty-first
anniversary this past December, along with all the holidays, then
pushed the thought aside. This was a fresh start, a new beginning
for them, and she was going to trust Naaman completely. She had
to. Faith, hope, love—and trust—were the foundations for a good
marriage.

They ate their lunch in relative silence, commenting on two

squirrels chasing each other nearby and how much the creek was up from the recent rains. When they were done, Levina packed everything except their plastic tea glasses back into the basket.

"That was wonderful, Levina." Naaman lay back on the blanket and rested on his elbows, then he crossed his ankles, cringing as he did so.

"Your hip still bothering you?" Levina had noticed him still limping a little.

"Not as much as it was. The doc in Middlefield said it would just take awhile to heal. I hope it doesn't take too much longer; there's much to be done around the farm, and I don't want this holding me back."

Levina glanced around. Not a soul anywhere. She lay down on her side, propped her head in her hand, and faced her husband.

"We've had a *gut* life, haven't we?" Naaman reached over and grabbed her hand.

Levina grinned. "You make it sound like our life is over. I choose to believe that it's just beginning."

Naaman intertwined his fingers with hers and gave her a gentle squeeze. "Today can be the first day of the rest of our lives."

Levina giggled. "Naaman! I've heard that before. It's a popular catchphrase the *Englisch* use." She pulled her hand from his and pointed a finger in his direction. "You're going to have to do better than that."

He twisted around and lay on his side, facing her, but groaned as he did so. He chuckled. "I sound like an old man." He reached for her hand again. "Do you remember the day Rosemary was born? The way it was storming, and we worried how we would get to the hospital? That was back before phones were allowed in the barn." Naaman shook his head. "I reckon that's the most scared I've ever been in my life. Scared me to death that you might have that baby at home."

"Women do it all the time, but with midwives—not a husband

who is in a complete state of panic." Levina laughed at the recollection of Naaman's actions that day. "Remember how you
flagged down that car on the highway? Those two *Englisch* teenagers didn't know what to think."

"But they helped us. That boy helped me get you into the car,
and the *Englisch* girl was wise enough to ask if you'd packed a bag."

"Which I had. She went and got it for me."

They were quiet for a few moments, the gentle breeze rustling
the leaves overhead as the sun continued to shine brightly.

"We've been *gut* parents, haven't we?" Naaman squeezed her
hand again and smiled.

"*Ya*, I think so. And we are blessed that all five of our *kinner*
chose to be baptized into the faith and stayed in this community."

They were quiet again, and Levina was sure she could read
Naaman's mind. Raising children had been something that they'd
partnered on in every area, making sure the children had complete understanding of the *Ordnung*. They'd worried together
when each one ventured into their *rumschpringe* and held steady to
their faith through the challenging teenage years. All of their children loved the land and worked hard, even the girls, who Levina
believed had turned out to be better cooks than she was. Yes, she
and Naaman had been the best parents they could be.

Naaman avoided her eyes, tucked his chin. "I am so sorry,
Levina. I am so sorry that I left."

She squeezed his hand. "I know you are, Naaman. And I've
thought a lot about it, even more so now that you're back." She
paused in recollection, intertwining her fingers with his. "I think
that once we'd done our job as parents, we didn't know what to
do with each other. It's been so long since we focused on just us."

"That's what I want to do now. Focus on us. Tell me what
would make you happy."

Levina filled with warmth as she thought about some of the
things she'd dreamed of doing with Naaman. She let go of his

hand and tapped her finger to her chin. "Let's see. Do you really want to know? Because you might be very surprised."

His eyes swept over her face as he smiled. "Surprise me."

"Okay." She bit her bottom lip and thought for a minute. "It would make me happy to eat at Yoder's Pantry once a week, since we don't have *kinner* to feed."

Naaman nodded for her to go on.

"I would like to fly a kite."

Naaman chuckled, and Levina playfully held up a finger. "*Ya*, I know it is something *kinner* usually do, but I have never flown a kite. I want to shirk work one afternoon and run barefoot through the grass in the far pasture on a sunny summer day when the winds are high . . . and fly a kite."

"Do we own a kite?" Naaman lifted his brows.

"Not yet."

Naaman smiled. "Go on."

"I would like to go to Florida. So many folks in our community vacation in Florida. I would like to see the ocean in Florida."

"Then we will." Naaman shifted his weight a bit. "And?"

"And I would like to paint a picture. A landscape painting that Bishop Ebersol would approve of. I'd like to do it on real canvas with real paints." Levina felt her face turning red. She shook her head. "I know that sounds so whimsical, but I've always wondered what it would be like to—"

Naaman reached over and pulled her into his arms and kissed her on the neck.

"Naaman! Someone might see." She tried to push him away. But she didn't try very hard.

"Who?" He glanced around them. "The trees?" He chuckled, then went on. "You are going to do all of those things, *mei lieb*. And much more. I'm going to make sure that you are happy always."

Levina forced herself out of his embrace, then sat up and crossed her legs beneath her. She gazed into his eyes. "Now,

Naaman . . . you tell me what you would like to do during this second half of our lives."

Naaman took a deep breath. "Levina, I don't feel worthy. I already did something I wanted, without ever even consulting you. Let me spend the rest of my life making you happy."

Levina smiled and shook her head. "We are partners, Naaman. We always have been. It's just that in the past we focused all our efforts on the children and everything else but ourselves. In this second half of our life, we'll still be a partnership. What is something you would like to do?"

Naaman sat up and faced her, looping his thumbs beneath his suspenders. "I would like to make furniture and sell it to the local shops. I've made things here and there for pleasure, for the children and for friends, but I'd like to spend more time doing that."

Levina nodded. "I think you should, then. What else?"

"I would like never to have to eat shoofly pie again the rest of my life."

Levina widened her eyes in shock. "What?" She slapped her palms on her legs. "What in the world are you talkin' about?"

Naaman shrugged. "I don't care for it."

Levina crossed her arms across her chest. "Naaman, everyone likes shoofly pie."

"Not me."

"Then why have you been eating it all these years?" Levina narrowed her eyes at him.

"Because everyone says yours is the best in the county, and . . ." He shrugged. "What kind of Amish man doesn't like shoofly pie?" He grimaced. "I reckon I don't really care for molasses at all."

Levina couldn't speak or close her mouth. Finally she shook her head. "Now, Naaman, how could I have not known that?"

"That's what this is about, no? Getting to know each other better."

Levina threw her head back and laughed until Naaman was laughing so hard with her that both of them struggled to catch their breath.

"I reckon so, Naaman. I reckon so." She struggled to compose herself. "So, what else? What else would you like to do?"

"I'd like to play that guitar in the basement, the one Freda brought into the house while she was in her *rumschpringe*."

Levina arched one eyebrow. "It's against the rules, Naaman. You know that the *Ordnung* says that musical instruments invoke unnecessary emotion. That's why we stored it in the basement."

"In the big picture of rules to be broken, Levina, I reckon I just don't see the Lord minding if I strum that guitar from time to time when no one is around."

Levina smiled. "All right, Naaman. What else?"

Naaman leaned slowly forward and kissed her on the lips. "I want to love you for the rest of my life."

Levina kissed him back, again and again . . .

Chapter Twelve

LARRY ENJOYED HIS THIRD HELPING OF RASPBERRY YOGURT with a generous amount of fresh granola on top. Two other couples were just leaving when he sat down at eight forty-five. This seemed like a good time to inquire about Naaman Lapp.

"I just can't seem to get enough of this yogurt. I sure would like to take some back to my wife, if I can stuff one more thing in my suitcase." Larry smiled at Barbie Beiler as she placed a few fresh pancakes in the warming tray on the counter.

"I have a friend who makes and sells it. If you're not traveling too far, I bet it would keep until you get home. I'll call her if you're interested in purchasing some."

"Thanks. That'd be great." Larry stood up, then helped himself to all the pancakes she'd laid out. "I'm looking for an Amish fellow by the name of Naaman Lapp. Do you know him?"

Barbie stopped wiping the counter behind the food trays. "I'm sorry. I'll be right back. I need to check my pie in the oven."

She stepped through the door to the kitchen and closed it behind her.

After about ten minutes Larry figured she wasn't coming back. Maybe Barbie was avoiding his question because she'd heard he was a sheriff. He'd been sure to wear his street clothes after the first evening, but the woman who checked him in might have told her.

He opened the newspaper on the table, knowing he had some time to kill before church. He'd ask again about Naaman after he attended Mass and before he got settled in for his ball game on television. He looked down at his protruding belly, then he slathered butter all over his stack of pancakes before soaking them with maple syrup. *Patsy would have a fit.*

LEVINA OPENED HER EYES SUNDAY MORNING, AND NAAMAN was propped up on his elbow staring at her.

"*Guder mariye, mei lieb.*" Naaman draped an arm across her. "How did you sleep?"

"Better than I have in . . ." She paused, not wanting to bring up the past. "In a long time."

"I love you so much, Levina." Naaman leaned down and snuggled close to her.

Levina chuckled.

"What?" Naaman sounded alarmed.

"I was just thinking . . . what kind of a girl does this . . . you know . . . on her first *date?*" Levina smiled. She didn't think she'd ever been happier than at this moment. Last night there was an honesty between them that seemed new, fresh, and alive.

"*Ya.* Shame on you, *mei lieb,*" he teased as he pulled her closer.

They lay quietly for a while, and Levina was wishing they could lie there all day, but today was worship service—at Adam's house.

"We have to get up and get ready, Naaman." She eased away from him.

Naaman rolled on his back. "*Ya.* I know."

"I'm sure everything will go fine with Adam. I'm hoping you get to talk to him alone. Maybe you can find out what is going on with him."

"Levina, Adam doesn't even want to be around me, so I reckon I don't know why you think he'll open up to me."

Levina pulled her robe closed and lifted her chin. "Because you are his father. That's why."

Naaman scowled. "Can't we just stay in bed all day and play sick?" He grinned as he folded his hands behind his head.

"We cannot. Now get up and get ready, Naaman Lapp." Levina arched her brow. "Before I go bake you a shoofly pie and serve it to you for breakfast."

Naaman let out an exaggerated moan as he climbed out of bed. "If I have to."

"Up! Up!" She snapped her fingers and walked to the bathroom, humming.

Today was going to be a good day. The best day. She could feel it.

ADAM SET THE LAST OF THE CHAIRS IN THE BARN. FOUR rows of ten for the women, four rows of ten facing those for the men, and six chairs in the middle for the bishop and deacons. He dreaded having to face his father, but it was a day of worship, and he would be respectful of the day and the situation at hand.

"I wish we had a bigger *haus* so we didn't have to have worship in the barn."

Adam turned when he heard Hannah. "Our *haus* is fine. We only hold worship once every nine or ten months anyway."

Hannah shrugged, and Adam fought the urge to say something. He started straightening the chairs in the rows.

"Adam, I hope things go *gut* with your *daed* today."

He looked up at her as he moved one chair in line with the others. "I won't be disrespectful, if that's what you're worried about."

Hannah didn't say anything. She just stood watching him work, twisting the string on her *kapp* with her finger.

He put the last chair in line, then put his hands on his hips. "What is it, Hannah?"

She shrugged again, and Adam took a deep breath and glared at her. "I have work to do out here."

"I was just checking on you, Adam. I just wanted to tell you that I hoped things went *gut* with your *daed*. That's all."

"*Danki.*" He got the broom and started sweeping around the chairs, but Hannah just stood there. "Anything else?"

"Adam, what is wrong with you? Why are you acting like this?" Hannah's voice cracked as she spoke.

Adam felt like a *dummkopf*. But he didn't have time to get into this now. "Nothing, Hannah. Nothing is wrong."

"Something is wrong, Adam. Something has been wrong for a while, and I don't understand." She wiped a tear from her cheek. "It wonders me what is going on with you. Please talk to me."

"Hannah . . ." Adam stopped sweeping and closed his eyes for a moment. When he opened them, he caught her brushing away another tear. He couldn't stand to see her cry, but now was not the time to have a serious talk about anything. He leaned the broom against one of the chairs and went to her. "Hannah, can we talk about our problems later?"

"I didn't realize we had any, Adam. We're so blessed, in so many ways."

Adam hung his head. "I don't want to talk about it right now."

Hannah spun around and ran back to the house, crying. Adam wanted to go to her, to comfort her, tell her how much he loved her. But his feet were rooted to the wooden floor in the barn.

Lord, why am I so confused? What is wrong with me?

NAAMAN ENTERED HIS SON'S HOUSE WITH LEVINA. ALL OF his children, their spouses, and his grandchildren were already there when they arrived, and each greeted them when they walked in the door. Even Adam.

Adam's greeting was forced, barely a nod and a hello, but it was better than total avoidance. But Naaman was confident that

Adam would be respectful, no matter his ill will. He'd have his mother to answer to otherwise.

Naaman turned to Levina, feeling more in love with her than ever before. They were going to spend the rest of their lives living out their dreams. Going to Florida, flying kites, and—he smiled—no more shoofly pie.

Following the three-hour service, they all shared a meal on tables set up outside the barn. Then, as was customary, the men began to gather together on the far side of the barn to talk and tell jokes while the women finished cleaning up.

Naaman had heard enough jokes in his day. He didn't want to leave Levina for one second. "Let's just stay on the porch together," he said.

Levina grinned. "And do what?"

Naaman grabbed her hand and brought it to his lips. "I just want to be with you."

Levina giggled like a schoolgirl as she playfully pulled her hand away. "Naaman, people are watching, and I need to go help the others make things tidy."

"What are they *doing*?" Rosemary grabbed Freda by her sleeve and pulled her to the window. "Look. Just look at them!" She shook her head. "It's embarrassing, them acting like this."

"Let go of me." Freda shook loose of Rosemary's hold. "They're just standing there."

"Well, you should have seen them a minute ago. *Daed* picked up her hand and kissed it, right there on the front porch. No tellin' who saw. They are acting like teenagers."

"*Ach*, Rosemary, I'm sure it wasn't as troubling as you're making it out to be."

"Oh no?" Rosemary grabbed Freda again and turned her toward the window. "Look at that!"

"Keep your voice down. Others will hear." Freda parked her gaze on their parents, and Rosemary watched as Freda's jaw dropped. "They're kissing. In public!"

"I'm going to go out there and tell them that they are acting inappropriately, and that it's embarrassing."

"I think it's sweet."

Rosemary and Freda turned to see Tillie standing behind them, looking over their shoulders, a grin on her face.

"Sweet?" Rosemary folded her arms across her chest. "It's not proper for two middle-aged people to act like that, especially in light of *Daed's* absence the past year."

"Maybe they have found their way back to each other and fallen in love all over again." Tillie's eyes glowed with romantic illusions, and Rosemary rolled her own eyes.

"I've said it before, and I'll say it again . . . all this lost-and-found business is *dumm*."

Freda gasped. "Look! He kissed her again. On the mouth!"

"I think it is beautiful to see our parents like this, and shame on both of you for not being happy for them." Tillie scowled and walked toward the other room.

Rosemary tried to organize her thoughts. "Freda, you agree, no? They are behaving badly."

Freda kept her eyes on her parents, who were now just gazing into each other's eyes. "I don't know. I want them to be happy, but maybe we should go and talk to them nicely about these public displays."

"*Ya*. Let's do that." Rosemary moved toward the door and Freda followed.

"Hello, girls," their mother said as Rosemary and Freda approached them on the porch. "Lovely service today, no?"

"And a lovely day," their father added with a strange, dreamy tone to his voice. Rosemary looked at Freda briefly, then she lifted her chin and faced her parents.

"We—we just wanted to talk to you for a minute."

"Of course, dear." *Mamm* pushed back a strand of hair that had fallen from beneath her *kapp* and smiled. "What is it?"

Before Rosemary could answer, *Mamm* had already turned back toward their father.

Is she batting her eyes at him?

Rosemary searched the area to make sure no one was in earshot, then she leaned closer to her parents. "What are the two of you *doing* out here?"

Mamm narrowed her eyebrows. "What do you mean?"

Rosemary let out a big gasp. "All this nonsense." She raised her arms in frustration and waved them in the air. "This . . . kissing." She glanced around again. "Someone is going to see, and it's—it's just not right."

"Hmm. I see." *Mamm* grinned at *Daed*.

"I'm not sure you do," Rosemary said, folding her arms across her chest.

"Levina, I think the girls are right." *Daed* latched onto *Mamm's* hand. "Let's go where we can be alone." Then he winked at their mother.

"Where are you going?" Freda asked.

"Home." *Daed* put his arm around *Mamm*.

Rosemary squeezed her eyes closed for a moment. *Please, Freda . . . don't ask any more questions.*

"To do what? It's still early. No one leaves so soon after worship service." Freda glanced at Rosemary, who was too fearful of her parents' answer to move.

Mamm glanced toward the sky. "Hmm. It's windy."

"*Ya*. It is."

"Should we? What do you think?"

Rosemary and Freda watched the private conversation unfolding between their parents.

Then *Mamm* whispered in *Daed's* ear.

"*Ya.* I reckon you're right," *Daed* said to *Mamm*. "We will be staying awhile longer."

Rosemary looked back and forth between them and wondered if Freda was half as perplexed as she was. "*Gut.* Now try to behave yourselves, for goodness' sake."

Rosemary nodded, then she and Freda turned to walk back into the house. She'd almost cleared the distance between her and her parents when she heard her mother say, "Kiss me again, Naaman."

Rosemary slammed the door behind her. *Silly, silly parents.*

Chapter Thirteen

NAAMAN CHUCKLED AFTER ROSEMARY AND FREDA WERE back in the house. "You sure played that up, Levina."

"It was great fun to watch their expressions." Levina smiled. "Shame on us." She sighed. "I hope our children will always be as happy with their spouses as we are at this very moment."

"I pray for that too."

"When are you going to talk to Adam? It looks like the last of the guests are leaving, except for our immediate family."

"I'd rather go home and snuggle up with you."

"I thought we were going to fly a kite."

Naaman dabbed his tongue to his first finger, then held it up. "Wind is dying down. I think snuggling sounds better."

"Talk to Adam. Make things right, and see if you can find out what is going on with him." Levina grinned. "Then home to snuggle."

Naaman couldn't remember the last time he felt this content, but the situation with Adam lingered like a dark cloud above them. Naaman needed to talk to him, but he had little hope that Adam would give him the time of day just yet. Pushing him might be the wrong thing to do. But Levina sure did seem worried about him, for reasons that seemed to have nothing to do with Naaman.

Naaman crossed the yard and met Adam and Hannah. "It was a *gut* service today."

Adam nodded but didn't make eye contact with his father.

"So glad you're here, Naaman." Hannah gave Naaman a hug, and over her shoulder Naaman could see Adam scowl.

"*Danki*, Hannah." He eased out of the hug. "Would you mind if I talk to Adam for a few minutes?"

"Of course not." Hannah smiled, but before she even walked away, Adam spoke up.

"We don't have anything to talk about." He folded his arms across his chest.

"Maybe no, maybe yes." Naaman held his position as he looped his thumbs beneath his suspenders.

Hannah stepped toward Adam, and Naaman saw tears in her eyes. "Talk to your father, Adam."

"This is not your business, Hannah."

Naaman was shocked by the way Adam spoke to his wife, and as Hannah's cheeks turned a rosy shade of pink, Naaman was wishing Adam was still of the age to be taken behind the woodshed for a good spanking.

"Please, Adam." Hannah dabbed at her eyes. "Your father is a wise man. Whatever is bothering you, or if you're angry at him—or me—or . . . I just don't know, but maybe you should talk to him."

"It's all right, Hannah. I'm sure Adam will come to me when he's ready."

A tear rolled down her cheek. "It might be too late by then," she said as she turned and ran back toward the house.

"Adam?" Naaman took a few steps closer, but Adam clenched his jaw tight and stared at the ground. "I know you are angry with me, and I don't blame you. I also know that there is something else going on with you. Your mother senses this, and I can see it now too." Naaman paused with a sigh. "I am here for you if you want to talk to me."

When Adam didn't move, Naaman reluctantly turned to go find Levina, but the sound of his son's voice caused him to turn back around.

"Must be nice to leave all responsibility for a year-long vacation, no?"

Naaman walked back to his son. "Is that what you think it was—a vacation?"

"*Ya*. That's exactly what it was."

"I should not have left, Adam. I regret it."

"But you did it, just the same."

"*Ya*. I did."

They stood quietly for a few moments. Naaman could see his son's bottom lip trembling.

"Don't you think we'd all like to do what you did? Just leave?" Adam glared at his father with such loathing that Naaman was tempted to walk away, but now he saw the deeper issue.

Beneath the outpouring of anger, Naaman could see the pain his son was in. Now how was he going to explain to Adam that his feelings are normal but that they should not be acted on as Naaman had done? He chose his words carefully.

"Is that what you want to do, Adam? Leave your family?"

"Of course not. I would never abandon Hannah and the *kinner*."

Naaman studied him for a moment. "Let's go for a walk, Adam."

Adam grunted. "I'm not going on a walk with you."

Naaman looped his thumbs beneath his suspenders. "*Ya*, you are. Let's go." He hoped the firmness of his tone would coax his son to remember that Naaman was still his father.

Naaman set off, and slowly Adam joined his side. Neither of them spoke until they reached the barbed-wire fence separating the cows from the yard. Adam put a foot on the bottom wire and pushed it back and forth as he stared at the ground. Naaman rested an elbow atop a fence post and waited.

"I–I would never leave my family."

Adam's words stung Naaman, even though he was glad Adam repeated his earlier comment.

"But—I think about what it would be like, to go into the world, to see things, and not have responsibilities. Like you did." He narrowed his eyes at Naaman.

"I regret what I did, Adam." Naaman sighed. "I ask the Lord's forgiveness every day, and I try not to question how my leaving could have been His will." Naaman paused. He knew he must speak candidly. "Your mother and I spent most of our years raising you *kinner*, and once you were all gone, it felt—lonely. I didn't really know your mother anymore. We were just two people sharing meals. That's how it seemed anyway. But, Adam . . . leaving was not the answer. And I didn't leave to go see the world." He raised his brows. "I had an active *rumschpringe*, and I saw all I needed to. If that were what I'd been seeking, I wouldn't have gone to Levi's home in Ohio. I just felt like I needed to be alone."

"You weren't alone there, *Daed*. Levi and his family were there."

"No, I wasn't alone. There were people around me, but a man can be alone in his heart if he chooses. And for reasons I didn't even understand, I chose to be alone."

"Why did you come back?"

"I missed your mother and all of you." Naaman shrugged. "No amount of distance was going to cure the mixed-up feelings I had. I knew I needed to come back and face my fears."

Adam stopped popping the barbed wire back and forth with his foot, and for the first time he looked directly at his father. "What kind of fears?"

Naaman wished he didn't have to have this awkward conversation with his son, but if it helped Adam not to make the same mistake, it would be worth it.

Please, Lord, help me to help Adam through my mistakes and experiences.

At that moment Naaman speculated whether or not his leaving could have been part of a larger plan, God's plan. Could the choices he'd made ultimately affect Adam's future decisions?

Naaman took a deep breath and released it slowly. "I was afraid that your mother and I would never reconnect with each other—that we'd been wonderful parents but lost the love we once shared."

Adam looked at the ground and kicked at the grass. "That's how I feel sometimes. I work all day, and Hannah works hard too. By the time we tend to the *kinner*, there ain't much time left for—for us."

"Adam, I've made mistakes. All I can do is tell you what I've learned. A marriage has to be nurtured the same way you nurture your *kinner*. Your *mamm* and I stopped doing that somewhere along the way and woke up one day to realize we didn't really know each other anymore . . . that is, we didn't know each other the way we once did, when we were young and in love."

Adam gazed out toward the pasture.

"Do you love Hannah?" Naaman moved closer to his son.

"*Ya.*" Adam turned to Naaman. "But she gets on my nerves sometimes."

Naaman chuckled. "And I'm sure you get on hers. That's just part of a relationship." He rubbed his forehead. "In some ways I don't feel like I have the right to talk with you about this, after what I did. But, Adam, if it helps you not to make the same mistakes I did, then perhaps this was God's plan."

Adam continued to gaze into the pasture.

"When is the last time you and Hannah had a date? Just the two of you? Maybe a night out to dinner or a picnic?"

Adam grunted. "*Daed*, I don't remember us doing that since before the *kinner* were here."

Naaman ran his hand the length of his beard. "I wish your *mamm* and I had made more time to spend with each other while you children were growing up."

Adam nodded, then looked Naaman square in the eyes. "I love Hannah, *Daed*."

"I know you do, *sohn*." Naaman took a chance and put a hand on Adam's shoulder. "Don't make the same mistake I did. I never stopped loving your mother. Distance might make the heart grow fonder, but it also puts a wedge in something beautiful that's not meant to be separated." He pulled his hand back slowly. "Why don't you and Hannah plan a night out soon, or even a whole day together? Let your *mamm* and me keep the *kinner*."

"A whole day? What would we do?" A grin tipped at the corner of Adam's mouth.

Naaman raised his brows. "Anything you want. You said you wanted to get out and see things, go places . . . Take Hannah somewhere with you."

Adam ran a hand down his beard. "Hannah and I used to like to go to Pequea Creek, have a picnic, and go fishing. I don't even remember the last time . . ." He shook his head as his voice trailed off. Then he scowled. "But I reckon the *kinner* would like to go to the creek too."

"And you should take them sometime. But there is nothing wrong with you and Hannah having some . . . some romance, by yourselves."

Adam's face turned a tad red, but Naaman continued. "Your *mamm* and I just had a picnic at Pequea Creek."

"I still don't understand how you could just leave *Mamm* . . . and us."

Naaman resisted the urge to hang his head in shame and instead looked his son in the eyes. "I don't understand either. But I'm home. In time, I hope you can forgive me."

"You know that it's our way."

"And I also know that forgiveness does not always come easily—for any of us. I'm sorry for the hurt I caused you, your brother and sisters, and mostly *Mamm*."

"I think I'd like to go talk to Hannah."

Naaman nodded, then he watched as Adam walked away.

Adam took about ten steps before he turned around. *"Danki, Daed."*

Naaman smiled, then followed Adam toward the house to find Levina.

Chapter Fourteen

LARRY ROLLED OVER AND PRIED ONE EYE OPEN TO LOOK AT the clock. How in the world had he slept until nine thirty? Worst part was, he'd missed breakfast downstairs. No homemade yogurt with granola on top today. He rubbed his eyes, then forced himself to sit on the side of the bed.

He had planned to pin down the owner this morning and get an address for Naaman Lapp. His stomach growled as he headed to the shower, past an empty pizza box and two beer bottles. It had been a great ball game, but he probably should have foregone the late-night movie—and the beer.

Once he was shaved and in his street clothes, he flipped through a binder that listed the recommended eateries nearby. After reading brief descriptions of each, he decided on Yoder's Pantry. *Authentic Amish food—breakfast, lunch, and supper.*

Maybe the folks there would know where to find Naaman Lapp. And maybe they would have that yogurt he'd missed out on this morning. Surely Patsy couldn't fault him for the yogurt. He was pretty sure it was good for him.

His knees popped on every single stair on his way down to the car, but once he pulled out, it was only a five-minute drive to Yoder's Pantry.

When he walked into the restaurant, a young Amish woman was placing jars of jams and jellies on a rack by the door.

"Hello." He waited for her to put the last jar on the shelf. "I need a table for one. Also, I was wondering if you know where I can find Naaman Lapp. I'm an old friend of his."

The girl looked up at him with stunning blue eyes that seemed to see right through him. "I don't work here. The hostess should be out in a minute."

"I'm sorry. I saw you putting the jellies on the shelf, so I just assumed you worked here."

"That's all right." She fumbled with the jars, using both hands to line them up side by side on the shelf.

"So do you happen to know Naaman Lapp?"

"*Ya*, I know him." The girl looked up at him, but again she seemed to be staring through him.

"So . . . can you tell me where I can find him?" Larry saw her face muscles tense.

"I'm not sure."

"Maybe an address?" Larry saw two other Amish women in the distance, but they were scurrying to deliver food.

"I don't know the address."

Larry raked a hand through his hair and sighed. Most Amish folks he knew back in Ohio had a phone in the barn, even though phones weren't allowed in their homes, but he doubted this woman was going to share any information. "Well, could you give me directions?"

"I don't think so."

Larry pulled a card from his pocket. "Can you ask him to call this number, if you see him?"

"If I *see* him, I will."

When she didn't reach for the card, Larry placed it on the shelf near the jams. "Thank you."

A moment later a much more chipper Amish woman hurried across the floor toward him.

"Hello!"

She jumped up a bit on her toes, which caused Larry to grin.

"How many? Would you like a window seat or a booth?"

"Uh, just me." Larry started to follow her, but the other

woman started speaking loudly to her in Pennsylvania *Deitsch*. He recognized the dialect from back home.

His hostess stopped, turned, and glared at him. It was a look of obvious displeasure, and Larry raised his brows and waited. Then she pointed to a booth right inside the entrance. "This okay?"

Before he could answer, she'd scooted back to the other woman.

"Sure," he whispered to himself as he sat down.

TILLIE HURRIED BACK TO ELLIE. "WHAT DO YOU MEAN HE'S a sheriff looking for *mei daed*?"

"Irma, who works for Barbie Beiler, said that a man came into the bed-and-breakfast on Friday, dressed as a sheriff. The next day that same man asked Barbie where he could find your father. When this man started asking questions, I couldn't help but worry it's the sheriff Irma was talking about."

"What did you tell him?" Tillie twisted to look briefly at the man, then turned back to Ellie.

"He asked if I knew the address, which I really don't. Then he asked if I could give him directions. And I really can't, because we go a different way from home than going from here."

"Then what happened?"

"He asked if I saw your *daed*, would I tell him to call him." Ellie grinned. "I told him that if I *see* him, I will."

Tillie smiled. Ellie had been blind for the past several years, due to optic nerve damage. Most people couldn't tell because her eyes looked fine—although after a short while you noticed that her line of vision was always a little off.

"I don't think he and *Mamm* are coming in today, but you did *gut*, Ellie," Tillie said. "*Ach!* I need to go tell the other girls to avoid his questions. I don't want anyone to lie—just avoid him."

"Why do you think he's looking for your *daed*?"

"I don't know. But things are going so *gut* with him and *mei mamm*, I don't want to stir up trouble. Besides, I know *Daed* couldn't have done anything bad."

"He left a card." Ellie felt around the shelf, and Tillie saw a white business card next to a jar of jam.

"I got it." Tillie picked up the card and read *Larry Dozier*. And there was a phone number. She tucked it into the pocket of her apron. "I'm going to go warn the other girls."

LARRY HAD NEVER SEEN SUCH A SPEEDY GROUP OF WAIT-resses in his entire life. They bustled about like there was a fire in the building.

"Here you go, sir." An Amish woman he hadn't seen yet placed a small bowl of cheese spread and another bowl that looked like peanut butter spread alongside a basket of pretzels. Larry had noticed the sign outside proclaiming the "best pretzels in the county."

"Thank you. I'm ready to——"

But she was gone. Scooted right off before he had time to order. He glanced around at the four servers waiting on other customers. In between taking orders and delivering food, they would gather in a circle, then look in his direction. He wasn't imagining it.

Everyone buzzed about, but they didn't seem in any hurry to take his order. Finally the bubbly girl who had met him at the door showed up. "And what would you like, sir?"

"I'll have the meat loaf with mashed potatoes." Patsy hated meat loaf, so this was his opportunity to splurge on something he didn't get at home. "And ranch dressing on my salad."

"Sure." She spun on her heel.

"Miss?" Larry made sure he said it loud enough that she couldn't ignore him.

When she turned around, her face dropped into the saddest frown he'd ever seen. *"Ya?"*

"I just wanted to ask you if you knew where I could find Naaman Lapp? I'm a friend of his, and—"

The girl bit her bottom lip so hard it hurt Larry to watch.

"I have to turn in your order. We're very busy, and if I don't, it could take forever to get your food!" She spun around and was gone.

Larry sat motionless, watching her. "Okay," he said again to himself.

He dipped a warm pretzel into the cheese sauce and brought it to his mouth, dripping a tiny bit on the white table. Closing his eyes, he savored the salty taste against his tongue before biting into the moist bread. This was comfort food at its best, and Larry knew he agreed with the sign outside. This was the best pretzel in the county. Perhaps in the world, he thought, as he dipped the remainder into the peanut spread. Equally delicious. Right up there with the homemade yogurt.

The doctor, along with Patsy, had said to cut back on carbs, but today was not the day for it. He reached for another pretzel and decided to double-dip—first into the cheese sauce, then the peanut butter spread. *Pure heaven.*

He was appreciating the last little bit of the pretzel when every waitress in the joint suddenly darted toward the front door. Larry strained to see what they were doing, but they rounded the corner and were out of sight. He shoved the last bite into his mouth, hoping his salad would arrive soon. Or that more pretzels would be forthcoming.

TILLIE MADE IT TO HER FATHER AHEAD OF THE OTHER GIRLS and pushed him back toward the front door of Yoder's Pantry.

"*Daed*, what are you doing here?"

Her father scowled as he stumbled backward. "Your *mamm* asked me to drop off this casserole dish you left at Adam's yesterday. And she has some raisin puffs for you and Rufus." He narrowed his eyes at her. "What is wrong with you?"

Tillie motioned with her hand for the other girls to go back around the corner, then she whispered to Annie. "Go make sure that man doesn't get up or try to go to the bathroom or anything."

"How will I stop him?" Annie's eyes rounded with surprise, but she nodded and left.

"Stop *who* from going to the bathroom?" *Daed* took a step forward and leaned his head around the corner, but Tillie grabbed his arm and coaxed him back toward the entrance.

"We're just very busy, *Daed*. Tell *Mamm danki*, and I'll see you later." She opened the door of the restaurant for him to leave.

"*Mei maedel*, it wonders me what is wrong with you." *Daed* shook his head but he did back out the door, and Tillie breathed a sigh of relief.

What had her *daed* done to make a sheriff come to town looking for him?

Chapter Fifteen

AFTER HER SHIFT AT YODER'S PANTRY WAS OVER, TILLIE stopped by Freda's house on the way home. She was tethering her horse when Freda met her in the yard.

"Hi, Tillie." Freda took a bite of a banana as she glided across the yard barefoot.

Tillie put her hands on her hips. "We have a problem."

Freda swallowed. "What kind of problem?"

"Our father, that's what!"

Freda's expression grew concerned. "Did something happen? Is he sick? What is it, Tillie?"

Tillie turned her head from one side to the other, scanning the area. With no one in sight, she still felt the need to whisper. "Our *daed* is a wanted man!"

"Tillie, what are you talking about?" Freda folded her hands across her chest, the hint of a smile on her face.

"It's not funny, Freda. There is a sheriff in town looking for *Daed*. He must have gotten in trouble while he was away."

"What kind of trouble?"

Tillie lifted her shoulders, then dropped them. "How should I know? The kind that makes a lawman come lookin' for ya. A tall man with beady eyes and a big belly came into Yoder's Pantry. He was asking where to find *Daed*." Tillie took a deep breath. "This sheriff man is staying at Beiler's, and he asked Barbie too."

"Tillie, are you sure about all this?" Freda thrust her hands onto her hips. "Because you make such a big deal outta every little thing."

"Well, I reckon a sheriff looking for *Daed* is a big deal, no?"

"What could he have done?"

Tillie paced the yard for a few moments. "I don't know, but things are going so *gut* between him and *Mamm*. And he's home. I just don't want him to have to leave again. For prison! *Ach*, Freda, what are we going to do?"

"Tillie, that man will find *Daed*. You can't stop him. *Daed* ain't that hard to find."

"Hmm . . ." Tillie tapped her finger to her chin. "I wonder how long he's planning to stay. Maybe he'll get tired of looking and go back home."

"Probably depends on how bad a thing *Daed* did."

"What do you think it could be?"

Freda shrugged. "I don't know. It's hard to imagine *Daed* in trouble, enough to make a lawman come lookin' for him."

"The girls at Yoder's Pantry are helping me spread the word not to tell that beady-eyed man anything about *Daed*."

"Tillie, are you asking folks to lie?"

"Of course not." Tillie lowered her chin, then raised her eyes to Freda. "Just to avoid the truth. I have to go. But make sure that Jonathan knows. And . . ." Tillie twisted her mouth from side to side as she thought. "Might be best not to mention this to Rosemary or Adam just yet. Adam might haul *Daed* straight to the man, happy to have *Daed* spend the rest of his days in a jail cell!"

"Tillie, stop being so dramatic. Besides, *Mamm* said that Adam and *Daed* talked yesterday after worship service, and things are on the mend between them."

"Just the same, I reckon we don't say anything just yet. Maybe just to Jonathan."

"Whatever you say, Tillie. But I think maybe you should at least talk to Rosemary. She'll know what to do."

Tillie shook her head. "No, no. Rosemary tells *Mamm* everything. You know that. I'm going to go spread the word to everyone

I can think of. *Mamm* and *Daed* need time to work on their relationship, alone and with no troubles." She gave a taut nod of her head.

Freda chuckled. "Tillie, you read too many of those magazines at the doctor's office."

"This is not funny, Freda. Not funny at all! Make sure you tell Jake to let everyone know not to tell."

"Tillie, *Daed* is not above the law for whatever he did. Just like the *Englisch*, we're responsible for our actions. It's just a matter of time—"

"Don't say that." Tillie pointed a finger at her sister, then she turned to leave, still wondering what law their father could have broken.

BY LATE AFTERNOON LARRY KNEW HE WOULD BE STAYING AT least one more day in Lancaster County, since Naaman Lapp was proving to be the most elusive man he'd ever pursued. Every person Larry had come in contact with today had avoided him like he was . . . a sheriff in pursuit of a criminal. Larry shook his head and smiled as he walked into the small breakfast area at the B & B.

"I'm going to need to stay at least one more night," he told the same Amish girl who'd been there when he arrived.

"Sure. That's fine. But the rest of the week is already booked up." She smiled as if this was the best news on the planet. "I'm sorry."

"What? I thought you said I wouldn't have to worry about it until the weekend. This is only Monday."

Still smiling, the woman shrugged. "Big group of ladies called to book four rooms, starting tomorrow."

"Couldn't you have checked with me?"

Her smile fell. "I'm sorry, Mr. Dozier. We have to accept

those who are a for-sure thing. You didn't think you'd be staying past today. I'm sorry for the inconvenience."

Larry sighed. "So I need to check out tomorrow morning?"

The woman smiled again. "Yes, sir. By noon, please."

Larry eyed some sticky buns on a plate near the woman. "May I?"

"Sure." She pushed the platter toward him.

Patsy would have my behind for this. He took a bite as he walked out the door. He hoped he could find Naaman in the morning, then be on his way back home by tomorrow afternoon, instead of having to find another place to stay.

LEVINA WASN'T SURE EXACTLY WHAT HER TWO YOUNGEST daughters were trying to pull, but Rosemary had gotten wind of their antics first thing this sunny Tuesday morning and had come straight to tell Levina about it.

"I heard it from Rebecca, who heard from Sarah, that *Daed* is on the run from the law. Sarah heard from her husband, who heard it at the market in Bird-in-Hand. And Paul Dienner said that Big John at the hardware store said *Daed* is going to prison for a very long time. And Tillie and Freda are running around town telling everyone not to tell where you and *Daed* live. Evidently the sheriff man went into Yoder's Pantry looking for him."

Levina turned off the water in the sink, dried her hands on her apron, then spun to face her daughter. "What for? What did he supposedly do?" She wasn't sure what was more upsetting— Naaman's crime or the fact that the entire community was talking about it and bordering on breaking the law themselves by hiding Naaman. Just when she thought they could put embarrassment behind them, this happens.

"I don't know, *Mamm*." Rosemary sat down at the table.

"Where are my grandchildren?"

"Glenn is with them." Rosemary reached for a leftover biscuit. "He thought I should come right over here and tell you."

"Did he, now?" Levina opened the refrigerator and pulled out a jar of rhubarb jam. She pulled a spoon from the drawer and placed the spoon and jam in front of Rosemary.

Rosemary piled the jam on one half of the biscuit, then she began talking with her mouth still full. "What are you going to do?"

Levina sat down. "What do you mean?"

Rosemary swallowed. "Are you going to ask *Daed*?"

"I am not going to disrespect your father by asking him about petty rumors." Levina's stomach churned, though she was doing her best not to let Rosemary know.

"But, *Mamm* . . . there is a lawman lookin' for *Daed*. He did something."

Levina put her head in her hands, then looked back up at Rosemary. "The good Lord will provide the answers when He's ready. And so will your father."

Rosemary stuffed the other half of the biscuit into her mouth. "I can't believe you're not gonna ask him about this."

I can't believe it either.

Things were better between her and Naaman than they'd ever been. Levina recalled the past couple of days. Sunday night after worship at Adam's, they cuddled together on the couch, holding hands and reading the Bible. Monday they'd each worked hard all day, but after supper they'd taken a walk, then gone to bed early. Levina smiled. Things were perfect. If her world was getting ready to fall apart again, she wanted to enjoy these special moments while they lasted.

NAAMAN PUT THE LAST COAT OF VARNISH ON THE OAK dresser, then he stood back to inspect his work. It was small, perfect for a baby's room—for whichever of his youngest daughters needed it first.

"Very nice," Levina said as she strolled in holding two glasses. "I brought you some sweet tea."

"*Danki.*" He accepted the tea, took a large gulp, then set it down on his workbench. "I reckon this will be for either Tillie's or Freda's *kinner.*"

"It seems to be a race between those two." Levina grinned. "What are you going to do if they both get pregnant at the same time?"

Naaman pointed to his right, to a stack of wood he planned to use for his next project. "I'm prepared."

It was only midmorning, so Naaman pushed back thoughts of a nap with Levina. All he could think about these days was holding her in his arms. He was like a teenager in love, and he wanted to spend every waking minute with her.

She edged closer and smiled, the type of expression that made Naaman think perhaps a nap was in order after all. "What's your plan for the day?"

Naaman smiled and lifted his eyebrows up and down. "Depends. What are your plans?"

"Stop that, Naaman." Levina waved him to shush, but with a grin on her face. "With the *kinner* gone, I reckon our days aren't as full, but there is still much to be done around here. I'm planning to finish the wash this morning before lunch and get it out to dry."

"When did wash day change from Monday to Tuesday?"

Levina crossed her arms across her chest. "When you returned and we started taking naps all the time." She lifted her chin, still grinning.

"*Ach*, I see." He took a swig of his tea. "What did Rosemary want this morning?"

"Just to chat." Levina shrugged.

"That reminds me. Tillie acted mighty strange yesterday when

I went to drop off the things you sent. It was like she couldn't get me out of Yoder's Pantry fast enough." He scratched his chin. "That girl was hiding something, but I reckon I haven't a clue what. You know anything?"

Levina shrugged again. "You know Tillie. She always has something going on, and if she doesn't she creates something to keep herself entertained."

"Hmm . . ." Naaman eyed Levina and tried to figure out if she was being completely truthful. His wife always knew what the *kinner* were up to.

"Hannah stopped by while you were tending to the cows in the pasture yesterday afternoon. She was glad that you and Adam talked. Whatever you said to him, she said he seems like a much happier person. I was so glad to hear that."

Naaman nodded. "They are young, but I think they will be fine."

"What about you and Adam?"

Naaman pulled his straw hat from his head and wiped his forehead. "I think things will be all right. Just gonna take Adam a little time to understand why . . ." Naaman trailed off, not wanting to bring up the past.

"I'm going to get the wringer going and start on those clothes. I've got some beef stew simmering on the stove."

"Sounds *gut*. I'm going to put the knobs on this dresser, and then it will be ready for whichever *dochder* needs it first."

"It's a beautiful piece of furniture, Naaman."

He smiled, not sure if life could be any more perfect.

Chapter Sixteen

TUESDAY MORNING LARRY CHECKED OUT OF BEILER'S B & B and into a small hotel at the edge of town after not being able to find a room at any of the other bed-and-breakfasts in the area. The first two Amish-owned establishments told him they were full, but not until after he mentioned his name. He ventured into two more B & Bs in Gordonville, and although the places weren't Amish-owned, he'd spotted some Amish women outside in the yard. These inns were full, too . . . after they asked for his name.

It didn't take a brain surgeon to figure out that the community was protecting Naaman Lapp from the big bad sheriff. Larry smiled as he settled onto the bed in the small room, then he picked up the phone.

"Bill, I need you to get an address for an Amish man named Naaman Lapp. He lives in Lancaster County, Pennsylvania, in the town of Paradise."

"You mean to tell me that you can't track down one Amish fellow in that small town?" His partner chuckled.

"Yeah, I know. I think folks around here are hiding him, so to speak. It's a pretty close-knit community."

"Let me get you an address, and I'll call you back."

Larry hung up, propped the pillows behind him, then flipped on the television. He couldn't believe he was still here after four days. But there were worse places to be when one was avoiding the in-laws. Besides, Patsy would be thrilled with the quilt and all the trinkets he'd picked up for her. And he was enjoying some mighty good food.

He crossed his ankles and starting switching the channels. It wouldn't take long for Bill to get him an address, and Larry planned to head to Naaman's place right after lunch. Maybe lunch at Yoder's Pantry again. More of those warm pretzels dipped in cheese sauce and peanut butter spread. Just thinking about it made his mouth water.

LEVINA PINNED THE SHEETS TO THE LINE WHILE NAAMAN cleaned the stalls in the barn. Hard as she tried, she couldn't shake her conversation with Rosemary. She'd prayed hard about it all morning, asking God to guide her to do the right thing, and she knew she needed to confront Naaman about what Rosemary said. She didn't want there to be anything between them. They were in a good, honest place, and she'd never been happier. This new information made her uneasy, and she couldn't stop wondering what it was that Naaman had done to bring a sheriff to town. Her healing heart was still fragile, but she would have to know the truth.

She trembled as fear overtook her like a winter's wind slapping against her bare skin. *Please, God, whatever Naaman did, I pray it wasn't too bad. Please don't take him from me again.* Naaman was a good man, and even if he'd done something he shouldn't have, he wasn't the type of man to run away.

Levina froze as she realized that he was *exactly* the type to run away. He'd proven that. Then it hit her—hard. Maybe that was the reason her husband had come home—because he was in trouble with the law. Her head began to spin. Would Naaman have ever come home if there hadn't been trouble in Middlefield? Maybe he didn't have a choice. Maybe home was the only place he had to go. *Did I get him back by default?*

She took a deep breath, then blew it out slowly as she pinned the corner of the last sheet.

By the time Naaman came in for lunch, Levina had dreamed up every possible scenario as to why a sheriff would be looking for him. Did he leave Ohio owing someone money? Did he drive a car while he was there and get a violation of some sort? Maybe he'd had an accident? The "maybes" kept going through her head, but logically she couldn't wrap her mind around the idea of Naaman doing anything illegal, much less not fessing up to it. She was just going to have to ask him.

"Something smells *gut* in here." Naaman walked into the kitchen, put his hat on the rack, and wasted no time wrapping his arms around her waist as she stirred the stew. Just the feel of his arms around her sent a shiver of longing through her. They were on their second honeymoon, and Levina wished it could go on like this forever. Maybe she'd wait to ask him about the sheriff.

When they'd finished eating, Naaman kissed her on the cheek while she washed the dishes. Then he did something he'd never done. He began to dry the dishes and put them away.

"Why are you doing that?" She asked the question with a sharper tone than she intended as she turned to face him.

His jaw dropped slightly. "Just trying to help you."

She forced a smile, but her thoughts returned to a bad place. *Maybe you are just trying to solidify your place in our household so that I will stand by you when the lawman comes. Maybe the only reason you came back is because you have nowhere else to go.*

"That's not where that goes." She dried her hands on her apron, then pulled the large spoon from the drawer where Naaman had put it. She hung it on the rack near the stove.

"Levina, is everything all right?" Hesitantly, Naaman picked up another plate and started to dry it.

"*Ya.*" She walked back to the sink and resumed washing, but didn't look at him. "I—I have some errands to run this afternoon."

"I can finish up in the shop and go with you." He smiled as he put away a plate in the cabinet.

"No." She shook her head. "You would be bored. I have to go by Rebecca Deinner's house to pick up some cookbooks to take to Yoder's Pantry, and I have to stop by Barbie Beiler's Bed-and-Breakfast." She quickly looked at Naaman to see if the mention of Beiler's B & B generated any kind of reaction. Nothing.

"Well, okay. I'll take the spring buggy to pick up some parts I need to fix one of the generators." He kissed her on the cheek again. "But I hope to meet back here before too long." He winked at her as he put the last dish up. Then he pulled his hat from the rack and headed out the door.

Levina dried her hands and took a deep breath. She couldn't take this anymore. She'd just go find the sheriff at Barbie's B & B and find out exactly what he wanted. Waiting around for him to just show up was going to make her crazy.

LARRY SCRIBBLED DOWN NAAMAN'S ADDRESS ON A PIECE OF hotel stationery, thanked Bill, and hung up the phone. No time like the present, he figured. Once he found Naaman Lapp, he could head back home to Patsy. He was missing her more than ever by now, and she'd said during their phone conversation earlier that morning that her parents were leaving. Patsy's parents were good people, but they rode him even more than Patsy about his diet, the occasional beer, and his lack of exercise. And it wasn't just that. Patsy's mother had a high-pitched voice that sounded sweet the first few minutes you were around her, but after about an hour it turned into an annoying, almost yappy little squeak. Fortunately Patsy hadn't inherited that trait.

An hour later he was pulling into the driveway off Black Horse Road. He was impressed by the way folks around here kept their property. Nothing out of place, and yards that would make any homeowners' association proud. Naaman's homestead consisted of a freshly painted white clapboard house surrounded by a white picket fence, and a large barn on either side. He didn't see any buggies, though.

He waited an ample amount of time at the door, but when no one answered, he headed back to the car, stopping to pet an Irish setter on the way out. "Where's your owner, buddy?"

No problem. He'd catch some overdue lunch, then try again later. No shortage of good food in these parts, that was for sure.

LEVINA WHISKED INTO THE BREAKFAST AREA OF BEILER'S Bed-and-Breakfast. Empty. She knocked on the kitchen door, then she pushed it open a few inches. All dark. Her friend was probably cleaning one of the guest rooms. She went around the corner just in time to see Irma walking out of a first-floor guest room, toting a cleaning bucket filled with supplies.

"Levina, what brings you here?" Irma smiled as she approached her.

"I–I know you're probably not supposed to do this, Irma, but I'm looking for a lawman that I think was staying here. I need to talk to him." Levina scrunched her face up and bit her lip, not sure if Irma would help her or not.

"You mean the big man who is looking for Naaman?" Irma looked like she was holding her breath.

So much for the embarrassment of this whole thing.

"Ya. I really need to talk with him. Can you tell me what room he's in?"

"He checked out. I mean, he wanted to stay, but he only had the room until Tuesday noon, and we had a last-minute group of ladies call for the only four rooms we had left." Irma leaned closer and whispered, "Is Naaman in trouble?"

Levina grinned and waved her hand at Irma. "No, no. It's nothing. Do you know where he went?"

Irma shook her head. "No. But Tillie and Freda made it a point to tell everyone around here not to tell the lawman where Naaman lived. So I reckon some folks might not rent to him either."

My girls should know better than this. "Irma, I'm sure that Naaman didn't do anything, but we can't have the community trying to hide him. It isn't right. Do you know if this policeman is from Ohio?"

"I reckon I don't know. He didn't say. He's a sheriff, though. He had on a sheriff's uniform when he checked in."

"Hmm . . . All right. *Danki.*" Levina waved as she turned to leave.

"Hope everything is all right, Levina!"

So do I. Levina nodded.

PARADISO WAS RIGHT DOWN THE BLOCK, AN ITALIAN REStaurant Larry hadn't tried since he arrived. Another place probably filled with forbidden foods. He smiled as he walked in.

The smell of garlic and oregano filled his nostrils, and a hostess seated him right away. He scanned the menu, not even allowing his eyes to peruse the healthy section. Patsy always wanted to eat heart healthy. *Gotta love her.*

"Would you like to try our special?" The waitress pointed to a large chalkboard on her right. Larry squinted to have a look. Baked lasagna, salad, and garlic bread.

"That looks good." He handed the woman his menu. "I'll have the special. Ranch dressing, please, ma'am."

After his salad, Larry savored the rich taste of the lasagna and cleaned his plate. Truly some of the best Italian food he'd ever had.

Then he got the strangest pain in his chest.

Chapter Seventeen

LEVINA TRIED TO FIND THE SHERIFF AT FOUR MORE BED-and-breakfasts, but she decided there were just too many places to check. Next stop—Yoder's Pantry. Tillie was probably almost through with her shift, and Levina had a few questions for her.

"*Mamm!* I'm just getting ready to clock out for the day. What brings you here?"

Levina put her hands on her hips. "Tillie Mae, is it true that you and Freda have been running round town telling people not to tell a certain sheriff where your father lives?"

Tillie lowered her chin and twisted her mouth from side to side. "Hmm. You found out about that, no? How?"

"Rosemary heard from Rebecca, who heard from someone else, who heard from someone else."

"Figures that she would tell you right away."

"You should have told me, Tillie. I heard that he came here." Levina glanced over Tillie's shoulder to make sure no one could hear, but lowered her voice anyway. "Did he say why he is looking for your father?"

"I didn't talk to him. Ellie did. But I saw him. He's a big, scary-looking man with a big stomach." Tillie clasped her hands in front of her, looked down, and shook her head. "What do you think *Daed* did, *Mamm?*"

"We don't know that he did anything, Tillie, but you can't involve the entire community by asking them to hide your father." Levina let out a heavy sigh. "It could be a misunderstanding or any number of things."

"Like what?"

"I don't know, Tillie. But let's not presume the worst. Maybe your *daed* drove a car without a license or some other thing of little worry. The man, the sheriff, has already checked out of Beiler's B & B, but—"

"*Gut!* Maybe he's gone."

"No. He wanted the room for another night, but Beiler's was full. He's around here somewhere." Levina shrugged. "No use lookin' for him, I guess. I'm sure he's going to find us, so we'll just wait."

Tillie stood quietly for a while, which wasn't like her. Then she gazed into her mother's eyes. "Don't let him leave again, *Mamm*. Whatever you do."

Tillie's eyes were brimming, and Levina swallowed back her own tears.

"I don't want your *daed* to go anywhere, but if he did something wrong, Tillie . . ." She stopped when Tillie dabbed at her eyes. "Try not to worry, and I'll let you know when I find out what's goin' on." Levina pulled Tillie into a quick hug, then she decided there was nothing to do but go home.

As she left Yoder's Pantry, her heart was heavy. *Please, Lord, give me strength.* She couldn't help but fear that Naaman was only home because of whatever trouble he'd gotten into in Middlefield. Yet she'd allowed him back into her heart, further than he'd been in many, many years. She swiped at a tear as she flicked the reins, unsure whether to say anything to Naaman or just wait for the sheriff to show up.

LEVINA SEEMED NERVOUS AS A CAT. NAAMAN ASKED HER several times throughout the course of the evening what was wrong, but she said her stomach was just a little upset. It was more than that, he knew, but whatever it was, she wasn't talking.

He looked over the rim of his reading glasses. Levina had her head buried in the Bible, but he didn't think she'd turned a page since they sat down on the couch an hour ago.

"Levina, are you sure you're all right?" He pulled his glasses off and closed his own Bible, then twisted slightly on the couch to face her. "I see you lookin' out the window from time to time. You expecting someone?"

She pushed her reading glasses up her nose and kept her head in the book. "No. Are you?" She looked up at him, raised her brows.

Naaman grimaced. "No. I'm not expecting anyone. Should I be?"

Levina let out a heavy sigh. "I reckon not."

"Do you want to go to bed?"

She glowered in his direction. "It's too early for bed, Naaman. It's not even dark yet."

Her sharp tone of voice didn't leave room for discussion, so he stayed quiet. They'd been going to bed early all week. But something had changed, and Naaman was desperate to find out what.

Two hours later nothing had improved, and Naaman was tired. "Do you mind if I go on to bed?"

She didn't look up. "No, that's fine. I'll be there shortly."

He took two steps and turned around. "Levina?"

This time she looked up and raised her eyes above her glasses. *"Ya?"*

"I love you with all my heart. I'm glad to be home. And I'm sorry, still, for everything."

Levina swallowed hard. "I know, Naaman. I love you too."

He kept his eyes locked with hers for a few moments, trying to figure out what was on her mind, but there were no clues in her staid expresssion. When she lowered her head, he eased up the flight of stairs to their bedroom, longing for his wife to join him and wondering what had changed between them.

Larry sat down on his bed at the hotel and put his arm across his full belly. This was surely the worst case of indigestion he'd ever had. Bad enough to keep him from going back to Naaman's house, and he'd been anxious to take care of things with Naaman so he could get home to Patsy. He popped two more Tums in his mouth, then he decided to take a shower before he called his wife.

He'd barely wrapped a towel around himself when he heard his cell phone ringing—a zingy little ringtone that Patsy had assigned herself.

"Hello, dear. Miss me?" Larry smiled as he spoke, hoping to forget about the heartburn that had settled in the middle of his chest.

"Have you not found that man yet, Larry? Good grief. You're an officer of the law, for goodness' sake."

"Well, you know . . . the first day, there was shopping to do for my lovely wife. Then I didn't want to bother the Amish folks on a Sunday, and yesterday I struck out. Not a soul around here would tell me where that man lives."

"Why didn't you just ask Bill to get the address?"

"I finally did, and I went there earlier today, but no one was home. I was planning to go back this evening, but I'm telling you, Patsy, I have the worst case of indigestion I've ever had in my life." Larry cringed, wishing he could take back the statement.

"Larry Dozier, what have you been eating? You haven't been sticking to our diet, have you? What have I told you about eating fat-filled, cholesterol-soaked foods that aren't good for you—"

Larry held the phone a few inches from his ear as she went on. *Good to be loved.*

"Yes, dear. Yes, dear." He just kept agreeing with her. Always best.

"You know I only tell you these things because I love you."

"I love you, too, dear. And tomorrow morning, first thing,

I'm going to Naaman Lapp's house. I'll catch the first flight out after that."

"I can't wait to see my quilt!"

Larry smiled. He loved to hear Patsy happy, and he couldn't wait to see the look on her face when she saw the quilt. "I'll call you tomorrow when I have my business wrapped up."

"I love you. I'll talk to you tomorrow."

"Love you, too, dear."

Larry changed into his pajamas, took two more Tums, then folded himself onto the bed. He flipped the channels on the television, but he couldn't concentrate. The tightness in his chest was getting worse, not better, and he was having trouble catching his breath.

Oh no. As the possibility of having a heart attack hit him, he reached over to grab his cell phone, but he quickly fell back against the pillows. He was being crushed, something so heavy on his chest, he couldn't breathe.

Why am I not breathing? He wanted to breathe but nothing was happening, and the weight on his chest was unbearable.

Dear Lord, am I dying?

Yes.

Larry heard the voice loud and clear, and he knew who it was.

I'm afraid, God.

Patsy's face flashed in front of him, then each of his three children's faces, then his entire life began to play in his mind like a slide show. He thought about how he had only recently turned his life over to God, after years of doubts as a nonbeliever. Six months ago he'd even been baptized. Patsy, who'd always been strong in her faith, said it was the happiest day of her life. Larry agreed with her. Getting to know God and His Son, Jesus, had changed his life.

My life. It's over, isn't it?

He heard the soft voice again. *Yes. Don't be afraid.*

His body wasn't moving. There was no air coming out of his lungs. But a white light filled the room and gave him an immediate sense of comfort.

And he was no longer afraid.

Chapter Eighteen

Two days later Levina was still on edge, watching the window and waiting for the sheriff to break whatever bad news was forthcoming. *But why is he waiting?*

Maybe there was another Naaman Lapp somewhere else, outside of their town of Paradise. Or maybe he just changed his mind.

She thought about how happy she and Naaman had been since his return.

"Guder mariye, mei lieb." Naaman walked in full of smiles and kissed her on the cheek.

Levina took a deep breath and tried to fend off her worry. *"Guder mariye."*

She stared at her saucepan on the burner and waited for the water, brown sugar, and butter to come to a boil. Then she poured it into a casserole dish and set it aside. Naaman loved the syrupy pancake bake she'd learned from her mother years ago. Both her parents had passed away, and Levina always thought of her mother when she made this favorite of Naaman's.

Levina wondered if things would have been different if Naaman's parents were still alive. Would he have confided in his father about his problems? Like Levina, Naaman had been an only child—something uncommon in their community. She'd always wondered if that was one of the many reasons they'd taken to each other so easily.

Naaman sat down at the table and started reading the *Intelligencer Journal* while Levina combined the rest of the ingredients to put on top of the first layer of their breakfast—an egg, milk, salt, sugar, butter, flour, and some baking powder. The pancake bake was a little too sweet for her taste, but it had been a favorite of the children's as well as Naaman's.

"Is that pancake bake I smell?" Naaman raised his eyes above his reading glasses.

"It is. Just for you." Levina placed the casserole dish in the oven. "But it will be about thirty minutes." She closed the oven and turned to face him. "The girls are coming for lunch today. Will you be here?"

"No." Naaman pulled his glasses off and smiled. "When Jonathan was here last time, I showed him the dresser I'd made. He told the folks at the furniture store where he works, so I am supposed to go meet with them about doing some special-order projects."

"Naaman, that's great. I know how much you're enjoying that." Levina sat down at the kitchen table. "And it would be nice to supplement our income, since we don't do as much farming as some of the folks around here."

"I won't let this take away from my chores around here, though."

"*Ach*, I know. But it's nice to have something on the side. I enjoy taking jams, jellies, and crafts to Yoder's Pantry."

Naaman reached across the table and latched onto Levina's hand. "Life is good. God is good. We have so much to look forward to." He grinned. "And we will fly a kite, and we will go to Florida."

Levina thought again about the sheriff, but she pushed her doubts about Naaman's return to the back of her mind. If he had done something all that bad and was on the run, the sheriff would have found them by now.

After they chatted about various home repairs they hoped to do, they enjoyed Levina's casserole. Naaman helped himself to

BETH WISEMAN

seconds . . . and thirds. As sunlight crept above the horizon, the kitchen began to fill with natural light. Levina turned off the two gas lanterns; then she began to clean the kitchen. She busied herself, even humming, as Naaman finished reading the newspaper.

The *Intelligencer Journal* was the most-viewed newspaper in the county—by both the *Englisch* and Amish. Most of those in their district subscribed to it, in addition to *The Budget* and *Die Botschaft*, both of which served Amish communities throughout the country.

The more she hummed, the more it quieted the worry in her heart. She was looking forward to Rosemary, Tillie, and Freda coming for lunch. Tillie had the day off, and they'd made the plans days ago. She hoped that the conversation wouldn't focus on the sheriff, or the past. Levina wanted to simply enjoy what the future held for them.

She'd just put the last of the clean dishes in the cabinet when she heard Naaman stand up. She turned to see him pulling his hat from the nearby rack. As he placed the hat on his head, his mouth was pulled into a frown, and his eyes were glassy with emotion.

"Naaman, what's wrong?" Levina dried her hands on the dish towel and moved toward him. "What is it?"

Naaman tried to smile, but Levina could see the muscle in his jaw quiver as he blinked his eyes. "Uh . . . nothing. Just lots on *mei* mind. I need to go." He hurriedly kissed her on the mouth, then he was out the door before Levina could say anything else.

She needed to dust and then run the floor sweeper over the downstairs before the girls came at noon, but there was plenty of time for that. She pulled out a chair at the kitchen table and sat down, then pulled the *Intelligencer* toward her. The headline that caught her eye caused her heart to skip a beat.

Middlefield Sheriff Found Dead at Junction Inn.

Levina brought her hand to her chest and tried to calm her rapid heartbeat. She leaned closer to the paper, but all the lines blurred. She reached across the table and grabbed Naaman's reading glasses, which he'd hastily left behind.

After adjusting the glasses, she began to read beneath the picture of a man with balding brown hair and solemn expression, wearing a sheriff's uniform.

Larry Dozier, 58, a sheriff from Middlefield, Ohio, was found dead in his room at the Junction Inn in Paradise on Wednesday. Authorities say that Dozier was in town on business when he apparently had a massive heart attack in his room on the second floor. Dozier's body was found in his bed the next morning when an employee at the inn entered to clean his room.

Dozier was a 30-year veteran of the Geauge County Sheriff's Department. He is survived by his wife, Patsy, two sons and a daughter.

Levina reread the article two more times, but her heartbeat didn't slow down. She said a quick prayer for Larry Dozier's family before she stood up and began to pace in her kitchen.

Is that why Naaman ran out the door? Did he realize that he'd been found out for whatever it was that he'd done? Would he run again? Levina breathed deeply and tried to keep her thoughts clear. When that didn't work, she decided to start on her housework. Cleaning had become a stress reliever over the past year. She probably had the cleanest house in the district, and it really didn't need dusting, but she gathered her dusting rag and set out to work, hoping and praying her nerves would settle before her daughters arrived.

NAAMAN STEERED HIS BUGGY ACROSS LINCOLN HIGHWAY and headed to the furniture store where Jonathan worked, a place filled with various handcrafted fixtures and furniture, much of it

BETH WISEMAN

made by Amish men in the area. He was excited about the prospect of adding his furniture to the inventory. But he couldn't stop thinking about Larry Dozier and the family he'd left behind. As he wondered why the Middlefield sheriff was in Lancaster County, Naaman suspected that it had something to do with him.

He parked his topless spring buggy outside of Lyman's Furniture, then he tethered his horse. Jonathan met him as he walked in the entrance.

"Mr. Lyman is waiting to talk to you, *Daed.*"

Naaman nodded and tried to clear his mind so that he could make a good business presentation to Doug Lyman, but his thoughts kept veering back to the sheriff.

LEVINA GAVE THE KITCHEN FLOOR ANOTHER ONCE-OVER, which it certainly didn't need, but staying busy was all that was keeping her sane this morning. She looked at the clock and realized her daughters would be here any minute. She poured herself into a chair in the kitchen, then she read the article about Larry Dozier one more time and tried to decide whether or not to show it to the girls.

Rosemary would likely push her to question Naaman about it. Tillie would try to persuade her not to say anything, for fear it would push Naaman away. Levina didn't know what Freda would think. Freda was less predictable than her other two daughters.

It was five minutes later when they all trailed up the driveway. Rosemary had baby Leah and the twins with her. Levina put the newspaper on top of the refrigerator, then met all of them in the yard.

"It's so nice out here, I thought maybe we could eat lunch outside." Levina pointed to the picnic table in the yard covered with a red-checked tablecloth she'd picked up at the savings store in town.

"I love this time of year!" Tillie skipped across the yard, then she wrapped her arms around Levina. "Beautiful day to eat outside."

Freda also greeted her with a hug, but Levina knew right away that Rosemary was unhappy about something. She set the baby carrier on the ground, barely hugged Levina, then urged the twins to go play in the sandbox that Naaman had built for them last spring.

"I saw the article in the newspaper about the sheriff from Middlefield. Did you see it, *Mamm*?"

"What article?" Freda leaned down to pick up Leah from her carrier, then stood up and faced her mother.

Tillie looked at Rosemary, then at her mother. "*Ya*, what article?"

"A sheriff from Middlefield, Ohio, died at the Junction Inn Tuesday night." Rosemary put her hand on her hip. "Sure would be a coincidence if it wasn't the same sheriff lookin' for *Daed*."

As much as Levina wanted to avoid the conversation, she knew there was only one way to find out for sure. "I'll be right back."

Levina came back toting the newspaper, still opened to the article, and she pushed it toward Tillie. "Is this the man you saw at Yoder's Pantry, the one asking about *Daed*?"

Tillie gasped as she brought her hand to her mouth. "That's him all right. Isn't he scary-looking?" She pulled her hand down and grimaced.

"Tillie. Don't speak that way about the dead." Levina folded her arms across her chest and waited for Tillie to read the article, then Freda.

"Guess we'll never know what *Daed* did, huh?" Freda handed the *Intelligencer* back to Levina.

"*Ach*, I'm sure they'll send someone else," Rosemary said.

Ignoring Rosemary's smart tone, Levina chose to answer

Freda's comment. "I have told all of you, we don't know that *Daed* did anything. Did any of you mention this to Adam or Jonathan?"

"Not about the man dying. But Adam and Jonathan both know someone was looking for *Daed*," Tillie said. "They said they wouldn't say anything to *Daed* until you had a chance to talk to him. So, did ya?" Tillie's eyes widened.

"No. Not yet."

"Why not, *Mamm*? You're going to have to ask him about it." Rosemary stuffed her hands in the pockets of her apron.

"No, she doesn't, Rosemary! *Mamm* does not have to ever mention this." Tillie's eyes pleaded with her mother's. "Don't do anything to make *Daed* leave again. He's home. That sheriff man is—is dead. This whole thing will just go away."

Levina narrowed her eyes at Tillie. "I didn't realize I did something to make *Daed* leave in the first place."

"That's not what I meant." Tillie hung her head.

Levina turned to Freda and waited for her to voice her opinion.

Freda looked at Tillie, then at Rosemary, and finally back at Levina. "I think you need to ask him about it, *Mamm*. Otherwise it is going to bother you—the not knowing."

Levina was quiet for a moment. "Since all of you know . . ." She glared at Tillie. "As well as most of the town—I don't see how I can avoid talking to your father about this. No tellin' what sort of rumors are already spreading."

Freda let out a heavy sigh. "Well, I–I hate to say it, but there is already a nasty rumor floating around the district."

Levina's stomach dropped. *What now?*

Chapter Nineteen

LEVINA PACED THE FLOOR IN THE DEN FOR A LONG WHILE after her daughters left. She'd been fighting back tears from the minute Freda informed them that folks not only thought Namman was on the run for a crime he'd committed in Ohio but also suspected he had another woman there. Levina had never felt so humiliated in her life . . . and she couldn't help but share some of their suspicions.

She thought about how things had been since Naaman's return. So loving, so passionate. Levina hadn't felt so alive and in love in years. To have a glimpse of what the rest of her life could be like, only to have it threatened by her own lack of trust, was not an option. She had to clear the air. Naaman had never told a lie in his life, that she knew about, so she tried to prepare herself for the truth—whatever that might be.

When he walked in about ten minutes later, Levina knew right away that something was wrong by the look on his face.

Naaman took off his hat and set it down on the coffee table, then he sat down on the couch. He put his head in his hands for a moment, then looked up at her and shook his head. "I don't understand it. Last week Mr. Lyman was all excited about carrying some of my furniture in his store. Today when we sat down to talk, he couldn't seem to look me in the eye, and then he told me that he already had too much inventory. I asked him about special orders, but he wasn't interested." Naaman rubbed his forehead. "He excused himself after our brief visit and said he had another appointment."

Levina sat down beside him. Despite all her worries, her heart hurt for Naaman. "I'm sorry, Naaman. I know you were hopeful about working with Mr. Lyman. But our income is fine, and——"

"It's not that. I know we're all right financially. But that represented part of our new beginning, and . . ." He paused. "I had the strangest feeling that Jonathan knew Mr. Lyman's reasons, but he wouldn't share them."

Levina couldn't decide if this was the worst possible time or the best to have the much-needed conversation with Naaman. She wanted to wrap her arms around him, but darkness hung between them. For there to be peace, she knew, there had to be honesty.

"Naaman . . ."

He looked into her eyes, and Levina didn't think she had ever dreaded having a conversation with her husband this much. She took a deep breath. "People are talking around town. Lots of people."

Naaman furrowed his brow and sat up taller. "What people? What are they saying?"

Levina felt her heart beating way too fast. "They . . . they are saying you might have had a woman in Middlefield."

Naaman latched onto her shoulders. "Levina, no. Levina, no, no, no." He hung his head for a moment, then he looked back in her eyes, which were starting to tear up. "Never. I have no explanation for what I did, but I would never, ever betray our wedding vows. I've told you all this."

Levina knew she needed to bring up the sheriff, but one crisis at a time was all she could handle. "But you did betray our wedding vows when you left, Naaman." She pulled away from him and stood up. "And it's hard for me to trust you."

"Levina," he pleaded as he stood up. "I thought we were past all this. And folks will stop with these silly rumors. Surely you don't think I would——"

"I don't know anything anymore, Naaman!" She stomped her

foot and let the tears pour down her face. "I don't know! I don't understand! I'm confused about everything!"

"Levina," he said tenderly as he tried to pull her to him. "Things have been so wonderful between us. This is the happiest I've ever been in my life. And I meant what I said. I will spend the rest of my life making it up to you. Please don't let this set us back. I love you so much."

She stepped back away from him and swiped at her eyes. "I love you, too, Naaman. And I've been happier than I can ever remember being."

"Then, Levina, let's don't worry about anyone else. It's just you and me, and I love you."

She sniffled and held her chin up slightly. "There's more, Naaman."

"More what? What are you talking about?"

"There's been a sheriff in town looking for you."

Naaman hung his head. "I figured that out when I saw an article in the newspaper about his death."

"What did you do, Naaman? Did you only come home because you were in trouble?"

"No! No, Levina."

They heard a car coming and turned toward the window. The timing couldn't have been worse.

Levina wiped her eyes on the sleeve of her dress and tried to gather herself. "Are you expecting anyone?"

"No."

Naaman looked like a broken man, and part of her wanted to comfort him, but she just stood there. Then she shuffled to the door, feeling more than a little broken herself. She looked through the screen and watched a woman getting out of a white four-door car. As the woman shuffled through the grass, she kept her head down, and Levina couldn't see her face. But when the woman reached up and dabbed at her eyes, Levina felt weak in the knees.

BETH WISEMAN

Now what? Why is an Englisch *woman here crying?*

When the woman reached the porch, Levina talked to her through the screen. "Can I help you?"

The woman was short and plump, with graying brown hair, and her eyes were heavy with sadness. "I'm looking for Naaman Lapp."

Before Levina could answer, Naaman was at the door. He eased Levina out of the way, pulled the screen door open, and embraced the woman. "Patsy, I'm so sorry. I'm so very sorry."

The woman cried harder as Naaman held her in his arms.

Levina didn't move, didn't speak. She felt like a stranger to her own husband at this moment.

Finally he pulled from the hug and motioned the woman inside. "Please sit down, Patsy." Then he turned to Levina. "Levina, this is Patsy."

As the woman sat down on the couch, Naaman continued. "And, Patsy, this is my wife, Levina."

Patsy raised her hand to Levina as she sniffled. "I've heard so much about you, dear. So many wonderful things."

Levina smiled and shook her hand, knowing she couldn't return the sentiment. She had no clue who this woman was.

Naaman sat down on the couch beside Patsy, and Levina slowly backed into a rocker in the corner and watched the scene unfold.

"Larry was a *gut* man, Patsy. He will be greatly missed."

Levina held her breath for a moment. *Larry?*

"He was indebted to you, Naaman." Patsy dabbed her eyes with a wrinkled tissue she had in her left hand. "He might not have known how to say it, but he loved you like a brother."

Naaman hung his head, then Patsy put her hand on his cheek. "You are a good man, too, Naaman." She looked across the room at Levina. "I can't tell you how grateful we are that Naaman showed up in Middlefield." She shook her head.

Levina could barely force a smile as she struggled to put the pieces of this strange puzzle together.

"Of course he belonged here with you, Levina," the woman added. "And I knew the Lord would guide him back to his home." She smiled a bit. "But I'm so glad we met him first. Naaman introduced Larry to the Lord. I'd tried for our entire married life, but he had so many doubts." She turned back to Naaman. "I don't know what you said to him, Naaman, to make him turn his life over to God, but it gives me great peace to know that when Larry left this world he went to be with God."

Levina swallowed hard and thought about all the times she'd questioned God's plan.

Naaman's head was down as he spoke. "And we know that all things work together for good to them who love God, to them who are the called according to his purpose." Naaman looked up, smiling slightly. "It's not our way to minister, but from the time I met Larry, I felt the Lord guiding me to share my faith with him."

Patsy turned to Levina and eased into a smile. "We've been friends with Levi and Mary for years, and we were at their house having supper the evening that Naaman arrived. He and my Larry hit it off right away." Her expression grew somber. "They were both lost souls, each with his own problems. But I believe that sometimes the good Lord introduces people who can guide each other onto the path God has planned for them." Her face brightened a bit as she continued. "In the months that followed, Larry would drop by their house, and he and Naaman would talk for hours out in the barn while doing various projects. I don't know what those men talked about, but I do know this . . . Naaman is home where he belongs. And my Larry is with our Lord in heaven."

She took a deep breath, then she reached into the small black purse in her lap. "This is why Larry was looking for you." She pushed a small box in Naaman's direction. "You left before Larry had a chance to tell you good-bye, and it was important to him for you to have this."

Naaman eyed the small container, not bigger than a pillbox, and Levina watched him remove the small lid. His eyes watered almost instantly as he pulled out a man's gold ring.

Patsy put her hand on Namaan's. "I know you folks don't wear jewelry, but I believe you know why Larry got this ring?"

Levina watched her husband blink back tears. "*Ya*. His police department gave it to him because he saved a life."

Patsy patted Namaan's hand. "And Larry said you saved *his* life. He wanted you to have this as a remembrance." She pulled her hand back and placed it in her lap. "And I think, Naaman, that Larry just wanted to thank you in person. You left so quickly and all."

Naaman glanced at Levina, then back at Patsy. "When I knew it was right in my heart to come home, I just wanted to leave right then."

"I understand." Patsy stood up. "I need to go now."

Naaman and Levina both walked her to the door. Levina wondered how different life would have been for everyone if Naaman hadn't left. For starters, she and Naaman might have spent the rest of their lives the way they were before, instead of falling in love all over again and sharing a new honesty and intimacy that they'd never had. Would their oldest son have made a terrible mistake by leaving his own family at some point, if not for Naaman sharing his experience? And what about Larry Dozier? What if Mr. Dozier had never met Naaman Lapp?

"A man's heart deviseth his way; but the Lord directeth his steps."

Levina smiled as the Scripture came into her head. The Lord always had a plan, and Levina felt more grounded in her faith than she had been in a long time. She'd been raised not to question the will of God, yet she had recently. But as the door closed behind Patsy, Levina felt a sense of calm that she hadn't felt the past few days.

She and Naaman waved as Patsy got into her car and pulled out of the driveway.

"I love you, Naaman." Levina touched her husband's cheek. "And Patsy is right. You are a *gut* man."

Naaman put his hand on top of hers and pressed her palm closer to his face. "I should have never left you."

Levina smiled. "It wonders me how differently things might have turned out if you hadn't." She pulled her hand from his face, intertwined her fingers with his. "I'm sorry I doubted you, Naaman."

He gave her hand a squeeze as he smiled back at her. "I don't blame you, Levina. My actions—"

"No, Naaman." She put a silencing finger to his lips. "My doubts drove a wedge between us." She cupped his cheek in her hand. "There must always be trust. From now on."

Naaman nodded as she pulled her hand away, then he gently kissed her on the lips.

After he slowly eased out of the kiss, Levina gently led him across the den, toward the stairs. "I think it's time for a nap." She winked at him as they headed upstairs.

Chapter Twenty

LEVINA FLOATED AROUND HER KITCHEN WITH THE ENERGY of a woman half her age and the heart of a giddy teenager in love. It had been almost a month since Patsy's visit, and since then, she and Naaman had resumed their role as newlyweds. They'd even flown a kite, but instead of doing it alone, they'd shared the experience with Adam and Hannah's children one afternoon while their son and his wife enjoyed some time alone together.

Levina and Naaman had agreed that there is no greater joy than to see happiness in the eyes of children at play. And it was refreshing to see Adam and Hannah's relationship taking on a new closeness that Levina could identify with. She was glad Adam and Naaman had patched things up and that Adam and Hannah had come for Saturday supper today along with the rest of her children, their spouses, and all her grandchildren.

Two weeks earlier Mr. Lyman had come to the house to talk to Naaman about stocking furniture at his store, and he apologized for listening to nasty rumors. The men shook on a deal, and Naaman was on top of the world. Their fields were filled with the promise of a bountiful harvest, and Levina wasn't sure life could be any grander. Today as her family gathered together for Saturday supper, festivity and fellowship were in the air.

After the meal the older children were playing a game of tag while the adults sat around the picnic tables outside. Levina was holding Leah. Sunshine mixed with a cool breeze to make for a perfect day.

"I have some news," Tillie announced as she grinned at Rufus.

Levina smiled as she readjusted Leah in her arms. She'd noticed all afternoon a certain "glow" about her youngest daughter. "What's that, Tillie?"

Tillie stood up from the picnic table and bounced on her toes, as she was known to do. A smile filled her face as she blurted, "We're in the family way!"

"*Ach*, Tillie! That's wonderful news!" Levina handed Leah to Rosemary, then she walked to Tillie and gave her a hug. "I suspected as much," she whispered to Tillie, who just giggled.

"So, *Daed*. I was wondering about that beautiful chest you just made, the one in the barn." Tillie giggled. "The one perfect for a baby's room!"

Naaman grinned. "Well, Tillie, I reckon——"

"Wait a minute!" Freda stood up. "I have news too."

Levina brought her hand to her chest and wondered how she could have missed it. She'd known every time that Rosemary was pregnant as well as both her daughters-in-law. Could it be . . . ?

"I am also in the family way!" And to everyone's surprise, Freda began to jump up and down.

"Oh my!" Levina ran to her other daughter. "*Two* new grandbabies for me to love!" She threw her arms around Freda. "I'm so happy for you, Freda."

Freda eased out of the hug and turned to Naaman. "And I'm the oldest. I think I should have the chest."

Naaman's face split into a wide grin, and Levina wasn't sure if it was because both his young daughters were with child or because they both wanted the chest he'd worked so hard on.

"No, no." Tillie wagged a finger at Freda playfully. "I asked first."

Freda thrust her hands on her hips. "I say whoever's baby comes first should have the chest. When are you due, Tillie?"

"March the second. When are you due?"

Freda frowned. "That's the same day I'm due!"

But instead of bickering, Tillie and Freda hugged each other. "How exciting for us," Tillie said. "This will be so fun."

"*Ya, ya,*" Freda said, smiling.

Naaman stood up and looped his thumbs under his suspenders. "Well, this will give me plenty of time to make a second chest. Then both my girls will have a new chest of drawers for these new additions to our family." He glanced around at his family. "And I'll start on the new piece of furniture as soon as I get back from my trip."

Levina couldn't breathe. She couldn't move. *What trip?* She reminded herself that she trusted her husband, and she refused to allow herself to take a step backward, but as she waited for him to go on, her heart thudded against her chest. No one spoke, and Levina kept her eyes locked with Naaman's as she spoke in a whisper. "What trip?"

Naaman glanced around at their children and grandchildren. "I'm afraid that all of you will have to do without me for two weeks."

He walked closer to Levina, and she was relieved to hear him say he would only be gone for two weeks. *But where?*

Naaman put his arm around her and stood taller. "And you're all going to have to do without your *mamm* for two weeks too." He reached into his pocket and held up a small envelope, then waved it in the air as he grinned. "Because we will be traveling by bus to Florida." He smiled at Levina, gazing into her eyes as he spoke. "Your mother wants to see the ocean."

Levina gasped as she threw her arms around his neck. "*Ach,* Naaman!"

He gently eased her away, then kissed her on the lips.

"*Ach,* stop! Your *kinner* are watching!" Tillie giggled, and Levina heard the rest of her loved ones snickering and poking playful fun.

She didn't care. She kissed her husband again. "I love you, Naaman."

He held her tight. "I love you, too, *mei leib.*"

Reading Group Guide

A CHOICE TO FORGIVE

1. Throughout the book, Lydia struggles with forgiveness. First she must find it in her heart to forgive Daniel, and later she must forgive her deceased husband. Have you ever found yourself in a situation where you needed to forgive someone who has passed on? Did forgiveness give you a sense of peace or resolve, even though you were not able to voice your feelings directly to that person?

2. Anna Marie is experiencing her running-around period (*rumschpringe*). Is her behavior different from that of *Englisch* teenagers at this age? If so, how? Is Lydia more trusting about her daughter's actions than *Englisch* parents might be, or is this simply reflective of a generational shift across both cultures? For example, Lydia states that her parents would have been much stricter with her if they'd caught her sneaking out of the house. Are you less strict with your children than your parents were with you?

3. The Amish believe that all things that happen are of God's will. Is Lydia being true to her faith by questioning the way things happened, harboring ill will, and struggling to forgive—or is she just human? Have you ever questioned God's will in a situation where a different outcome would have affected far more people than just you?

4. Daniel and Lydia were each other's first loves, yet they went on to live separate lives. Do you know anyone who has reunited with his or her first love? Did it work out?

A CHANGE OF HEART

1. Leah's father worries throughout the story that Leah will not master the skills necessary to become a good Amish *fraa*. At what point does he begin to realize that Leah's stories are much more than just a frivolous waste of time?
2. Aaron agrees to read Leah's books as a way to get close to her. What are some of the things Aaron learns about Leah by reading her stories?
3. Auntie Ruth nudges Leah and Aaron together by writing notes to each of them. What do you think would have happened if Ruth hadn't done this? Would they eventually have found their way back to each other? If so, who do you think would have initiated a get-together?
4. Leah's *Englisch* friends, Donna and Clare, are not at the same spiritual place in their lives as Leah. Can it be in a person's best interest to avoid people with whom they are unequally yoked, as many Amish believe? Have you ever been friends with someone with whom you were unequally yoked spiritually? How did it affect you?

HEALING HEARTS

1. Adam has the most trouble accepting his father's return, more so than his other siblings. Why do you think that is?
2. What does Levina struggle with the most when Naaman returns and throughout the story?
3. What are some of the signs that Naaman and Levina are falling in love with each other all over again?
4. What are some things that married couples can do to nurture their relationship amid busy jobs and raising children?

Amish Recipes

Marian Petersheim's Tomato Pie

1. Mix until right consistency to press into bottom of pie dish:

> 2 cups Bisquick
> 1/2 cup milk

2. Slice 2 medium tomatoes and line the crust.
3. Sprinkle with:

> 1 teaspoon basil
> 1 teaspoon parsley flakes
> 1/2 teaspoon thyme leaves
> 1/2 teaspoon oregano
> 1/2 teaspoon onion powder
> 1 teaspoon brown sugar
> Salt and pepper

4. Mix together and spread over tomatoes and spices:

> 1 cup mayonnaise
> 3/4 cup shredded American cheese

5. Bake at 350 degrees for 35 to 45 minutes until golden brown.

Syrupy Pancake Bake

Syrup

> 2 teaspoons water
> 1 cup packed light brown sugar
> 1/2 cup butter

Top Layer

> 1 egg

1 scant cup milk
½ teaspoon salt
2 tablespoons sugar
2 tablespoons butter, melted
1 cup flour
1 teaspoon baking powder

1. Bring syrup ingredients to a boil in small saucepan. Pour into a 9 x 13 inch glass baking dish. Set aside.
2. In large mixing bowl, combine all top layer ingredients and beat well. Pour over syrup.
3. Bake at 350°F for 30 minutes.

—Compliments of an Amish Friend

MOLASSES CRINKLE COOKIES

1. Mix together well:

3 cups vegetable oil
4 cups brown sugar
1 cup molasses
4 eggs, beaten

2. Add:

8 teaspoons baking soda
1 teaspoon salt
2 teaspoons cinnamon
1 teaspoon nutmeg
1 teaspoon ground cloves

3. Stir well. Mix in the following with your hands:

2 cups whole wheat flour
6 cups all-purpose flour

4. Form into 1-inch balls and roll in white sugar. Bake at 350° for 10 minutes.

Makes approximately 10 dozen—plenty for sharing!

Source: Courtesy of an Old Order Amish friend.

Acknowledgments

A Change of Heart:

SPECIAL THANKS TO MY HUSBAND, PATRICK, AND MY FAMILY and friends. I'd never make it without your support and encouragement. To Barbie Beiler, thank you yet again for reading the manuscript to verify authenticity. You're the best! Thanks also to nurse Melissa Gips for verifying medical accuracy. Much appreciated!

To my fabulous fiction team at Thomas Nelson, you guys and gals are awesome. And special thanks to LB Norton for your editorial assistance. Thanks to my agent, Mary Sue Seymour.

My most heartfelt thanks goes to God. Without Him, there would be no books.

Healing Hearts:

TO MY HUSBAND AND BEST FRIEND, PATRICK. YOU ROCK, baby! And I couldn't write these books without the support of my family and friends—or without my mother-in-law, who cooks for us twice a week. Love you all! Heartfelt thanks to Barbie Beiler, the folks at Thomas Nelson, and particularly to my editor, Natalie Hanemann, who holds a special place in my heart. And LB Norton, it is always a pleasure to work with you! Special thanks to my mom, who continues to inspire and encourage me. I love you, Mother, and I think Daddy is smiling from heaven. To my agent, Mary Sue Seymour—thanks for all you do, my friend. Blessed be to God, who continues to put the stories in my head that He wants me to share.

A Choice to Forgive:

Thank you to my friends and family who continue to support me on this incredible journey. With each new book, I am learning to balance my time a little better, and your patience with my tight deadlines is much appreciated. My friendships and personal relationships are important to me, and I will always find the time to nourish them.

Patrick, thank you for providing me with an environment that affords me this grand opportunity to live my dreams—dreams of writing full-time and of living the rest of my life with you, my forever love.

Eric and Cory, dreams do come true. Work hard, strive to be the best you can be, and maintain a relationship with God. Talk to Him as you would a dear friend. He listens. He blessed me with the two of you.

To Natalie Hanemann—I'm so blessed to have you in my life, as both editor and friend. You push me to hit my writing potential, and I always end up with a better book after your input. Equally important is the friendship we share. God puts people in our life for a reason, and I feel sure He was smiling when He introduced the two of us. Thank you for everything.

My entire fiction family at Thomas Nelson is awesome. I am so honored to be a part of this group. I thank God for each and every one of you.

Thank you to LB Norton for your editorial assistance. It was a pleasure to work with you.

A sincere thanks to my dear friend, Barbie Beiler. As always, your Amish and Mennonite background helps me to keep the books authentic. You always make time amid your busy schedule to read the manuscripts prior to publication, and I am so grateful to you. You are a blessing in my life, my friend.

To Anna B. King, thank you so much for the time you spent

on the phone with me, making sure that I understood the details of Christmas as celebrated in an Old Order Amish community. By the time this book goes to print, I will have met you in person in Pennsylvania, and I am really looking forward to that—to meeting Barbie's mom!

Thank you to my agent, Mary Sue Seymour. You are a special person, and I value our professional relationship as well as our friendship. Thank you for everything.

Special thanks to those "first responders" who read behind me as I write—Reneé Bissmeyer, Rene Simpson, and my wonderful mother, Pat Isley. You all keep me on my toes and push me forward to completion. Rene, thank you for reading behind me on this particular novella and for all your input.

To my friends and "sistas" who constantly promote the books, thank you so much. Just to name a few—Laurie, Dawn, Melody, Valarie, Pat, Carol, Amy, Bethany, and Gayle. You gals are great!

And always, my most heartfelt thanks goes to God for providing me with this wonderful opportunity to spread His Word through inspirational stories about faith, hope, and love.

The Daughters
of the Promise novels

What would cause
the Amish to move to Colorado,
leaving family and friends behind?

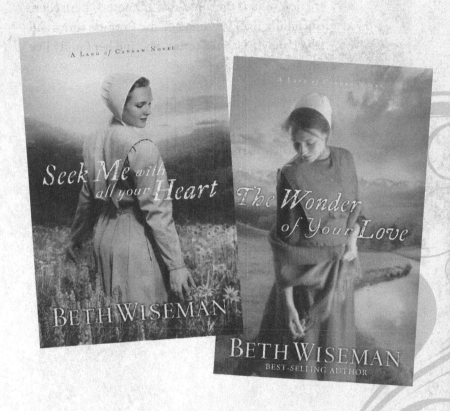

The Land of Canaan Series

About the Author

BETH WISEMAN is hailed as a top voice in Amish fiction. She is the author of numerous bestsellers including the Daughters of the Promise series and the Land of Canaan series. She and her family live in Texas.

PHOTOS BY LYDIA, Weimar, Texas

Visit BethWiseman.com